THE LEGACY

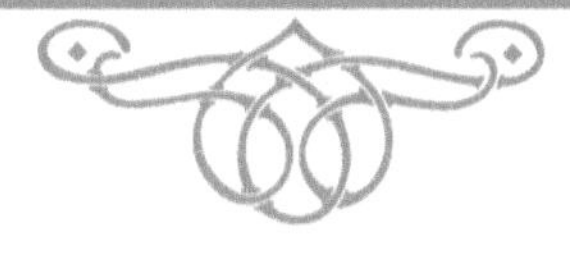

LIGHT *in the* EMPIRE

THE LEGACY

CAROL ASHBY

CERRILLO PRESS

THE LEGACY
Copyright 2017 by Carol Ashby

Publisher's Note: This novel is a work of fiction. Names, characters, places, and incidents are either products of the author's imagination or used fictitiously. All characters are fictional, and any similarity to people living or dead is purely coincidental.

Some Scripture quotations are from the Holy Bible, English Standard Version, copyright © 2001, 2007, 2011, 2016 by Crossway Bibles, a division of Good News Publishers. Used by permission. All rights reserved.

Some Scripture quotations are from the Christian Standard Bible®, Copyright © 2017 by Holman Bible Publishers. Used by permission. Christian Standard Bible® and CSB® are federally registered trademarks of Holman Bible Publishers.

Cover and interior design by Roseanna White Designs

Cover images from Shutterstock.com

ISBN: 978-1-946139-04-7 (paperback)
        978-1-946139-05-4 (ebook)
        978-1-946139-14-6 (hardcover)

Cerrillo Press
Edgewood, NM

Let all bitterness and wrath and anger and clamor and slander be put away from you, along with all malice. Be kind to one another, tenderhearted, forgiving one another, as God in Christ forgave you.

Ephesians 4:31-32 (ESV)

Beloved, never avenge yourselves, but leave it to the wrath of God, for it is written, "Vengeance is mine, I will repay, says the Lord."

Romans 12: 19 (ESV)

All that the Father gives me will come to me, and whoever comes to me I will never cast out.

John 6:37 (ESV)

To my children, Paul and Lydia,
for their love, support, and encouragement,
to Mom and Dad, who passed on their legacy of faith,
and especially to my husband, Jim,
who'll always be a hero in my own life story.

And most of all, to Jesus.

Soli Deo gloria.

Legacy. It's a word that calls up images of wills and lawyers, of our parents' house or the family farmland, of stocks and bonds and bank accounts, of family heirlooms and...the list goes on.

But we leave behind a legacy much more important than material possessions. Is there a person alive who doesn't want those they love to share the highest values that inspire and define their lives? As mothers and fathers, how many hours do we spend teaching our children what we know about God and praying for them to grow to know and love Him like we do?

I can think of no greater legacy that I could pass on to my family and friends than the knowledge of how much God loves them and how Jesus's sacrifice on the cross opened the door to eternal life, if they only choose to accept the forgiveness and salvation He freely offers.

I'm not sure there could be anything more gratifying than knowing your grown children have passed through the questioning years and decided their faith in Jesus is no longer a second-hand version of yours, but a deep, abiding, personal commitment of their own. Yet no matter how hard we try to pass on the legacy of faith, we can only plant the seeds and pour on water. It's God Himself who brings the harvest.

But what if you come to know and love Jesus after your children are grown? What if they are content with the culture that questions and rejects what you long to share? What if they have no interest in the faith you would be willing to die for?

The Legacy is the story of Publius Drusus and his three grown children. In middle age, he leaves behind the philosophies that had directed his life to become a God-fearer, following the God of Abraham, Isaac, and Jacob. Then he learns about Jesus and embraces Him as Savior. But his oldest son wants him dead so he can be free of his father's control. Lucius betrays his father and arranges Publius's execution as a Christian. In the face of impending death, what can a father do to pass on the legacy of faith to his other children, Titus and Claudia? How will God answer a father's final prayer for his children's salvation?

When we reach the point where we have done all we can, when time and opportunities have run out, there is One who loves our children more than we ever could. We might only set the ball in motion, but He can bring others into their lives to get it to the final goal. I hope you'll enjoy this story of the faith of a father who plants the seeds but must trust God for the harvest as much as I've enjoyed writing it. May we all know the joy of passing on a legacy of faith in the Lord we love.

Carol Ashby

Characters

CLAUDIUS DRUSUS FAMILY, SERVANTS, AND SLAVES
Publius: (49) Father of Lucius, Titus, and Claudia; Decimus's mentor and friend
Lucius: (33) Publius's oldest surviving son
Titus: (24) tribune serving in Perinthus of Thracia, Publius's youngest son, Decimus's best friend
Claudia: (16) Publius's only daughter
Cornelia: (31) Lucius's wife
Malleolus: (61) freedman steward of the Claudius Drusus family
Miriam: (19) secretly Christian slave bought by Titus

ARISTARCHUS OF THESSALONICA FAMILY AND FRIENDS
Aristarchus: (50) wealthy Greek with merchant fleets and many estates, leads house church in Rome
Philip: (25) youngest son, controls Thracian fleet and estates, leads house church in Perinthus
Ariadne: (23) sister who is very close to Philip, lives in Thessalonica
Penelope: (16) sister going to Perinthus with Philip to marry
Nicanor: (33) Philip's oldest brother, lives in Thessalonica
Junia: (30) Penelope's maid
Hector: (32) Philip's captain and best friend
Phoebe: (23) Philip's former betrothed and Ariadne's good friend
Nestor: lent to Titus by Philip to be house steward

CORNELIUS LENTULUS FAMILY
Tiberius: (47) governor of Germania Superior, Decimus's father and close friend of Publius
Decimus: (25) Titus's best friend; senatorial tribune of XXII Primigenia Legion, son of governor Tiberius

VALERIUS CORVINUS FAMILY
Marcus: (33) Lucius's best friend
Septimus: (20) Marcus's brother, tribune posted to Perinthus

OTHER IMPORTANT CHARACTERS
Appius Manlius Torquatus: close friend of Publius
Quintus Flavius Sabinus: powerful Senator, friend of the Emperor; political power broker

1) Rome and Portus, Rome's port where the Tiber enters the Mediterranean Sea
2) Thessalonica, capital city of Macedonia
3) Perinthus, capital city of Thracia
4) Byzantium
5) Odessus, town in Moesia
6) Pontus Euxinus

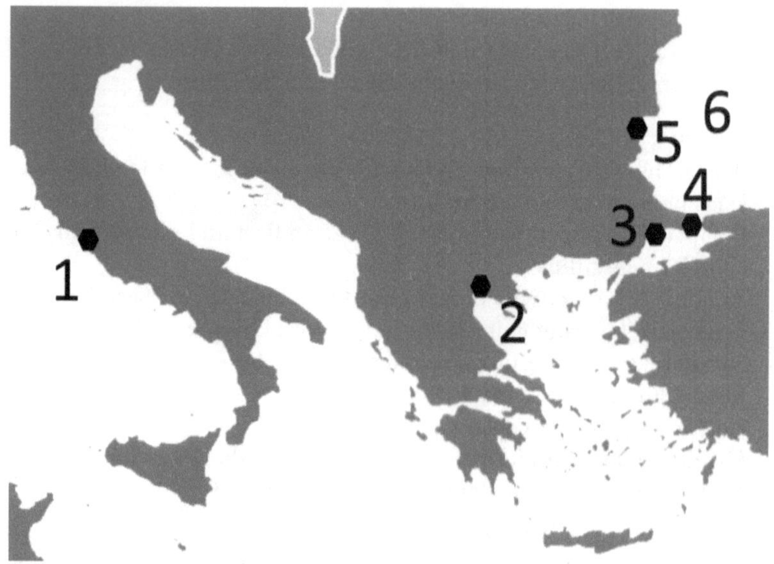

Chapter 1

ALMOST CONTENT

Rome, AD 114

Saying goodbye was always hard. When it was your youngest daughter, that punched a hole in a father's heart.

Aristarchus stood in the doorway, watching Penelope chat with her maid under the grape arbor. His lips tightened as his mouth drooped. His last child was about to leave Rome for good. A lovely young woman of sixteen, ready to marry and discover the joy of having children of her own. She was ready, but he would never be.

Philip walked up behind him. "Don't worry about Penelope, Father. I've found three young men who would be good husbands for her. They're all strong in the faith, and every one of them would cherish her and care for her well. She'll get to know them over the next few months so we can wisely choose the one God intends for her."

Aristarchus's gaze swung to his youngest son before he sighed. "I am sure you have done as well as I could myself, but I will miss having her here close to me."

Philip's hand rested on his father's shoulder. "You and Mother will just have to come to Perinthus more often. I'd like that as much as Penelope."

"I plan to." Aristarchus rubbed his bearded chin. Philip would not like his next words. "You have found good men for Penelope, but when are you going to find a good woman for yourself? It is time you married and started a family. At twenty-five, I already had Nicanor and Leander."

Philip shrugged. "As Solomon wrote, 'For everything, there is a season.'" His gaze shifted to the floor, then back to his father. "But not for me. Not yet. I can marry anytime I want. If I let it be known that I'm looking for a wife, fathers as far away as Byzantium will line up to offer their daughters to the merchant prince of Perinthus." His mouth twitched up, then straightened. "But I don't want someone who only wants to marry me because I'm rich."

"Any woman would grow to love you deeply, no matter why she first married you. Phoebe was too young and foolish to see your true worth as a husband."

Philip adjusted the strap of his eye patch. "I don't want to force some woman to marry a man she could only stand to look at on a moonless night. Phoebe only said what any woman would think. She was right to be honest about how she felt. I'm glad she found a man she can love even when her eyes are open."

Aristarchus's brows dipped before he shook his head. "You are wrong, son. Women do not just care how a man looks. I was never a handsome man, but the best and prettiest woman on earth was happy to marry me and not for my fortune. Your mother has blessed my life in so many ways that I could never tell you all of them. I want that for you, too."

Philip's eye focused on distant nothing before he turned it back on his father. "It's your love for me that keeps you from seeing the truth, Father. Phoebe made the way women truly feel very clear. If it's God's will for me to marry, then I'll marry, but I haven't seen any sign that it is. He allowed the burns and scars. I've just learned to be content with the results." He rubbed the back of his neck. "Most of the time, anyway."

Aristarchus saw the wistful look flit across Philip's face, and then it was gone. "Never underestimate the power of God or His desire to give you what is best for you, son."

"I never do." The shrug that accompanied Philip's weak smile signaled his eagerness to change the subject.

"Mother has some things she wants me to take to Ariadne, so I'm planning to land briefly in Thessalonica. Did you have anything for her or Nicanor?"

Aristarchus switched to the new topic for Philip's sake. He didn't like to see any of his children in pain, and the memory of Phoebe's rejection seven years earlier was still a poorly healed wound in Philip's heart, no matter what he might say to the contrary. Only the love of the right woman would let it finally heal.

But first, Philip had to be willing to risk being hurt again to find that love. Aristarchus would be praying for that kind of courage for the best of his sons.

Chapter 2

What a Girl Wants

Publius Drusus leaned back in his chair and flexed his shoulders. He'd been sitting too long, but the new history on the conquest of Dacia had enthralled him.

The music of Claudia's laughter and her maid Graecia's response reached his ears before his daughter swept into the library and came to the desk to give him a kiss.

"It was lovely at the baths today, Father. Lucretia and Portia were there. Portia had the most exciting news."

Her head tipped as a teasing gleam brightened her brown eyes. "Well, aren't you going to ask me what it is?"

Publius set the scroll aside. A smile lifted the corners of his mouth as he turned to look up at her. "Could I keep you from telling me, even if I wanted to?"

"No." She picked up a stylus and rolled it between her fingers. "I have two things, actually. Lucretia's betrothed is coming home from Britannia. He'll have a posting in Rome, and their marriage will be the first auspicious day after he returns."

Publius tipped his head to acknowledge her first report. "And the second?"

"Portia is now betrothed to Quintus Palma."

The corner of Publius's mouth twitched. "I'm sure her parents are ecstatic about that. I've met young Quintus. I wasn't impressed, but his father is very wealthy and a leader in the Senate. He has the emperor's ear as well. That will open better opportunities for Portius's sons if their sister's father-in-law decides to promote their careers." He shook his head. "Not the best reason for arranging a marriage. But maybe his sons want the political life." The corner of his mouth lifted. "I never did."

"I'm glad you didn't, Father. I'd miss you terribly if you were off leading a legion in some frontier province. It's bad enough that Titus has been tribune in Thracia these past four years."

She placed the stylus back on the desk. "Portia's happy with the choice, but I wouldn't be. He's so...dull. I've never heard him talk about music or philosophy or poetry. It's always which faction won the most at the races that week and how much he won gambling." A short giggle brightened her eyes. "He never says how much he lost."

She held out her arms and twirled one circle. "I know what I want in a husband."

Publius was hard pressed not to laugh. "What is that?"

Her eyes turned dreamy. "Someone as handsome as Titus, as big and strong as a German warrior, and as brilliant and kind as you."

The laugh escaped. "That's a challenging list. Just where do you think I'll find someone like that?"

"I know one already. Guess if you can. You should be able to. You've known him for years."

Publius's eyebrows shot up. "Really? I can't think of a single young man who is all that."

"Of course you can. It's Decimus Lentulus."

Publius smiled as he shook his head. "No, I don't think he'd suit you. Decimus is all that, except maybe the kind part, but you couldn't find a man more driven by political ambition. He'll need a wife from a family with great political influence, and ours is exactly the opposite. Even if we were what he needs, would you want to be a political wife with your husband always focused on something other than you and your children?"

Claudia shrugged. "Well, maybe not. I'd rather be a scholar's wife so we could talk about the things I love." Her eyes clouded. "I'd never do what my mother did. I'll be the best wife and mother a man could ever want."

As her smile faded, Publius stood and took her in his arms.

"I know you will. I just need to find the right man for you." He stepped back and rested his hand on her cheek. "I'll keep your list in mind as I look for him."

She flashed him a fresh smile and strolled into the atrium.

Publius sighed. His little girl was a woman now. As much as he hated the thought, it was time for her to marry and start her own family. But how was he ever going to find a husband who would protect and care for her like he had?

Chapter 3

TIME FOR A CHANGE

It isn't fair. Fathers shouldn't live as long as mine has.

Lucius Drusus swirled another bite of peacock in the red wine sauce and placed it on his tongue. It had been a superb banquet so far, but he wasn't enjoying it.

His closest friend, Marcus, was celebrating becoming head of the Corvinus family and inheriting its fortune with an extravagant banquet for only his most trusted friends. Celebrating his father's demise would be considered shameful, were it generally known. Under the Roman law of *paterfamilias*, the father owned all the property and could dictate everything his sons could do, no matter how old they might be. Only a father's death gave true independence to a son.

Lucius flipped his frown into a smile when Gaius Barbatus strolled toward him. Barbatus was no friend. He'd always resented the great wealth of the Drusus family. He took perverse delight in taunting Lucius since his father, Publius, put an end to his orgies of drinking and womanizing three years earlier.

"Lucius, I saw your father in the forum last week with his philosopher friends. He looks almost as young as you. Should be a long time before you give a banquet to mourn his death."

Lucius's fake smile masked his fury at the snide laugh that followed Barbatus's prediction before he sauntered away. It was best if no one suspected what he was thinking at that moment.

He glanced around the room at his friends. Many were now masters of their own lives. He was tired of living on an allowance and being subject to his father's will. He was thirty-three and ready to be in control. He'd begun planning for that years ago.

Father always thought the death of his older brother had been a fluke accident when the wheel came off his chariot during a friendly race between brothers. He thought it was grief that made Lucius kill the slave who was supposed to care for the chariots.

The corner of Lucius's mouth lifted. He covered his mouth and drew his hand down to wipe off the smile that might draw questions. He'd promised that slave freedom if he tampered with the wheel so it would come off in a sharp turn. He kept his promise. He freed him with a sword thrust to his heart.

That had been almost ten years ago. It wasn't fair that he was still under his father's thumb. Father was almost fifty, but he was as vigorous as many men only two-thirds his age. He could easily last another ten or twenty years. Lucius didn't want to wait.

Money wasn't the problem. His allowance earned the envy of his friends since the Drusus fortune was more than five million denarii. He lived with his wife and children at the villa east of Rome that was better than the ones his friends had inherited. The problem was his father.

Father hadn't cared how he spent his allowance. His friends all enjoyed wild living, and their parties often lasted past dawn. He'd already produced three boys as future heirs, so he no longer felt he had to waste his evenings with the high-born woman he'd married.

Then Father became a God-fearer and followed the Jewish rules for living. The things Lucius enjoyed were condemned by the Jewish god, and Father cut off his spending on the long nights of too much wine and loose women. He'd been told to restrict his activities to that plain, passionless woman he'd married and to at least try to stay sober at banquets.

He'd obeyed, but it convinced him it was time to replace his father as head of the Claudius Drusus family. The problem was how to do that without being executed for killing his own father. Rome was a city where almost anything goes, but patricide was one thing that still remained beyond the pale.

Chapter 4

Dilemma Resolved

It wasn't considered dignified for a man of his status to scurry, but Publius could hardly wait to get home to share with Claudia what he'd just learned at the synagogue. It solved the conundrum that had disturbed his peace of mind for many months.

He found her sitting under the grape arbor with the codex of poetry he'd left as a surprise for her that morning.

She looked up at his approach. "Father, I love this new poet." She pressed the open codex to her breast. "His phrases are exquisite. Thank you for finding this for me."

"I'm glad you like it." Publius kissed the top of her head before he sat down beside her. "I learned the most wonderful thing at synagogue today."

"What, Father?" Claudia closed the codex and focused her full attention on him.

"I don't have to worry any more about the end of the sacrifices in Jerusalem. How anyone could approach God when there was no way to pay for sins—that has haunted me. Well, today I met someone who explained it all."

She pressed her lips together and shook her head. "I'll never understand why you worry so much about paying for your sins." Her eyes warmed as her smile returned. "I think you're the perfect father, and all our slaves would tell anyone what a wonderful master you are. No one is wiser or kinder. I don't think anyone could be less of a sinner than you are. Your god should be happy to have a wonderful man like you as his worshipper without any sacrifices."

Publius took her hand. "You don't understand what sin is, child. It's anything that separates someone from Holy God. That can be as simple as thinking I'm good enough when my life is less than totally perfect. God requires perfection. It's not enough to just be very good or even better than other people."

"Well, you're as close to perfect as anyone could be, and that should be good enough for your god. I don't understand why the most wonderful man in the world would ever think he's a sinner." An encouraging smile graced her lips as she patted his arm.

Her response saddened him. She wasn't interested because she didn't understand him or God. She'd been so heartbroken when her mother abandoned her, so he'd showered her with his love and tried to shield her from life's ugliness. Now she couldn't see that people were naturally sinful even when they were doing their best. His sweet, brilliant daughter didn't feel she was a sinner. But she was choosing to be separated from God, and that made her a sinner no matter how she felt. Until she understood that, what he learned today wouldn't mean a thing.

She kissed him on the cheek and opened her codex of poetry again. "Would you like me to read to you? I have a new favorite. The phrases are so elegant and the images extraordinary."

"Later, my dear." He stood and kissed her again on the top of her head. He received a loving glance and sparkling smile in return before she turned her eyes back on her codex.

How could he excite her interest in the solution? Perhaps, if he started with one of their discussions of philosophy that she loved, he could lead her toward God. It was too important to drop the subject for long.

He left her in the garden and walked to his bedchamber. There he unrolled the scroll of his Greek version of the Jewish Scriptures that included the writings of Isaiah. He wanted to read again all the prophesies about the Messiah that foretold how He would be the sacrifice for the sins of all men and the reconciler of man with God.

Those parts of Isaiah used to confuse him, but now he understood them clearly. At long last, he knew who the Messiah was. God had placed the right man in his path today to resolve his dilemma.

What had started as a discussion of the state of the Roman economy with the Greek merchant, Aristarchus, had turned into something of much greater importance. It was Aristarchus who finally knew the solution to the riddle that had plagued Publius for many months. As a result, he had just taken the next logical step in his faith and accepted Jesus of Nazareth as the Jewish Messiah, the Son of God, and his own Savior.

Chapter 5

THE NEWEST BROTHER

Publius burned with anticipation as he set out the next morning for his first Christian worship service. Malleolus, steward of his house in Rome and overseer of all the Drusus estates, had not returned from Lucius's villa when Publius retired for the night. That was disappointing. Next to Claudia, there was no one he was more eager to tell about his life-changing discovery.

As he was walking through the *vestibulum* on his way out, Malleolus was admitted by the door slave.

Publius clasped Malleolus's upper arms. "I may be gone for most of the day, but I have the most amazing thing to tell you when I return from the house of Aristarchus of Thessalonica."

"If I need to find you, master, who is that and where does he live?"

"Aristarchus owns a fleet of merchant ships and estates in several eastern provinces. His house is just south of the Gardens of Maecenas this side of the Porta Esquilinas. We had a fascinating discussion about his views on the financial state of the Empire yesterday. He's also a scholar of history, and I count him among my close friends now."

Publius left Malleolus standing in the *vestibulum* as he hurried out the door. He had some distance to walk, and he didn't want to be late for the start of the worship.

◆

Malleolus concealed his surprise at his master's destination. He'd never heard of Aristarchus before, and he was certain he knew the names of all the master's good friends. Master Publius was very selective about whom he chose to call a close friend. There were only a handful, and Malleolus had known them all for years. What could have so suddenly made a wealthy Greek merchant a member of that elite group?

When Publius knocked on the door at Aristarchus's house, a small window in the door opened rather than the door itself.

"Whom shall I say is seeking admittance?"

The question struck him as odd. The synagogue was open to all without question.

"Publius Claudius Drusus. Aristarchus invited me yesterday."

"Please wait a moment." The window closed.

Publius waited longer than he expected before the door finally opened. Aristarchus himself stood before him with a delighted smile and outstretched arms.

"Come in, come in. I am so glad you decided to join us today, Publius." He closed and bolted the door behind them. "I am sorry to have kept you waiting. We have to be careful here in Rome these days. Next time my doorkeeper will recognize you and admit you right away. You picked a very good day to join us for the first time. Come meet my son. He will be teaching today."

Aristarchus led Publius toward a brawny young man who was standing with his back toward them. "Philip, I want you to meet our newest brother, Publius."

When Philip turned, Publius was unprepared for what he saw. A warm and welcoming smile spread across the young man's face, but Publius's gaze fixed on the hideous scars covering his right cheek and extending down his neck to disappear beneath his tunic. More scars swirled where his bushy eyebrow should have been and around the patch over his right eye. He was, without doubt, the ugliest young man Publius had ever seen.

Philip offered his arm, and Publius grasped it. "Father told me how God led you two into your discussion yesterday. You made the wisest choice when you decided to believe in Jesus as God's perfect sacrifice for our sins. You'll never regret that decision." The enthusiasm in the young man's deep voice was contagious.

Aristarchus placed his hand on his son's shoulder and beamed at him. "Philip leads a house church in Perinthus. He will be returning to

Thracia in about three weeks. We will miss him here in the fellowship. When he teaches, we truly hear the word of God."

Philip's fleeting smile betrayed his discomfort with his father's effusive praise. "Please excuse me, Publius. I need to prepare since we'll be starting shortly." With another welcoming smile, he moved away.

Aristarchus's eyes glowed as he watched his son. "Philip is my youngest son, but God made him the smartest of them all. He is only twenty-five, but he is wise beyond his years. I am glad you will hear his teaching today." He placed his hand on Publius's shoulder. "I would be honored if you would sit beside me."

The two men sat down and waited for Philip to begin. Publius had never felt such intense anticipation for any lecture at the forum or teaching at the synagogue.

An odd fire lit the eye of the ugly young man standing before them. Philip picked up a codex and held it close to his chest as he closed his eye. Then he lifted it up and faced the open sky above the garden where all were seated.

"Dear Father, may my words be inspired by the Holy Spirit and bring honor to You and to my Lord Jesus."

Publius was transfixed as Philip began to teach from the gospel written by the apostle John. He spoke about God's love for the world shown by the Father sending His only Son in the body of a man as the perfect sacrifice for sin so that everyone who believes in Jesus would have eternal life with Him. Publius's heart swelled with inexpressible joy as Philip spoke of God's love and sacrifice. His mind knew and his heart burned with the knowledge that God had done it for him. It seemed too soon when Philip concluded his teaching.

"Brothers and sisters, there's no need to live in fear once we choose to follow Jesus. Remember that He said, 'I am the resurrection and the life. Whoever believes in me, though he die, yet shall he live, and everyone who lives and believes in me shall never die.' This very week, some of our fellow believers will face the lions in the emperor's arena for refusing to call Trajan lord and god, but our God is greater than any emperor. Jesus has promised us that the man who loves his life will lose it, while the man who hates his life in this world will keep it for eternity. Jesus has promised that He will be with us always, and we can live free from the fear of death."

Publius leaned forward in his seat, hanging on every word as Philip continued. "Remember Jesus's words, 'But the Counselor, the Holy Spirit, whom the Father will send in my name, will teach you all things and remind you of everything I have told you. Peace I leave with you. My peace I give to you. I do not give to you as the world gives. Don't let your heart be troubled or fearful.' So, in spite of the dangers of living among men who would destroy us because we love our Lord, we can rest on Jesus's promise of eternal life and not be afraid."

When Philip finished, Publius turned toward Aristarchus. His beaming smile was mirrored by his friend.

Aristarchus raised his eyebrows. "Are you ready to declare your faith in Lord Jesus before us today?"

"Yes! Today and for the rest of my life."

Philip stepped close and offered Publius his hand. "Come."

Publius knelt before the gathered believers as Aristarchus and Philip placed their hands upon his shoulders. Philip spoke, "In the presence of all gathered here, tell our Lord your decision to love and serve Him, and receive the Holy Spirit as He promised."

As Publius spoke his heart, the indescribable presence of God surrounded him, and he offered praise to his new Lord in a language he never knew before. When he finished, the whole congregation rose to offer their praise and thanks to God. Publius didn't know all the words yet, but he sang along as best he could. As he listened to the closing songs, it was as if he were listening to the choirs of heaven itself.

Chapter 6

Fathers and Daughters

As the food for the fellowship meal was being carried out to the serving tables, Aristarchus turned to the beaming Publius.

"It does my heart good to see such joy on your face, my brother, but I must warn you."

Publius's brow furrowed. "Warn me?"

"Yes. You will want to tell everyone you see about our Savior, but you must be careful. Rome is an enemy of the followers of Jesus. It is very dangerous for the wrong person to know you are one of them. If they report you, you will be asked to deny Jesus and offer sacrifice to Caesar before they will let you go. Refusing could put you in the arena, so do not tell just anyone. The Holy Spirit Himself will reveal whom you should tell and whom you should not."

Publius nodded. "I understand. I can see where discretion is needed. I'll be careful."

Aristarchus waved at a girl to get her to come over. "Publius, this is my daughter, Penelope. She is my youngest, only sixteen, and to have her as my daughter is truly a blessing from God." He wrapped his arm around her shoulder as he smiled down at her.

"The true blessing from God is to have you as my father and Philip as my brother." She kissed her father's cheek before smiling at Publius. "I'm so glad you came to worship today, Publius. I love to be there when someone joins us following Jesus."

Publius beamed at her. "Today is the best day of my life. Nothing, not even the birth of my children, has given me such...such sheer joy!"

Aristarchus placed his hand on Publius's shoulder. "It was a blessing for us all to be with you today."

Penelope's eyes sparkled as she nodded her agreement. "Please excuse me, Father, Publius. I want to hold the new baby." With another flash of her sweet smile, she moved away to join the other young women cooing over the new baby girl.

Publius watched her cuddle the baby. "Your daughter is charming. She reminds me of my own daughter, Claudia. They are the same age. It would be good for our girls to become acquainted."

"If we had met sooner, yes, but Penelope will go to Thracia with Philip. My son has found three good Christian men for her, and she will choose the man she wants to wed."

"You are fortunate to have so many choices. Claudia is almost seventeen. She should be betrothed by now, but I haven't found even one man who would be the right husband for her."

The corner of Aristarchus's mouth lifted. "It can be a challenge."

"Claudia has both my wife's rare beauty and my love of learning. Her beauty is attracting the interest of many men—too many, in fact, and for the wrong reason. The problem is she's likely to be much smarter than her husband, and most men don't want that. I don't want her to have to hide her intelligence or have her husband try to crush her love of learning."

Aristarchus nodded. "My Ariadne is also very smart. I looked for a husband who would value that. God provided a man who is proud of her gifts."

"There's a bigger problem. When Claudia was three, her mother decided she didn't want a scholar like me as her husband anymore. She divorced me and married a man who has power and influence with the Senate and the emperor. She wanted nothing to do with me or our children after that. My boys were older and didn't care, but Claudia is still hurt by her abandonment. An unfaithful husband...I fear that would wound her heart beyond healing.

"To have her mother do that..." Aristarchus tightened his lips as he shook his head.

"I've always tried to let her know how much I love her to make up for her mother's rejection, but a father can only do so much."

Aristarchus nodded in sympathy. "A mother's love—nothing can fully replace that." He scanned the gathering until his gaze rested on Philip. "His mother's love and care pulled Phillip through when he was burned."

"These last three years, I've been a God-fearer. She isn't, but I still want to find her a husband who worships the God of Israel, if I can. So far, I haven't found a single man who fits all three requirements."

"If she were a Christian, Philip would be the perfect husband for her. He enjoys the company of very smart people, and no one is kinder or more faithful."

Publius glanced at Philip. He would have been ugly even without the scars. With them, ugly was too kind a description. Claudia always mentioned handsome first when describing the ideal man.

"Yes, that's exactly what Claudia needs, but I don't want her living so far away. I would almost never see her if she moved to Thracia. I need to find someone who lives nearby."

Publius had no doubt that Philip was a kind, faithful, smart man who wouldn't be intimidated by his daughter's intelligence, but there was one glaring problem. Claudia would be repulsed by his appearance. A rare beauty like her would never want to be married to a man so ugly she couldn't bear to look at him. It was hard to imagine that any young woman would.

Publius was beaming as he entered his house. The slave who opened the door scarcely had time to step back before Publius placed his hands on both his shoulders.

"It's a great day. Best ever."

The doorkeeper's eyes saucered. "Yes, master."

His slave's surprise drew an even bigger grin. "Where's Malleolus?"

"He left for the northern estate shortly after you left this morning, master. He hasn't returned yet. He expected to be gone until tomorrow."

"As soon as he returns, tell him I have something exciting to tell him."

The slave bowed his head. "Yes, master, as soon as he returns."

Publius hurried away to look for Claudia. He stuck his head into the library first. That was usually the best place to start looking. Their mutual love of learning was the thing he enjoyed most about his precious girl. The many hours they'd spent together as he taught her had been pure pleasure. If she had been a boy, he could have shown off her intelligence to his scholarly friends. As a girl, she wouldn't have been welcomed. Too bad; she was smarter than most of the men in that elite group.

The soft sound of a lyre drew him into the garden. Claudia was reclining on a couch, her eyes closed and a smile on her lips.

Publius paused beside the musician. "That's enough for now." Aristarchus's warning echoed in his memory. He would speak with her alone.

The musician bowed and left the two of them alone in the garden.

Claudia opened her eyes and sat up. "You look so happy, Father. What has you smiling today?"

"Remember yesterday when I was telling you about how the destruction of the temple in Jerusalem was such a problem for me? Well, it isn't a problem at all. Not for anyone. The temple was no longer needed for sacrifices because sacrifices were no longer needed. Jesus of Nazareth made the final and perfect sacrifice for my sins, for everyone's sins for all time."

Claudia was gazing up at his face. He picked up both her hands as he stood before her.

"I don't ever have to worry about being able to approach God again. I've accepted Jesus as my Savior. I've met God...I actually met Him today. He's right here with me, right now."

Claudia's eyebrows shot up. Then she lowered them and tipped her head. "You met God?"

"Yes. I wish I could explain to you how that feels. I never imagined it was possible. It's...it's...I just can't find the words right now."

She bit her lip before taking a deep breath. "I don't know what to say either. I've always thought your god would be pleased to meet you. Anyone would."

Publius laid his hand on her cheek and stroked it with his thumb. "I know that sounds insane to you, but it's not. Before you understand, we'll have to talk more about why I need a savior, why you need a savior."

"We'll have to do that, Father."

Her gaze dropped to the floor. When it came back to his eyes, her unease was too obvious.

"You don't want to right now, do you."

Claudia paused. "Not really, Father." She offered a weak smile. "But we can if you want to."

Publius leaned over and kissed her forehead. She wasn't any readier to understand today than she had been yesterday. Now was not the time. "We can talk later when you're ready."

Claudia's relief was palpable as her smile broadened. "Later sounds good."

Publius gently squeezed her hand before letting it go. He turned and walked back into the house. She wouldn't listen to the truth yet, but as soon as she let him tell her, anyone as smart as Claudia would surely understand and turn to Jesus as Lord.

Chapter 7

Unsuitable Prospects

Publius was in his library the next morning when the door slave came to him.

"Master, you have a visitor. Flavius Sabinus is here, and I have seated him in the atrium."

Publius's eyes narrowed. Sabinus had never visited before, so why would the notorious political manipulator visit now? His wealth was legendary, and he used it without scruples. He had the ear of many in the Senate and even of Emperor Trajan himself.

Publius's nose twitched as if assaulted by the stench of a rotting carcass, but he put on a pleasant face as he entered the atrium. Even when he despised a man, he treated him with respect.

"Flavius Sabinus. This is a surprise. To what do I owe this unexpected visit?"

Sabinus smiled at him. Calculating eyes, stiff lips exposing crooked teeth—the resemblance to a crocodile was unmistakable. That seemed appropriate. If even half of what Publius had heard about Sabinus was true, he and the crocodile had more significant similarities than their smiles.

"Ah, Claudius Drusus. It's good to see you again. I understand you often speak about history in the forum, but I haven't had the time lately to have the pleasure of hearing you."

"I believe you're better known for making history than for studying it, Sabinus."

Sabinus's smile warmed at what he took for a compliment. "True. Very true."

Then fake sadness dragged his mouth down. "You may have heard of the tragic, untimely death of my dear wife." He drew a deep breath to support the sigh he added for dramatic effect.

"My condolences to your children and to you, Sabinus. I'd heard that your wife was a very loving mother. Her children must be missing her." Publius ignored most gossip, but he believed the rumors that Sabinus had beaten his wife badly enough to cause the miscarriage of what would have been their sixth child...and her death.

"That is true, and a man must consider remarrying quickly when he has children to care for. I am deeply grieved, but life must go on."

Publius watched Sabinus's eyes. He was about the same age as Publius and had been an infamous womanizer for years. Not even a flicker of warmth was there to mask his indifference to his children's suffering caused by their mother's death.

"That's why I've come to you, Drusus. I know your Claudia is an extraordinarily beautiful woman. I hear, too, that she is a very kind woman who would be a wonderful mother to another woman's children. I would like to discuss her becoming my next wife."

Publius's inner urge was to strike Sabinus for that offensive request and throw him out of his house. To even suggest that he would marry his daughter to this wife-beating old lecher was an insult to his honor as a father. Instead, he responded graciously.

"Claudia is only sixteen. She's still very much a child herself. I don't think she's ready to be a mother."

Publius's attempt to deflect the proposal made Sabinus's eyes even more eager. "A child? I think not. I've seen no other with more womanly charms." The crocodile smile accompanied his shrug. "But children can always be cared for by slaves. If she wanted, she could simply be my wife."

Publius had managed to keep his face passive, but any desire to make the refusal gracious was gone.

"It's my intention to marry her to a man closer to her own age. Neither you nor I are young men anymore, Sabinus."

"True. But young men can't afford to express their appreciation of her unique beauty like I can. Even 50,000 denarii would not be more than I would consider offering for her."

Publius placed his hands behind his back so Sabinus wouldn't see his fist clench. "Money can't change my decision, Sabinus. My daughter is not a slave to be sold to the highest bidder." Publius's eyes flashed as he frowned at Sabinus.

"I would never suggest that you would sell your daughter, Drusus. I only meant to express my great admiration and appreciation of her worth."

"There really is nothing more for us to discuss in this matter. You're just not a suitable husband for my Claudia." Publius forced a calm voice and demeanor even though he wanted to grab Sabinus by the back of his tunic and hurl him out the door. "I'm sure you have other pressing business, so I won't detain you here any longer."

◆

Drusus's summary dismissal was oil on hot coals, but Sabinus masked his anger. It never paid to get an enemy's guard up too soon, and he was expert at manipulating men of the highest rank. He would marry the unparalleled beauty, even if it took a while to find the key to swaying her father. Crocodiles are patient when waiting for their prey. All it took was one small weakness to be revealed, and then...

"Quite right. I'm on my way to the imperial palace, and I shouldn't delay any longer."

Sabinus offered his most gracious smile before turning and walking away. The door slave opened the door and bowed deeply as he walked out.

After the door closed, Sabinus glanced back. He would have Claudia Drusilla as his wife. No one said no to him like that and got away with it.

Publius was furious with Sabinus for trying to buy Claudia, but his visit did focus Publius's attention back on the problem he'd rather ignore. Claudia was sixteen. Most Roman girls were married or at least betrothed by her age. As much as he would love to have her live with him for the rest of his life, that wasn't right for her. It was time to get serious about finding her a good husband.

Back in his library, he settled into his desk chair and picked up the gold-tipped ivory stylus. As he rolled it between his fingers, his lips tightened. There must be some young man who'd make a proper husband for Claudia.

"You wanted to see me, master?"

Malleolus's greeting pulled a smile. Publius had freed him years before, but "master" had remained the steward's most common mode of address even though he'd been told he should use Publius. He waved his hand at the chair across the desk from his own. "Sit a while. We need to talk."

Malleolus lowered himself into the chair and leaned forward. "Is there a problem?"

"I just had a most unpleasant visitor."

"Flavius Sabinus? I passed him as I was entering our street. He didn't look happy."

"He had the gall to offer me 50,000 denarii if I would let him marry Claudia."

"That doesn't surprise me. Men like him think they can buy anything."

"Well, he'll never have my precious girl."

"No, he won't."

"But I do need to find her a husband. A good man who'll care for her when I'm gone. A man who'll appreciate her intelligence and never do anything to betray her trust. But who can that be?"

Publius ran his hand through his hair and sighed. "She just suggested Decimus Lentulus. I considered him once myself. He was here so often with Titus that he was almost my son already, and I knew he'd be a faithful husband. He's a smart man himself, and he would enjoy having a smart wife."

Malleolus nodded his approval. "He's a fine man. Except for Titus, I can think of none better."

Publius started rolling the stylus again. "I even approached his father with the idea just before he left for his post as governor of Germania Superior. The first girl betrothed to Decimus died before they could marry, and Tiberius hadn't lined up another wife yet." Publius smiled wryly as he remembered. "Tiberius graciously declined my request."

He hadn't told Malleolus this before, and the astonishment that anyone would turn down Claudia as a daughter-in-law showed on his steward's face.

"You needn't be so surprised. He was right. It really wouldn't be a good match. Decimus is destined for a political life. He needs a worldly wife to help him navigate the shoals of Roman power. She needs to be a reader of people, not a reader of poetry, and a woman able to entertain dishonorable men without either offending them by her own high standards or being dragged to their low level. Claudia's never going to be that type of woman."

"No, she would never be happy in that life."

"It's a problem that she's even more beautiful than her mother was. I was enthralled by that beauty when I was only fourteen. It's why I was so glad when my father arranged for me to marry her, but what did I get? A hot-tempered, selfish, cold-hearted beast inside a beautiful shell." He shook his head as he gazed out the window. "Life can be misery when you marry the wrong person."

He focused on Malleolus again. "Too many men want Claudia for her beauty alone. I'm not going to make the mistake of letting her marry that kind of man. She's so much more than an ornament to satisfy some man's vanity."

Publius ran his fingers through his hair and shook his head. "What am I going to do? I haven't been able to think of a single man who's worthy of her, who'll treasure her like she deserves."

"I don't know who, but there must be such a man. A man like you or Titus."

"There must be, but we need to find him soon. I'm not a young man, and I don't want Lucius making the choice."

One corner of Publius's mouth lifted. He was approaching this the wrong way. God would help him find the right man for his precious girl. Thinking was good, but praying was better.

"We don't need to solve this today, but keep thinking about it. I have something much more important to tell you."

"Is it what you mentioned yesterday as you were leaving?"

"Yes. I met someone at the synagogue who knew the answer to why God let the sacrifices be stopped when His temple in Jerusalem was destroyed. It's all so simple once you know the answer." He chuckled. "So many difficult questions are that way—totally obvious once you know the answer."

"What is the answer?"

Malleolus was not a philosopher, but for many years he'd been the sounding board for Publius's ideas before he presented them to his scholar friends. Publius valued the practical intelligence of his talented steward as he refined his thoughts. He grinned as he anticipated his friend's response to the logical solution to the ultimate problem.

"Jesus. Jesus of Nazareth was the final sacrifice made almost forty years before the temple was destroyed. God Himself came as a man and made the final sacrifice so the temple was unnecessary. It actually got in the way by letting men think they still needed to make animal sacrifices for their sins."

Malleolus had been nodding his head as he listened, as was his custom in such discussions. He stopped nodding, and his face turned grave.

Publius's mouth curved at the transformation. "Yes, you understood me. I've moved past being merely a God-fearer. I've become a Christian."

"That's a dangerous choice."

"I know. I was warned to be careful whom I told, but I know I can trust you with anything, and I need people to share my happiness. Claudia knows, too, but no one else. Would you like to hear more right now?"

Malleolus took a deep breath. "If you want to tell me, I'll listen."

So many years together let Publius hear what wasn't spoken. Malleolus wasn't a mere servant; he was a trusted friend. Publius would discuss Jesus with him, but not now. If a man really wasn't interested, it was better to wait.

Publius laid his hand on his steward's shoulder. "I hear your 'no,' and that's fine. We can talk again later when you think you might want to."

The tension drained out of Malleolus. "Did you need me for anything else?"

"No. Not right now. You can go." Publius picked up the stylus and began rolling it between his fingers again as his faithful servant bowed and left the room.

Publius shook his head. Neither Claudia nor Malleolus were ready to listen and understand, but he was a patient man. There would be many opportunities to share with them about Jesus and the joy that came from believing in him. The day would come when they would believe, too.

Publius's first week as a follower of Jesus had been more wonderful than even he had expected. Reading the Scriptures, saying his prayers, even just walking in his garden, everywhere he went and everything he did—he felt the closeness of God.

He went to the synagogue on the Sabbath, as he had been doing for the past three years. The Jewish Scriptures seemed even more alive now he knew Jesus was the fulfillment. Sabbath was good, but it was the second Sunday worship at Aristarchus's house that he could hardly wait for.

This time, when he knocked at the door, the doorkeeper admitted him immediately. Aristarchus was delighted to see him, and they sat together while Philip taught more on the gospel of John. His heart soared toward heaven as they sang the songs. He'd learned all the words of one they'd sung the week before, and they kept playing in his mind. Aristarchus introduced him to several of the brothers, and he thoroughly enjoyed their conversation.

As Publius walked home, he found himself more at peace than he'd ever been. His only regret was that he hadn't learned that Jesus was his Savior years before. Soon he would convince Claudia and Malleolus to join him as believers. When Titus returned from Thracia, he would convince him, too, and then all those he loved would share his joy.

Life was very good, and he was content.

Chapter 8

As Publius walked home from worship the next Sunday, he tried not to grin at total strangers. To think that only three weeks ago he had still been worrying about how his sins could be covered so he could approach God without temple sacrifice. After only three gatherings with his new Christian friends, he already felt like part of a big family. Aristarchus was more of a kindred spirit than any of his closest friends whom he'd known since childhood. And the teachings that Philip shared—Aristarchus hadn't just been a proud father exaggerating when he said you could hear the words of God when the young man spoke.

Contentment colored the smile he gave his door slave as he passed through into the atrium. It felt like it might be a good day to try to tell Claudia about Jesus again, so he walked through the house and out into the garden. He found her sitting under the arbor, reading as usual.

◆

Claudia looked up from her codex when she heard her father's footsteps. He'd been blissfully happy for the past two weeks. His mood had never stayed so high for so long before. Every time he came back from meeting with his new Christian friends, he almost had a glow about him.

He walked over and kissed her on the top of her head. "What are you reading today?"

"The new codex you got me. Maybe you could read me some of the poems again? Especially the one that's your favorite right now."

"Of course. Anything you'd like."

She beamed up at him. "I love it when you read to me, Father."

She held out the codex and patted the bench next to her. He took it and sat down. He opened the codex to a poem near the middle, but he paused before beginning to read.

"It was another wonderful worship time today. I learned even more about how much God loves us all. Knowing that Jesus set me free from my sins—I can't describe how wonderful that feels."

It was obvious something unusual had happened to Father, but Claudia couldn't imagine what that might be. Maybe it was time to ask.

Father took her hand. "I know you haven't been interested in the past in hearing about sin and forgiveness and the sacrifice God Himself made, but I would love to tell you everything as soon as you care to hear it."

For a moment, she considered telling him she wanted to hear.

"Aemilia is already expecting me this afternoon. She was planning to show me some new jewelry that her father just bought her, and then we were going shopping for some new sandals to wear with it."

She paused. As she looked into her father's eager eyes, she almost asked him to tell her right then.

Then the stable slave entered the garden and bowed. "Your sedan chair awaits you, mistress."

Claudia placed her hand on her father's arm as she stood. "I would love to have you tell me more later this week, when we have time for a long talk." She kissed his cheek and turned to follow the slave from the garden.

◆

Publius's smile broadened as Claudia disappeared through the portal. He'd watched her face closely, and for the first time, he didn't see that artificial smile she used to politely remove herself from an uncomfortable conversation. His precious daughter was almost ready for the discussion that might transform her life, just as it had his.

Lucius had been to the Baths of Trajan, and he'd decided to drop in to visit his father. It was, after all, his duty as a son, even though he and Father had nothing in common. If the truth were known, it would have shocked both Claudia and Father that he was hoping to find their father developing a health problem. Anything that would hasten Father's death and bring freedom from his control would be welcome.

His father's obvious vigor was a disappointment, but there was something different since Lucius had seen him a month ago—something he couldn't explain. Father seemed too happy. Usually when Lucius visited, his father's facial expressions were at best neutral and more often disapproving. Today, Father had smiled broadly when he first approached and spoken words that sounded like he was really glad to see his son. It had been years since he'd had that kind of response to his visit.

◆

Claudia had thoroughly enjoyed shopping with Aemilia. Her best friend wasn't a scholar or even remotely interested in the deep subjects she loved discussing with her father, but she was a dear friend with a kind heart and a generous spirit. The girls loved spending time together.

It was almost time for dinner when she returned home. As she walked into the atrium from the *vestibulum*, Lucius entered from the library.

"Lucius! What a nice surprise. Are you going to join us for dinner?"

"Not today. I was just at the baths and thought I'd drop in to pay my respects to Father before I went home."

"I'm sorry. It's been much too long since you spent some time with Father and me. It would have been so nice if you could have stayed."

Lucius and Father disagreed about so many things since Father became a God-fearer. Too many times, she'd heard Father criticizing Lucius for something, and then they would argue. Lucius usually left angry, and Father was always sad for a while after that. If only they got along better. She sighed. A nice dinner together might have helped.

◆

Lucius pasted on a fake smile. "I already have an engagement for this evening. I'm sorry I can't stay. Father seemed unusually happy today. I haven't seen him this happy in a long time. Do you know why?"

"Yes. He's become a Christian."

Lucius couldn't believe his ears. Being a Christian was a capital offense in parts of the Empire, and Father becoming one presented the perfect opportunity. One of his good friends was a praetor who hated Christians, and he would be glad to interrogate and condemn Lucius's father if he wouldn't worship Caesar. This was even better than finding his father was sick.

He concentrated on keeping his smile from becoming a smirk. "Really? Is that why he's so happy today? I thought something must have happened. When did he do that?"

"About two weeks ago. He's been happy all the time since then."

"I knew he was happy as a God-fearer, but I didn't expect him to become a Christian. Do you know who talked Father into this? Was it one of his good friends?"

"I don't really know. He just came home from his meeting at the synagogue two weeks ago and told me he thought Jesus was the solution to all his worries about being a sinner. Other than that, I don't know anything about why he decided to become one."

Lucius fought to suppress a grin. This was the solution to all his problems. A single conversation with his friend, and he would be well on his way to being the new head of the family.

"Thank you, Claudia."

As Lucius walked through the *vestibulum* and the door slave opened the door for him, Claudia stood staring at his back. What on earth could he possibly be thanking her for?

The bright morning sunshine was streaming in through the window of Claudia's bedchamber. Graecia had almost finished pinning the last of the curls in her elegant hairdo when Claudia heard the commotion in the atrium. The sound of tramping feet was followed by a man's voice barking commands. She rose from her vanity stool and hurried to the door. Her father was facing a centurion, who stood with his hand resting on his sword.

"Are you Publius Claudius Drusus?"

Father's head tipped. "I am. What's your business here?"

"I am here to arrest you for the crime of treason."

Her father's head snapped back. "Treason? I am a loyal son of Rome. I have committed no treason."

"You are charged with being a Christian, and you are summoned to answer the charge. You will come with us now."

Claudia ran from her room to throw her arms around her father. "No! You can't take him. He's never done anything wrong."

The centurion stared at her stone-faced, unmoved by her distress.

Publius kissed his daughter's forehead. "It's all right, child. I knew this might happen, and it's all right."

He extracted himself from her arms. "Graecia. Come take her."

The maid hurried over and wrapped her arm around Claudia. Publius rested his hand on his treasured daughter's cheek and wiped away some tears. She grabbed his other hand and held it to her chest.

"Don't grieve for me, child. No matter what happens, don't grieve. Jesus paid for my sins, and I don't have to be afraid, even if I die. I just wish I'd had more time to explain it all so you'd understand."

"No, Father! Please. Tell them it's all a mistake. Tell them you're not a Christian."

"I can't do that, Claudia. I can't deny my Lord just to stay here, not even for you. I love you, child, more than my own life, but I love Him even more."

Claudia sank to her knees, still clinging to her father's hand. She looked up at the centurion with pleading eyes. "Please! Don't take him."

The centurion pulled their hands apart and shoved Publius ahead of him. "Move."

Claudia leaped to her feet. Graecia wrapped her arms around her and held on as Claudia struggled to reach him one more time.

As they left the atrium, Publius turned to gaze one last time on his beautiful daughter. Then the centurion shoved him forward, and he lost sight of his greatest earthly treasure. His eyes must now be fixed on the heavenly one.

Chapter 9

THE LEGACY

The trial had gone exactly as Publius expected. He'd been given the chance to offer a sacrifice to Caesar as lord and deny Jesus. He had, of course, refused, and now he was in a tiny cell deep under the Flavian Amphitheater waiting for his execution.

A key rattled in the lock, the door swung open, and Appius Manlius Torquatus entered, accompanied by one of his slaves.

His friend strode over to him and placed both hands on Publius's arms.

"I couldn't believe it when I heard you were condemned to the arena for being a Christian. I can get you another hearing with a different praetor, and we can get you out of here. After you make the sacrifice to Caesar, we can put this all behind you."

Publius patted his friend's shoulder. "I appreciate you coming here to see me, my friend. I appreciate your offer to get me a second hearing with an impartial judge, but the result would be the same. But there is something you can do for me before I die."

"What is it?"

"I want to write a final letter to Titus. All my property has been seized. The letter will be the only legacy I can give him. I need to explain why I'm dying and to tell him why I do it willingly."

Appius's head bounced back. "You don't want to fight this?"

Publius shook his head as a slow smile formed. "No. I can't do what it would take to win. I can't sacrifice to Caesar without denying my Lord Jesus, and I will not do that."

Appius peered deep into his eyes before the slow nod came. He turned to his slave. "Glyptus, go buy pen and ink and plenty of papyrus sheets and bring it all back here as quickly as you can."

His slave bowed and hastened away to execute his master's command.

"I'll stay here until Glyptus returns to make sure he can get back in. He'll wait while you write and then bring the letter to me. I'll make sure it gets to Titus."

Appius lowered his head to stare at the filthy floor. He stood in silence, searching for something to say to a friend who was about to die. The pain in his eyes when he looked up again spoke volumes.

"Appius, you have been my best friend for more than thirty years. There won't be time to explain why I'm making this choice to die for Jesus so you could possibly understand. I want you to promise me you'll read what I write to Titus before you send it. Then maybe you'll see why I have no other choice."

Appius nodded without speaking. His jaw clenched. Publius had never seen him at a loss for words, even after the carnage of the battles they'd fought in their youth. A Roman was supposed to be strong, able to face anything stoically, even to joke about death. But it was obvious Appius couldn't bear the loss of his closest friend that way.

Publius chose his next words to soften the blow. "Did you make it to the lecture that Lartius Licinius gave yesterday on Vespasianus when he commanded the II Augusta Legion during the invasion of Britannia?"

"Yes." Appius's eyebrows shot up. Publius suppressed his grin. It was a very odd question from a man about to die.

"Good. I've always enjoyed Licinius's lectures on Britannia. I hope you can tell me some of the highlights while we wait."

"Of course. He thought the decision to move the II Augusta from Germania to Britannia was..." Appius began their last discussion of history with a sigh of relief.

Publius fixed his gaze on Appius and nodded at the important points. His friend couldn't speak the words he wanted to say, but Publius could let him think their discussion had helped him think of something other than the lions for the few remaining minutes they had together.

He didn't need the distraction, but his friend couldn't yet understand that. Perhaps after he read the letter, he would.

When the slave returned with the writing materials, Publius rested his hand on Appius's shoulder.

"It's time, my friend. Thank you for this last discussion. Remember your promise to read my letter before sending it to Titus."

"I will."

Appius stepped to the door and called the guard. When the door opened, he stood for a moment, his lips squeezed tight as his gaze lingered one last time on his best friend. Then he turned and slowly walked away.

Publius pointed to a corner. "There's a dry spot over there, Glyptus. Sit, if you wish. This will take some time."

As Publius began to write the most important letter of his life, he gave thanks to God for this last chance to share the faith worth dying for, first with his best friend and then with his best son.

When Malleolus walked through the atrium and past Claudia's room, he heard her crying...again. He wanted to cry himself. The master he'd followed into battle on the frontier before becoming steward—the master who'd freed him and called him friend, the master he loved like a brother—had been betrayed by the scum of a son that he now had to treat like the master himself.

He would do anything to save Publius, but what could he do? The great wealth of the Claudius Drusus family was, to a large extent, due to Malleolus's extraordinary skill in managing all the master's estates and other affairs, but none of it was his. He'd invested his own small salary, but he had too little to help the best man he'd ever known. If only there were something, anything, he could do to get Publius out of the cells beneath the arena.

Decimus Lentulus had just returned to Rome. His father, Tiberius, had finished his term of service as governor of Germania Superior and had chosen his son to command the cavalry troop that escorted him back to Rome. His father was planning to build Decimus's network of politically valuable acquaintances before he had to return to his post as senatorial tribune of a legion in Germania. A few months ago, nothing would have pleased Decimus more. He now had other priorities, and the need for a serious private conversation with his best friend, Titus Drusus, was uppermost in his mind.

When Decimus knocked on the door of the Drusus house, it was opened by a house slave he didn't recognize.

"I've come to see Titus."

"Master Titus is not at home."

"Do you expect him soon?" Disappointment dragged Decimus's mouth down.

"He is serving now in Perinthus in Thracia. He hasn't been home for more than three years, and we don't expect him within the next year."

Disappointment surged through Decimus, then his frown flipped into a smile. Publius would be even better for part of what he needed. Who better to consult than the man to whom he'd brought all his ethical quandaries during his youth? In all the ways that were important, Publius had served in the role of father when his own was too busy with political affairs.

"Is Publius here? I'll speak with him instead."

The door slave tensed at his words and glanced behind him before answering. "My former master doesn't live here anymore."

The news of Publius's death was like a punch in the stomach. "When did he die?"

The question made the door slave twitch. Before he could answer, the slender form of an older man stepped into Decimus's view of the atrium.

"Malleolus."

The man's gaze lifted from the mosaic floor and swung onto Decimus.

"Decimus?" Malleolus strode into the *vestibulum* and spoke to the door slave. "Admit him. I'll attend to this business."

The slave bowed to Decimus and swung the door wide open so he could pass. Malleolus motioned for Decimus to follow.

The old steward led him into a small room that opened to the right off the atrium. He walked to the far corner of the room and summoned Decimus with a wave of his hand.

As he stood with his eyes fixed on the doorway, Malleolus spoke in a voice that was barely above a whisper. "I am so glad to see you, Decimus. Terrible things have happened here this past week. Publius is no longer here, but he's not dead yet. I hope you can convince him to change his course so he won't be killed."

Decimus lowered his own voice to a whisper. "What's happened?"

"Publius has become a Christian and is now in the cells at the Amphitheater, waiting to be killed in the games this week. There is no one in Rome more loyal to Emperor Trajan than my new patron. Because of that, Lucius made the difficult choice of honoring Caesar instead of his father. May Rome have many more such patriotic citizens. He reported his father's treasonous rejection of the Roman gods. When my old master was charged with being a Christian, he would not perform the sacrifices to Caesar and was sentenced to die. In gratitude for his loyal service to Rome, the Drusus estates and other property were awarded to Lucius instead of being confiscated."

Malleolus's praise for Lucius and his treachery didn't fool Decimus. It was only for the benefit of anyone who might overhear their conversation. He had no doubt about the loyalty and affection the old steward had for his real patron.

"What would you have me do?" Decimus doubted anything could be done, but Publius's steward was as shrewd as they come. If anyone could devise a plan that might work, it was Malleolus.

"Master Publius has always loved you as if you were his own son. If he will listen to anyone, it's you. If you could go to him and convince him to deny the Christian god and return to the worship of the gods of Rome, he could be spared. That's all it would take."

Malleolus's eyes were pleading as he gazed at Decimus. "I would try myself, but it will take someone with influence and money even to gain admittance to see him. As senatorial tribune, you have both."

"I'll go speak with him this morning. Are you sure he's already in the cells at the Amphitheater?"

Malleolus took Decimus's hand in both of his as intense gratitude overspread his face.

"Yes. I overheard Lucius tell one of his friends last night."

Decimus placed his other hand on the old steward's shoulder. "I will do all I can, but I may not be able to convince him. The loyalty of Christians to their god is beyond what I understand. They will sacrifice what they love most to him, and nothing can turn them from that decision."

"It's enough that you even try."

Decimus squeezed Malleolus's shoulder. "I'll go right now. I will try, and we will see."

Malleolus escorted Decimus back to the door, and the door slave let him out.

◆

Decimus's visit brought a ray of hope to Malleolus. If there was anyone who might convince Master Publius to turn from the course that would kill him, it was this young man the master loved like his own son.

Malleolus started toward Claudia's room to tell her Decimus had gone to the Amphitheater to convince her father to offer the sacrifice. Before he reached her door, he changed his mind. If Decimus succeeded, she would soon know when her father returned to them. But if he failed...perhaps it was better to say nothing. It would be too cruel to raise her hopes only to have them dashed if her father insisted on dying rather than deny his god.

Chapter 10

HELP FOR HIS EXTRA SON

Publius was alone in his cell. The guards had just taken away the family who'd shared it with him. They'd spent the night singing and praying, and the time had passed quickly. The father had asked him to pray for the lions to take his children first in a swift, painless death. He was in the middle of that prayer when a key scraped in the lock. The door swung open, and a tall man carrying a torch stepped inside.

"Call when you wish to leave, tribune." The guard snapped a salute before he closed the door, leaving it unlocked.

Publius was sitting on the filthy floor with his back resting against the cold, damp wall. The tall man slid the torch into a ring on the wall and strode toward him.

"Decimus?" Publius could scarcely believe his eyes. "I thought you were in Germania."

Decimus took Publius's hands and helped him to his feet. "I escorted Father back to Rome. He's finished his term as governor. I'll be returning to the province soon."

Publius pulled Decimus into a fierce hug before holding him at arms' length. "I didn't expect to see you before I died. I thank God for this chance to say goodbye to my fourth son. How did you know I was here?"

"I went to your house to see Titus, and Malleolus told me. He sent me to persuade you to worship Caesar and be pardoned."

"He's a faithful servant and a good friend. I'm sorry my death is causing him such grief, but I won't change my course. I die gladly for my God. I can never deny Jesus to please Caesar."

Decimus stared at the ground as silence filled the cell. When he finally looked up, he locked his gaze on Publius's eyes. "I knew you wouldn't. That's part of why I came. You've always guided me in everything that's truly important, and I'm facing the most important decision I've ever had to make."

Decimus's eyes clouded as Publius watched his thoughts churn. Then Publius placed his hand on his young friend's shoulder. "What is it, son? Let me help you."

Decimus took a deep breath as he ran his fingers through his hair. "I'm in love with a Christian woman, and she loves me, too, but she rejected my proposal because I don't love her god. She loves your Jesus more than me, more than her own life, more than anything. I need to know why you're both willing to give up everything for him, and I need to decide if I can follow him, too." His voice broke. "Help me understand so I can decide."

Nothing Decimus could have said would have shocked Publius more. His almost-son had always been certain of his destiny to help rule the Empire and eager to pursue it. Publius had never seen a young man so sure of what he wanted and so committed to doing whatever it took to get it. He and Tiberius had agreed that Claudia would never be the right wife for him for that very reason.

Decimus's distress kept Publius's smile from growing too broad, but he thanked God for this chance to share his faith with the young man he loved like his own son. "Tell me all about it, and maybe I can tell you what God needs you to hear."

Decimus poured out his tale of being ambushed, how a Germanic Christian risked her life to save him because of Jesus's command, about the miracles of him not dying from mortal injuries and of his sight returning. He told Publius how she'd made him part of her family, how he read their Scriptures and heard their prayers, and how much she wanted him to believe like they did. He told of how he fell in love and asked her to marry him, and how she loved him too but rejected him because she thought marrying him would mean denying Jesus.

"And now I'm back in Rome, and I find the man I love and respect most in the world, the wisest man I've ever known, has made the same choice she did—to give up everything else for the love of Jesus. I must know why. How is it possible to love a dead man who claimed to be god enough to give up everything for him?"

Publius listened and nodded as Decimus poured out his heart. When he finished, Publius rubbed the back of his neck. How best to explain his journey to faith to his extra son?

"Let me tell you how I came to my decision. Maybe then you will understand."

It began like the many conversations Publius had enjoyed with Titus and Decimus in their teen years. He explained, Decimus asked questions, and Publius led his young friend through the failings of the philosophers that convinced him to follow the God of Israel. He explained sin and the way God covered it so people could approach Him, and how Jesus's bloody death on the cross ended the need for any future sacrifices.

Decimus's nods and questions were proof he was following the logic, but irrefutable logic wasn't all Publius had to share.

Publius placed his hand on Decimus's shoulder, and he felt the warm presence of God surround him. "And then I met God. He came to me and He lives in me. The day I decided to believe, to repent of my sins and commit myself to Jesus as my Lord, all the darkness and decay in my life was replaced by brightness and newness."

He stared past Decimus, his mind embracing something only he could see. "It was as if I'd never seen beauty before, never tasted sweetness before, never known what it meant to be fully alive. Following Jesus is like the finest marriage; denying Him would be like committing adultery against the most loving, beautiful, faithful wife a man could have. I could never betray my Lord that way."

Publius's eyebrows dipped as he lowered his arm. "When Lucius reported me as a Christian, I knew what my sentence would be. The praetor who heard my case is Lucius's good friend. He's well known to hate Christians, especially those of the senatorial and equestrian orders."

His smile broke free again. "But I have no regrets. I'm content to die because it isn't death that matters. It's whether you have accepted Jesus as Savior. Death is a tragedy apart from Jesus. Without Jesus, I would be lost, in hell, forever separated from God. With Jesus as my Savior, death has no power over me. I don't fear it. It will just usher me into life with Him in heaven.

"I know Lucius betrayed me because he wants full control of his life and the family fortune. He wasn't content to wait until I died naturally. I've forgiven him, and I pray that somehow God will reach him so he'll choose to follow Jesus, too."

The pain born of that betrayal triggered a deep sigh.

"I pray for Claudia and Titus, too." Wistfulness softened the tone of Publius's voice. "My only regret is leaving Claudia under Lucius's guardianship. I wish it was Titus. He would select the right husband. Marriage to the wrong man will crush her gentle heart. I know my arrest and coming death are devastating her, but I pray that God will care for her when I am gone.

"I've written Titus to tell him why I believe in Jesus, that I'm happy to die for Him so he is not to grieve, and that he must find a way to forgive his brother for turning me in. I've told him that I will be praying for all my children until I take my final breath and even after that in heaven."

Publius placed his hand once more on Decimus's shoulder and squeezed. In all their years together, Publius had never seen Decimus cry, but that touch almost breached the dam holding back his young friend's tears.

"I will pray for you as well. For many years, you've been my extra son. May Jesus claim your heart and mind as His own so you can know the joy and peace I've found."

Decimus ran his fingers through his hair and shook his head. "All you say makes sense, but how can I know it's true? Just because something is logical, that doesn't mean it's true."

"But it is true. Jesus told us that He is the way, the truth, and the life. He promised if a man would believe in Him and follow, he would know the truth and the truth would set him free. If you let Him, Jesus will show you what is true. Open your mind to Him, Decimus. Open your heart. Know the truth and be free like I am, even in this prison as I wait to die."

Decimus shook his head again. "I can't do that. I have to know something is true before I can believe it, not the other way around."

"Let God help you. Know that Jesus loves you and wants you to come to Him."

"That's what she said." Decimus's voice caught. "But I don't know, and I need more help to decide."

Decimus took a deep breath and released it as he squared his shoulders. "I'm not going to just leave you here to die. You'll be in the arena with the lions before week's end. I have enough money with me to pay the bribe to get you out. I know she'll gladly take you in for as long as you need. I can get you out of Rome and send you to her. You can safely follow Jesus there."

With both his hands resting on Decimus's shoulders, Publius gazed at the young man who loved him enough to risk everything by helping a condemned man escape. "My son, I don't want to get out unless it's God's will to free me without any bribery. There's nothing on this earth worth you dying to free me. The lions kill quickly, and then I'll be with my Lord Jesus forever."

Publius's mouth curved into a smile. "Death comes to every man, but mine will open the door to eternal joy and peace and perfect life without end. My brothers and sisters in Christ who have already died await me across the threshold. I'm ready to begin my new life with my Lord Jesus forever."

Decimus stared at him, Clearly, he still couldn't comprehend how Publius could be so at peace with his coming death. "But—"

Publius placed his finger on Decimus's lips and stopped him. "It's time for you to go. You shouldn't be here if the guards come again to take more of us up to the arena. They've already taken the people for the lions today, but they may take some for the gladiators this afternoon. I'll probably go up tomorrow. Don't grieve for me. Rejoice instead. I'm going to be with my Lord."

Publius wrapped his arm around Decimus's shoulders and guided him toward the door. "I'll be praying for you, Decimus. For you to hear God's call to you and choose to follow Jesus with your whole heart, as I have. Then this parting will only be a farewell, and not a goodbye."

He called through the tiny window, "Guard, we're through."

The hinges creaked as the door swung open. As Decimus stepped through the doorway, he looked back, and the sight of Decimus's clenched jaw as he fought against tears almost brought tears to Publius's own eyes. The pain in Decimus's eyes would be mirrored in Titus's when he heard of Publius's death. If only his letter could be the first announcement, so the pain of that loss could be soothed by the knowledge that he hadn't really died at all.

"Farewell, my son. I pray I'll see you again as my brother. May the grace and peace of my Lord Jesus be with you."

The guard closed the door and locked it.

Publius shook his head as he stared at the door. Decimus had always preferred history to philosophy and had dreamed of making history himself. Now he was on the verge of abandoning everything in his search for God because of the love of a Christian woman.

Publius's only regret was that he would never get the chance to lead Claudia and Titus to know the God he now loved more than anything. Perhaps, as for Decimus, God would bring true loves into his children's lives who could help them find their way. Until death, that would be his most fervent prayer.

As he closed his eyes to pray, a song of thanksgiving filled his heart with peace. Jesus had sought and found him. Surely Jesus could reach his beloved children as well.

Malleolus had waited eagerly for Decimus's return, but he wasn't surprised when he heard that Publius refused to change his mind about not worshiping Caesar. Publius had even refused to let Decimus pay a bribe to get him out before he was killed. Now there was no hope that Malleolus's dearest friend would live past the end of the week. It was good he had said nothing to Claudia. First to hope and then to have that hope ripped away would have been more than she could bear.

Barely picking at her food, teetering on the verge of tears all the time—that worried him greatly. What if crushing grief carried her past tears to something that led to her death?

Malleolus had always scoffed at the idea that someone could die of grief, but now he wasn't so sure.

Chapter 11

New Head of the Family

As Publius and the other believers walked out of the tunnel that led into the arena the next morning, he was almost blinded by the brightness of the sand and sky after the darkness of his cell. The small girl who walked beside him covered her face with her hands and froze. Before the soldier escorting them could jab her with his sword, Publius knelt beside her and eased her hands away from her face.

"Look at me, child."

She opened her eyes and gazed into his. With eyes showing no fear, he smiled at her.

"Take my hand, and we'll walk together to join Jesus in heaven. He's waiting for us right now with open arms. We're almost there."

She slid her small hand into his large one. Together, they walked to the center of the arena.

Chains rattled as the mesh gate of the lion cage was raised enough to let the big cats enter.

Publius knelt beside the little girl. "Look up. See Jesus?"

She tilted her head back, and a bright smile appeared as she nodded.

"Now close your eyes, and don't open them until you're in his arms."

While his left hand enveloped hers, he raised his right toward heaven and began to sing the song of praise he'd learned that first day at Aristarchus's house.

The two lionesses hit them almost simultaneously. One quick bite to the neck, and Publius was free forever.

Lucius had already moved into the town house, and he expected to spend very little time in the near future at the estate that had been his home. His wife was there with their children, and the way Cornelia looked at him since his father was arrested...a loathsome bug would have felt more respected.

With Father dead, he was *paterfamilias* now. If it weren't for Cornelia's dowry money, he'd divorce her. That and not wanting a scandal so soon after Father's death. He felt the condemnation in the gazes of many at the forum. Cornelia had many friends, and her brothers were too important to have as enemies. But at least he didn't have to spend his evenings with her anymore. That thought drew a smile.

By moving into town, he'd also escaped the nuisance of his daughter crying at night. For some unfathomable reason, Cornelia had chosen to nurse herself, and more than once his sexual pleasure had been interrupted by the infant's greedy cries. The baby was almost two but she still made much more noise than he liked.

He'd left the baby behind, but he hadn't escaped the sound of a bawling female. The slightest thing triggered Claudia's tears since Father had been taken away, and he was sick of it. He would never have admitted it to anyone, but her tears pricked what little conscience he had over getting his father killed.

As he walked toward her room, he heard the sobs yet again. It was long past time that she should have that under control.

When he stepped into the room, Claudia's maid was standing at her bedside. He flicked his hand to summon her before he stepped back into the atrium.

The maid bowed her head and clasped her hands at her waist as she waited for his orders. He kept his voice low. What he told any slave of his was none of Claudia's business.

"What are you doing to get Claudia to stop this constant fussing?"

"Whatever I can, master. I hold her hand. I rub her back. I sit with her after the nightmares."

Lucius's brows dipped. "It isn't enough. I want this crying to stop. Father is dead, and it's time she accepted it and moved on. You're the closest one to her. I expect you to start cheering her up. Now...or there will be consequences for you."

The maid's eyes widened. "I truly am trying, master, but nothing I've tried seems to work. I just don't know what will."

"Figure it out. If she keeps this up, she's going to make herself sick. I'll give her two more weeks, and then...it has to stop. See to it that it does."

She lowered her eyes. "Yes, master."

With a flick of his hand, he sent her back to her mistress.

Lucius walked on to the library and seated himself at his father's desk. The chair was comfortable; it was a pleasant place to spread a scroll and read. A matching chair gave equal comfort to someone who might sit across the desk for a board game. Father and Claudia had played there often. The painted seascapes and mountain views that adorned the walls made it easy to forget the urban congestion of Rome waiting outside. The barred window near the ceiling was too small to admit a thief while it added to the light streaming in from the atrium. The library had been Father's favorite room. It had already become his.

Lucius picked up a bronze-tipped ivory stylus and drummed on the desktop. Crying herself sick—that could ruin Claudia's beauty and diminish the money he expected to get for betrothing her in the next few weeks.

Father had turned down too many marriage proposals. Claudia was already sixteen; she should be married. Now that Father was dead, some of the wealthy patrician families that he'd refused were approaching Lucius. He would soon be making his selection.

Roman marriage didn't officially involve payment of a bride price, but money often changed hands to sway the choice of a guardian. He hadn't quite decided whether he would place more weight on the importance of the family or the amount of money they were offering to encourage him to give them Claudia. Most of the offers were impressive on both counts. The best were more than enough to repay him for the dowry he planned to provide her. He wouldn't mind coming out money ahead when he made the final decision.

Lucius was reading some satirical poetry by Lucilius when the door slave came to announce a visitor.

"Master, Flavius Sabinus has come to see you. I have seated him in the atrium."

"Bring him here to me." Lucius rubbed his cheek. He hadn't expected such a distinguished caller so soon after assuming headship of the family. He'd heard many things about Sabinus, most of which made it clear that he was not a man to be trifled with. His sudden appearance made Lucius a bit nervous.

Lucius stood respectfully as Sabinus entered the room.

He held out his hand to offer his influential visitor the guest chair. "You honor me with your visit, Flavius Sabinus. I've never had the pleasure of receiving a pillar of Roman society like yourself before."

◆

Sabinus looked around the room at the many shelves of codices and scrolls. The room reflected the personality of its former owner, yet the current one seemed more at home in it than he expected. Still, his inquiries about Lucius suggested the son would be much more receptive to his proposal than the father ever would have been. A man who would betray his own father to inherit early was a man he could deal with.

"I thought it appropriate to pay my respects to a man who loves Rome so much that he would choose her over all else. Rome should have many more sons who would choose her even over family loyalties." His lips smiled, and he willed his eyes to be warm instead of coldly reptilian.

"It was the most difficult thing I've ever done. My father was a fine man until he chose to abandon his duty to Rome. His absence from this house has brought great sadness to us all."

Sabinus was expert at reading people, and watching Lucius was entertaining. The new head of the Claudius Drusus family was still an amateur at the game of deceit, but he had the potential to become a master.

"I believe your sister Claudia was especially close to your father. She must be greatly affected by his death."

"Yes. Father doted on her, and she almost worshiped him. This is very hard for her." Lucius started to reach to rub the back of his neck, but stopped himself. Sabinus suppressed a smile. He liked to make people nervous, but he didn't want this one to know that...yet.

"I have observed that the quickest way to get over a loss is a change of scenery. To remain in this house, with all its memories of better times, is very bad for her."

"It's hard for us all. I'm sure she will recover in time."

"Perhaps I can help with that." The crocodile began positioning himself to capture the prey. "I was in conversation with your father about marrying your sister just before he was arrested. While many fine Roman families might now be unwilling to accept the daughter of one who rejected his duty to Rome, I am a man who does not hold the crimes of the parent against the child. I'm still interested in taking her as my wife."

Lucius's two fast blinks ushered in a broad smile. "That's extremely generous of you, Flavius Sabinus. We are honored that you would still consider Claudia worthy of your regard."

Sabinus almost let his self-satisfied smile out, but he replaced it with a friendly one before Drusus should have seen.

Lucius's brow began to furrow, then it smoothed. "I'm glad to say that many of the finer families in Rome share your generous spirit. Several have already let me know they would welcome Claudia as a daughter-in-law despite my father's unfortunate choice."

Sabinus kept his friendly smile, but he did not like that response. The son should have been easier to manipulate than the father. Competition for anything he wanted was unwelcome, and he wanted Claudia.

"That does them credit. She is a beautiful girl, and I am glad she won't have to suffer rejection by Roman society."

"As far as I can tell, she's as sought after now as she was before. My father had turned down several marriage proposals. I believe most of those families are still eager for my sister to join them."

◆

Lucius saw a flicker of emotion in the reptilian eyes. It might be anger, but it was gone before he could be certain.

"Yes, but their eagerness may not be equal to my own. Your father and I were discussing 50,000 denarii as a token of my great esteem for your sister."

Lucius hoped he hadn't let his amazement at the size of the offer show, but he was new at this game. Something about Sabinus wanting his sister that badly made his skin crawl. He'd heard the rumor that his last wife had died from a beating at his hands. Lucius wasn't close to Claudia, but even he wasn't eager to send his little sister into the hands of that kind of man.

"That's an extraordinarily generous offer. There are some that are comparable, but that is certainly one of the most generous."

"Your sister is an extraordinary beauty, worth the price."

"This is a great compliment to her. I'll be considering what will be best for Claudia over the next few weeks, and I will certainly take your admiration and respect for her into strong consideration as I choose her husband."

Sabinus's eyebrow rose, then settled. Lucius's response was clearly not the one Sabinus had expected and certainly not the response he wanted.

"I am sure that, upon reflection, you will come to a wise decision that will benefit both yourself and your sister. An alliance with my family can be a great advantage that would extend far past my monetary expression of appreciation of her worth. Having the right friends and avoiding the wrong enemies can be of immeasurable value."

A chill ran up Lucius's spine as he looked into the predatory eyes of the cold-blooded power broker. He wasn't sure just how dangerous it might be to cross him. He didn't especially want to sell Claudia into a bad marriage, but if it came down to a question of selling Claudia or risking harm to himself, the sale would go through.

"Her grief is so intense right now that I'm reluctant to commit her to a marriage for a few weeks. I can assure you that your kind interest will not be forgotten when the time comes."

More than anything, Lucius wanted to end this audience with the crocodile as soon as possible. He'd never before had the feeling of being no more than a bug to be squashed if he got in the way.

"I quite understand. A proper time of grieving must be allowed. My interest will remain when you think it's time for her to move on and marry."

Sabinus stood. "I have matters of state to attend to, so I must leave you now."

Lucius stood as well. "Thank you again for the honor of your visit. You'll be hearing from me when it's time."

"I'm sure I will."

The crocodile smiled at Lucius before turning to leave. Lucius escorted him through the atrium to the door personally. One more cold-eyed smile from the crocodile at the doorway drove home the importance of making the right decision when the time came.

Lucius returned to the library and seated himself at his father's desk. He was certain Father would never have taken the 50,000 denarii to marry Claudia to such a man. He knew he shouldn't, either. He'd delayed having to turn Sabinus down, but he would have to respond to the offer sometime. Maybe something would come up so he didn't have to make an enemy of one of the most powerful men in Rome.

Chapter 12

Selling Claudia

Claudia tossed on her bed as the lions entered the arena yet again. The great male with the black mane stared at Father. As the lion started trotting toward him, she heard his first scream of fear. He turned and ran, but the lion was much faster. The beast leaped upon him and began clawing his back open. So much blood. His screams changed from fear to agony. He rolled over and struggled to hold the lion's fangs away from his face. Finally, he could resist no more, and the beast's jaws clamped down on his head. Then everything turned red.

She jerked awake, shaking uncontrollably. In the darkness, she curled into a tight ball. First came the silent tears, then the sobs she couldn't control.

Graecia came into the room. "Mistress? Do you need something?"

"Yes…I need my father." Great hiccupping sobs made further words impossible.

Claudia rolled on her stomach, buried her head in the pillow, and continued sobbing.

◆

Graecia sat on the bed beside Mistress Claudia and slowly rubbed her back. Tears filled her eyes as she watched the mistress suffer. If the last few nights were any indication, it would be at least an hour before the mistress cried herself to exhaustion and finally went back to sleep.

When Lucius walked into the garden, he heard the sound of Claudia crying...again. He would never have believed that one girl could possibly shed so many tears. He followed the sound and found her sitting under the grape arbor.

"Do you have to cry all the time, Claudia? It's time for you to stop. Father's dead, and tears won't change that."

She stared up at him as she flicked away some tears. "How can you be so unconcerned that Father's been killed? It's as if you didn't love him at all. I know you and Father fought a lot, but he always loved you."

"Do you really think so? I don't. All he ever did was criticize me. And making me live like one of those God-fearers? He made my life miserable these last three years. I'm glad he's dead."

Her eyes saucered. "You can't mean that. No son ever had a better father."

"No son had a worse one. He disgraced our family name and betrayed Rome by becoming a Christian. I love Rome, Claudia. More than I ever loved him. It was my duty to report him." Lucius hadn't intended to tell her that, but somehow it felt good to get it out in the open.

Claudia was thunderstruck. "You? You had Father killed? For Rome?"

She was shaking. As she stared at him, he shifted under her penetrating gaze. Then her eyes flared as the truth struck.

"No. You didn't do this for Rome. You did it for yourself. You wanted Father dead so you could have all the estates and the money and do whatever you wanted. You murdered him as much as if you stuck a dagger into his heart yourself. You should be flogged and sewn into one of those leather bags and tossed in the Tiber. I'd gladly use the scourge myself."

She rose from the bench as her voice rose in pitch and volume. "You don't deserve to inherit and lead this family. You should be dead instead of Father. I hate you!"

She raised her hand to strike him, but Lucius caught her wrist in an iron grip. "That's enough. You will not speak to me like that."

Claudia jerked away from him. "Don't you touch me. I don't want to be anywhere near you. Ever."

The hatred blazing in her eyes triggered his anger. How dare she insult him like that? He was head of the Claudius Drusus family now, and he'd teach her to show him the respect the *paterfamilias* deserved.

"You won't have to stay in my house much longer. Flavius Sabinus has offered me 50,000 denarii for the privilege of marrying you. I was going to think about his offer for a while, but no more. You will marry him."

Claudia's eyes saucered as Lucius declared her fate. "No! He's so old, and I've heard such horrible things about him."

"He's the head of a noble Roman family with great wealth and political influence. You should be honored that he wants you. The decision is not yours, anyway. It's mine, and my decision is final."

Claudia swayed and sank to the ground.

Lucius turned to the slave who was working in the flowerbed. "Take her to her room, then come to me in the library."

The slave lifted her from the ground and supported her as he dragged her, sobbing, back to her bedchamber.

Lucius strode into the library. He picked up his father's stylus and drew a small wax tablet from one of the desk drawers. By the time the slave came from delivering Claudia to Graecia's care, he had written his acceptance of Sabinus's offer.

He handed the tablet to the slave. "Deliver this to Flavius Sabinus."

"Yes, master." The slave bowed and left.

Lucius stood and walked back into the garden. So Claudia wanted him dead and didn't want to stay in his house. He would give her half of what she wanted. Sabinus should be very pleased to receive the tablet saying he had given serious consideration to the proposal and had decided Sabinus would be the ideal husband for his sister. Claudia would be getting what she deserved for saying what she did, and he'd be 50,000 denarii richer in the process.

It was almost time for the Sunday worship to begin, and Publius still had not appeared. Aristarchus was surprised and more than a little concerned. As Philip lifted the gospel by John and asked the Holy Spirit to inspire his teaching, Aristarchus offered a prayer that everything might be all right with his good friend, but he had an uncomfortable sense that it wasn't.

Lucius was in the library, examining the writings his father had acquired over many years. Some he would keep; many he would sell. He was mentally sorting the titles when the door slave entered.

"Master, Flavius Sabinus is here to see you again."

"Bring him to me."

The slave left to bring Sabinus from the *vestibulum* where he was waiting. Lucius had not expected a personal visit by Sabinus that morning. There were many men he would rather see than his future brother-in-law, but he expected to feel more comfortable around the power broker as he got to know him better.

Sabinus was all smiles as he entered the library. "It is good to see you again so soon, Lucius Fidelis."

Lucius's look of surprise at the name brought a cool smile to Sabinus's face.

"In my letter to Trajan yesterday, I mentioned your exemplary dedication to Rome in reporting your father's treasonous decision. He will agree with my suggestion that he bestow a new name upon you, along with a monetary token of his appreciation of your loyalty as a true son of Rome. An emperor at the head of his fighting legions always values such devotion at home. It will take some time for the imperial messenger to return, but I wanted the pleasure of telling you myself right away."

Lucius couldn't have been more surprised, and Sabinus chuckled at his incredulity as he stood momentarily speechless.

"As I told you before, an alliance with my family can be a great advantage."

Lucius finally found his tongue. "I am honored beyond what I can express."

He knew Sabinus had influence with the Emperor, but he never expected this.

"I'm sure you are." Sabinus's lips curved up in a smug smile. "Now to the real reason for my visit. I have come to see my beautiful future wife. It's time for her to begin getting to know me."

"Of course. I'll have her summoned right away."

"You can have your slave take me to a suitable place in your garden. A beautiful woman can best be appreciated in a setting of equal beauty."

Lucius indicated with a wave of his hand that the slave was to escort Sabinus into the garden and then fetch Claudia.

As he watched Sabinus walk out of the library, a satisfied smile overspread Lucius's face. His earlier concerns about dealing with Sabinus seemed rather foolish now. The master of Roman influence would likely turn out to be a very good brother-in-law.

Claudia had been crying, and her eyes were red and puffy. Graecia had just brought some cool water to wash her face after the latest bout of tears when the door slave came to her room.

"Mistress, Flavius Sabinus has come to see you, and I've seated him in the garden, as he requested. He would like you to come to him."

"Tell him I have no desire to see him."

Graecia stepped forward. "What the mistress means to say is tell him she will be there shortly." The slave bowed and left to convey Graecia's version of the message.

"That's not at all what I meant to say, Graecia. Everything I've ever heard tells me he's a horrible man, and I don't want to see him at all."

"I understand, mistress, but Master Lucius has promised him that he will be your husband. I'm afraid of what a man like him might do if you refuse to see him. It will be so much better for you if you can somehow bring yourself to be nice to him. If he likes you, maybe it won't be so bad being his wife."

"Oh, Graecia. How could Lucius give me to a man like him? I know I made Lucius mad when I accused him of murdering Father, but I never dreamed he'd sell me like this. I've never done anything to deserve this."

"I know, mistress, but now that he has, you just have to try to make the best of it."

"But I don't know how I'll ever be able to do that."

"You can start by going out to him in the garden and trying to be nice to him. Please try, mistress. I don't want to see him hurt you, and if he likes you, he might be good to you." As Graecia watched the tears trickling down Claudia's cheeks, her own eyes filled with tears.

Claudia wiped the tears from her cheeks and sighed. "I know you're right, and I'll try. Give me that hideous necklace he sent yesterday. He'll probably want to see me in it."

◆

"Yes, mistress, I'm sure he will."

Relief surged through Graecia. Her young mistress was at least trying to do what Master Lucius wanted. The master expected Graecia to get Mistress Claudia to stop being such an emotional fool, or he'd hold her responsible. She suppressed a shudder as she considered what that might mean. Master Lucius wasn't a patient man, so it was important for the mistress to stop all this crying and get on with life. The sooner she did that, the better for everyone.

Sabinus was beginning to wonder if the lovely Claudia was ever going to appear, and his patience was wearing thin. Then he saw her enter the garden, and the wait was almost worthwhile. Her eyes were puffy from crying, but she was still as exquisitely beautiful as her reputation had promised. She was, in fact, a trophy worth acquiring.

"My dear Claudia, what a vision of loveliness you are today."

◆

The look in his eyes was one of hunger, and it sent chills up Claudia's spine. He was seated on a bench and waved his hand to invite her to join him, but she stopped just in front of him and remained standing.

"I am sorry for the delay in welcoming you, Fabius Sabinus, but your visit was unexpected." She tried to smile at him, but her smile was a tenuous one. She hadn't expected him to be so old and ugly. He was even older than Father, and there was that worn look about him that bespoke the long nights of drinking and women that Aemilia had told her about.

"Call me Quintus. I see you appreciate the necklace I sent as a small token of my regard. I'm glad to see it on you." His raspy voice showed the effects of his excesses. "Your exquisite beauty enhances its own."

His response to her wearing the hideous necklace was exactly what she expected from a man like him. He could buy her from Lucius with money, but if he thought he could buy her affection with expensive gifts, he was wrong. "It was a surprise when such an extravagant gift arrived yesterday. My brother was quite delighted with it."

"A beautiful woman like yourself deserves to be adorned by the most beautiful jewelry." His lips curved into a smug smile as he obviously congratulated himself on her appreciation of his gift. Then he caught the flicker of disdain that crossed her face before she could stop it. His lip twitched as he grasped the subtle sarcasm of her response.

"When you move into my villa, you will find many pieces of jewelry for your enjoyment. I have been acquiring beautiful pieces to adorn my wives for many years."

Claudia fought to suppress her cringe. He was planning on her wearing the jewelry he'd bought for the wife he'd just beaten to death.

◆

Sabinus stood and stepped close to her. The necklace was a 4-inch wide plate of gold suspended from a heavy gold chain and encrusted with seven rubies and ten emeralds. He reached out and fingered the necklace. Then, as he smiled his crocodile smile, he traced its outline where it rested against her breast. She shivered at his touch and stepped back.

She was an unspoiled beauty, and he was not surprised that she withdrew from his intimate touch. He would enjoy their first night much more than she would, but that was fine with him. He really didn't care if she ever enjoyed anything as long as he got his pleasure.

◆

A lecherous gleam appeared in the reptilian eyes. Claudia could stand no more. "If you will excuse me, Flavius Sabinus, I haven't felt well at all today, and I really must leave you now and rest."

"Of course, my dear. We will have years to get to know each other well. Very well, indeed." His smile was a cruel smirk. "I look forward to sharing that intimate knowledge with you." He traced her upper arm with his middle fingertip. "And you should call me Quintus now."

Claudia tipped her head to him and turned away. She would have run from the room, but she forced herself to stroll. He would have liked her to run for the pleasure of watching her distress. Those hungry eyes...she'd never felt so exposed before, and he found pleasure in her fear. He was even colder and almost certainly much crueler than anything Aemilia had suggested.

Lucius must cancel the betrothal. He simply must. She could never stand being married to this horrible man. She would rather die.

◆

Lucius startled when Sabinus stepped into the library unannounced. The old man's lips were tight, and Lucius was instantly nervous in his presence again. He pasted a smile on his own, trying to conceal the effect the crocodile had on him.

Sabinus stood so close to the desk that Lucius had to tip his head back to look into the reptilian eyes. "I'm disappointed in how my future wife's recovery from her grief over her father's death is progressing." His lips smiled but not his eyes. "I'm eager to take her to complete the marriage ceremony and install her in my villa."

"I quite understand your eagerness. She is still deep in her grief, but I think she's beginning to improve. I expect she'll soon be happy to join your family in your home."

◆

Sabinus's gaze raked Drusus from head to lap and back. This son of the scholar wasn't a practiced liar. He hadn't mastered the art of making his eyes and his lips convey the same emotion when it was false. Sabinus had, when he wanted to, but today it would be much better for Drusus to read his thoughts in his eyes rather than believe the lies on his lips.

"I was glad to see your sister's beauty is undiminished. It was good to see her wearing my necklace, although I'm not sure she appreciates its true worth and what it means when she wears it."

He dropped his gaze to the desktop as he drew his index finger along it, then inspected it for dust. When he raised his eyes to meet Drusus's, he let the ice form. "I expected a warmer reception. She is still very young, but she must learn that a woman's role is to get her own pleasure from giving pleasure to her husband. That is something the *paterfamilias* should have under control."

Sabinus smiled stiffly, but the coldness of his eyes fully made his point.

◆

Lucius's stomach knotted under the crocodile's stare. "She's had no mother since she was three, and the duties of a good wife are a mystery to her. Perhaps I should have my own wife talk with her so she has a clearer understanding."

The crocodile smiled again. "That would be wise, for everyone's sake. Now, I must leave. I'm attending to a special matter for the Emperor, and even I don't like to keep Trajan waiting too long."

"Of course. I look forward to your next visit." As Lucius bowed his head, Sabinus turned and walked out.

Lucius looked at his left hand and gripped it with his right to stop the tremor. In his anger with Claudia, he'd foolishly closed the door on any possible escape from becoming permanently tied to one of the most dangerous men in Rome. If only he'd waited. Maybe something would have prevented him from having to be frequently in the company of a man who, quite frankly, scared him half to death.

Chapter 13

No Way Out

Lucius sat at his father's desk, rolling his father's stylus between his fingers when Claudia entered the room. With quick steps, she approached and stopped right in front of the desk.

"Lucius. Please. You've got to get me out of the betrothal to Flavius Sabinus. He was just here, and I tried to be nice to him, but..." Tears began trickling down her cheeks. "Oh, Lucius! He's the most horrible man I've ever met. The way he looked at me, the way he touched me. You know he beat his last wife to death. Please. Don't send me into his house to suffer like she must have before he killed her."

She reached across the desk and gripped his hand. "Please, Lucius. Don't do this to me. I'll never say you murdered Father again. I'll marry anyone else you pick without complaining, but please...don't make me marry him."

As Lucius looked at her agonized eyes, he knew he should tell her he would end the betrothal. He should never send her off into certain suffering and maybe even an early death. He shouldn't make her marry Sabinus...but he was going to, anyway. If he didn't, he would be the victim of some horrible revenge from the crocodile. As much as he might like to spare his sister from what he'd done in a fit of anger, he was much more concerned with protecting himself.

He shook her hand off. "I've given him my word that you'll marry him. I keep my word, Claudia. We'll have no more talk of you not marrying Sabinus. He's from one of the noblest families, he's extremely rich, he moves in the highest social circles, and he tells me he has great admiration for you. He's proving that by paying me 50,000 denarii for the privilege of marrying you. No man spends that kind of money on a woman he plans to harm. The rumors that he killed his wife are only vicious, jealous gossip about a great Roman. You should be honored that such a man wants to marry you. Now leave me, and don't talk to me about this again."

He pulled a wax tablet in front of himself and began writing on it.

Her tears transformed into sobs as she whirled and ran from the room.

Lucius watched her with some regret. Regret that he couldn't go back in time to before Sabinus came to his house and made that wretched offer. If only he'd never met the man. But he had, and to cross one of the most powerful men in Rome, a man whose threats were hardly even veiled, was not a risk he was willing to take. It was much better for Claudia to suffer than to end up suffering himself.

Lucius's wife, Cornelia Scipia, would not have come to the town house from the eastern estate to visit her husband, but she was more than willing to make the trip to visit poor Claudia.

She'd always liked Publius and considered him one of the finest men of her wide acquaintance. Claudia had been the joy of her father's life, as he had been of hers. His gruesome death because of Lucius's betrayal must have devastated her.

Claudia was the same age as her own oldest son, so she was more like a niece than a sister-in-law. The poor girl had no mother, and Cornelia had tried to befriend her, but the eastern villa was far enough from the town house that she hadn't seen as much of Claudia as she probably should have. She could have performed many of the roles of a real mother if she'd lived closer.

Cornelia left her litter in the stable yard and strolled through the peristyle to the atrium. Her nose twitched when she glanced toward Publius's library, where her scum of a husband probably was.

Pain and anger simmered near the surface. Lucius abandoned their marriage bed as soon as his father was arrested. For seven years, she'd endured his many rejections after the birth of their third son ten years earlier. She was a proud daughter of one of the noblest families, and she had never allowed Lucius to see how much it hurt when he chose to spend his nights with promiscuous Roman ladies and even prostitutes rather than with her.

He would have mocked her if she'd ever told him how delighted she'd been when Publius became a God-fearer and told Lucius that the only woman he was allowed was his own wife. Too often he'd complained that she didn't know how to satisfy him like the wanton women Publius had denied him. But their beautiful little daughter, who was now almost two, had been born while Lucius was really her husband again. With Publius dead, Lucius had returned to his womanizing ways. Once more, he'd hurt her deeply, but her pride had carried her through the first round of rejections, and it would carry her through this one. At least she had her precious daughter as consolation.

When Cornelia entered the bedchamber, Claudia was lying facedown on her bed, her shoulders shaking as she cried. Graecia stood beside her mistress, helpless to stop the tears.

Cornelia sat down beside Claudia and rested her hand on the broken-hearted girl's back. She began to rub it. "I'm so sorry about Publius. I wish with all my heart that I could undo what Lucius has done."

Claudia rolled over onto her back. Red-rimmed eyes and the puffiness beneath them marred her usual beauty. "Everything is so horrible. First Lucius had Father killed, and now he's making me marry Flavius Sabinus. You know what he is."

Claudia's breast jerked as she fought against a new flood of tears. "Oh, Cornelia, what am I going to do? I've begged Lucius to release me from the betrothal, but he's going to get 50,000 denarii for marrying me to that horrible old man. He told me there's no way he'll get me out of it."

Claudia's hands clenched. "I hate him! I hate him with every fiber of my being for murdering Father. I hate him for selling me. I wish he was dead. I'd gladly kill him myself if I had the chance."

Cornelia let the threat against her husband's life pass without comment. She'd felt that way many times herself during the years when he'd rejected her. The thought had crossed her mind again this past week.

"He betrothed you to Quintus Flavius Sabinus?" Claudia's nod was accompanied by another jerk. "But he's your father's age."

Cornelia had heard for years about Sabinus's sadistic behavior and studied cruelty to both his now-dead wives.

"Please, Cornelia. Will you go to Lucius? Will you talk him out of doing this to me? I just can't marry that monster."

Cornelia swept some tears from Claudia's cheek. "I'll try, but I don't expect it to do any good. Lucius hasn't cared what I think since before you were born."

"You have to convince him. You're my only hope. If you can't change his mind, life won't be worth living."

"That's not true. Even when all your dreams turn to ashes, life is still worth living, if only to make Lucius see that he hasn't won. You can't let him think he's won. The ultimate revenge is to deprive him of enjoying his victory."

Cornelia offered her sister-in-law a smile that she hoped was encouraging, but the sadness in her own heart over her husband's latest rejection and the death of the father-in-law who'd always been a good friend made her smile a sad one.

"I'll go talk to him. I doubt that he'll listen to me, but I'll try."

The gratitude in Claudia's eyes almost broke Cornelia's heart. She'd be willing to bet nothing would change, and this sweet, beautiful girl would be made to suffer for years. She'd suffered herself, but at least Lucius wasn't a violent man. Despite all his cutting words and cruel neglect, he'd never hit her even once. From all she'd heard, she didn't expect Claudia to have even that small consolation as the wife of Sabinus.

◆

Cornelia found Lucius seated at the desk in his father's library. He was rolling a stylus between his fingers. When she entered, he set the stylus down, and a smile appeared.

"Cornelia. Just the person I need right now."

Cornelia's eyebrow rose at those words. He'd already made it abundantly clear that he didn't need or want her anymore.

"You surprise me, husband. What do you need from me?"

"It's Claudia. She doesn't want to marry the man I've betrothed her to. He's concerned that she doesn't know what's required of a wife. I told him I'd have you talk with her about what makes a good wife."

"You promised her to Quintus Sabinus. Of course she doesn't want to marry him. He's an evil, violent man who will beat her and maybe kill her, just like he did dear, sweet Augusta. You know that. How could you sell your sister to that monster even for 50,000 denarii?"

"You've never had to talk to him. Do you have any idea what kind of power he wields in Rome? He made it very clear that I can't refuse his offer."

"Of course you can. You're Claudius Drusus, not some servile freedman. How can you do this to your sister? Are you a man or what? A real man wouldn't sell his sister for any amount of money just because he's afraid. Would you sell your own daughter? No. And you shouldn't sell your sister."

"For that kind of money from a man who's made it perfectly clear it could prove fatal to refuse him, yes, I'd sell Drusilla. I'd sell you, too."

His words should have shocked her, but they didn't. In her heart, she knew they were true.

"If you were even half the man your father was, you'd stand up to him and stop this."

Lucius's brows slammed down as his fist struck the table. He shot to his feet.

Cornelia swallowed hard, but she rested her hand on her own throat and raised her chin to conceal that from Lucius. The comparison with his father may have been one step too far.

"That's enough. This marriage is going to happen no matter what you or Claudia say. I won't cross a man who could crush us if he chooses. He'd even enjoy doing it."

Cornelia faced her husband with her fists on her hips and eyes flashing with anger. His greed, his cowardice, his failure as a brother and husband—how could a son of Publius have turned out like this?

Disgust and condemnation burned in Cornelia's eyes. That ignited flames in Lucius's eyes as he read her revulsion. He was now *paterfamilias*. He might expect the respect due the head of the family, but she would never give it to a worm like him.

"Enough! You will not speak to me about this again. Go back to the villa. You can teach Claudia her duties to her husband just before the marriage. You seem to forget that obedience and respect are your first duties to me. I have plans with another woman this evening, and I want you gone before she arrives. I'll send for you if I ever want you."

"Don't bother. I won't come merely because you summon me."

She squared her shoulders and tipped her head to look down her nose at him, even though he was several inches taller. "I leave gladly, Lucius. The sight of a man who could betray his father and sell his sister sickens me."

With head held high, she made an elegant turn and walked out of the room.

Cornelia paused outside the door to Claudia's room, but she couldn't make herself enter. It had gone even worse than she expected, and she hadn't the courage to tell Claudia it was even more hopeless than the poor girl already believed.

Her face was an emotionless mask as she passed through the peristyle and into the stable yard where her litter waited. With confident grace, she sat and swung her legs in. As the slaves placed their shoulders under the poles and lifted, she let down the curtains. Then she buried her face in her hands. Her body shook in silence as she wept hot, bitter tears: tears for Claudia, tears for Publius, and tears for the wreck of a marriage she was trapped in herself.

Chapter 14

A True Friend

Too often when Malleolus passed Claudia's bedchamber, her hiccupping sobs were like hammer blows to his heart. Lucius kept complaining about her endless tears. It was time to help her stop.

As he approached, sobs turned to silence. When he entered her room, she was sitting at her dressing table with her back toward him. No sound, but the small jerks of her shoulders revealed her weeping.

In the polished brass mirror, he saw what she held in her hands. She drew a finger along the blade of a small dagger. She turned it in her hands, and then...she turned it toward her breast and raised in into position.

"Claudia!"

She twisted to face him, but she didn't lower the dagger.

Malleolus strode to her side and seized her wrist. "You mustn't do this."

With his free hand, he loosened her grip on the dagger and dropped it on the floor.

The anguish in her eyes matched the quaver in her voice. "But Lucius is going to marry me to that horrible Sabinus. He's older than Father, and I've heard such terrible things about him. Aemilia said he beat his last wife to death. I'd rather die by my own hand than marry him."

Tears dribbled down her cheeks. "Lucius had Father murdered just so he could do whatever he wanted. I can't bear to live here with him, either."

Malleolus enfolded his precious mistress in his arms. She clung to him as silent sobs shook her body.

What was he to do? She had been Publius's greatest treasure, and he loved her as much as her father had. To see her in such pain...it was almost more than he could bear.

"Don't do this, Claudia. It's the last thing your father would have wanted."

Claudia fought to get her tears under control as she gazed up at him. "But I'd rather die than be Sabinus's wife. There's nothing left worth living for."

Malleolus saw more than grief in her anguished eyes. He saw despair. Then it hit him.

He spoke his next question very softly; he wasn't sure where Graecia was. "What if I could keep you from having to marry Sabinus?"

Her eyes widened. "How is that possible? Lucius is the only one who can change that, and he's giving me to Sabinus to punish me for what I said about him murdering Father. He'll never change his mind."

Malleolus knelt before her and took both her hands. He lowered his voice to a whisper in case unfriendly ears might be listening. "I wasn't planning on Lucius changing his mind. What if I could sneak you out of Rome and send you to Titus in Thracia? Would you go?"

Titus still had five years to complete his mandatory ten-year military service. He was permanently assigned to the palace detail in the capital city of Thracia, so he would have regular lodging and not have to travel. If Malleolus could only get her there, Titus should be able to have her live with him.

Claudia's face brightened. "Can you? I know Titus would welcome me, but I have no idea how I could get there safely. It's so far, and I've read how dangerous travel in the eastern provinces can be. I've never been farther from here than the eastern estate." The fleeting look of hope began to fade.

"I know of someone who might help us. Promise me you won't do anything foolish before I see whether I can get you to Titus."

She forced a shaky smile. "I promise. Do whatever it takes to get me out of here. If anyone can save me from Lucius and Sabinus, it's you."

"Say nothing to anyone. Even Graecia. The walls have ears, and Lucius mustn't suspect what we're planning."

She glanced around the room as she nodded.

He rose and walked to the door, but he turned in the doorway to look back at her. Hope shone in her eyes as her tentative smile brightened them. Somehow, he must find a way to rescue Publius's treasure... and his own.

When Malleolus told the door slave he was going to the eastern estate, the slave simply replied, "Yes, steward." Malleolus often took care of business where Lucius's wife and family lived. He didn't mention the extra stop he would make on the way.

What good fortune that he'd asked Publius where his newest close friend who owned merchant ships lived. To reach Lucius's villa, he passed through the city wall at the Porta Esquilinas, so he knew exactly where the Gardens of Maecenas were. It was simple to find the house of Aristarchus of Thessalonica just south of the Gardens.

Simple to find, but not what he expected. It was in a good neighborhood on the eastern end of the Oppian Hill, but it was modest in size and devoid of any ornamentation that might lend it distinction. If this Aristarchus truly was a man of great wealth with a merchant fleet and estates all over the eastern Empire, why didn't he live in an opulent town house or a luxurious villa outside the city?

But Malleolus knew of no other friend who might help, so the Greek merchant, whatever his true situation, was his only hope. He drew a deep breath and knocked.

A small window in the heavy door opened. "Yes?"

"The steward of Publius Claudius Drusus needs to speak with Aristarchus of Thessalonica. It's a matter of great urgency."

The door swung open, and the doorkeeper motioned Malleolus to enter. Then he closed and bolted the door. "Follow me, please, and I will see if my master can speak with you now."

He led Malleolus into a small room off the atrium. "Wait here, please."

Malleolus paced as he waited. Sooner than he expected, a large bearded man of about fifty entered with a welcoming smile on his face.

"I am Aristarchus. What is this urgent matter for my brother Publius?"

Malleolus kept his eyebrows down, but for this Greek to refer to Publius as brother was surprising. And also promising. He wasn't quite sure how to make his request to this total stranger, but Claudia's survival hung on whether the merchant would help his dead "brother."

"My master told me you were one of his close friends, so I have come to beg a great favor from you." He swallowed hard before proceeding. It still hurt to speak of what had happened. "Publius has been killed in the arena for refusing to sacrifice to Caesar and deny his Christian faith. His daughter Claudia is now in great danger if you can't help her."

The smile vanished, replaced by an expression both sad and serious.

"I am grieved to hear Publius has been killed. Tell me what the problem is and how you think I can help solve it. I will do what I can."

Relief flooded Malleolus. He'd been afraid this man he first heard of three weeks ago wasn't a close enough friend to help, in spite of what Publius said.

"It's a shameful thing that has led to my master's death and his daughter's desperate need. His oldest son, Lucius, was the one who betrayed him to the authorities. He did it so Publius would be executed and he could become head of the family, free of his father's control. Claudia accused Lucius of murdering their father, and he decided to punish her by marrying her to Flavius Sabinus, who offered 50,000 denarii for her. Sabinus is a cruel man who wants her only because she's so beautiful. Claudia was about to take her own life to avoid the marriage when I stopped her. It was only by promising to get her to her brother Titus that I was able to convince her not to kill herself this morning."

Malleolus paused before asking the question that would be the true test of the friendship his master claimed to have with the Greek merchant.

"Lucius must not know that she's gone to Titus, or he'll try to get her back and force her to marry Sabinus for the money. I have some money, but not enough to get her safely to her brother in Thracia. He's a tribune posted to the governor's palace in Perinthus. He said he didn't need an allowance, so he hasn't been getting one. He has only his officer's pay, and all he would have inherited from his father has been given to Lucius instead. He might not have enough money to pay back whoever might bring her to him."

Aristarchus waved his hand before Malleolus could even ask the final question. "That is not a problem. I will gladly take care of everything. In fact, I know the perfect way to get her to her brother without Lucius ever knowing what has happened to her. However, she would have to leave immediately and leave almost everything behind."

"I'm sure she would be willing to do both."

"Good. It is best that you not know exactly what is to be done. Then you should be safe from Lucius suspecting your part in the affair. Does Claudia often go to the Baths of Titus or Trajan?"

"Yes, to the Baths of Titus."

Aristarchus rubbed the back of his neck. "She must be there in two days right after the baths open. She can bring one small box, like she might normally take to the baths. It must be light enough for a woman to carry by herself. She should plan on walking several miles. A woman will meet her in the women's dressing area just inside the entrance. She will identify herself to Claudia with her father's name.

He stroked his beard. "Claudia must find some excuse to send her maid away before she undresses. The woman will contact her as soon as her maid leaves. She will take Claudia to the one who will transport her to Thracia. She will never come to this house, so there will be no way for Lucius to know I have played a part in her escape. He might figure out what has happened to her if he knew about me."

Malleolus's whole body relaxed. "What you propose sounds so simple."

Aristarchus placed a hand on his shoulder. "I will leave all the difficult details to the best strategic mind I have ever known. I expect no difficulty in rescuing Claudia from her evil brother and delivering her to the good one. Now, can you give me a good description of your mistress so the woman meeting her can recognize her?"

"Claudia Drusilla is about chin-high on you. Her hair is naturally blonde with a reddish tint. The color is quite unusual. She has large brown eyes with very long lashes."

A smile tugged at the corner of Aristarchus's mouth. "Publius told me his daughter is unusually beautiful, but to every father, his daughter seems the most beautiful woman alive. Is it so?"

"To call her unusually beautiful doesn't do her justice. Many would call her the most beautiful young woman in Rome. The Roman ideals of beauty come to life in both her face and figure, and Publius turned down ten marriage requests from some of the finest families in Rome. Yes, I would call her an extraordinary beauty in every way."

"I think the reddish-blonde hair and brown eyes will be enough for her contact to find a famous beauty. Now the plan. I will know nothing of the details of the escape myself. I have already told you what is needed to start her escape, and that is all you will know. You should do everything you can to find her, as if she had run off on her own. That way Lucius will not blame you for her disappearance."

The half-smile broadened into a full one. "I will entrust all the planning and execution to a brilliant man who will spare no effort to make certain Publius's daughter reaches her brother in Perinthus. I can guarantee that the plans of the man in charge of her escape will be clever enough to prevent any discovery, no matter how hard you search."

◆

Aristarchus planned to hand the entire affair over to Philip. His son would devise some clever way to get her out of Rome so she could not be traced and forced to return. He would even relish the opportunity to conceive and execute the rescue of the poor girl.

"I can't thank you enough for your kindness to Claudia...and to me. I've served Publius since before she was born, and she is...was his greatest treasure." Malleolus tightened his lips, but his eyes moistened anyway.

Aristarchus placed his hand on Malleolus's shoulder and gently squeezed. "You need not worry any more. I will get your precious Claudia safely delivered to her good brother. You need only to return home and have her prepare for her escape. Be sure to have her at the Baths of Titus with her single small box right after they open in two days. Leave the rest to me."

Aristarchus guided Malleolus back to the door himself and opened it after looking out the small window to be certain no one was watching. He patted the steward on the back as he prepared to walk out the door.

"You can rest assured that you have entrusted your Claudia to the best man possible. She will be with her brother very soon."

Aristarchus closed and bolted the door after Malleolus left. Yes, she would be in the best possible hands with Philip, and Aristarchus would be praying for the poor child who was broken-hearted over the death of her father. She did not follow Jesus, so she had no way of knowing that her father had not really died at all.

Chapter 15

REASON TO HOPE

When Malleolus returned, Claudia was pacing in her room.

"May I speak with you, mistress?"

She took his hands. For the first time since her father was killed, hope lit her eyes. "You were gone so long. I was afraid..."

"I went to the eastern estate as well in case Lucius asks where I went."

"Will he help?"

Malleolus scanned the room to make sure no one was listening. Graecia might be more loyal to Lucius than to her mistress.

"The day after tomorrow, you'll go early to the Baths of Titus. You must be at the women's bath as soon as possible after it opens. You can take one small box. It must be light enough for you to carry by yourself. When you get there, you need to stay in the women's dressing area just inside the entrance, but do not get undressed.

"You must send Graecia away, maybe to fetch something you would use at the baths, something special so she has to come home to get it. A woman will approach you right after you send Graecia away. She will identify herself using your father's name. Graecia must be gone long enough for the woman to take you away without her seeing you leave. She will lead you to the man who will get you to Titus."

"Who will she be taking me to and how will he get me to Titus?"

"For your safe escape and for my safety after you've gone, you won't know before you meet her, and I will never know."

"But can we trust these people?"

"I watched his eyes as I told him about your father. I saw sadness when he heard. I think we can trust him. He had no doubt that the man who will plan your escape can get you safely away from here and take you to Titus."

She fingered a strand of her long, flowing hair. "I can't marry Sabinus, and I can't stand staying with Lucius even one more day, but how can I decide to do this when I don't know anything about what I'll be doing?"

Claudia hugged herself as she rocked a little. "I really have no choice, do I, Malleolus?" She spoke her decision in a trembling voice, afraid to stay, afraid to go.

Malleolus sighed. "No, you don't. And you mustn't tell Graecia anything about this. I'm not sure whether she's loyal enough to you to risk your brother's wrath. She might betray you."

The corners of his mouth drooped. First, he'd lost Publius. Now he would be sending Claudia away with someone he didn't know to get her to Titus in some unknown way that he couldn't be sure was safe for her. It would be months, if not years, before he even knew if she made it to Thracia. He was as worried as she was, but he didn't let it show. She would lose her courage and stay, and that could end in her death.

Claudia's shoulders slumped at the prospect of Graecia's betrayal, but she nodded in agreement. Then she drew herself up to her full height and raised her head.

"Then I'll do it. Titus will know what to do when I reach him. He'll make everything right. Somehow, he'll make Lucius pay for killing Father." Her voice started strong and brave, but it was quavering by the time she said 'Father.'

Malleolus glanced at her dressing table. It was time to focus her on the plan before she dissolved into tears again.

"You'll need a small box."

"It can't be too small. I have to put some of my poetry codices and scrolls into it. As many as I can and still carry it."

"Won't that make Graecia suspicious?"

"I'll tell her I am taking some of my favorites to share with Aemilia in the garden at the baths. Graecia knows we often talk there, so she won't think it too odd that I want to get her interested in my favorite poets."

"I have what you need. It has a handle on each end, and it's shaped right for holding a good number of codices. Gather what you want from the library today so it won't seem like you're packing tomorrow."

Claudia cradled her face in both hands. "I don't have any money to take, but I can take some of my jewelry. I can sell it if I need to. I can hide some at the bottom of the box, but I want to save most of the space for poetry. I'll wear my large gold headband and hair net, my largest gold ring and the ruby one, and the gold tunic clips."

She felt her neck. "I hate that ugly, heavy necklace that Sabinus gave me, but it is worth a small fortune, so I'll wear that, too. And some gold bracelets. I can't wear too much or Graecia will be suspicious. It's too bad she helps me dress, or I could hide some under my tunic."

"Taking your jewelry is an excellent idea." Malleolus smiled at the change. She had turned her mind away from dark thoughts of death toward planning for her escape.

The quaver returned to her voice. "This is the right thing to do, isn't it?"

"Yes. You must try to act like nothing is going on so Graecia won't become suspicious and tell Lucius."

"I can do that."

Malleolus masked the worry churning within him as she took his hand and squeezed it. His young mistress had been a sweet, protected child, but her determined smile revealed the woman ready to face uncertainty on her own. She was very beautiful and very smart; now she would have to be very brave.

"I must return to my duties now."

"Yes, and I need to go to the library and make my selections."

She headed toward her father's library. It was hard, but Malleolus managed to keep the tears from forming as he watched his beloved mistress for almost the last time.

Chapter 16

PREPARATIONS

When Aristarchus entered Philip's room, his son had almost finished packing the eight boxes of codices and scrolls that he was adding to his library.

"I have a problem for you to solve for me, son."

Philip greeted him with a smile. "What, Father?"

"I need you to get Publius's daughter to his son in Perinthus right away."

Philip turned his attention back to getting the final two codices snuggly packed in the last box. "That's not much of a problem. I can give her my room in the cabin and sleep with my boxes. She'll have Penelope and Junia to entertain her."

"There's much more to the problem than her berth on your ship."

Philip's eyebrow rose as he straightened. "More to the problem?"

The corner of Aristarchus's mouth lifted at Philip's response to the chance to solve a tricky problem. "His son Lucius told the authorities that his father was a Christian, and Publius has been killed in the arena."

The smile vanished from Philip's lips. "I'm sorry to hear that, Father."

"It gets worse. Publius's daughter, Claudia, was very close to him. Her brother is planning to marry her to Flavius Sabinus for a large amount of money. To put it bluntly, Sabinus is an evil man, and her life would be a living hell. Publius's steward just came to beg me to get her away from Rome immediately and deliver her to her other brother.

He's a tribune serving the governor in Perinthus. It was only his promise to get her to Titus that stopped her from killing herself."

Philip took a deep breath and blew it out slowly. "So you want me to devise an escape plan to get her away from Lucius without him suspecting where she's gone."

Aristarchus smiled. "That should be simple enough for the best strategic thinker in Rome."

Philip's lips twitched up while he shook his head. "Not the best in Rome, but I'm certainly willing to do the best I can."

"Too modest, son. I meant what I said. I know you sail on the evening tide in two days, so I told Publius's steward to have her at the women's dressing room of the Baths of Titus right after they open that morning. She will have a single small box light enough for her to carry, and she will be expecting a woman to meet her and take her away after she sends her maid off on some errand. I expect Junia will help with this part. She is to identify herself to Claudia with Publius's name. I thought you could devise the rest of the plan."

Philip placed his hand over his mouth and rubbed his scarred cheek with his thumb as he thought for a few moments. "This shouldn't be too difficult. I can get Lucius looking for her in the wrong place while I get her to my ship. Leave the details to me, Father."

Aristsarchus's smile broadened. "I told Publius's steward I knew the perfect man for this job."

Philip let the compliment pass. "What do you know about the girl?"

"Publius told me she is the most beautiful in Rome." He chuckled. "All fathers think that of their daughters, but, according to the steward, she really is an acknowledged beauty. That is why Sabinus wants her. She is sixteen, has reddish blonde hair and brown eyes, and her face is the perfect image of beauty, by Roman standards. Her figure is perfect, too, and she stands about this high." He tapped his chin.

"Stunningly beautiful...That makes it harder to sneak her out of Rome if all the men she passes are going to stare at her, but I have an idea for that."

He turned back to finish tightening the strap around the last box.

"Do you know where Penelope is? The first thing I need to do is send her shopping for...Claudia, is it?" Philip grinned. "I'm quite certain my baby sister will be happy to help with that part."

Aristarchus grinned back. "Claudia Drusilla. I am sure she will, too. I think she is in the garden."

Philip tightened the strap and straightened up. "Leave the lovely Claudia Drusilla to me, Father. She's as good as in Perinthus already."

A satisfied smile curved Aristarchus's lips as he left Philip's room. Once Philip put his mind to something, it was as good as done. Publius's precious daughter would be in good hands.

It was late afternoon by the time Penelope and her lady's maid, Junia, returned from buying all the clothing and accessories that Penelope thought necessary for a young lady. The only restriction had been that everything must fit in the two chests that would be stowed under her bunk. Philip had given his sister a large sum of money for the purchases. The poor girl was leaving everything she owned behind, and he didn't want her to feel destitute.

By then, Philip had devised a plan that should get her safely to his ship in the early afternoon, leaving some margin in case something delayed her arrival, while misdirecting any efforts that Lucius might launch trying to find her. It was so simple that only Junia, his ship's captain, and he needed to know the details. It didn't require precise timing for any particular step after Junia met her at the bath, and it should leave Lucius searching in a different part of Rome for a nonexistent accomplice in the escape.

He excelled at games involving strategy, and he welcomed this chance to use his skills to help someone in desperate need. It was good that Father had offered him the chance to do one last thing for Publius. If those in heaven could still see what took place on earth, his newest brother would be pleased.

Philip loaded his travel chest, his library boxes, and the chests for Claudia into his father's *raeda.* He'd chosen that carriage because its solid wooden walls could conceal the passengers within. Carriage travel in Rome was banned for most of the daylight hours, so he'd been forced to wait for the lifting of the ban in early evening. He needed to get to the harbor at Portus as soon as possible to get his captain, Hector, prepared for his role in the escape. Junia already knew what she had to do. He wouldn't see her again until she came to the ship with Claudia in two days.

After saying farewell to his parents, Philip climbed aboard the driver's seat and clucked to the mules. The night was going to be clear, and the moon was close to full. He had about twenty-five miles to travel, so he should arrive at the ship before midnight if he could keep the mules mostly trotting once he got out of the city. That would allow a half day of rest before he drove them fifteen miles north on the Via Portuensis. He'd leave the carriage at the family warehouse closest to the edge of town, where wagon traffic was still allowed during the day. The riding horse tied behind would get him back to the ship after he walked the planned escape route to identify potential problems. It would also carry Hector from Portus to Rome for the actual rescue.

The daytime carriage ban within the city was unfortunate. Claudia had to walk across most of Rome since he couldn't risk revealing her escape route with a sedan chair or litter. It crossed a rough part of town where the normal travel mode of a wealthy woman would draw too much attention. He also didn't want to risk the slaves who carried her revealing where she'd gone. He was helping her escape from her legal guardian, and that could be considered kidnapping if Lucius Drusus wanted to claim it was. He would rather not be charged with a capital crime.

The plan was sound, but there was one part he regretted. The escape party must pass unnoticed through several miles of Rome in the middle of the day. He would have preferred to fetch her himself rather than have Hector do it. It was enough to risk the arena himself without dragging his captain and best friend with him. But his scars always drew the attention of people when he was in public, and that would put her in danger. It was much easier to conceal an unusually beautiful woman than a truly ugly man. A stunning beauty with an ugly man like him—that would be ludicrous enough to catch the attention of almost everyone.

His father had required all his sons to work a shipping season as a crewmember on one of the family's merchant ships that hauled cargo along the northern coast of the Mediterranean. That summer, he learned all he'd ever need to know about his ship, including the proper way to load the cargo. He would take over Hector's job while Hector performed his.

Chapter 17

Slipping Away

Claudia was already tired when she rose early the morning of her escape. Between the nightmares about the lions and the worry about what lay ahead today and into the future, she hadn't even slept two hours. She joined Lucius for a light breakfast of bread, fruit, and cheese. She only picked at it, and Lucius scolded her about making herself sick if she didn't eat. They'd had that conversation every day since he betrothed her to Sabinus, so it should suppress any suspicions he might have if she seemed too happy.

Graecia had laid out a fine linen tunic and was getting ready to spend the hour it would take to do Claudia's hair.

Claudia swallowed hard as she glanced at the box of poetry. It was time to begin her escape. "I don't want to stay here this morning. I need to get away from this house, to think about something different. Lucius is so mad at me for crying all the time, and I've got to do something to stop."

She tried to keep the building excitement from her voice. "Aemilia was planning to go to the Baths of Titus this morning. I think I'll join her. A refreshing bath, some time in the gardens together—maybe I can start acting more like Lucius wants. I want to go early so I won't miss any time with her."

"Yes, mistress. I'll prepare what we need to take."

Claudia's heart began to beat faster. What if Graecia noticed? She took several deep breaths, and it slowed.

She waived her hand at the box by the side of her bed that held her treasured poetry. "Good. Oh, and be sure to take that small box of poetry for me. I've been telling Aemilia about some of my favorites that she hasn't read. I want to show her some of my own poems as well. We can read some in the gardens after we bathe."

"Yes, mistress. I'm sure Master Lucius will be pleased that you're trying."

As Graecia packed her perfumes, Claudia took note of which were left behind. She would insist that she absolutely had to have one of those, one of the rare ones that couldn't be bought in the shops at the bath. When she sent Graecia home for it, her escape could begin.

Claudia walked over to the dressing table where her hair accessories were stored. "I want to wear my hair simple today since I'm only going to bathe."

She picked up the solid gold headband. "I think this and a gold net is what I want."

She opened her jewelry box and took out the gold and ruby rings and the two gold bracelets. She slid them on.

"I think this necklace from Sabinus is horribly ugly, but if I wear it today, then Lucius can tell him I'm wearing it. He keeps telling me I have to be nice to Sabinus since he's going to be my husband and there's nothing I can do about it." She sighed to make it seem like she was finally reconciled to the match.

"Oh, and I want the gold tunic clips. I think they'll help draw attention away from that ugly necklace."

Claudia closed the jewelry box after taking out all the items she'd mentioned. She didn't want Graecia noticing that some of the other gold pieces that were now hidden at the bottom of her poetry box were missing from their usual places.

As Graecia swept Claudia's hair into the simple style, Claudia watched her in the brass mirror. The smile on Graecia's lips...was it because she was glad to see Claudia a little happier or because she could report to Lucius that her opposition to the match was over? Was Malleolus right that Graecia was more loyal to Lucius than her?

Graecia caught her watching, and the smile she gave Claudia seemed like one that showed she cared. Was Lucius going to do something terrible to Graecia for letting her escape?

She suppressed a sigh. She had to leave. She could only hope that Malleolus and Graecia wouldn't pay a terrible price because she did.

Junia was already waiting at the bath when it opened. Now she sat in the women's dressing room, pretending to be waiting for her mistress while she held a small bag of clothes.

It felt like she'd been sitting there for a very long time. She glanced at each young woman as she entered the room, but none had been what she'd call stunningly beautiful. She'd seen a few natural blondes, more than a few bleached blondes, but no reddish blondes with brown eyes. Was Master Philip's description only the result of the imagination of people who loved the girl? Had she missed her?

When Claudia finally entered the dressing room, Junia breathed a sigh of relief. There could be no mistake. The stunningly beautiful young woman of about sixteen with thick, reddish-blonde hair and large brown eyes walked past her. Close behind her came an unhappy slave with two boxes stacked in her arms. Now all Junia had to do was wait for Claudia Drusilla to send her maid away, and the execution of Master Philip's plan could begin.

◆

Claudia glanced around the dressing room as she headed toward a quiet corner. Several lady's maids sat on benches, waiting with varying degrees of patience. Was one of them the woman she was supposed to meet? If only she had some idea what the woman looked like or what she'd be wearing or something.

What if she sent Graecia away when the woman wasn't there yet, and she returned before the woman showed up? All the plans might be for nothing. Graecia would be suspicious if she tried to send her home a second time.

But it was definitely past the time the woman was supposed to be there. She couldn't wait until she was sure since there was no way for her to be sure. It was time.

"Graecia, I want that new perfume from Spain."

"I brought the attar of roses and the lavender perfume that are your favorites."

"But I don't want those. They make me think too much of Father because he loved them."

She blinked fast a few times, like she did when she fought the next flood of tears. "If I wear them, I won't be able to keep from crying, and I must stop that. Father never cared for that one from Spain. Nothing else will do. Go home and get it for me. You can leave both boxes. I'll watch them here in the dressing room and read some poetry until you return."

"Yes, mistress. I'll hurry back as quickly as I can."

◆

The lady's maid bowed to her mistress and walked out of the room. Junia rose and approached the beauty.

"Excuse me, mistress."

Claudia turned to face her, a look of nervous anticipation in her eyes.

"Publius Claudius Drusus would have you go with me."

"I'm ready."

Claudia leaned over and picked up her box. She leaned back as she held it against her stomach.

"Let me take one handle, mistress."

Claudia set the box down, and they each took one handle before lifting. Junia's eyes widened at the weight.

"I know it's heavy, but I could never replace what's in it."

"It's not too heavy, mistress. Do you have friends named Lucretia or Portia?"

◆

Claudia's head tilted. "Two Portias and a Lucretia." What an odd question.

The woman led her toward the entrance of the dressing room, where there were several slaves stationed to help the patrons. She steered them close to one who was looking right at them. As they passed close to the slave, she began talking as if they'd been carrying on a conversation.

"Yes, but we must hurry. My mistress Portia is planning to have a carriage waiting for us just outside the city gate at the Via Tiburtina. We'll be on the Via Valeria before nightfall."

Claudia nodded, but she fought to keep her surprise from showing. How strange that her guide was revealing the roads they would be taking to the east where anyone might hear.

Her guide led her out of the Baths of Titus and turned east along the north wall. Rising just to the north and east were the much larger Baths of Trajan, which had been completed only five years earlier. They hurried across the space between the two large buildings. They walked along the wall of Trajan's Baths until they reached an entrance. The woman turned inside and headed for the women's dressing room. When they entered the dressing room, she led Claudia over to a corner.

"I'm Junia." Her guide offered a warm smile. "That went well, but we still need to hurry."

She pulled a sack from the bag she'd been carrying.

"You're going to change, mistress. Here, place all your jewelry in this. Your headband, too."

Claudia complied, leaving only the fine gold netting on her hair.

Junia unfastened the gold tunic clips and dropped them into the sack as well. Then she drew the drawstring tight and put the sack into the larger bag. She took out a plain off-white tunic, a beige stola that was worn only by married women, and a nondescript off-white palla.

"We must get you changed quickly, mistress."

She helped Claudia out of her expensive pale blue tunic and into the plain one. Then she helped her into the stola. Claudia was instantly transformed into a young merchant-class married woman. Finally, Junia draped her with the palla, pulling a fold of it up over her hair so she would not be identifiable from the side or behind. She folded Claudia's fine clothes and slid them into the bag, which she hung over her shoulder.

"Let's go."

Chapter 18

FLIGHT TO FREEDOM

Junia picked up one handle of the box and waited. After Claudia picked up the other, she led them toward the northern exit from the massive bath complex.

Claudia glanced at her guide. She was setting a pace that was brisk but not so fast it would draw attention. When they'd gone about an eighth of a mile, she made a sudden left turn into a narrow street and headed back toward the west.

Claudia glanced over her shoulder. No one seemed to be following. A smile tugged at the corner of her mouth. Junia was clever, leading them one way as far as anyone at the baths might notice and then backtracking.

But maybe the clever one wasn't Junia. Malleolus had said a man chosen by Father's friend would take her to Titus. But when would he appear? What if he didn't seem trustworthy? A tingle shot up her spine. Trustworthy or not, she couldn't go back to Lucius. Nothing could be worse than marrying Sabinus.

They had walked a block when a brawny, bearded man stepped into the street right in front of them. He wore a short sword under the cloak that partly covered his beige tunic, but the dark eyes that were framed by his curly black hair and short beard held no threat.

His voice was deep. "Don't be afraid, Claudia. I'm Hector, your escort for the rest of the trip today."

Junia set down her end of the box, so Claudia did as well. The man picked it up and balanced it on his shoulder. His eyebrows rose.

Claudia shrugged her apology. "I know it's heavy, but I only brought what I couldn't bear to leave."

A smile tugged at his mouth. "I've carried much heavier. We need to make good time, so let's go."

Hector led the way west toward the Clivus Suburanus, the major street that led from the plateau where the baths were situated to the valley floor. Soon they were descending between the Cispian and Oppian Hills to the Subura valley below.

Claudia hadn't planned on walking a long distance. She'd worn sandals that were pretty but not walking shoes. As they headed down the sloping road into the lower-class neighborhood that lay in the valley below them, her left sandal was starting to rub. There wasn't a blister yet, but there soon would be. Would they be walking much farther? She hoped not, but it appeared likely they would. They were somewhere in the middle of the city, so no matter which way Hector took them, the city gate would be too far to avoid the blister.

She'd lived in the Fagutal, an elite section in the upper-class Carinae section of the Oppian Hill. She'd never before walked through the lower-class parts of the city. As the trio reached the valley floor, the streets became narrower, dirtier, and more crowded with people whom she found rather frightening.

◆

Hector shifted the box to his left shoulder to free his sword arm. "Both of you, stay close to me. Claudia, walk between the two of us and keep your face down."

Something made the skin at the back of Hector's neck begin to crawl. He glanced back across his shoulder. Three men seemed to be following them.

"Pick up the pace. We need to move faster."

He didn't want to frighten the women. He hoped he was wrong, that the men just happened to be walking the same way. When he sped up, perhaps they wouldn't do the same.

When he glanced back again, the men were gaining on them. Their eyes were tracking him. They kept getting closer. He flipped his cloak back to give free access to his sword.

The men meant trouble.

"We're being followed. When I set the box down and turn, I want the two of you to get behind me. If I say run, run as fast as you can. Go down past the forums to the river, cross the Aemilius Bridge, and take the Via Portuensis to the warehouse. The carriage is there. Junia, ask for the steward. He'll have someone drive you down to Philip."

◆

Claudia glanced over her shoulder and saw the three men. They were getting closer, and at least one of them had a sword at his side. When she glanced at her escort, the grim set of his mouth raised her heart rate. The man who was leading her to safety was about to be in mortal danger, and it was her fault.

"But what about you?" Claudia's voice quavered as she asked the question that she was afraid she already knew the answer to. There was no reply.

Hector set her box down and drew his sword as he turned to face the three men. Junia moved closer to her and gripped her hand.

The men fanned out in front of Hector, making it harder for him to watch all three closely. The one in the middle stepped forward, and a cruel sneer twisted his mouth.

"Looks like an interesting box you have there. Heavy. Real heavy. Maybe filled with money? Maybe something gold or silver? Looks like it's slowing you down, too. We'd be happy to lighten your load so you can get where you're going faster."

The other two men began moving forward, trying to flank Hector. His grip on the sword tightened. "Get ready."

"Wait! There's nothing here you want." Claudia pulled her hand from Junia's grip and knelt by her box to open the lid. "There's no money. It's only poetry."

She lifted two scrolls out of the box and held them high for the robbers to see.

The leader scowled when he saw they weren't worth robbing, and he raised his hand to stop his men. Then, as he watched her wave the scrolls, he burst out laughing. He signaled for his men to follow him before he turned, and they walked away.

◆

Hector slid his sword back into its scabbard. Claudia had already replaced her scrolls and closed the latch on the box when he turned to face her.

She was still kneeling as she looked up at him. "Maybe until we get past this part of town, Junia and I should carry the box? So you can get your sword faster if you need to."

One corner of his mouth pulled up into a crooked smile. "It's only a short distance now to the area of the forums. We shouldn't have any more trouble. I can carry it for you."

He hoisted the box back onto his shoulder, and they resumed their walk toward the forums and the river beyond. He glanced sideways at Claudia. An eye-catching beauty who had chosen to fill her one box with poetry. Would Philip ever be surprised...and pleased. The voyage would take about four weeks. Philip would much rather spend that kind of time with a lover of poetry than with a pretty girl. This trip he'd be getting both.

Ahead of them rose the magnificent stone and concrete buildings that graced the center of Rome. Hector felt the tension drain from his body when they finally emerged from the narrow, dirty streets into the city center. The most hazardous part of their route was past. Now it was just a matter of getting to the carriage at the family warehouse without anyone recognizing Claudia.

He glanced at her. She was much too pretty, and the palla had slipped, exposing some of her hair and too much of that eye-catching profile.

"Junia, fix Claudia's palla."

As Penelope's maid adjusted the fabric, another smile tugged at the corner of his mouth. A poetry-loving woman gorgeous enough to serve as the model for a sculpture of Venus. Philip was in for a big surprise.

◆

Claudia tried to keep her eyes focused on the buildings that lay ahead of them, but she found them being drawn toward the Flavian Amphitheater off to her left. Her throat tightened, and tears started to pool in her eyes. As she gazed at the monumental arena, she fought to push the thought of the lions tearing her father to pieces from her mind. Now was not the time for tears; she must hold herself together at least until they reached the carriage that her escort had said was waiting.

Hector shifted the box from his left shoulder to his right and glanced at her. "Are you all right, Claudia?"

She didn't want him to know she was on the verge of crying uncontrollably. She wasn't sure she could speak without her voice betraying her, so she simply nodded.

"We're going to pass through the forum area as quickly as possible. Claudia, keep your palla pulled forward to hide some of your face and look down as much as you can. We don't want anyone who knows you to see us passing this way."

He led them past the Forum of Augustus and the Forum of Caesar. As they approached the Basilica Julia, he skirted the building, leading them along the northern wall.

Claudia's heart rate ramped up. The basilica was the most popular meeting place for the elite of Rome. Father had spoken there often with his scholar friends. What if one of them saw and recognized her? She swallowed hard and kept her head down, looking at Hector's feet instead of the white stone buildings all around them. They continued past the Capitolium and the massive Temple of Jupiter. Finally, he guided them into a street that led down to the river.

She had never been to the banks of the Tiber before. The river was much wider than it looked from the top of the Oppian Hill. As the trio started across the beautiful seven-arch stone bridge, her gaze was drawn to the large island just to the north. Some other time, she would have paused to watch the river flowing under the bridge, but her escort showed no sign of slowing down, much less stopping to enjoy the scenery.

Her eyes narrowed. Lucius should have been sewn into a leather sack and thrown into the river from that bridge. She would have gladly swung one of the clubs used to beat him before that toss. She blinked hard and shoved that thought from her mind, but the beauty of the river had already been ruined by it.

A brief stop would have been so welcome. She'd worn the wrong sandals. The bands of leather that crossed her toes had rubbed a blister on top of her left foot as they came down the sloped street in Subura. Every step hurt, but she wouldn't complain. She wasn't going to say anything that would slow their progress to whatever the destination was. Any delay might lead to Lucius catching them, and she couldn't bear living with him again.

More than a week had passed since she'd had a good night's sleep, and that was taking its toll. Exhaustion stalked her as they started southwest on the Via Portuensis. Claudia had no idea where they were going first on the way to Titus, but this was the road to the port. Whatever the plan, a sea voyage must be part of it.

The blister had long since popped. The toe strap was now rubbing against raw flesh, causing more pain than she'd ever felt before. To make matters worse, a blister had formed where the strap of the other sandal was rubbing on the back of her heel. Between the fatigue and the pain, she wasn't sure how much farther she would be able to walk at this pace.

Hector frowned as he caught her favoring her left foot. "It isn't far now, Claudia. The ban on carriages goes one mile past the gate, and the warehouse is only a quarter mile past that."

She tried not to cringe, but another mile and a quarter?

The frown straightened. "We'll slow down a little. We've made good time, but there's still fifteen miles over the hills and across the plain to reach Portus. But you'll be in a carriage after we reach the warehouse."

Claudia's popped blister made each step agony. She fought tears, not from grief but from pain. They'd walked past building after ugly building, but at least there were wagons on the road. The warehouse must be close.

At long last, Hector turned in through a gate in a wall surrounding a large grain warehouse. A black *raeda* hitched to two bay mules stood by the building. A riding horse was tied to an iron hoop on the wall next to the team. Hector opened the carriage door and slid the box under the seat.

"We won't be walking any farther today. Philip wanted me to apologize for making you walk so far so fast, but it couldn't be helped, given the tight schedule for traveling the necessary distance."

He offered Claudia his hand to help her into the carriage. "Allow me."

With almost her last ounce of strength, she took his hand and climbed aboard. She settled into the rear seat and leaned against the carriage wall for support. Junia climbed in and sat beside her. Hector closed the carriage door. He led the riding horse to the back of the carriage and tied it there. Then he untied the team from the iron hoop.

The *raeda* creaked as Hector climbed up into the driver's seat. He backed the mules up until he could turn the carriage enough to head out through the gate. He clucked to the mules, and Claudia was jerked back into the seat as the carriage moved forward. As soon as they were through the gate and heading south, he slapped the mules with the reins and urged them into a trot.

Claudia settled back into the seat with a sigh. Her feet hurt in general, the blisters hurt horribly, and she was more tired than she'd ever been in her life. But she'd made it out of Rome and was on her way to Titus. Somehow everything would be better after she reached the brother who loved her.

She closed her eyes. The rocking of the carriage soon lulled her into sorely needed sleep.

◆

Junia watched the poor girl begin to doze. She, too, was tired by the walk, but a satisfied smile overspread her face. The hard part was behind them. Fifteen more miles with the mules doing all the work—this part of the escape route would be so easy. She settled back into the seat and enjoyed the view out the carriage window as the mules began the climb into the hills on their way to Portus.

Chapter 19

The Ugliest Man

Claudia didn't awaken until the carriage jerked to a stop in the heavy traffic near the wharfs. The three-hour nap had taken her from exhausted to merely tired, but that was still an improvement. During most of the nights since Father died, she hadn't had more than three hours of uninterrupted sleep anyway.

The palla had slipped off her head as she slept. Junia leaned over and adjusted it to hide her hair again.

"We're almost there, mistress. It's only a short walk to the ship from where we'll leave the carriage. In case anyone asks, you're a married woman, Livia Marcella, going to meet your husband in Thessalonica. I'm your maid, Junia."

The *raeda* moved forward, then slowed, then stopped. Claudia's heart began to beat faster. A few steps more, and she'd be on the ship that would take her to Titus. She'd be free from Lucius and Sabinus and all the horrible things he would do to her.

Hector opened the carriage door and stood waiting to help. Junia hung the bag of clothes on her shoulder and climbed out unassisted. He offered Claudia his hand.

She took it. The mules shifted, and the *raeda* moved a little as she was stepping down. He tightened his grip to steady her, and she was glad. Despite the rest, she still felt a little unsteady.

The smells of the harbor assaulted her nose. The slight odor of dead fish wasn't strong enough to make her gag, but it was not pleasant. Loaded freight wagons moved in while empty wagons moved out.

Dockhands moved barrels and crates on handcarts to get them shipside for loading into the waiting cargo holds. An overloaded handcart had tipped, spilling sacks down a ramp. An overseer cursed, and the snap of a whip made Claudia cringe.

Hector hoisted her box back onto his shoulder. "Follow me. The ship is just over there."

He strode toward a ramp that led down to the pier.

Junia started to follow, then turned back with her hand outstretched. "Come, mistress. Just a little farther, and you can rest."

One deep breath, and Claudia started walking. Her feet ached, and her blisters burned and stung with every step. But each step made her heart feel lighter. She was very close to escaping from Lucius now, and there was every reason to think she really would escape. Soon she would be with Titus, and somehow, he would make things better, just like Father always had.

Junia stepped aside and waited for her to precede her down the ramp and along the pier where her escort had gone. He was already some distance ahead of them, striding toward the ship that would carry her to freedom.

Claudia had never been near a merchant ship before. Her breath caught as her eyes swept the length of the *corbita* on which she would sail. It was more than 90 feet long and 25 feet wide. A large cabin, about 10 by 20 feet, sat toward the rear with a canopy almost half that size attached to it. A carved neck and head of a swan rose just past the canopy. The two large rudders, one on each side, had poles that extended up to the cabin roof where whoever was steering would stand. One huge mast, about a third as tall as the length of the ship, rose just a little forward of the ship's center, and a second smaller mast about a third as long as the tall one stuck out at an angle past the front end.

A powerfully built man in a white tunic stood with his fists on his hips, watching a crane swing a large crate toward him. His back was toward her as he turned his head left to speak to the man beside him. That crewman pointed toward her escort, causing him to turn to his left again. He slapped the man's shoulder before trotting down the gangplank and striding toward them.

Hector increased his pace until he reached the man in white. They exchanged words that Claudia couldn't hear, and her box was transferred to the man's shoulder. Hector strode up the gangplank and took charge over the loading process as the brawny man continued walking toward her.

◆

Philip's father had told him Claudia was a beautiful girl, but no words could have prepared him for what he saw. In all his travels to the port cities of the Empire, he had never beheld such an extraordinary beauty. The symmetry of her face was perfect with arched eyebrows and high cheekbones. The longest lashes he'd ever seen framed her brown eyes, and the palla drawn over her head didn't completely conceal the rare beauty of her reddish-blonde hair. Any man with even one eye could see why a rich old lecher would be willing to pay a small fortune to marry such a beauty and why her father had been so unwilling to give his precious daughter to just any man who wanted her, no matter how rich or powerful. Most only wanted her for the obvious reason.

◆

Claudia was struck by her rescuer's appearance, but it was not a pleasant surprise. Before her stood the ugliest man she'd ever seen. His bushy eyebrow, large ears, and prominent nose were enough to make him unattractive, but the horrible scars that covered the right side of his face took him past ugly to hideous. The patch over his right eye actually improved his appearance by hiding some of the scarring.

Sheer willpower kept her gaze upon him as he walked toward her. He mustn't suspect how repulsive she found him. She didn't want to hurt the feelings of this man who'd saved her from the horrible fate decreed by her brother. To look but not to stare—how was she to manage that? His scars would draw stares wherever he went. Did children run from the monster? What pain that must bring, for surely he knew why they ran.

But she'd have to look at his face when he first spoke to her. Perhaps, if she focused on his one good eye, she could do it. Friendliness radiated from it, and a welcoming smile greeted her as well. That friendly eye and pleasant smile—locking her gaze on them should help her pretend she didn't see the grotesque scarring.

When he reached her, the friendly sparkle of his eye brightened as his smile broadened. "Welcome to my ship, Livia Marcella. I'm delighted to have you aboard, and I trust you'll enjoy your voyage with us to join your husband in Thessalonica." His deep, booming voice drew the gaze of the nearby dockworkers. "Please follow me, and I'll get you settled in your room."

With a sweep of his hand toward his ship, he swung around and led her to the gangplank. He took two steps up, then turned to offer his hand. She placed her palm on his, and his fingers wrapped around her hand as if it were a child's. She stepped onto the boards that moved up and down as the ship rode on the gently lapping waves. With her box balanced on his shoulder as if it weighed nothing, he walked up the gangplank beside her. She focused her gaze on where she placed her feet so she wouldn't have to look at him.

At the end, he stepped off ahead of her. "Watch your step."

Only after she stepped safely onto the deck did he release her hand.

His broad shoulders and brawny arms dominated her view as he led her and Junia past the large opening in the deck through which the cargo was being lowered. His large hand pushed open the door to the cabin near the back of the boat. A sweep of that hand invited her to enter ahead of him.

The door opened into a room with a counter and cabinets on one side.

"This is the galley. Food is prepared here." His hand reached past her and swept the wall opposite the door. "And these are the passenger rooms."

There were four small rooms about six feet deep and five feet wide opening to the right off the galley. Each had a small window and contained a set of bunks, a small table beside the bunks, and a chair that fit under the table. The small lip around the table edge would keep anything from sliding off in rough seas, and above each table was a specially shaped oil lamp that couldn't be tossed from its rack to start a fire even when the sea was running unusually high. The lower bunk was high enough to slide chests underneath for storage of clothing and other personal items during the voyage. The headroom above the lower bunk was enough for a man to sit up comfortably. The upper bunk was close enough to the ceiling that it was clearly meant only for sleeping.

The ugly man stepped past Claudia and led her into the slightly larger room that was farthest from the cabin door. He set her box down on the table. Junia placed the bundle of clothes and jewelry on her bed and left.

As he turned to face her, she braced herself to once more pretend she didn't see the scars.

The deep voice that had boomed on the pier spoke quiet words in the cabin. "I'm Philip, and I'm very pleased to be of service to you, Claudia Drusilla. My father and yours were friends, and I had the pleasure of talking with your father as well. I offer my deepest condolences for your loss."

Despite the slight quiver of her lips, Claudia managed a weak smile. In silence, she looked past him out the window as she struggled to keep her emotions under control. She didn't want to start crying again, and a single word might breach the dam holding back the torrent.

The soft, deep voice pulled her mind back to the cabin. "I apologize for not coming for you myself. I would have, but you needed to pass unnoticed through the center of Rome. My face doesn't allow me to blend into a crowd. People tend to remember a large ugly man with so many scars and only one eye. I can't imagine why."

Even looking past him, she saw him shrug.

Her eyebrows started up but she forced them back down. He had almost chuckled as he described himself. Was he truly that unconcerned about his grotesque appearance?

"Anyway, I knew Hector would execute the plan at least as well as I could myself, and I trust his judgment if unforeseen complications force a change.

"I apologize for your long walk, but I thought it best to make a false trail and then get you here as quickly and inconspicuously as possible. A litter or sedan chair would have been much slower and would have drawn too much attention along part of your route. I did leave the carriage as close to town as I could."

As uncomfortable as it was, she made herself look at him when she replied.

"I'm so grateful for your help in getting me to Titus. Everything you've done...I can't thank you enough. I only hope Malleolus isn't punished for my disappearance. And my maid, Graecia, too."

She bit her lip as she thought about what Lucius might do to the dear old man if he suspected anything.

"I don't think that will be a problem. Your maid only obeyed your command, and there was nothing odd about what you told her. The worst, or maybe the best, that will happen is she'll be sold to someone who wants the hairdresser of a famous beauty. All your steward knows is that you've disappeared from the women's bath. He never met me, and he only came to my father's house once as a secret side-trip on the way to your father's eastern estate. That's when he was told to have you bring your box to the baths today. I only shared the plan with Hector and Junia. Not even my father knows what we've done. Junia laid a false trail for them to search for you meeting a woman on the east side of the city."

He hooked his right fingers on the lip of the upper bunk, and he seemed to fill the whole room as he stood with his left thumb hooked on his belt.

"Your steward was told to launch a thorough search for you, just as he would if you'd disappeared on your own. Your brother should be convinced he had no part in it. By the time they decide they can't find you in Rome, we'll be well out to sea.

"The dockhands all think this ship is only carrying my sister and a married woman going to Thessalonica, and my own crew is completely trustworthy. I believe I can guarantee your safe delivery to your brother Titus without harm to anyone you care about who's left in Rome."

His plan, both clever and simple, really did get her out while protecting those she left behind. He was right; Lucius would never suspect anyone except her and the imaginary woman who was helping her flee to the northeast.

He lowered his arm. "I'm sorry you could bring so little, but the plan only allowed for one small box. My sister Penelope will be making the voyage with us. She's about your age. I had her buy a few things she thought a young woman would need. Junia is her maid, and she'll be helping you both."

He pulled the larger of two chests from beneath the bed and opened it. It was filled with clothing made of the finest fabrics in a rainbow of colors, perfectly suited to a young Roman noblewoman. He pulled out the smaller chest and opened it to reveal all the personal items and accessories that a wealthy young woman would need or even want.

"Please check to make sure nothing you need is missing. One of my crew can escort Junia to the market this afternoon to buy anything else you might want. We'll be sailing on the evening tide."

She blinked several times as her gaze swept the luxurious contents. What had all this cost?

"This is much more than I expected, and I don't want to cause you extra expense. I don't have any money to pay you for all this now. I did bring some of my jewelry to sell so I can pay you later, or maybe Titus will."

"No payment is needed. It's my pleasure to help the daughter of any friend of my father."

A slight breeze brushed her cheek, carrying the smell of the harbor through the window, but the room was still stuffy.

Philip glanced over his left shoulder toward the window. "I'm sorry, but I have to ask you to stay in the cabin to avoid being seen while we're still docked. I'd rather your brother not connect my ship with your disappearance. Any woman as gorgeous as you is certain to be noticed by every man who sees her. I suspect you draw almost as many stares as I do."

The corner of his mouth lifted as he shrugged. "Once we're at sea, you can spend as much time on deck as you wish. I realize this room is very small compared to what you're used to, but it's the biggest I have. There's ample room for relaxing under the canopy on deck, and my passengers usually find it very pleasant there. I hope it won't be too uncomfortable in here for the next few hours."

He'd spoken the truth. Men always turned their heads to watch her. She hated the way some men looked at her. Just thinking about it could make her blush. Being too beautiful was definitely a drawback when a person was trying to be invisible.

"I'm sure I'll be comfortable in here, and staying out of sight would be wise. Too many men do stare."

She cast him a quick glance. An ugly man and a beautiful woman had something in common after all.

Chapter 20

MORE THAN A BEAUTY

Philip rested his hand on her box. "Where would you like me to put this before I leave you? If it contains anything that might break, the floor would be best."

The box was very heavy for its small size—probably full of perfumes and beauty preparations or maybe gold and silver jewelry.

"There's nothing breakable in it. What I hate leaving most is our library. I brought as much of my favorite poetry as I could fit in it. Maybe under the table where I can get to it easily. Or will water come in through the window?"

A beauty like her choosing poetry over perfumes and jewelry? His eyebrow started to rise, but he settled it back in place. It wasn't fair to judge her by her looks. He should know better since strangers often underestimated his intelligence because he was so muscular and ugly. Father had said Publius was a renowned scholar in history and philosophy. It made sense that his daughter would love to read. A woman could have both beauty and brains. His sister Ariadne certainly did.

"No. It should stay dry there." He lifted her box from the tabletop and set it on the floor. After turning it so it would be easy to open, he slid it between the legs of the chair and under the table. When he stood up, a broad smile curved his mouth.

"I have something in my room that you might enjoy during the voyage."

◆

Claudia pressed her back against the wall so her rescuer could slip past her into the galley. He pushed open the door of the room next to hers. The lower bunk was covered with boxes. When he released the straps and lifted the lid off the closest one, Claudia drew a sharp breath. It was full of codices.

The corner of his mouth tipped up. "I always add to my library when I visit Rome. Feel free to read anything you find here. The voyage will take about four weeks, and you might find it boring to sit on deck just watching the shoreline go by for that long. I find that a good history or some poetry makes the time pass more enjoyably."

She'd glanced at his face long enough to see his half-smile, but she didn't let her gaze linger. Eight boxes of writings were only an addition? No one would suspect this man with a laborer's build who made his living shipping cargo was a scholar with a large library.

Her hand went to her throat. "Thank you. I can't imagine anything that I would enjoy more. You said you have poetry?"

His smile broadened as she stated her preference. He reached into the first box and lifted out three codices.

"Here are some. There are many others. The boxes are only sorted into scrolls or codices, so you'll have to look for them."

◆

Philip leaned over to open another box to show her some of what it contained. He glanced up to see if anything interested her. How intelligent those beautiful eyes looked as she clasped the first three codices to her breast while she focused on the others he held out to her. An unexpected opportunity was presenting itself.

"I find poetry is much more enjoyable when it's read aloud, but I seldom have someone to read with onboard. Perhaps we can read to each other after we're at sea."

"My father and I often read together."

He took that to mean she would like to read with him, and he smiled at the thought. Her voice was musical and just as beautiful as her face. Listening to it reading poetry should be enchanting.

He straightened up and looked down on the crown of her reddish-blonde hair as she scanned the first page of a codex. The promise of many stimulating conversations during the voyage drew a broader smile. His sister was a sweet person, but she wasn't interested in scholarly things. A long voyage could get boring without intelligent conversation. It wouldn't hurt that Claudia was so beautiful. A feast for the mind and the eye—a few weeks with such a companion would be a pleasant reward for his willing efforts to help her escape.

"I must return to the work on deck. If you need anything, just call from the cabin door, and someone will come get me."

"Thank you, Philip."

She didn't even glance at him as he left the room. Her eyes remained on the poems. He didn't blame her, given the alternative.

As he walked back to join Hector, a satisfying thought played in his mind. Who would have predicted that a renowned beauty would be as intelligent as she seemed to be? He'd expected she would be company for Penelope, not a stimulating companion for himself. This was likely to be the best voyage home he'd ever made.

◆

Claudia watched Philip's back as he walked away. Two things amazed her: how a scholar was concealed in that laborer's body...and how he joked about being so ugly, as if he didn't care at all.

She walked back into her own room and stood looking at the chest of beautiful clothes. She hadn't known exactly what to expect when she reached her rescuer, but this certainly wasn't it. She'd expected her life of luxury to end the moment she walked out of the Drusus house. The provisions this total stranger had made for her were better than she could have brought herself. He barely knew her father and he didn't know her at all, yet he'd provided all this. He was only a Greek with a merchant ship, yet he was the most generous man she'd ever met.

She turned at the tap on the open door behind her. Junia was standing there with a bucket of water and two basins.

"Master Philip sent me to attend to the blisters on your feet."

Claudia's eyebrows shot up, and Junia smiled.

"You'll find that almost nothing gets past the master's notice. He wants me to clean your feet well so they can heal quickly. He told me to tell you that you should go barefoot until they heal if Mistress Penelope doesn't have some sandals that won't rub the blisters."

Claudia sat down on the bed so Junia could wash her feet. "It was a long walk for you as well. Did you get blisters, too?"

"No, mistress. I knew how far we would be walking, and I wore the right sandals."

When Junia finished and left the room, fatigue crashed down on Claudia. She'd hardly slept at all last night as she worried about the escape plan. But that wasn't the whole problem. She hadn't slept through a night since Father was killed and the nightmares came.

In the excitement of her escape, she'd been distracted. Now the suffocating sadness descended on her again.

One of the poetry collections Philip had handed her was one her father had loved. She opened it to his favorite poem and began to read. In her mind, she could hear his voice once more reading the poem to her and see him smiling at a particularly beautiful phrase or the choice of a special word.

She closed the codex and clutched it to her breast as she flopped sideways on the bed. Tears began to flow as she curled into a fetal position, and she suffered in silence until exhaustion overcame her and she finally fell asleep.

Penelope arrived at the dock mid-afternoon. Her father's slaves followed her, bearing her three chests and the chest belonging to Junia. Dockslaves were still carrying cargo into the hold, but only a few small crates remained on the pier. As soon as Philip saw her, he left Hector's side and trotted down the gangplank to greet her.

She walked up to Philip and gave him a big hug. He draped his arm across her shoulders and kissed her cheek in return.

"Running a bit late, sister dear. I guess I should expect that with you being a woman now." His indulgent smile triggered her grin. He still called her "baby sister" sometimes, but she was now sixteen and looked every bit like the woman she had become.

"As long as I beat the tide, I'm right on time." She poked his stomach. "Father and Mother send their farewells and prayers to you."

He turned to the slaves, who awaited his commands.

"Leave all the chests on deck outside the cabin. I'll see to the stowing later. You can take the extra carriage and horse back as well."

He didn't want any of the family slaves to see Claudia. None of them would reveal her presence with him voluntarily, but Roman law required the interrogation of any slave be conducted with torture. Even the most loyal slave might crack under such pressure.

He stood with Penelope on the pier until the last of his father's slaves had returned to the carriages and driven away.

◆

Penelope craned her neck as she scanned the ship's deck. "Is she here, Philip? Tell me about her."

"Too soon to know much, but she must be a brave girl. She didn't faint at the first sight of me." The corner of his mouth lifted.

Penelope slapped his arm. "Of course she didn't. Where is she? What's she like?"

"I put her in my room since it's a little bigger than the passenger rooms. I moved in with my boxes, so Junia will be sharing with you. She seems nice. Intelligent, too. She was delighted when I showed her what I bought for my library. If she's a scholar like her father, I expect some interesting conversations during the voyage. She loves poetry, so I'll have someone to read with as well. I told her to stay out of sight until we leave the harbor. She's even more beautiful than Father told me, and any man who sees her couldn't help remembering she was on my ship if her brother comes looking for her in Portus."

Penelope tried to keep her face straight, but her curiosity was raging. Philip was smiling as he described the mystery girl. Usually he was very reserved in his comments about eligible young women.

Mother and her older sister, Ariadne, kept telling him he'd find the right woman to marry if he'd just look. He was such a kind brother; he'd be exactly the sort of husband Penelope wanted herself. Since the fiasco with Phoebe, he was convinced no woman could ever desire an ugly man with so many scars. He didn't want to marry someone who only wanted him because he was rich. But not all women were so shallow that they only looked at the surface of a man.

Philip led a house church, and he'd often told her he'd only marry a Christian woman. That narrowed the field of possibilities even further. Father had said their secret passenger wasn't a Christian even though her father had just died for his faith, but only God knew what she might become.

◆

Philip's head tilted. Why that amused look and sly smile on his sister's face as he was talking? Women—they were beyond comprehension for him. Growing up with two sisters hadn't helped that at all.

Chapter 21

It was Philip's custom to serve only a light supper of bread and cheese on the day he left Portus. They would sail with the evening tide, and that didn't leave time for a regular meal.

Penelope and Junia were eating under the canopy at the stern of the ship. He intended to join them after taking Claudia supper in her room. He filled a plate with cheese and some chunks of bread and carried it to her closed door.

A soft knock drew no answer. He knocked again. "Claudia Drusilla? I have your supper."

Still no answer. She couldn't have failed to hear him. He wrapped on the door even harder.

"Are you all right in there?" Silence. "I'm coming in."

When she failed to answer again, he opened the door and stuck his head in. What he saw surprised him.

She was lying asleep on her bed with one of his poetry codices clutched to her heart. She was on her side, curled up like a kitten, with some reddish blonde tendrils trying to escape from the gold hair net.

The vision of beauty cuddling his codex drew his smile. She must have been exhausted to fall asleep that way. He didn't want to disturb her, so he tiptoed into the room and placed the plate on the table. She could eat whenever she awoke.

Claudia had been sleeping deeply. It was the first undisturbed sleep she'd had since her father was killed. She began to awaken when she heard someone knocking. Philip's deep voice slowly penetrated her consciousness, but she didn't stir right away. When he closed the door, she finally roused enough to open her eyes. There on the table was a plate of bread and cheese. She sat up and stretched. She really wasn't hungry, but she needed to eat, especially since Philip had been thoughtful enough to bring her supper.

She'd almost finished when she heard two quick knocks.

"Come in."

The door swung open, and she turned in the chair to see Philip, smiling at her. She focused again on his good eye and that welcoming smile. She was getting better at ignoring the scars each time she saw him.

"The rowboats are here to pull us out of the harbor. As soon as we're past the breakwater, please join us on deck for some fresh air. The evening should be lovely."

"Thank you, Philip. I'd love to join you and meet your sister if you come get me when you think it's safe."

"I'll be back for you soon."

He left the door to her cabin open when he withdrew. A light breeze blew in the window, through the room, and out the open door. The last trace of stale air was borne away, just as the last bit of tension flowed out of her as it sank in that her escape was a fact.

Through the window, she heard the captain barking orders to the crew as they cast off and moved away from the pier. As she sat at the table gazing out the window, the ship was towed past many others awaiting their turn to dock. She watched the lighthouse as the ship passed through the channel between the breakwater where the lighthouse sat and the massive rocky barrier that separated the harbor built by Emperor Claudius from the open sea. She'd gotten used to the soothing rocking of the boat on the gentle waves in the harbor. The boat began to rock more as it left the quiet waters of the harbor behind.

Claudia inhaled the salt air and let it out slowly. Her escape from her murderous brother and that horrible man he was selling her to was assured. That really was what it would have been—a slave sale where the price was a small fortune. Sabinus was so powerful in Rome that he could have done anything he wanted with her. Lucius would never have let her divorce him, so she truly would have been sold into slavery, just like a household slave.

Philip had rescued her from certain misery, and he appeared to have spared no effort or expense doing so. The things in the chests he'd provided—nothing she could possibly want was missing. The tunics and *pallae* were exquisite and probably more expensive than anything she owned. The hair accessories and tunic clips were elegant and reflected the latest fashion. They were made of gold and silver, and some even had jewels on them. Three expensive perfumes in swirled glass bottles nestled in a carved sandalwood box. The table mirror was even polished silver, not brass like the one she'd left behind.

The whole affair was so risky for him. If he was caught helping her leave against her guardian's will, he'd be charged with kidnapping. Lucius would make sure of that, no matter what she said to defend him. He wasn't a Roman. He'd be in the arena or nailed to a cross for helping her. When she reached Titus, the two of them could try to repay Philip for his expenses, but money alone could never repay all she owed.

Claudia was expecting Philip when she heard his steps coming through the galley. He stooped as he stuck his head into her room.

"Now you can go wherever you want on board. My sister, Penelope, is eager to meet you. Care to join us under the canopy?"

"I would like to very much."

She stood to accompany him, and the rocking of the ship made her almost lose her balance.

He offered his hand. "It takes a little while to get your sea legs."

His big hand engulfed hers completely. When they stepped through the cabin door onto the deck, he placed hers on his arm and escorted her to a collection of chairs, a couch, and some small tables under the canopy. She kept her eyes on the deck as she walked. She still wasn't quite sure how to look at him without it feeling awkward, like she was either staring or trying not to.

Seated there were Junia and her mistress, a pretty girl with dark brown hair, sparkling brown eyes, and a cheerful smile. Claudia couldn't see any family resemblance between her and Philip, but she'd tried hard not to look at him too closely, so there might be one she'd missed.

Penelope stood and held out her hand. "Come sit with us. What should I call you? My brother gave me money to buy everything I thought you'd need, but he wouldn't even tell me your name or who we were taking you to." She slapped his arm and got an indulgent smile in return. "He was so secretive about you, like he couldn't even trust his own sister."

"Please, call me Claudia. I'm going to my brother, Titus Claudius Drusus. He's a tribune serving the provincial governor in Perinthus."

"That's where Philip lives. He controls part of our merchant fleet and all the family estates in Thracia and Moesia from there. I'm going there to live with him for a while."

Claudia glanced at Philip. She'd thought he was the owner of this ship or maybe only the son of the ship owner. He couldn't be much older than Titus. He was lounging in one of the chairs with his legs stretched out and his hands clasped at the back of his head, watching and listening with a relaxed smile. In his plain white tunic, he didn't look or act at all like the rich man he must be. He smiled at her, but she looked away quickly and turned more toward Penelope. She still found it hard to look at all his scars.

"Do tell me more about your brother." Penelope leaned toward her.

"Titus is twenty-four, and he's been serving in Thracia for four years. He's the best brother—so kind and thoughtful and smart and... well, I just couldn't have a better brother than Titus. He'll try to make everything right. If he'd been in Rome, I wouldn't have to be here now."

Her voice filled with passion. "He would have killed Lucius for betraying our father. Then he would have hunted down and killed that horrible man who told Father about that Jesus and convinced Father to follow him. He's responsible for Father's death as surely as Lucius is. I hate the blood of the games, but I'd gladly watch the lions do to him what they did to Father. I'd love to wipe Lucius's blood off Titus's sword. I could kill them myself if I had the chance. I hate the two people who took Father from me. I want to see them bleed and die just like my father had to."

Penelope's head snapped back as her eyes saucered. Claudia hadn't meant to say what she'd just said, but somehow it had just come pouring out.

Philip sat forward in his chair, and he was looking at her oddly. It was the first time she'd seen him without a smile. He looked surprised, then serious, then sad. Why would that be? Surely any man would understand and agree with her desire for revenge.

Tears began to pool in Claudia's eyes. The last thing she wanted was to cry in front of these strangers who'd been so kind to her.

"Please excuse me. I really don't feel very well."

She turned and hurried back to her room. She closed the door, threw herself on the bed, and let her tears flow as she buried her face in the pillow to muffle the sound.

◆

Philip was shocked to hear such hatred spewing from those beautiful lips in that beautiful voice. She had just lost the person she loved most and left behind everything she'd ever known. It was her grief speaking, but it grieved him that she could feel that way, that she wanted revenge so passionately because she didn't know how to forgive or the freedom from pain that forgiving would give her.

He stood and motioned for Penelope and Junia to follow him toward the bow of the ship. He normally used the room he'd put her in. She would hear any conversations under the canopy just outside her window.

When they were well out of earshot, he began his warning. "Be careful what you say under the canopy. It can be heard inside the cabin. You can hear what's being said in the adjacent bedrooms, too. When we carry passengers, we always give thanks for meals silently if we don't know they're all believers. Given what we just heard, we need to avoid saying anything about Jesus where Claudia might hear."

He shook his head as he crossed his arms and looked at the deck. "Her hatred for Father and me could extend to other Christians, and I don't want to put you at risk from anything she might say or do after we land. Her brother is a Roman officer, and he'll probably share her hostility. I'll tell Hector to warn the crew as well."

Penelope nodded; then she put her hand on his arm. "Oh, Philip. She's in such pain. Just watching her makes me want to cry."

He nodded and uncrossed his arms to place his hand on top of hers. Her compassionate eyes mirrored his own feelings. "It's a good thing her steward came to Father for help. She needs our prayers even more than she needs me to take her to her brother."

Penelope brightened. "Maybe the weeks with us on the ship will change her mind. Maybe God will use us to reach her. I'll be praying for that."

"Maybe, but don't say anything to her about Jesus without talking to me first."

Philip placed his hand on Penelope's cheek and stroked it with his thumb. Her faith was so simple and strong. She hadn't seen the ugly side of life yet. She hadn't seen how a gentle soul could be made to suffer unbearably by the evil choices of others. She hadn't seen the bitterness that suffering could cause. But Penelope knew the power of prayer, and Claudia needed their prayers more than anyone he'd ever known.

He led them back to the canopy to watch the sun set the clouds on fire as it descended toward the horizon. It was a beautiful evening, but it was marred for them all by the occasional soft sound of Claudia weeping in her room.

Finally, Junia rose. "I'm going to go see if Claudia is ready for me to help her get ready to retire. I think she needs me before you will tonight, mistress."

Penelope nodded her approval.

Claudia raised her head from the pillow at the gentle knocking on her cabin door. "Yes?"

"It's Junia, mistress. Are you ready for me to help you prepare to sleep?"

Claudia brushed the remaining tears from her cheeks and sat up. "Come in."

She pressed on the puffy areas below each eye that revealed how hard she'd been crying.

Junia pulled the larger trunk out and removed a clean tunic from it. "Let's get you into something fresh for sleeping. I helped Mistress Penelope choose your clothes. Our choices may be a bit more Greek than Roman, but I hope they'll still please you."

Claudia smiled weakly. "What you chose is lovely. I really am grateful for everything you all have done."

Junia pulled the stola and plain tunic over Claudia's head. She transferred the shoulder pins to a clean linen one before helping Claudia into it.

"Would you like your hair brushed tonight, mistress?"

"Maybe a little."

As Junia removed the clips and spun-gold hair net from Claudia's hair, her thick blonde tresses tumbled down her back. When Junia began to brush them, Claudia sighed. She would miss Graecia styling her hair and the visits with her friends at the women's bath. Everything and everyone were gone now, but at least she'd escaped the marriage that would have been a living hell. When she got to Titus, somehow things would get better again.

As Junia pulled the brush through for the last time, Claudia forced a smile. "That felt wonderful. Please thank Penelope for sharing you with me."

"It's a pleasure for both of us to have you on this voyage."

Claudia placed her hand on Junia's arm. "And thank you so much for the risks you took in getting me here."

Junia's smile was remarkably like Philip's when she'd given him thanks. "I was glad to help. If you need anything in the night, I'm in the upper bunk in the first room with my mistress."

"I think I'll be fine."

In truth, she was afraid she wouldn't be. She hadn't been fine at night since Father had been killed by the lions, and she was beginning to fear she would never be fine again.

As Junia closed the door behind her, Claudia lay down on the bunk, closed her eyes, and began the long night of wanting to sleep and being afraid to because the dreams would come.

Philip and Hector stood by the rail, watching the moonlight reflecting off the crests of the waves.

"It mostly went smoothly getting her today. There was one moment with the robbers in Subura. You were right about taking a sword. I thought I was in for a real fight until she showed them what was in the box. I didn't expect a pampered rich girl to be so cool-headed. She stopped them dead in their tracks when she held up the two scrolls."

A crooked grin accompanied the shake of Hector's head. "You should have seen the look on the leader's face. Anyway, I'm sure your plan to get her away unseen worked."

"Only because of you, Hector. I appreciate you taking the risk for me. It would have been the arena for both of us if we'd been caught. I wish I could have done it all myself, but my face would have put her and all of us in danger of discovery. Her brother's a bad piece of work. I can't understand a man getting his father killed just to become the patriarch or selling his own sister to an abusive womanizer, even for a small fortune."

Philip rubbed his hand back and forth on the smooth wood of the railing.

"I am concerned about how much she cried today. I know she's grieving her father's death, but still... The Drusus steward asked Father to get her to her brother because she was about to kill herself rather than marry that old lecher. Telling her that he'd get her to Titus was the only thing that stopped her."

He looked out at the waves again.

"She's probably going to be fine now that she's on the way to her brother, but I'd appreciate it if you'd help me keep an eye on her for a few days until we're sure."

"Of course."

Philip placed his hands on the top of his head and arched his back. "It's been a long day. I'm ready for a good night's sleep."

Hector nodded, and the two men walked back to the cabin to retire.

After closing his door, Philip lit the lamp and opened each of the boxes to extract the Christian Scriptures that he was carrying home for some of his friends. He repacked the Septuagint, several copies of each gospel, and three bound compilations of the letters of Paul into a single box. He placed it back against the wall at the foot of his upper bunk. She was too short to notice it back there.

Now she wouldn't find anything related to Jesus when she looked through his boxes. He would hate to have her deliberately damage any of the Scriptures. They were hard to come by and precious, and his friends were eagerly awaiting these copies of the word of God.

It made it safer for Penelope, too. Claudia wasn't ready to know that Penelope and he were believers. Hatred and a desire for vengeance can make people do what they normally wouldn't. She might try to hurt any Christian she met because she hated the ones who led her father to new life at the cost of his old one.

Philip jerked awake in the middle of the night. The sounds of Claudia sobbing passed through the thin boards that formed the wall between them. He rolled from his side to his back and listened for what seemed a very long time. He was about to rise and knock on her door to see if he could get her something when the sobs finally died away.

He rubbed his scarred cheek. He hadn't expected her to be so devastated by the loss of her father. She was truly suffering. Maybe he could figure out something tomorrow that would help. He rolled back onto his side and drifted off to sleep after one more prayer for her deliverance from the pain.

Chapter 22

DISTRACTIONS

Philip had been up since the first hints of dawn. He loved the first full day at sea. After a few weeks ashore, it felt good to be in the company of his crew, all men he'd known for years. Only at sea was he free from the stares of curious strangers and the quickly averted eyes when he looked directly at someone.

As he stood with Hector by the poles that controlled the rudders from the roof of the cabin, Claudia came out the cabin door much earlier than he expected and went to the rail. She gripped the smooth wood and stared down into the water. The way she leaned over the rail—something wasn't right. The look of desolation on her face—that triggered deeper concern.

He climbed down and joined her at the railing with her just to his left. He always stood to the right of people so he didn't have to turn his whole body to see them.

For someone bothered by his appearance, it also gave less of his scarred face to look at. If looking away or down while talking made someone more comfortable, that's what he did. While he'd mostly reconciled himself to how ugly his scars made him, he still saw how they repelled some people...especially young women.

It was too obvious that Claudia found him hard to look at. She'd tried not to look at his scars from the moment she met him. No surprise in that. Of course someone so beautiful would feel uncomfortable with ugliness.

The puffiness under her eyes showed she'd been crying again, but she was still the most beautiful woman he'd ever seen.

She pulled her gaze from the deep water. A fleeting glance and smile at him, then she looked once more at the waves.

"Good morning, Claudia. I hope you slept well."

Her smile was sad. "Not really, but thank you for asking."

She was trying to veil the grief in her eyes. It was plain she didn't want to talk about it.

"The first night out is hard for many people. I hope tonight will be better for you."

She smiled again and nodded.

In silence, he stood beside her, leaning with his forearms on the railing, watching the ship cut through the waves.

She said nothing and continued staring at the deep water.

After many minutes, he spoke again. "Breakfast will be served soon. I hope you'll enjoy it."

As he rejoined Hector, something about her made him very uneasy. Watching her stare into the water had done nothing to reduce his concern. He continued to watch her from the cabin top.

After one final look at the deep water flowing past the ship, Claudia returned to the cabin to prepare for breakfast.

After breakfast, Philip walked the ship, checking on his crew before joining the three women under the canopy. Penelope and Junia were watching the shoreline move past the ship, each occasionally pointing out something interesting.

He focused on Claudia, whose eyes were pointed at the shore, but she seemed miles away. From the droop of her mouth and the dullness of her eyes, she was probably dwelling on the horrible things that had happened in Rome.

It was time to give her something else to think about.

"Claudia, I hope you enjoy games. Penelope is never interested in playing with me, but I hope you will."

Penelope pulled her gaze from the shore to face him. "I never play with you, dear brother, because you're just too smart for me and I lose every game. You know that's not fun for me or you."

She turned to Claudia. "Do indulge him in a few games. He really is a gracious winner. Maybe you can help me find out if he's a gracious loser, too."

Claudia shifted her gaze from the shore to Philip.

His hopeful smile and raised eyebrow should convey his desire for an opponent, but would she say yes? She could look at the board, not him, so maybe she'd be willing.

"I'd be happy to play with you, Philip. Father and I used to play Jackals and Hounds..."

The aura of sadness surrounding her deepened when she said "father." It would be a bad idea to play a game that she'd often played with him.

"Let's play something you don't already know." He grinned at her. "I'll have a better chance of winning. Have you played Conquest?"

"No..."

"Good. I'll teach you. It's a strategy game from Macedonia. You try to conquer the world, like Alexander the Great. You'll love it." He grinned again. "But I must warn you that I'm famous for my skill at it. Well, maybe not exactly famous..."

◆

Claudia forced a smile at Philip's attempt to entertain her. Playing with him was the least she could do to show her appreciation for all he'd done, even though playing a game was the last thing she felt like doing. After so many sleepless nights, she barely had energy for anything. But it might help take her mind off Father and everything else she'd lost, and that could be worth the effort.

Her fake smile drew his genuine one in return. "I'll get the board. It will only take a moment to set it up."

She watched his back as he walked away. He was so muscular, and he moved like a trained athlete. It seemed odd that a man like him would be so fond of playing board games. Then again, maybe it wasn't. It made sense for a man who loved reading to enjoy the challenge of matching wits with another person. She'd always enjoyed strategy games herself.

Several games later, Claudia was surprised by how much fun it had been to play with Philip. He was amazingly good at teaching her how to play. During the first game, he almost played both sides, explaining what her response to his moves ought to be and why. During the second game, he let her play mostly by herself with occasional explanations of why she just lost a battle and what she could have done to avoid it. The third game he didn't help her at all. He did win, but he told her she was a worthy opponent.

Penelope leaned forward and stared at the board as the fourth game was coming to a close. "I can't believe it, Claudia. You're going to beat him."

"Shhh, sister dear. I'm concentrating."

Philip stared intently at the remaining pieces. His left hand rubbed the back of his neck as he scowled at the board. Finally, he sighed and moved his last piece.

"I hate to admit it, but you have me." He looked up at her with a twinkle in his eye. "I could say that I let you beat me, but that would be a lie. Well done."

Claudia's smile started small and grew as she raised her gaze to his face. It was an excellent game, and he was a challenging opponent. Best of all, it really had taken her mind off everything else while they played.

"Perhaps we can play again later, and you can have a chance to regain your honor." She grinned as she made the offer.

"Your challenge is accepted."

As he spoke, the ship's cook came from the galley with their lunch of bread and cheese. He nodded and smiled at the cook to acknowledge the arrival of their food.

"But first we eat. Maybe you won't be quite so sharp when you're relaxing after a good meal."

As Claudia ate, she found herself feeling better than she had since the soldiers took Father, and it was all due to Philip. He was sitting with his scarred side toward her as he talked with his captain. She'd found his appearance repulsive when she first met him. Now that she'd spent so much time looking at him while they played, his scars weren't so hard to look at. They hadn't affected his smile at all.

After lunch, Philip excused himself and joined Hector on the cabin top. For a while, Claudia watched the passing shoreline with Penelope and Junia, but soon her thoughts returned to her father and what Lucius had done. The more she thought, the harder it became to hold back the tears.

♦

Junia watched Claudia's descent into silence and sadness. The poor girl was trying to bear her grief with no one and nothing to help her, and she appeared to be failing. When the tears began to pool in Claudia's eyes, Junia decided it was time to do something.

"Excuse me, mistress. I need to walk a little."

Penelope smiled and nodded her approval. Junia walked to the front of the cabin where Claudia couldn't see and waved at Philip for him to come down. His brows dipped, then rose before he nodded. He climbed down the ladder and joined her. She motioned for him to follow her toward the bow of the ship, where their conversation wouldn't be overheard.

"I'm worried about Claudia, master. She was so terribly sad last night. Now she's been too quiet for too long, and she looks like she's trying very hard not to cry. You cheered her up so well this morning. Can you maybe do something to distract her again?"

Philip rubbed his scars. "It's good you told me. I think some poetry reading might be in order. That should prove an effective distraction."

◆

They returned to the stern. While Junia walked back to resume her seat beside Penelope, Philip went into the cabin to select something suitable. He chose a codex by a little-known poet who wrote elegant lyrical poetry on topics more uplifting than the odes glorifying licentious behavior and political satires of the most popular poets.

As he shuffled through the box, looking for a second codex, a smile tugged at the corner of his mouth. Claudia must have liked the one he'd seen her sleeping with before they sailed. What better to read to her?

The door to her room was open, and he could see it on the table. He stepped in and picked it up before heading out to the canopy.

He found her sitting in a chair, drooping as she gazed at the passing shoreline. Junia was right; Claudia definitely needed something to cheer her up.

Philip sat down in the chair just to her right. She turned slowly to look at him. Her eyes swam in tears that threatened to escape at any moment.

"Claudia, you promised me yesterday that we could read some poetry this afternoon. I hope now is a good time for you."

Her smile wavered a little, but her eyes seemed eager for a distraction, any distraction, from the thoughts that were haunting her. "I would enjoy that very much, Philip."

He handed her the codex by the new poet while keeping the one she'd liked yesterday to read himself.

"I haven't read much by this poet, so we can explore the intricacy of his writing together. I did find the first poem striking when I was selecting this trip's additions to my library. Would you like to read first?" His eyebrow rose and his entreating smile mirrored the request.

"I would enjoy that."

"As you wish, Philip."

He leaned back in his chair, stretched his legs out, and rested his clasped hands on the back of his head. Elegant words for his ears and a vision of loveliness for his eye—the corner of his mouth lifted in anticipation.

◆

Claudia had already seen Philip in that position several times. He looked so relaxed and content. How she wished she could be that way again.

She turned to the first page and the first poem. "Ever the beauty of sunrise graces my eyes, filling my heart with joy. Oh, for the peace of..."

As she read, she found the images striking and the choice of words sometimes surprising but always beautiful. She'd never heard of the poet before, but his writing was enchanting. She glanced at Philip. He had excellent taste in poetry. With his seaman's tunic and his bulging muscles, he looked like a laborer, not a scholar. He was a surprising man.

She read several pages, savoring each line. Finally, she closed the codex and looked up at him. He was listening with his eye closed, the corners of his mouth turned up in a satisfied smile. He was a very ugly man, but he was not as unpleasant to look at when he was so obviously enjoying the poetry.

"Your turn, Philip."

Philip picked up the codex he'd placed on the table and turned to a poem toward the middle. As he began to read, an icy hand gripped her heart and began squeezing. He'd chosen a poem that Father had read to her the day before his arrest.

◆

When Philip glanced at her at the completion of the first eight lines, he was stunned by the anguish in her eyes.

"What's wrong?"

A tear trickled down her cheek. "Father loved that poem. He read it to me often...." She flicked the teardrop away.

Philip closed the codex. "I'm certain no one can read it as well, so let me read something different."

He set the codex aside and lifted the other one from her hands. He thumbed through until he found where she'd stopped and began to read. "The wind's caress stirred the grass and made the flowers dance. Such grace..."

His voice was deep and resonant, and he read with feeling. Claudia tried to turn off her thoughts of death and focus on the beautiful visions of life in the poems. The tears dried, and she found herself caught up in the images so clearly drawn by his soothing voice.

His scars were too distracting if she watched him read, but if she kept her eyes closed, she could forget and be swept up in the images his rich voice was describing. She found herself smiling. Even though it was only a slight smile, it was still a smile.

Supper was a time of lively conversation for Penelope and Junia. Each had observed delightful sections of coastline that they described with enthusiasm.

Philip enjoyed watching Penelope's happy face. She'd been much younger the last time she made the coastal voyage, and that made each cliff and gently sloped beach seem totally new to her.

He watched Claudia, too, and he was not as satisfied with his observations. She tried to listen and smile at all the right times, but it was clear her thoughts were elsewhere.

After supper, they all sat for a long while, watching the sunset blaze and then gradually fade.

Claudia was in no hurry to retire. Her bed had become the source of terrifying nightmares of lions and screams and blood. Every night since her father died, the horrible images had come to torment her.

Junia helped Penelope prepare for bed first, then came back out to where Claudia still sat under the canopy in the fading light.

"Are you ready for my help, mistress?"

As much as Claudia hated to retire, there was no choice. "Yes."

She rose, sighed deeply, and followed Junia to her room.

Philip had remained with Claudia, watching the sky fade from orange to purple. She'd been lost in her thoughts and hadn't realized he was watching her even more than the sky. What he saw was deeply disturbing. She was a tormented soul.

What could he do to help? She'd probably be angry if she even suspected that the ugly man who'd rescued her from her brother was praying to the God she now hated, asking Him to rescue her from her anguish and give her peace.

It was near midnight when Philip woke again to her muffled sobs. He lay awake for more than an hour, listening to the sound of her breaking heart and praying for her pain to end.

Chapter 23

Pleasing the Crocodile

It had been two days since Claudia disappeared from the women's dressing area in the Baths of Titus, and Lucius was deeply worried. He wasn't worried because he cared about his sister's safety; he was worried about what her disappearance meant for his own.

When Graecia had run back to the house after discovering her mistress had vanished while she was fetching some perfume that Claudia insisted she must have, Malleolus had immediately mobilized a search. The good thing—one of the attendants had overheard some strange woman telling Claudia that Portia would have a carriage just outside the city gate and they would be taking the Via Tiburtina and Via Valeria. The bad thing—Claudia was going with the woman willingly. It wasn't a kidnapping; it was an escape attempt.

With the daytime carriage ban inside the city, the women had to walk or use litters, and the slaves Malleolus sent running along the streets to intercept them should have had no trouble catching up. No such luck. For the last two days, his steward had posted slaves to watch continuously at each of the five city gates that someone heading to the east or northeast would have had to use. Again, no luck.

Graecia knew of two girls named Portia who were Claudia's friends. Malleolus had visited their houses to make sure they hadn't given her refuge there, but both claimed they hadn't even spoken with her since her father died.

Malleolus had also gone to the home of her best friend, Aemilia, and tried to learn something that might give them a clue to where

Claudia might have gone. Aemilia had heard about Lucius's plan to marry Claudia to Sabinus, and she refused to tell him anything. Malleolus had then checked at the homes of every one of her friends that Graecia could name. Finally, he'd sent a slave to each of the three Drusus estates near Rome to see if she'd gone to one of those to hide. No luck.

Claudia had vanished into thin air, and neither Lucius nor Malleolus had the slightest idea of where to look for her next.

When the door slave entered the library to announce that Flavius Sabinus awaited Lucius in the atrium, it was with some trepidation that he instructed the slave to escort Sabinus to him.

Lucius stood as Sabinus entered the room. "Another unexpected pleasure to see you today, Flavius Sabinus." He smiled what he hoped was a welcoming smile.

"It's good to see you as well, Lucius Fidelis." There was a smile pasted on Sabinus's face, but his eyes reminded Lucius of a cat playing with a mouse before it killed it.

"I've come to visit my future wife. Our conversation was cut short earlier this week when she felt ill. I trust I'll find her in undiminished beauty and more receptive to my attentions today."

Lucius's stomach knotted. "Unfortunately, she won't be able to see you this morning. She's gone out."

That was certainly true.

"When will she return?"

"I'm not quite sure."

That was also most certainly true.

Sabinus walked over to the desk and picked up the stylus that Lucius had set down on his wax tablet. He began slowly rolling it between his thumb and middle finger.

"I heard a most surprising rumor this morning."

Sabinus fixed his reptilian eyes on Lucius. A chill ran up Lucius's spine. It was all he could do not to visibly shiver.

"What would that be?"

"I heard you were searching for Claudia all over the city. I heard she had run away because she didn't want to be married to me."

Lucius swallowed hard. He had no idea what to say.

Sabinus gripped the stylus like a dagger and drove it into the wax tablet. Lucius jumped.

"I'm sure you know that no one…no one…ever runs away from me unless I allow it. If they try, they don't get far."

The crocodile fixed his eyes on Lucius. "And no one who does anything to damage my reputation walks away unscathed."

Lucius swallowed hard again.

"You should have told me yourself, Lucius. As soon as you knew she'd disappeared. I don't like finding out two days later than everyone else. I have many contacts throughout the city, and I could have found her right away, before she got herself hidden so well."

The crocodile's eyes remained locked on Lucius. It was unnerving to keep looking into them, but he instinctively knew not to take his eyes off a predator.

"You have caused me embarrassment, Lucius. I expect you to fix it. You are to squash that rumor and replace it with another that Claudia has been kidnapped."

"I'll do that right away. This very day, I'll offer a large reward for information leading to her return and the capture of the kidnappers. How best can I do that to quickly let the most people know who need to know?"

"I can take care of that. You merely need to provide the 10,000 denarii that will be the reward."

The crocodile pulled the stylus out of the wax, then drove it in again with even more force before dragging it across the tablet diagonally.

"And then you will find her and bring her back here to marry me."

He dragged the stylus back across the wax tablet.

"That is, if I decide I still want her. I don't accept damaged goods, Lucius, or used ones, or anything that's gone out of fashion."

He lifted the stylus from the wax and snapped it.

"There's a time limit on my patience, Lucius."

He held the two broken pieces out in front of him before slowly opening his hand to allow them to fall to the floor.

Lucius stared at him, frozen in place.

"Well, Lucius?"

"Yes, absolutely. It's a terrible thing that a girl could be kidnapped in broad daylight in the heart of Rome. I'll gladly offer the 10,000-denarii reward for the safe return of my sister. Did you want me to draft the reward announcement? Perhaps you'd prefer to do it so it's done exactly as it should be."

The crocodile smiled with his lips, but not his eyes. "I would be most happy to help my future brother-in-law by getting the announcement out. You've chosen wisely in offering a reward that shows how serious you are about rescuing your sister from the kidnappers. Very wisely, indeed. My people will be looking for her as well. You will pay me the reward if they find her."

"I can't tell you how much I appreciate your help in rescuing my sister."

"I'm sure you can't." Sabinus stood staring at Lucius for much too long without speaking. Finally, he turned to leave.

"I'm expected at the imperial palace. I'll take care of the message. You be ready to pay the reward."

He paused at the door. "You don't want to disappoint me, Lucius. You really don't."

Lucius sat down as soon as Sabinus left the room. His knees felt weak, and his hand was trembling when he looked at it. At that moment, he'd give anything to be able to go back to the day before he betrothed Claudia to Sabinus.

Father had always said that only a fool chose to spend his time with dangerous company. His father had been right.

Chapter 24

A Good Day

They had been at sea for a week, and everyone had settled into the ship's routine. Philip still heard Claudia crying every night. It kept him from getting a full night's sleep, and it made him wonder if she slept at all. Every morning she rose puffy-eyed to stand by the railing, staring into the water. That still worried him, but at least she wasn't crying during the day.

He'd discovered a rhythm for the daytime that seemed to help. A few games of Conquest in the morning and poetry reading in the afternoon kept her from grieving all the time. He found it enjoyable as well. It had been a long time since he'd faced as good an opponent, even though she'd just learned the game. Her reading poetry was a feast for both eyes and ears. All he needed to do was make sure they read from something that hadn't been a favorite of her father.

◆

Claudia had just finished reading a poem by another gifted poet that she'd never heard of before Philip introduced her to him. When she looked up, Philip was lounging in his chair with his legs stretched out and his clasped hands resting on the top of his head. He was smiling contentedly as he gazed at her. She was used to men staring at her, but he was different. He looked at her like she was a real person whose company he enjoyed, not just something to desire.

He was an enigma. How could someone who was so horribly disfigured be so happy all the time? Something terrible must have happened to him, but it didn't seem to affect his positive outlook at all. How could that be?

"May I ask you something personal, Philip?"

"Anything you want."

"What happened to your face?"

She spoke the question gently, not fully expecting he would tell her. It surprised her when he smiled and shrugged.

"My scars are from a burn. When I was six, my little sister Ariadne wanted some of her favorite soup. It had just been lifted from the fire and was sitting on the counter. I thought I was big enough to get her some if I used a stool. When I was climbing, I tipped the pot over. It poured down one side of me. It burned my face, neck, part of my chest. It scalded my eye, too."

"That must have been horrible!"

◆

Sympathy filled Claudia's eyes, but not pity. That was good; Philip didn't need or want her pity. He'd grown content enough with the way he was. He'd decided a long time ago there was no point in being otherwise.

"The pain was bad, and it took a long time to heal, but I'm glad it was me who got burned and not Ariadne. It doesn't matter much that I have scars, but it would have been hard for a girl to have her beauty ruined."

"You could grow a beard to hide them."

"No beard will grow on the scar." He smiled wryly as he rubbed his scarred cheek. "I guess I could grow half a beard and always stand so you only see my good side in profile. Or I can just shave the hairy side and look Roman instead of Greek. At least shaving only takes me half as long."

Her eyes widened as he joked about it.

He faked a sad face as he slowly shook his head. "It is very hard for a Macedonian to have to settle for looking like a Roman."

He didn't get the response he intended. He'd expected a laugh or at least a smile, but she didn't realize he was joking. Now she was looking at him like she felt sorry for him, and he didn't want that. No man would, but he really didn't need her pity because he actually was content enough with the way he looked. There was a time when he would have given almost anything not to have the scars, but a man has to decide to be content with what can't be changed. One more attempt at humor, and maybe she'd get it.

"I really don't mind being ugly, Claudia. It has some advantages. It makes it much easier to know if a pretty woman wants me for my handsome face or my family's fortune."

He winked as he smiled broadly at her, and she returned his smile. The look of pity was gone.

"If she were smart, she'd want you for your kind heart. That's what I like most about you. Anyway, you're not really that ugly."

A chuckle escaped as he shook his head at her unsuccessful attempt to give him a compliment so he'd feel better. Unless she wanted to lie, there wasn't much she could say. She clearly didn't understand him, but he didn't expect that a beauty would. He was an ugly man on the outside, but it was only what was inside a man that mattered. For the most part, he was content being the man God had made him.

"Maybe not ugly enough to scare away small children, but pretty women—that's another matter."

There was only one pretty woman Philip didn't want his appearance to scare, and she was sitting contently next to him and looking right at him. His ugly scars didn't seem to bother her anymore since she'd just asked him about them. She was the first woman who ever had.

◆

Claudia watched the twinkle in Philip's eye. How could he be so unconcerned about his appearance that he could joke about it? Appearance mattered so much to her friends. They all wanted to marry a handsome, rich man from a prominent Roman family.

"Well, you might not be as handsome as my brother Titus, but you're at least as nice. He's not married yet, either. He hasn't found the right woman to marry even though he's very good looking." She smiled at him. "Anyway, I enjoy your company no matter what you look like."

"And I enjoy yours. Now, shall I read again, or would you like to?"

"You read. I think you have a beautiful voice for poetry. I love to close my eyes and let your voice wrap around me."

She leaned her head against the back of her chair and did just that. With her eyes closed, she could imagine that wonderful voice coming from the handsomest face. Or from no face at all—just a gorgeous voice floating over the images being painted by the words.

◆

As Philip resumed reading, he was glad she liked his kind heart even if she closed her eyes because she didn't like looking at him. No woman could actually enjoy looking at him. He'd accepted that fact years ago. But the heart of a man was so much more important than his appearance. As he glanced at the beauty lounging in the chair beside him, he found himself wishing she might be a woman who would agree with him.

Claudia sat watching the beginning of the sunset. It had been a good day. Philip was so kind to spend much of his time with her. She wasn't sure what he would normally have been doing onboard, but whatever it was, he was willing to not do it so he could help her. He had a gift for pulling her out of the black thoughts that dragged her downward, for focusing her mind on something other than Father and his death.

When they were playing Conquest, she could focus so completely on military strategy that only the game and her clever opponent seemed real. Reading with him wasn't quite as effective as playing the game, but it was still much better than staring at the shoreline or trying to talk with Penelope and Junia.

She looked over at him. His blind side was toward her, so she could look at him without him knowing. He was an ugly man, but she didn't mind looking at him anymore. His scars had become something familiar, and that made them no longer grotesque.

Junia had already helped Penelope prepare for the night, and she came from the cabin for Claudia. "Are you ready for me, mistress?"

"Yes. I'm coming."

As she rose from the chair, Philip rose as well.

"Thank you, Philip, for helping me have such a good day."

"It's been a good day for me, too. I trust you'll have a good night as well.

For the first time since Father was killed, she'd made it through a whole day without tears. It had been a very good day, and she expected a good night, too.

The lions came at midnight, with the screams and the blood flooding Claudia's mind. She woke in a cold sweat, and the tears began. She thought she'd turned the corner, that the horrors in her mind were over. But they weren't. The night was as if the good day had never happened. The flood of desperate tears soaked into her pillow, and it seemed they would never end.

◆

Philip awoke to the sound of her sobbing...again. It would be another short night's sleep. He ran his fingers through his hair. He'd figured out how to keep her reasonably cheerful during the day, but what on earth could he possibly do to help her at night? He really had expected tonight to be different.

He rolled on his back and stared at the ceiling, asking God to give her relief from the anguish that was ripping her apart, until the sobs finally died away.

Chapter 25

SOMEONE TO CLING TO

It was shortly after dawn, and Philip stood on the cabin top with Hector. Claudia was sobbing again in the room beneath his feet, and he was trying to decide whether he should go to her or get Junia. Suddenly, the sobbing stopped. Claudia stumbled out the door and over to the railing. He was already halfway down the ladder when she started to climb over. He jumped the remaining distance to the deck and ran toward her.

He reached her just in time to wrap his arms around her as she began to step off into the sea.

She struggled against him, twisting her body, slamming her head back into his chest, trying to break free and complete her step into oblivion, but she was no match against the muscular arms that encircled her, holding her firmly against his chest.

"Let me go! I just can't bear it anymore. Please!"

"I won't let you do this to Titus. You can't make him lose both you and your father. If you won't try to go on for yourself, do it for him."

Her struggles ceased. She went limp, and a torrent of tears began to flow. While one arm still held her tight against his chest, he slipped the other behind her knees so he could scoop her up and return her to the deck. He'd released her and taken a step back when she spun and wrapped her arms around his chest, clutching him as if she'd die if she let go. Racking sobs shook her whole body.

At first, Philip hesitated, his arms held away from her. He'd never been in the arms of a woman who wasn't a blood relative before. Then he wrapped his arms around her trembling body and held her tight, just like he would a frightened child. As her tears soaked into his tunic, he placed his hand on the back of her head and stroked her hair. Penelope had always liked that when she came to him for comfort when she was a little girl. He had no way to know what grown women liked, crying or otherwise.

"It's going to get better, Claudia. Just give it time, and it will get better."

He longed to tell her how Jesus knew all her pain and how he could help her bear it, but she wouldn't listen, and she couldn't possibly understand, even if she did.

Her voice was muffled against his chest. "I can't do it anymore. I can't stand the dreams every night. I haven't slept through the night since Father was killed. I'm so tired...I just can't go on like this."

◆

Claudia clung to Philip. He felt so solid, like a tree trunk that could never be moved, even by the strongest winds. She desperately needed something solid to cling to, someone to make it bearable.

She felt the steady beating of his heart against her cheek as he held her. There was something calming about that. Finally, the flood of tears turned into a rivulet. The racking sobs quieted into small, silent jerks.

◆

Philip looked down at her as she still clung to him so desperately, even though the tears had ended. "The dreams?"

She looked up at him with eyes like a rabbit dying slowly, painfully in a trap. "Every time I go to sleep, I see the lions, I hear the screams, I see the blood, and I wake up again. I just can't stop the dreams." More tears trickled down her cheeks.

She laid her cheek back against his chest, and he held her close, stroking her hair, for what seemed a very long time. It was so thick and soft that he wove his fingers in and slowly pulled them through. That brought a quiet sigh and a slight relaxation of her arms, but she still clung to him like a drowning sailor with only a single plank of wood between himself and a watery grave.

Claudia finally released him and stepped back. She hung her head, and her shoulders drooped, as if it took every bit of strength she possessed even to stand. He wiped the last of her tears away with his fingertips before placing his hands on her upper arms to steady her.

"If you can't sleep at night, then I'll help you sleep now."

"Can you do that?" Both desperation and hope filled her eyes. "How?"

"Come with me."

He placed her hand on his arm and covered it with his own. She rested her head against his shoulder as he led her back to the canopy.

Penelope and Junia had come from the cabin to stand beside them as he held her, and they followed.

"Penelope, would you please get me the scroll about India that's sitting on my table?"

She hurried into the cabin to fetch it.

Philip led Claudia to the couch and had her sit down beside him.

He placed a pillow on his lap and patted it. "Lay your head down here."

She complied, and her thick tresses fanned out across the pillow. The early morning sun turned them into shimmering strands of reddish silk.

Claudia bit her lip to stop the quiver. "I'm sorry to be such a terrible bother. I'm not even a paying passenger."

Philip gazed into her grief-stricken eyes. How could he take the sadness from them? He pushed some strands of hair behind her ear. Her eyes still glistened with tears.

"You're not a bother at all. It gives me pleasure to help you."

Somehow, Claudia knew he wasn't just saying that. He truly meant it. Some tension drained away as she floated in the peaceful, caring depth of his single eye. His warm smile replaced the snarling jaws of the lions at the top of her consciousness. It was funny how she didn't usually notice the eyepatch and the swirling scars surrounding it now. In fact, he didn't seem so terribly ugly anymore, especially when he was looking at her like he really cared. Looking at him made her feel better, even with his scars.

As his fingers swept her forehead, pushing back a lock of hair, she took a deep breath and slowly released it.

"Now close your eyes." He began massaging her temple.

The soft touch of his fingertips as they made small circles released the last of the tension. It was as if she were melting in the warmth of his kindness.

Her eyes popped open as footsteps came around the corner. After Penelope handed Philip a scroll, she perched on the edge of a chair, watching with her hands clasped to her breast.

Claudia's gaze flipped back to Philip's gentle smile.

"You need to keep your eyes closed. Just relax and listen."

She nodded her head and obeyed.

"I have long desired to write a full and orderly account of the land of India and of my journey to its farthest reaches..."

She let the soft cocoon of his deep, resonant voice wrap around her. It became fainter and fainter...

Philip stopped reading when her slow, steady breathing assured him she was deeply asleep. He sat for a long time with her head cradled in his lap, gazing at the beautiful face that looked more peaceful than it ever had since he first met her.

He knew exactly what could give her lasting peace, or rather Who, but there was no way he could tell her right now. She wanted nothing to do with Jesus, and she hated his father for telling her father about Him. She'd hate him, too, if she knew what he'd done.

As he gazed at her, he sighed and slowly shook his head. She was so smart, so beautiful, and so totally lost. He began what were now his daily prayers for her to accept the Lord and receive His peace.

When Claudia awoke several hours later, Philip was sitting in the chair next to her, reading one of his new histories. The scarred side of his face was toward her.

The swirls and ridges ran from where his right eyebrow should have been, down his cheek, barely missing his mouth, onto his neck, and under his tunic. He'd suffered horribly, but he always seemed content, even happy. How could he look so peaceful all the time? What was his secret?

Then he felt her gaze and turned so he could see her. "Did you sleep well?"

"Oh, yes. How did you know that would work?"

"It almost always worked for me. My mother used to rub my temple and tell me stories when I couldn't get to sleep because the burns hurt too much. It helped me focus on something other than the pain. I could usually doze off after a while."

"Was it so terribly painful?"

"At the time it was, but I scarcely remember the pain now. What I do remember is my mother's voice and the touch of her fingers. Time does that—blunts the pain and leaves the good memories. You'll see."

Her brow furrowed as she watched him, not quite able to believe that but hoping he might be right.

She sat up and laid her hand on his arm. "It feels so good to have just slept without those dreams. How can I ever thank you?"

He placed his hand on top of hers and lightly squeezed. "No thanks are necessary. I enjoyed watching a beautiful woman sleep so peacefully today." A smile lifted the corners of his mouth. "But I wouldn't mind you reading to me for a while."

"History or poetry?"

"History. Alexander the Great. Good training for future games of Conquest." His teasing grin made his eye twinkle. "It should give you a better chance of beating me."

She tilted her head as her grateful smile turned into her own teasing grin.

"But I can already beat you, at least occasionally."

"And the more you can beat me, the more fun it becomes."

She basked in his laughing eye and warm smile. Who would have thought there could be such a man, who could joke about being so ugly and enjoy losing if it meant a more exciting game? He was so unlike anyone she'd ever met. It was unbelievable good fortune that his father had been her father's friend. His clever plan had rescued her from Lucius. His soothing voice had given her a peaceful sleep for the first time in days. He would get her safely to Titus. How could she ever repay him...for everything?

Chapter 26

Lucius rolled a stylus between his fingers. Then he leaned his elbows on his desk and rested his forehead on his fists.

Malleolus sat across from him with his arms crossed. "I have no more ideas about where she might have gone. I've visited every girl that Graecia remembered Claudia ever visiting. Every woman or girl she saw Claudia talking with at the baths since Sabinus made his request. I spoke not only with the girls, but with their fathers as well. I made a list of all the families Claudia might know who have estates that are reached by the Via Valeria, and I visited them. No one knew I was coming, so they had no chance to hide her before I arrived. There's no trace of her anywhere."

Lucius rubbed his chin. "We're missing something. She can't have simply disappeared. We know some woman helped her. I'm certain the bath slave heard what she first told us. When I threatened to have the torturers take her in hand to make sure she spoke the truth...her terror was real, and the story didn't change."

He ran his fingers into his hair and rested his elbows on the desk again.

Then he snapped to attention. "A woman helped her, but there's no reason to believe what the slave heard was true. That could have been a false clue to hide where she was going." His jaw clenched. "And I know just the woman who's smart enough to sneak her out of the bath and leave a trail of lies to mislead us in the hunt."

Malleolus rubbed his cheek. "Who would that be?"

Lucius's eyes narrowed. "Cornelia. She opposed the marriage from the moment she heard of it. She even had the gall to come in here and tell me I should break my word to Sabinus and end the betrothal. She didn't care how dangerous that would be."

His lips tightened. "She acts the chaste, dutiful wife, but I don't believe it. Not after what she said that day. If Sabinus does something to me, our oldest son would become the new *paterfamilias*, and that would give her no end of satisfaction."

Lucius rose. "It's more than a week, so she won't be expecting me to question her now. A trip to the eastern estate is in order. She's either hidden Claudia there, or she's asked one of her brothers to do it. They're all too politically well-connected for me to bring charges and win against them, but they'll return Claudia to avoid the scandal." A sneer twisted his mouth. "No Cornelius Scipio would want a kidnapping charge to sully his reputation, even if he was never convicted."

Malleolus uncrossed his arms. "I don't think Cornelia would do that...but I suppose it's worth checking. Do you want me to go now?"

Lucius eyed Malleolus. His steward was fond of Cornelia. Would he confront her to get a confession or help her cover up whatever she'd done?

"No. I'll go myself."

He'd go himself, and he'd go immediately before Malleolus could get a message to his estranged wife. His steward's loyalty still belonged to Publius. Malleolus would continue dedicating his considerable skill to increasing the size of the Claudius Drusus fortune, but only for Publius's grandsons. In a contest between Cornelia and himself, he was certain Malleolus would not choose his side.

When Lucius trotted into the stable yard at the eastern estate, a slave scurried over to take his horse.

"Where's my wife?"

"In the garden, master."

Lucius strode through the archway that separated the garden from the stable yard. Cornelia was seated on a chair under a grape arbor, reading.

She looked up as the gravel crunched under his feet. "Lucius. To what do I owe the honor of your visit?"

Her tone as she said "honor" and the tilt of her head as she remained seated stoked his anger.

"You know why I've come." He planted himself before her with his fists on his hips.

She rose with a grace rivaling that of the Empress. "You are mistaken, Lucius. I haven't the slightest idea what would make you deign to visit without warning me of your coming. I could have had more suitable refreshments prepared for you." Palm up, she swept her hand toward the second chair under the arbor. Some bread, sliced cheese, and a bowl of fruit sat on the table beside it. "But since you are here, you may share what the chef prepared for my lunch."

"No need for the gracious act. I know you helped Claudia escape, and now you have her hidden somewhere. You're going to return her to me immediately, before Sabinus gets it into his head to strike at our family. It won't be just me he'll hurt. Our boys will suffer as well."

Her laugh had always been musical, but today it grated on every nerve he possessed.

"I'm flattered that you think I helped her escape Sabinus's clutches. I might have, if I'd thought of it first, and I could have devised a plan so clever you'd never find her before Sabinus got tired of waiting." The smile that curved her lips was too self-satisfied by far, and it drew his frown. "But I'm not responsible, and I have no idea who might be. I wish I did. I'd extend my heart-felt gratitude to them for saving the sweetest girl from the worst fate."

Lucius's gaze swept over her and locked on her sky-blue eyes. She was a master of the aristocratic art of speaking without revealing her true thoughts, but this time he believed her.

"You'd better hope I find her soon. I'm not sure how long Sabinus is willing to wait. If he doesn't lose interest in her and find some other girl to be his third wife, unpleasant consequences will happen. He's made it too clear there's a high price for disappointing him. I know you don't care at all what happens to me, but he has a reputation for hurting the whole family."

Cornelia didn't even blink at his statement. "I know as much about Sabinus and how he strikes as you, husband. I wish you'd stood up to him and spared Claudia, but since you didn't, I rejoice that someone did."

She took a step away from him, then turned to look over her shoulder. "It's getting late. You're probably entertaining yourself with some female at the town house this evening." Her nose twitched at the word female. "Don't let me detain you." After a fake gracious smile, she strolled toward the portico.

Lucius clenched his teeth. Cornelia had a rare gift when it came to irritating him, but she'd told him the truth. She wasn't the one who'd helped Claudia escape. But if she didn't do it, then who did?

Chapter 27

Sunsets and Stars

Dinner under the canopy had been relaxed and enjoyable, and Philip and the three women were watching the vibrant colors in the clouds as the sun set. After her undisturbed sleep on the couch, Claudia was in good spirits. Several hours of deep sleep free from disturbing dreams had refreshed her both physically and mentally.

Philip smiled to himself as he watched her chatting with Penelope and Junia instead of mostly just listening to their conversation. It was a great improvement. All it had taken to restore her spirits was letting her cry out some grief as he held her and helping her get some rest. Perhaps now she could begin to spend most of her time anticipating life in Perinthus with Titus rather than grieving over life in Rome without her father.

◆

Penelope was enjoying the conversation, but she was also watching Philip. He spent most of his time looking at Claudia. She couldn't quite decide if it was only because he was watching to see how she was doing or because he found her unusually interesting. He certainly seemed to enjoy himself when they played Conquest or read poetry together.

In fact, she'd never seen him enjoy the company of a woman so much. It might be because Claudia was very smart, and he found her intellectually stimulating. He was so intelligent himself that he took special pleasure in being with people who could challenge his mind, but maybe there was something more to it. Claudia seemed to enjoy his company as well. More than once, Penelope had heard Mother and Ariadne discussing what might get Philip to take a chance on liking another woman after being so cruelly rejected by Phoebe. Maybe a really smart woman was the answer.

She cast another glance at her brother. He was watching Claudia again. He really had spent an extraordinarily long time sitting with Claudia's head in his lap after she fell asleep, and that caring look was on his face the whole time. Her brother was the kindest person she knew, so maybe it was just because Claudia needed his help so badly. But maybe it was a sign of something more. She certainly hoped so, and she planned to do her part in encouraging them. No man alive was more capable of loving deeply or more deserving of being loved in return.

◆

The last of the orange was almost gone when Junia rose.

"Are my mistresses ready?"

Claudia had been reluctant to retire for most of the trip, but now she knew she could sleep without the nightmares. She was looking forward to a peaceful night of rest.

"I'm ready."

She turned to Philip and rested her hand on his arm. "Thank you for everything you did today, Philip."

◆

"It truly was my pleasure."

It was worth it for that smile alone. Add the sparkling brown eyes and the setting sun backlighting her hair to make the red highlights glow, and Philip was more than repaid for every moment he'd spent with her that day.

He watched her walk toward the cabin door with Junia and Penelope. It would be good to spend an undisturbed night without her sobbing in the room next door.

The blood-curdling scream tore into Philip. He sat up so fast he whacked his head on the ceiling and knocked himself back onto his pillow. He'd heard people saw stars, and now he knew that was true. There would be a lump in a few minutes, but he was still the first through her door.

Claudia sat upright in her bed, wild-eyed and staring right at him, although it was clear she wasn't seeing him. Hector came up behind him and looked over his shoulder.

"It's nothing. Just more nightmares. Go tell the crew all is well if any of them heard, then you can go back to bed. I'll take care of this."

Hector nodded and left the cabin.

Penelope and Junia were standing in the doorway by then. Penelope's eyes looked almost as scared as Claudia's.

Philip went to the side of Claudia's bed and shook her shoulder. Her head jerked, and her eyes focused on his face as she fully awoke to see him standing beside her.

"Are you all right now?" His voice was gentle as he tried to read her eyes in the moonlight.

She swung her legs to the floor, then stood up beside him.

"Oh, Philip!" The pain of the dream flooded her face as she tipped it up to lock her eyes on his.

She threw her arms around his chest and clung to him, just as she had that morning by the railing. "I slept so well under the canopy. I thought the nightmares were over, but this one was the worst ever."

Silent jerks accompanied the first teardrops as she clung to him. Once more he wrapped his arms around her and held her close. A torrent of hot tears soaked in and warmed his skin despite the wetness.

Penelope began crying as she watched Claudia suffer. Not a good thing for Claudia to see.

"She'll be all right now. I'll stay with her for a while. You two can go back to bed."

Penelope didn't want to leave, but when Philip flicked his head toward their room, Junia took her arm and led her away.

He held Claudia close, stroking her hair and entangling his fingers in it to massage the back of her head until the torrent became a rivulet and finally stopped.

It was then that she looked at his face and saw the purple bump on his forehead. She reached up to touch it, and he winced.

That drew a fresh trickle of tears down her already damp cheeks. "I made you get hurt. I'm so sorry...for everything."

He smiled as he shook his head. "The bump is nothing. I grew up with four older brothers. It's not the first time I've had a big bump on my forehead. It will go away quickly enough."

He swept some tears from her cheek with his fingertips.

"It's time to stop crying. It was only a dream, and it's over now."

The anguish in her eyes was worse than any he'd seen yet. She looked like a wounded animal, waiting and wanting to die.

"I thought the dreams were all over." Her voice was barely above a whisper as she hung her head and stared at the floor.

"I guess not yet, but I'm sure they will be soon."

He reached down and fluffed her pillow. "Now, lie down. I'm going to stay with you and read to you for a while so you can get some good sleep tonight. I'll get my scroll and be right back."

She lay down on the bed, but she remained propped up on one elbow until he returned.

He lit the lamp over the table and turned the chair to straddle it. That way he could get up and leave without moving it and making any noise that might awaken her.

Her eyes were pleading as she reached out to him.

"Hold my hand...please."

He gave her his left hand. She clutched it with both of hers and held it against her cheek as she lay her head down on the pillow.

He began to read. "The northern regions are dominated by the highest mountains..."

◆

As Philip's quiet voice painted images of that distant land, Claudia tried again and again to push away the thought that tormented her most. She thought the nightmares were over after sleeping so well that afternoon, but this really was the worst one yet. When would they end? Would they ever end? How could she bear even one more night like this?

◆

Whenever Philip glanced over at Claudia, silent tears were still flowing, sometimes trickling across his hand where she pressed it to her cheek. He'd read almost twenty panels before her grip relaxed. He read two more to be sure she was deeply asleep. Finally, he slipped his hand out of hers, blew out the lamp, and crept out of the room. He left both doors open so he would hear her if she needed him again.

He climbed into the upper bunk and lay on his back, wide awake for at least an hour, listening and praying for God to open the door for him to tell this beautiful, tormented woman how Jesus could save her and give her peace.

Chapter 28

Not Important After All

Philip was reading in his room early the next morning, waiting for Claudia to rise so he could check on her. Finally, he heard her moving and listened to her footsteps as she emerged from her room. When he stepped into the galley to greet her, she was at the work counter with her back to him. He was about to speak when she reached across the counter and picked up a knife. She raised it over her head as she prepared to plunge it into her heart.

"Stop!"

He leaped forward and gripped her wrist before she could drive the knife downward. He pried her fingers open and tossed the knife aside.

She turned her head to look up at his face. The black agony pierced his heart. He'd never seen total despair in anyone's eyes before.

Her lip quivered. "I thought they'd be gone, but they're never going to go away."

He turned her and encircled her trembling body with sheltering arms. She clung to him, once more the drowning sailor with only him to keep her from sinking into the depths of the sea. Her tears soaked through his tunic again. He stroked her hair, hoping that would comfort her as it had twice before.

"Yes, they will. It just takes time."

His heart ached for her. If only he could tell her about Jesus, how He loved her, how He saved her, how He would help her through this pain to find peace. But her hatred still burned, and she would never listen, even if he tried.

"But I can't take it anymore."

"Yes, you can. For Titus."

It hadn't been his intention, but somehow he'd become her anchor in a turbulent sea, holding her back from the whirlpool of misery that threatened to suck her under.

God, help me figure out what I can say or do right now to help her get past this.

She released him and stepped back. Deep sadness deadened her eyes as she looked up at him.

He pushed a strand of hair behind her ear. "And for me. Please don't make me have to find Titus only to tell him you killed yourself while under my care."

After resting his hand on her cheek, he wiped away some tears with his thumb. "He might kill me for letting you. There are things I'd gladly die for, but letting you kill yourself is not one of them."

◆

As Claudia looked at his unsmiling face, she knew Philip was right. Titus loved her as much as she loved him. He might seek revenge on Philip in his grief and anger over losing her. He always wore a sword on duty. He might strike if he blamed Philip for failing to stop her.

Her eyes filled with tears at that thought. If anything happened to Philip because of her...she couldn't think of anything more terrible than that. She never wanted to see him hurt by anything.

"I'll try...for Titus...and for you."

◆

Philip wiped away what he hoped were the last of her tears that morning. "That's better. I know you can do it, and I'll do whatever I can to help you."

When he smiled down at her, she tried to smile in response but didn't quite manage it.

"Breakfast is already served on deck. I'll walk you to the canopy when you're ready." He wasn't going to risk her trying to jump into the sea again. He might not catch her a second time.

He gazed into the depths of her lovely brown eyes. The deep despair had dulled them. Not good. Time to focus her mind on something that might bring some sparkle back.

"After breakfast, you owe me a few games of Conquest. I should have the advantage over you today, and I'm not about to miss this opportunity."

He grinned at her.

This time she managed a weak smile in return. "I don't know about that. I kept you up most of the night reading."

"You went to sleep quickly enough that you missed some of it. I'll have to read those parts to you again. Maybe this afternoon like we did yesterday."

She nodded in silent agreement. Her whole body seemed to droop as she bowed her head and stared at the cabin floor.

"I'm so sorry, Philip. I don't want to be such a burden to you. You've been so kind to me, and I have no way to repay you."

One small jerk told him she was about to cry again. He put his fingertips under her chin and lifted it until her beautiful eyes were looking into his.

"Don't cry. You don't have to be sorry. It's not your fault. Besides, helping you gives me pleasure."

He pushed another strand of hair behind her ear. Her eyes still looked so sad.

"Truly. I'm glad you're on my ship so I can."

Her eyes brightened a little. She believed him. She should. Each time he looked at her and thought about what would have happened if he hadn't intervened, he gave thanks that God had given him this chance to help.

"As soon as you're ready, we'll go eat." He turned her toward her door and gave her the gentlest push.

She looked back over her shoulder as she stepped through the door. Her smile was a little shaky, but it was still a smile.

When Claudia came out of her room, Philip was leaning against the counter, trying to adjust his eyepatch so the strap wasn't going right across the worst part of the big bruise left over from the bump. He grimaced as he repositioned it.

"Philip."

He turned to look at her. Her breath caught. His eyepatch. He wasn't wearing it last night. She'd never thought about whether it was uncomfortable for him. Maybe he wore it only when he had to. Maybe he was wearing it only to protect her from seeing something ugly.

"Don't wear this on my account." She slid the strap up and off his face. "It's bad enough that I made you hurt your head last night. I don't want you in pain because of me today."

His eye did look milky, and there was ugly, rippled tissue all around it, but it didn't look so bad that he needed to hide it from her.

"You don't look any better with it than without it."

He grinned at her clumsy choice of words. She felt the heat rising at her ears and across her cheeks. What she'd meant to say had come out all wrong and sounded like an insult.

"What I mean is, you don't look any worse without it so it's not worth wearing if it hurts."

That still came out wrong. His grin got bigger.

"No, what I really mean is you don't need to worry about what you look like on my account. The eyepatch doesn't make any difference."

A deep laugh rumbled up from within his chest. "What you really mean is that nothing I do can make me less ugly, so don't bother."

"No, that's not what I mean!"

He placed his finger on her lips to silence her protest. "You haven't offended me, Claudia. I know I'm ugly no matter what I do, but it will be more comfortable today if I don't wear it, so I won't."

He took it from her hand, stepped to the door of his room, and tossed it on the table.

"Now, shall we go to breakfast?"

He placed her hand on his forearm and then rested his hand on top of it. She looked up at his smiling face and found herself smiling in return. He almost always had that effect on her. He was the bright spot in her dark world. He was an ugly man, but she hardly noticed that anymore. She would never have expected that, considering how repulsive she'd considered him when she first saw him.

He was more than a bright spot; he was her safe haven in a world turned upside down. She would be dead if not for his quick actions. Twice. For Titus's sake, she was glad he'd been there to stop her. She wouldn't try again. Somehow, she would get through this...with Philip's help.

There were almost three weeks left in the voyage, and maybe he was right that the dreams would be gone by the end of their trip. He'd proven he could help her get at least some sleep without them. For now, that would have to be enough. But if the dreams weren't gone when they reached Perinthus, what was she going to do without him when she finally had to leave his ship?

Penelope and Junia were already under the canopy when they rounded the corner of the cabin.

Penelope smiled her usual happy greeting at her brother. "I see you finally decided to get comfortable. I was beginning to wonder if you would ever shed the patch this trip."

Claudia snapped her gaze upon him. He really had been wearing it only for her benefit.

"All it took was a bump on the head, sister dear. That finally overcame my vanity."

He reached over and flipped some of her hair that hung loose across her shoulders, held back from her face only by a broad headband of leather ornamented with gold. The simple style didn't need the hours of work by a hairdresser that so many Greek and Roman hairdos required.

"I think you look much better with your hair natural like this than with it all fancied up like you did in Rome. I don't know why you women spend so much time on your hair when it's much prettier down than up. I can't imagine a man spending that amount of time."

"Well, if women cared as much about what men look like as men care about how women look, maybe you'd spend more time, too."

"Maybe, but I doubt it. Some of us are lost causes."

They laughed together, and the conversation moved on to other topics.

When Philip left the canopy area with Hector, Claudia settled into her chair to await his return.

A mischievous smile played on Penelope's lips. "You've certainly kept Philip entertained this trip. He loves Conquest, and it's so seldom he can find someone who's a worthy opponent. It's so much fun watching you beat him sometimes. I always expected my brother would be a gracious loser, but you've proven it."

"I think he's playing just to entertain me. He's very kind."

"It may have started that way, but I don't think that's why he keeps playing. He really enjoys playing with someone who can beat him. He loves the challenge. You are right about him being kind, though. I don't think there's a kinder man alive than Philip. I'm really looking forward to being with him in Perinthus."

"Will you be there long before you go home to Rome?"

"Rome isn't really home. Thessalonica is, but I probably won't be returning to either. Philip is taking me to his home to meet several men he thinks might make a good husband for me."

Claudia's eyebrows rose. "Your father entrusted you to your brother to get you married in Thracia? He could have arranged a marriage for you in Rome."

Penelope took a measured breath. She needed to be careful what she answered. She couldn't tell Claudia that her father was afraid Rome might be too dangerous for his Christian daughter because the games often featured Christians now. Envy and greed made wealthier Christians likely targets there. He kept a low profile himself for that reason, and he was prepared to leave at a moment's notice. He didn't want to risk sending her to her brothers in Corinth or Thessalonica, either. Unlike those cities, Perinthus had no arena. Byzantium did, but that was more than a two-day hard ride from Perinthus, so the odds of her ending up in an arena were much lower with Philip.

"Philip doesn't get to pick. I'll get to choose among them, so I guess he's really entrusting the choice to me."

"I envy you that freedom. I might have chosen Titus's best friend, Decimus, if it had been up to me. He's handsome and strong and very smart. He was always kind to me when I was a child. Smart matters most. I would hate to end up married to a man who was stupid or a fool. I always loved talking with Titus and Father. I wouldn't want a man who bored me to tears."

A mischievous gleam lit Penelope's eyes.

"Philip is very strong and incredibly smart, too. He's always kind to everyone."

◆

Claudia nodded in agreement but said nothing. Penelope hadn't said anything about how he looked. He really was ugly enough to make most women not want him...or even want to spend enough time with him to discover he was a man worth wanting.

When Philip came around the corner of the cabin carrying the gameboard and the box of tokens, Claudia's heart fluttered. What if he'd overheard their conversation? Her cheeks warmed at the thought of him hearing them discussing his merits as a potential husband.

She felt his inquiring gaze as he noticed her blush. That only deepened her shade of pink.

"Looks like I missed something interesting. What was it?"

Penelope smiled her mischievous smile. "We were discussing your many fine qualities, brother dear."

"That must have been a short conversation." He chuckled, but Claudia saw his discomfort with them talking about him.

"Enough wasting time on boring topics. Time for the challenge of Conquest. Prepare to lose your armies, Claudia. I'm feeling particularly strategic today."

She gazed at him as he seated himself opposite her and began setting up the board. He really was very smart and extraordinarily kind. Maybe handsome wasn't that important for a husband after all.

Chapter 29

END OF DESPAIR

After lunch, Penelope and Junia resumed their conversation about the passing shoreline. Claudia tried to listen and take part, but she was so tired after sleeping so little the night before that she said very little. A nap would solve that, but what if the nightmare came again? She didn't want that with Penelope and Junia watching.

She slumped in her chair, desiring and dreading what closing her eyes might bring. Suddenly, Philip was standing beside her, holding the scroll about India.

"I promised you this morning that I would help you get some rest this afternoon. Would you like me to read to you now?"

"Will you rub my temple, too, like your mother used to?"

"If that's what you'd like."

She stood and moved to the couch. She picked up the pillow and patted where he should sit. "Please."

He sat down beside her. She laid the pillow in his lap and fluffed it. Then she lay down so she could look up into his face. He was smiling at her like something was funny.

"Is there something wrong?"

"No. I was just thinking about how surprised my mother would be to learn this has turned into one of the more useful skills she taught me. I'm sure she thinks it was all her efforts to turn her wild child into a civilized man that were her most valuable lessons." A playful grin punctuated his statement. "She can still take me out in public without worrying that I'll say or do something that will embarrass her."

Philip's eyebrow dipped when sadness clouded her eyes. Could the joke about his mother have caused that? "What's wrong?"

"I envy you, Philip."

His eyebrow shot up at her comment. "Why?"

"It must be wonderful to have a mother who loves you. I never had that."

Sympathy softened his gaze as he looked down at her beautiful face. "Did your mother die when you were a baby?"

"She hasn't died. She decided she didn't want to be my mother anymore when she divorced Father. I was only three, but I remember how she shoved me away and kicked me when I clung to her as she was leaving. She remarried into a powerful political family. She was strikingly beautiful then. I used to see her occasionally from a distance. She's still a beautiful woman." She paused. "She's never wanted to have anything to do with me."

The hollow longing in her voice made Philip want to draw her into his arms and stroke her hair again. "Beauty on the outside sometimes comes with ugliness on the inside. And stupidity, too. She would have found you a wonderful daughter if she hadn't made that foolish choice."

"I could never understand her leaving Father. He was so wise and kind and...he loved me as much as I loved him."

Tears filled her eyes and began to trickle down toward her ears as she lay looking up at him. He brushed them off with his fingertips.

"Your father wouldn't want you to grieve this way. He'd want you to remember the good times together, not just the pain of separation."

"I know. I just can't help it. It hurts so much, and I think about it all the time."

"Let's see if I can help you think about something else for a while. Close your eyes and relax."

He unrolled the scroll and began to read. "The jungles of western India are filled with the most amazing animals. Elephants roam..."

As his fingertips traced circles and spirals on her temple, she drifted off to sleep.

When her slow, deep breathing told Philip she was well asleep, he set the scroll aside. Again, he sat for a long time gazing down at that beautiful face.

What she'd told him was almost past believing. How could a mother reject her child like that? That abandonment had left a wound that still wasn't healed. She still yearned for the love of the mother she'd never really known.

No wonder she felt the loss of her father so deeply. His great love for her had mostly filled the aching places no child should have, and now he was gone, too. If only she knew Jesus's love. He could fill all the empty places, and He would never leave. But now was not the time to tell her. She wasn't ready to hear. Maybe there would be an opportunity before the end of their voyage. He would keep praying for that, and he would know when the time was right.

The sun was setting the western sky on fire as it slipped toward the horizon. Fear began to gnaw at Claudia as bedtime drew nearer. When she fell asleep, would the dreams come again?

She grew more agitated as the sun moved lower in the sky. Philip rose and moved to the chair to her right. The fear was at fever pitch when he turned his face toward her. Her hands were trembling slightly, and he reached over and took them in his own. She twisted her hands in his gentle grip so she could hang on tight to his.

"I don't want to go in there to try to sleep. What if the dreams come again? What am I going to do?" Her lips started to quiver as she fought the rising panic.

Philip's encouraging smile was not enough to calm her, but his next words should help. "I'll tell you what you're not going to do. You're not going to just lie there and cry. What you are going to do is come get me right away. I'll read to you and help you get back to sleep. It won't take me any time at all to get you sleeping soundly again."

"Really?" Her eyes filled with hope, like a small child who'd been promised a present. Then the hope faded into sadness. "I shouldn't ask you to do that. You need to sleep, too."

"I want you to promise you'll come get me. I'll sleep better knowing you will. Otherwise, I'm going to lie awake listening to make sure you're all right." The corners of his mouth lifted in a teasing smile. "Or maybe that's your plan. If you keep me awake all night listening while you sleep, you'll have an easier time beating me at Conquest."

His playful accusation got the response he wanted—a smile.

"I wouldn't do that to you. It would be cheating. I promise I'll come get you."

He stood and offered his hand to help her rise.

"Good. Now that you don't have to worry about what to do, you can go to bed for a good night's sleep."

He held her hand as he led her into the cabin. He didn't release it until they reached her bedroom door.

"When you go to bed, leave your door open so I can hear you if you need me."

Her eyes shone with gratitude as she stood looking up at him. Those eyes and her grateful smile were all the reward he needed. Helping her really had become a source of pleasure for him.

Junia came from her own room, where she had just finished helping Penelope. "Ready for my help, mistress?"

"Yes." Claudia smiled at Junia before turning to walk into the room ahead of her.

As soon as the door closed, Philip gathered all the knives he could find in the galley and carried them into Hector's room, where he laid them on the upper bunk. The cook was in for a surprise in the morning, but he wasn't going to leave any knives where Claudia could get to them in the night...just in case.

He entered his own room and climbed up on his bunk. He planned to get some sleep right away. He was fairly certain he would not be sleeping through the night.

It was shortly after midnight when the dream came. Again the roars, the screams, the blood—and then Claudia was awake, shaking, and the tears began to flow. But this time was different. She didn't lie in the darkness, alone and frightened. She rose and felt her way in the dark to his room next door.

"Philip?"

Against the dim light coming through the window, she saw him climb down from the upper bunk to stand before her.

"The dream?"

"Yes."

She was trying to put on a brave face for him, but her voice betrayed that she was crying.

"Don't cry, Claudia. Let's just go read for a while."

He turned to get the scroll from his table, then wrapped his arm around her shoulders as he guided her back into her room. He lit the lamp and set the chair so he could straddle it. She lay down on the bed as he prepared to read.

"Philip?"

"Yes?"

"Would you hold my hand again?"

"Whatever helps, that's what I'll do."

He offered his hand. She wrapped her fingers around it and placed it against her cheek. She rubbed her face against it, like a kitten.

He opened the scroll to the place where she dozed off in his lap that afternoon.

"The mightiest river is the Ganges. It begins in the mountains to the north, and..."

She closed her eyes and listened to the rise and fall of his deep voice. He was such a kind man—the kindest person she'd ever known. His voice became fainter and fainter until...

◆

Philip felt her hand relax and release his own. The satiny softness of her cheek had brought an unexpected warmth to his heart. He was almost sorry when she stopped nuzzling it, but his own pleasure had not been his goal. It had taken only a few minutes for her to get back to sleep. This was much better than lying wide awake in his bunk, listening to her cry her heart out for half the night.

He stood without making a noise and prepared to blow out the lamp. Before he did, his gaze lingered on her. Her long eyelashes rested against her cheeks, and a few strands of reddish-blonde hair had drifted across her lips. She was so beautiful. Simply looking at her was a pleasure, especially when she was sleeping and he couldn't see the pain in her eyes. A beautiful face and a brilliant mind. He'd never expected to meet a woman smart enough to beat him in strategic thinking.

His chest filled again with that unfamiliar warm feeling. She really needed him right now, and it felt good to be the one whose help she wanted.

Thank you, God, for bringing her to me so I can help her.

He could help her get enough sleep, and he could help her get to her brother in Thracia. If only he could help her discover that Jesus was the answer to all her suffering and pain. He remembered the look of joy on her father's face as he declared his faith. Nothing on earth would give him more satisfaction than seeing that same joy in her eyes.

Chapter 30

Philip was on the cabin top with Hector, but he climbed down when Claudia stepped out of the cabin to join the women for breakfast. She'd been sleeping soundly when he peeked in to check on her when he rose. She should feel better since she'd only lost a little sleep to the nightmares. He sat down in the chair to her right.

Her warm smile was just what he'd hoped to see.

"Thank you so much for last night, Philip. It was the best night I've had since Father died." Her deep gratitude shone in her eyes. "I don't know what I'd do without you right now."

"I'm glad we found something that helps. Do you have any idea why you're having the dreams every night? Maybe we can find some way to get them to stop."

◆

Claudia wasn't sure she wanted to talk about it. It hurt so much even to think about it, but maybe he was right. Telling Philip might help him find a way to make them stop. He was so understanding and so good at helping her. If anyone could figure out how to end the nightmares, it would be Philip.

"It's Lucius's fault. I never wanted to go to the games. Neither did Father, so I never went until Lucius made me. Father was out at one of the estates, and Lucius insisted that I go with him. He said all true Romans enjoyed the games, and he wouldn't take no for an answer. I tried not to watch, but I couldn't help seeing some of it. The worst was when they turned the lions loose on some runaway slaves. It was horrible, the way the lions ripped them apart and…and ate them. And the people next to me…pointing and laughing at two of them pulling on the same body until it ripped in two. That's what I keep seeing—the lions attacking Father."

◆

Claudia was getting agitated, and Philip was sorry he'd asked. This might not be helping, but she kept talking, so maybe…

"Lucius is seventeen years older than me. I never knew him really well, but I never dreamed he would betray Father. When he asked me why Father was so happy, I told him it was because he'd decided to be a Christian. I shouldn't have done that, but how was I to know he wanted Father dead so he could do whatever he wanted? I blame myself for giving Lucius the way to get Father killed." The tears pooled in her eyes.

"I hate Lucius! He should have been sewn in a leather bag and thrown in the Tiber for murdering Father, not given everything Father owned as a reward for his loyalty to Rome. I would love to take a knife and stab him over and over. I thought about sneaking into his room as he slept and driving a dagger into his heart, but that would be too quick and easy for him. I'd much rather poison his food with something that would make him die slowly in agony. He doesn't deserve an easy death after what he did."

Tears trickled down her cheeks. Hatred had twisted her beautiful face into something ugly.

As her anger spewed out, Philip recoiled inside, but he didn't let it show. As hard as it was to listen to, it was important to know.

"Killing Lucius wouldn't help, Claudia. Vengeance never satisfies. Only forgiveness can release you from suffering."

She stared at him as her jaw dropped. Then anger flamed in her eyes.

"How could you possibly know? You've never had anyone you love killed like that. Father was everything to me, and Lucius deserves to die for killing him."

As her anger burned, the tears stopped. She swept some old ones off her cheek with an irritated flick of her hand.

"I'd love to kill whoever got Father to become a Christian, too. If he'd just stayed a God-fearer, Lucius wouldn't have been able to get him killed. If I knew who convinced Father to follow that Jesus, I'd turn them in so they could die the same way Father had to."

The tears pooled in her eyes again. "I can't talk about this any-more."

Her chest jumped as she fought new tears. Her fists clenched.

Philip took her hand in his, and the fist relaxed to wrap her fingers around his hand. "Then we won't. Let's do battle and get your mind off this."

◆

Claudia smiled at him through her tears. He had a gift for knowing exactly what she needed. "I'd love to."

She was very glad to change the topic. Philip's face had turned serious as she was telling him. She'd seen that same look before. On her first day on his ship when she said she hated Lucius, he'd looked serious, then sad. She didn't want to make him sad again. She never wanted to cause him sadness or pain.

◆

As Philip walked into the cabin to get the game, he took a deep breath and blew it out slowly. She'd definitely given him some insight into why she was suffering, but he didn't like what he'd heard. She hated his father. She hated him, although she didn't realize either of them were the Christians that she wanted so passionately to see dead.

It was good he'd warned everyone on the ship to be careful about what they said. The way she felt about Christians right now, it was best she didn't know any of them followed Jesus.

After a few rounds of Conquest, Claudia felt much better. Philip had been rather quiet when they started, but he was soon back to smiling at her and teasing her about becoming the general who was his most worthy opponent ever.

Her lips curved as she watched him concentrate on his next move. Other than her father, he was the finest man she'd ever met. He was so very kind. He'd rescued her from Lucius even though he risked being arrested and killed for helping her. He was so understanding of her sudden fits of tears. He was willing to do whatever it took to help her through her grief. She couldn't possibly have a better friend than he'd become. He truly was a special man.

◆

Philip made his move and looked up at Claudia. "You shouldn't be smiling after seeing my last move. Your army is in grave danger."

"I know. I was just thinking about how nice you are to play with me like this."

"After I take your fortress city, you may not think I'm so nice."

"There's nothing you could possibly do that would make me think you weren't nice. You're very special."

The warmth in her eyes...he'd never seen that before when a woman looked at him.

"I think you're a pretty nice person, too, except when you're destroying my armies." He grinned at her. "But this game, you're not being as nice as you ought to be."

"I've been told that all's fair in love and war, and this is war."

She flashed a beautiful smile at him before turning her gaze on the board to plan her next move.

As Philip watched her focus, he gave thanks that his father had asked him to rescue her. It had become his greatest source of pleasure to do whatever he could to help. She'd become special to him, too.

At lunch, Claudia found herself enjoying the good-natured joking between Philip and Penelope as they shared funny family stories.

Penelope was just finishing one. "It still makes me laugh when I think of the look on Nicanor's face when his boys rode the goat into the house. It would have been nice if you could have brought them a couple of Father's ponies."

"True, but I didn't plan on shipping livestock this trip. There isn't room in the hold."

"You could have washed them."

Brother and sister burst out laughing so hard that Penelope had tears in her eyes. Claudia stared at them. What was so tremendously funny that even Philip was wiping at his eye?

Penelope glanced at her and grinned. "Oh, Philip. Claudia has to hear this story. Let me tell her."

He was still chuckling as he nodded his permission.

"When Philip was fourteen, Nicanor had this beautiful white colt that was almost two years old. He wanted to sell it, so he'd been telling everyone he knew about how big and strong that colt was and how gorgeous its mane and tail were. One of his friends had an uncle who lived about fifteen miles away. He was looking for a good horse, so he rode over to see it. When he got to our estate, Philip volunteered to bring it from the stable.

"What Nicanor didn't know was that Philip had taken the colt to his friend's house and brought back this really scrawny white cart horse that was only a little bigger than a pony. When the buyer saw the horse, he was furious with Nicanor for making him ride all that way for nothing. When Nicanor asked Philip what he'd done with his horse, Philip said he'd washed it and it shrunk. The buyer left mad and never came back."

Philip pulled a fake frown. "You didn't tell the whole story. I actually did Nicanor a favor. That colt has become the best stallion in his stable." His mouth relaxed back into a grin. "Besides, you have to admit it was funny."

"Father didn't think so at the time. He found a fitting punishment."

Claudia looked at Philip, who was wiping at his eye again. "What did your father do?"

Philip's face split with the widest grin she'd seen on him yet. "He made me wash all the horses and mules at the estate to see if any of them would shrink, too."

Penelope had to wipe at her eyes again when the fit of laughter struck her once more. Her laughter was so contagious that Claudia found herself laughing aloud for the first time since her father had died.

When her laughter subsided, she gave Philip the happiest smile since they sailed. "That's the funniest story, Philip. It must have been wonderful growing up in your family. Your father was so wise, just like Father…"

The smile faded from her lips. Her lower lip began to quiver as her eyes filled with tears. Pain clouded her vision as tears began to dribble down her cheeks.

"I'm sorry…sometimes I miss Father so much…I don't want to cry like this, but sometimes I just can't stop…"

Philip moved from his chair to sit on the couch beside her. He wrapped his arm around her shoulder, and she rested her head against his chest as the tears continued to flow.

"You can cry on me anytime. I don't mind."

She shifted to slide her one arm around his chest and let her tears soak into his tunic. Sometimes it hurt so much to remember how wonderful life had been with Father. All that was gone now.

Fear and loneliness wrapped her in pain, but the th-thud of Philip's heartbeat somehow calmed her fears and the warmth of his arm around her made her feel less alone. When he wrapped his second arm around her and held her close, she tipped her face to find comfort from gazing deep into his caring eye. She scarcely noticed his scars before resting her cheek against his chest again. A deep sigh escaped as she relaxed in the security of his arms.

Philip rested his unscarred cheek on the top of her head and felt the softness of her hair. She seemed so small and vulnerable as his arms felt her slowly breathing in and out, her breath occasionally catching as she wept.

God, please bring an end to this overwhelming grief and heal her broken heart.

He knew exactly Who could heal her, but right now she hated Jesus and those who follow him. She would hate his wise father if she knew he was the one who started Publius on the path to becoming a believer. He'd played a part himself by giving the teaching the day Publius publicly declared his faith. That might make her hate him as well if she knew, and he couldn't bear that now. He prayed for the end of her hatred as he cradled in his arms the tortured young woman with whom he was falling in love.

When the tears finally ceased, Claudia looked up at his face. There was a tenderness there that was exactly what she'd come to expect from him.

"I'm sorry." She rested her hand against his chest. "I got your tunic all wet again. I'm probably the worst passenger you've ever had."

"You're not even in the bottom half. A damp tunic is a small price to pay for having someone onboard who's the best general I've had the pleasure of crossing swords with."

"I don't think I'd be a very good general right now. I cried too much, and my head hurts terribly." She raised her eyebrows before she asked, but she already knew his answer. "Would you please rub my temple and read to me again?"

"Of course. There's no better way to spend some time after lunch than exploring India while I watch a beautiful woman sleep in my lap."

"You're just saying that so I won't feel like I'm such a bother."

"I keep telling you you're not a bother. You should stop saying you are." He stood and smiled down at her. "I'll be right back."

When Philip returned with the scroll, Claudia fluffed the pillow, placed it in his lap, and lay down.

"Thank you, Philip. I can't tell you how much this means to me."

The glow in her eyes as she looked up at him made his heart skip a beat.

"You don't have to. Just close your eyes."

A slight smile curved her lips as he began to read. Soon her breathing told him she was asleep.

As he gazed at the blonde-haired beauty sleeping so peacefully in his lap, his heart pulsed with long-dormant feelings. *She's so beautiful, so smart, so much fun when she's not crying her eyes out. The kind of woman any man would want to share a lifetime with.*

He shook his head. Time to banish those thoughts. He could easily fall deeply in love with her if he let himself, but nothing would ever come of that. Even if she were to become a Christian, which was essential for the wife of a leader in the church, a beautiful woman like her couldn't possibly fall in love with a hideous man like him.

Claudia was sleeping soundly, so Philip had succeeded in helping her get some rest after the latest attack of heart-rending grief.

Penelope watched him as he cradled Claudia's head in his lap. What she saw was both pleasing and a bit worrisome. At long last, Philip was letting down his guard with a woman. It had been seven years since his heart was shredded by his betrothed. Mother had begun to despair that he would ever take a chance and risk a broken heart again.

She watched him gaze at the sleeping Claudia. The tenderness there seemed to go beyond that of a kind man worried about a grieving friend. But then that tender look faded into one of sadness. Right after that, he carefully lifted the pillow so he could extract himself without waking her. Now he was standing toward the bow, leaning on the railing as he watched the ship cut through the waves. Usually he looked so peaceful when he did that, but now he looked sadder than she could ever remember.

Penelope left Junia to keep an eye on Claudia and walked forward to join Philip at the rail. He turned his head to glance at her and offered a weak smile before focusing again on the waves.

"What's wrong, Philip?"

"Nothing. Just thinking."

"Thinking about what?"

He didn't answer.

"Thinking about what, Philip?"

His lips tightened. He didn't speak, but she wasn't going to let him avoid answering her. Ignoring her or Ariadne only made them more persistent.

"Philip?" Still no answer.

She nudged him with her shoulder. "What are you thinking about?"

A small snort revealed his exasperation with her pushing the question, but he gave in. "How things might have been different."

"What things? Different how?"

He waved his hand as if to shoo away the question.

"Different how, Philip? You might as well tell me since I'm not going to stop asking until you do."

A sigh accompanied his surrender. "You win. Different if I hadn't spilled the soup. Different if I were a handsome man."

He glanced back toward the canopy where Claudia lay sleeping.

She placed her hand on her brother's arm. "You're too hard on yourself. Being kind is so much more important than being handsome, and any woman worthy of you would agree with your sisters about that. You need to trust that the right woman will be smart enough to see that. Nothing needs to be different for a woman to love you and want to marry you."

"You and Ariadne never leave it alone, do you. Even Father has started telling me it's time. I know you all want me to marry, and I will someday, if that's what God intends for me. I don't see it anytime soon, though." He sighed. "I wish what you say were true, but it's not. Contentment comes from accepting things the way they are and doing the best you can with what is."

She wrapped her arm around his and rested her head against his shoulder. "Promise me something."

"What?"

"Promise me you won't try so hard to be content that you miss seeing that God has brought someone special into your life. Maybe she's exactly the one you need." She squeezed his arm. "And maybe she needs you even more than you need her."

A glimmer of hope flitted across his face, but sad resignation soon erased it.

"But you've heard what she says about hating Christians. Even if she could stand me being so ugly, she hates the One I love most. She hates Father and me for leading her father to love Him, too. How could that ever work?"

"Wasn't the apostle Paul the greatest hater of Christians in all Israel? And didn't Jesus make him one of his truest disciples? Surely God can change her heart, too. Nothing is outside His control."

He slowly nodded, as if he knew she was right. All he'd really needed was for her to remind him.

He reached over and patted her cheek. "All right, baby sister. I'll keep one eye open to see if God has something different in mind for me." The corner of his mouth rose. "One eye, not two."

She slapped his arm. "Very funny, brother dear. Just remember what I said." His sad, wistful look was gone, and that drew her smile. "A smart woman knows the treasure is what's inside the box, not the box itself."

"When did my baby sister get so wise?"

"When I grew into a woman myself. I hope you didn't just line up handsome men for me. I want a kind one like you."

"Don't worry. I couldn't find one as ugly as me, but one of them is quite homely. All of them are kind."

She chuckled, and she got a genuine smile from him before she patted his arm and headed back to chat with Junia under the canopy, confident that she had convinced him to get out of his own way and let God work unhindered.

Chapter 31

Seeing True Worth

They had been at sea for two and a half weeks. Although they hadn't exhausted Philip's supply of poetry, Claudia was having difficulty choosing the one she wanted for their afternoon reading. Philip stood behind her, looking over her shoulder as she shuffled through his boxes. She turned to look up at his smiling face.

"You know, we haven't read from any of my collection yet. Why don't you choose today from my box?"

"An excellent idea. I've been curious for some time about which poets you thought most worthy of inclusion in your library."

He stepped back against his wall to let her pass ahead of him into her room.

She was about to kneel and wrestle the heavy box out from under the table so he could look in it.

"Let me get that for you."

She flattened herself against the wall so he could get past her. He had such broad shoulders. Whenever he was so close to her, she couldn't help noticing how muscular he was. Sometimes being close to him made her heart beat much too fast.

He gripped the handle with one hand and pulled it out as if it weighed nothing. When she pulled the box out, she had to lean back and use the weight of her body to move it.

He lifted the box, placed it on the bed, and stepped back so she could make her selection.

"I want you to pick, Philip. I love them all, so it's hard for me to choose."

His eye was drawn to one that was a set of individual sheets between two leather covers with ribbons holding it all together to make a codex. Nothing was written on the cover - no title, no poet's name.

"This looks interesting."

He reached very deliberately for the home-made codex. As he lifted it from the box, she took hold of it, too. His eyebrow rose, and she felt the heat to the tips of her ears.

"I don't think you want that one. It's my own poems."

The tease in his smile made her blush even more. "Then this is exactly the one I want. They say poetry is the window into a poet's soul. I'm sure what I'll see will be enchanting."

She tried unsuccessfully to pull it from his hand. He simply tightened his grip and chuckled at her attempts.

"No, you can't take it. You said I could choose, and this is my choice. The only choice you get is whether you read to me or I read to you."

His smile turned into a grin. "I'd much prefer the first. It would be very special to hear the beautiful words of the poet from the lips of the poet herself."

It was very clear she wasn't going to be able to take it away from him or convince him he didn't want it.

"Well, all right. If you're sure that's what you want."

"Absolutely." He smiled that same smile she saw when he'd just won a game of Conquest.

As much as she hated reading her own poems aloud to anyone, she hated the thought of disappointing him even more. If something as simple as reading them to him could make him this happy, she couldn't refuse his request. He'd done so much for her; how could she refuse him anything?

Philip carried the codex as they walked out to the canopy. Once Claudia was seated, he handed it to her.

"First read me your favorite. Then whatever you want."

He settled into a chair, stretched out his legs, clasped his hands behind his head, and gazed at her with anticipation.

She opened the volume to a poem in the middle of the collection. "In tunics of blue and purple, the flowers dance. Bowing and swaying..."

She kept her eyes fixed on the pages as she read. She was afraid to see his reaction. Maybe he would think the images from her heart were silly or boring. Maybe he would think her words and phrases were trite or clumsy.

When she finished reading, she raised her eyes and looked at him shyly. There was that broad smile that appeared when he was delighted with something.

◆

As Claudia read, Philip's admiration for her poetic skill grew. Her poems were elegant, filled with beautiful images, rich phrases, surprising words. She wrote as well as many of the poets in his library.

"I may have a new favorite poet. Your poems are beautiful, Claudia. You should never be afraid to read them to anyone."

She blushed, and the color in her cheeks made her even more beautiful, if that were possible.

"That's kind of you to say."

"Truth is truth. I don't have to be kind to say you're an excellent poet."

"Well, if you are kind, you won't say it too often."

"Fair enough, but you can't keep me from thinking it."

She blushed again. "Now it's time for you to read to me, Philip."

"Hand it over. I want to read some more of my new favorite."

◆

As Claudia handed her codex to him, he flashed that teasing smile. She settled back into her chair. As she listened to her own words being read in his deep, rich voice, she was glad she'd yielded to his request to read her poetry. His voice and her words were a combination she enjoyed at least as much as he'd enjoyed her reading.

She used to close her eyes when he read because she wasn't comfortable looking at his scars. How silly that was. Now she enjoyed watching him. It was fun to see which parts of each poem he liked best. They were almost always the parts she liked best, too. It was even better when she watched him watch her read. He would gaze at her and smile that delighted smile he reserved only for her. It made her feel all warm inside to give him such pleasure. Next time she read her own poems, she wouldn't be afraid to look up for his smile.

The next day, Claudia and Penelope were leaning on the rail by the canopy, watching the ship cut through the waves. Philip was up by the bow, talking with Hector.

Claudia had one nagging question about Philip, and his sister was exactly the person to answer it.

"Why isn't Philip married? He's rather old to be a single man."

"He's only twenty-five. All my brothers were at least eighteen when they married. Father had them work a full summer season as a crewmember on one of his ships before they married. Philip still enjoys being part of the crew when he sails. You'll see him up in the rigging before this voyage is over."

"Many Roman men are married by the time they're sixteen. The marriages are arranged by their fathers. My two oldest brothers were both born before Father was eighteen. My mother never really wanted to be married to Father, so he decided to do things differently. He let his sons decide whom to marry themselves because he hoped that would give them happier marriages than his was. Lucius married Cornelia before he was eighteen, but Titus is twenty-four and still hasn't found someone he wants to marry."

Penelope hesitated before speaking. "Philip was almost married when he was eighteen. The summer he was away at sea, Father arranged for him to marry a girl who was one of Ariadne's close friends. Phoebe was our age at the time. She was always cheerful and very pretty. I was only nine, but I remember how eager Philip was to make her his wife.

"He came home about three months before the wedding. She didn't know he was back, and he overheard her telling Ariadne that she was being forced to marry him. She thought he was hideously ugly. She said she'd rather die than be married to someone who looked like a monster, but her family wanted her to marry him because he was so rich.

"When he knew she felt that way, he didn't have the heart to make her go through with it. He broke the engagement and made sure everyone thought she wasn't to blame. But Ariadne knew better, and she had a very hard time forgiving Phoebe for hurting Philip so badly."

Penelope's eyes narrowed as her head tilted. "Since then, he thinks a woman could never want him except for him being rich."

Claudia shook her head. "But he shouldn't think that. He's a wonderful man. I've never met anyone kinder than he is or more interesting to talk with. There would be many women who would like him for himself, not just his money."

Penelope's eyes brightened as much as her smile. "That's what Ariadne and I think, but Philip's so modest he doesn't see it."

Penelope had been looking toward the bow where Philip and Hector were talking. When he started back toward them, she touched Claudia's arm.

"We need to talk about something else. Philip's coming, and I wouldn't want him to know we were talking about this." Her eyes turned serious. "Philip likes you very much, Claudia. Please don't hurt my brother."

Claudia turned her eyes on Philip as he walked toward them, smiling at her as always. She nodded her head in response to Penelope's heartfelt request. The last thing in the world she wanted to do was hurt this very special man.

Chapter 32

THESSALONICA

They had been at sea almost three weeks when the hills behind Thessalonica finally came into view.

As the ship sailed into the harbor, Claudia stood at the rail with Penelope. "I didn't expect the hills to be so close to the sea. The buildings go half way up them. Philip said there were 70,000 people here, but I never pictured it like this."

Penelope bounced on her toes. "Rome is magnificent, but I think Thessalonica is much nicer. It's been so long since I was here. This is home for our family. Nicanor still lives here. He's my oldest brother, and he runs all the Macedonian estates and shipping from here, just like Philip does in Perinthus. Ariadne and her family are here, too." She pointed toward the hills, green with gardens and vineyards, that rose from the shore west of the city. "The family estate I grew up on is over there."

Philip's footsteps came up behind Claudia, and she turned to smile up at him.

His gaze wrapped her in its warmth before he spoke. "We've brought some things for both of them from Father and Mother, so you'll get to meet more of my family today. We'll be in port for less than a day, but that's enough for a good meal and a hot bath. I'll find out as soon as we dock what the plans are."

"I can't wait to see Ariadne again." Penelope was beaming. "I was only twelve when Father took me to Rome, so she'll be surprised by how much I've changed."

Philip put his arm around his sister. "Now I have two of the prettiest women in the Empire for my sisters, and they're two of the nicest as well."

Claudia wished his arm was around her instead.

His smile broadened as he turned to Claudia. "Add to that the most beautiful woman any man has ever seen, and the men will be turning their heads in envy as I escort you through the city."

Claudia blushed at the compliment, which surprised her. She'd become so used to men commenting on her appearance that she usually didn't react at all. But when Philip said it, that was different. It meant something when Philip said it.

She flashed a smile at him. "And we'll be with the nicest man in the Empire."

◆

Penelope fought to suppress a smile as she watched them look at each other. She wasn't sure whose eyes sparkled more. Ariadne was in for quite a surprise when she met the woman who'd made Philip open his heart again.

The ship was tied securely against the pier and the gangplank was in place before Philip left the cabin top and came again to join the women at the rail.

"Stay on board until I talk with Nicanor to find out whether we go to his or Ariadne's house. I'll be back shortly."

Philip was eager to see his sister and brother again, but first he had to warn them to say nothing in front of Claudia that would reveal their faith. As soon as he sent word to warn both them and their households, he could bring his sister and the brilliant beauty who occupied so many of his thoughts into the city that had been home to his family for many generations.

◆

Claudia watched Philip as he strode down the gangplank and worked his way through the dockworkers who were preparing to unload some of their cargo and replace it with some goods bound for Perinthus.

"Will he be gone long?"

"I don't think so. The family shipping office is just above the wharfs. Nicanor is usually there this time of day."

Claudia swallowed hard. She was more than a little nervous about meeting Ariadne. If Philip were her own brother, she'd be very protective of him where other women were concerned. Philip and Ariadne were very close. How important it was to win her approval to keep Philip's remained to be seen.

It had been decided that everyone would gather at Ariadne's house for an early dinner followed by conversation for the men and a relaxing communal bath for the women. That would leave enough time for them to return to the ship for the night. They would sail for Perinthus very early when the tide was right.

Penelope and Junia chatted, but Claudia scanned the road until she saw Philip driving a two-wheeled, two-passenger cart toward them. A horse was tied behind.

He reined in and climbed down. "Ariadne's estate is a short distance west of the city."

Philip lifted Penelope into the *cisium* first and then Claudia. Claudia's eyes widened when he handed the reins to his sister without speaking before mounting himself. Penelope slapped the mules with the reins and clucked to start the team along the street. Philip trotted past and settled in just ahead of their two-mule team.

"You drive?" Claudia had never heard of a wealthy Roman woman who could drive herself.

"Of course. Father had all of us learn how to handle a team. He always said you never knew when it might be life-saving to know how. It's really fun to drive fast on the open road, but for that, I like a team of horses better than mules."

Claudia watched the passing scenery with great interest. This was where Philip had grown up, so she didn't want to miss anything. Near the harbor, there were so many different kinds of people and so much activity that she found fascinating.

It was very different from the elite parts of Rome she was familiar with, but one thing remained unchanged. Too many men were staring at her with the same look that men had in Rome.

She turned her eyes away from the men on the street and focused them on Philip. He rode just ahead of the cart, leading the way. He'd changed from his drab beige crewman's tunic into a white one like she'd seen him in that first day, but no one would suspect how rich and important he was just by looking at him. But he wouldn't care what kind of impression his outer appearance made. He only cared about what was inside a person.

A smile played on her lips. The best thing about being with him was how he didn't just see her as a ravishingly beautiful woman. He saw her as a general who was his strategic equal in Conquest and as a friend for long talks and companionable silences. When he looked at her, he really saw her, not just her beautiful face and lovely figure but the real woman inside the pretty package.

It was funny. When she looked at him now, she didn't see an ugly man at all. She saw the kindest, smartest, most wonderful man that could possibly be. More than that, she saw the man she wanted to marry so he would always be with her, lifting her spirits and making her feel like a real person, not just a beautiful trophy to display.

Beyond a doubt she was in love with him, but was he in love with her? Or was he just the kindest man alive who enjoyed spending time with a good friend who needed his help?

◆

Philip felt Claudia's eyes on him, and he twisted around to look back at her. Admiration lit her eyes and an affectionate smile curved her lips. He'd never expected any woman to look at him that way, and for a beautiful woman like Claudia to do it felt like a miracle. She could make his heart rate speed up just by flashing that beautiful smile or by resting her hand on his arm.

His heart swelled at the prospect that Penelope might have been right. God may indeed have brought a special woman into his life, someone who could see past all the ugly scars to the man inside. But if that really had happened, what was he supposed to do about it since she wasn't a believer...yet?

Ariadne had a banquet prepared for mid-afternoon. It was a small gathering. Nicanor's wife was missing because she'd taken their children to visit her parents at their country estate, and any message of Philip's unexpected arrival would reach her too late for her to return before they sailed. It would just be Ariadne's husband Lycurgus, Nicanor, Penelope, Philip, and the nonbelieving mystery woman named Claudia that Philip had warned them about.

The moment Ariadne learned he was bringing a passenger along to the intimate family dinner, her imagination ran rampant. For him to bring a young unmarried woman to meet them spoke of all sorts of possibilities, and she was dying to find out what was actually going on. Was she about to meet the woman who could draw Philip from his protective shell?

Since Greek women didn't recline at dinner, the family sat around two small tables that had been pulled together to make one large one. Ariadne seated Philip and the lovely Claudia next to each other and directly across from her. That gave her the best opportunity to watch both, and, for the most part, she liked what she saw.

Claudia was the most beautiful woman Ariadne had ever seen. Excessive beauty often came with arrogance and selfishness, but she'd seen nothing but politeness and genuine interest in her dinner companions from the lovely young woman seated across from her. Claudia hadn't spoken more than ten sentences before Ariadne could see she was very intelligent. She hadn't spoken more than five before Ariadne saw how Philip focused on every word his passenger spoke.

Philip and Claudia spent much of the time looking at each other when they weren't being directly spoken to by someone. Ariadne caught Penelope's eye with a question in her own, and her younger sister's wink and mischievous smile told her Claudia was much more to Philip than a passenger on his ship. The more Ariadne watched them, the more convinced she became that Philip was completely taken with the beauty. That in itself was surprising, given how guarded his response had been to every young woman he'd met since Phoebe's rejection. What was even more surprising was how the beautiful Claudia seemed just as interested in him.

Even before the second course was served, it was obvious that Philip didn't simply like this young woman. He was falling in love with her—if he hadn't already fallen. Philip opening his heart to love again was one of the things Ariadne wanted most, but if this gorgeous woman, who could easily have her pick of a dozen suitors, were to reject him like Phoebe did, then what? The privacy of the women's bath should let her discover how things stood between them and whether Philip was in danger of being hurt again.

The heated bath in Ariadne's house was large enough for at least six people. As Claudia slipped into the large tub and settled onto the submerged bench, a deep sigh escaped. After so long on the ship, she'd almost forgotten how wonderful it felt to be immersed to her neck in deliciously warm water for a quiet chat with a friend.

Penelope settled in next to her, and Ariadne sat across the tub. Speculation simmered under the cautious friendliness in Ariadne's eyes. Claudia was on her guard; an interrogation was coming.

Penelope pushed some water toward her sister. "I'm so glad Mother had some things she wanted us to deliver to you. It's worth a few extra days onboard to see you again, even if we can only stay for the afternoon." The water Ariadne pushed back swirled around her neck. "This water feels heavenly."

She leaned her head back against the edge of the tub, closed her eyes, and floated in sheer contentment.

Ariadne swished her legs in the water. "Nicanor and Philip often send ships between here and Perinthus, so we should be able to see each other a lot more often than when you were in Rome."

Ariadne's gaze locked on Claudia, and she tensed. The interrogation was about to begin.

"So, Claudia, I hope you've been enjoying the trip. Philip always tries to make the voyage pleasant for his passengers."

"I have. This is my first time at sea."

Ariadne's body looked relaxed, but her gaze sharpened. "What takes you from Rome to Perinthus?"

"I'm going there to live with my brother, Titus. Our father died recently, and I needed to leave Rome."

Claudia chose not to tell Ariadne the sad tale of Lucius's betrayal of first her father and then her. She still couldn't speak of it without anger and tears, and she didn't want to expose herself that way to Ariadne. She wasn't sure what to say next.

Penelope came to her rescue. "Philip is having so much fun with Claudia on the ship. I've come to love poetry listening to them read to each other. What's even better is how she actually beats him at Conquest almost half the time. Even you have never beaten him more than one time in ten."

Ariadne's appreciation of that feat was clear in the warm smile she directed at Claudia. "Philip's not that impressed by beauty, but he is by intelligence." Claudia felt his sister's eyes boring into her. "The combination...well, what man could resist that? I can see that my brother likes you very much, Claudia."

Claudia understood the question the statement implied. Ariadne was certainly not one to beat around the bush when it came to her beloved brother.

"I think he's the kindest man I've ever known, and I enjoy his company whether we're playing games or reading poetry or just talking. He's helped me so much as I've tried to get over my father's death."

Ariadne's smile remained friendly, but her eyes narrowed. "I'm glad you've had a chance to get to know Philip. Being onboard with someone for a few weeks lets you get past first impressions and appreciate the whole person. Penelope and I both think he's an extraordinary man that any woman would be lucky to marry."

Heat spread up Claudia's neck to the tips of her ears at the mention of Philip marrying. Her blush triggered Ariadne's knowing smile.

"You know, it's my fault he has all those scars."

"He told me about the accident with the soup. He thinks they make him ugly, but I don't. Well, I did when I first met him, but I don't anymore. He has the nicest smile."

"Did you know he was betrothed to my best friend Phoebe once? She hurt him terribly when he overheard her call him a monster because of the scars."

"Penelope told me, but Philip doesn't know that I know. You must hate her for hurting him so badly. If someone had done that to my brother Titus, I'd figure out some way to make them pay for it. What did you do to her?"

"It took me a while, but I forgave her. We're still very good friends."

Claudia's eyes saucered. "Does Philip know you're still friends with someone who hurt him so badly?"

Did Ariadne not see that her continuing friendship with Phoebe was a betrayal of Philip?

Ariadne tightened her lips to suppress a laugh. "Of course. Philip and Phoebe are good friends, too. Her husband is one of his friends as well. She and her husband would have been at dinner with us if she hadn't just given birth this week. She has a new baby girl who's the sweetest little thing."

Claudia didn't say anything, but she was beyond astonished that Philip could not only forgive the woman who broke his heart but even consider her a good friend. If it had been her, love would have turned into hate as soon as the pain passed and maybe even before.

Ariadne's countenance turned serious. "I do want to ask something of you, Claudia. I think Philip cares for you very much. I've never seen him like this with any other woman since Phoebe, and that was seven years ago. If you don't feel the same way about him, please don't lead him on to believe you might care for him as much as he cares for you.

If he were rejected once more by a woman he thought loved him, he'd never risk loving again."

"I would never do that to him. If anything, I care more for him than he cares for me. I would never deliberately do anything to hurt him."

"I'm glad. He really is the best of men. No one deserves to be loved more than he does."

Ariadne's nod and smile marked the end of the interrogation.

The conversation turned to other topics of interest to two sisters who'd been apart for four years, and Claudia listened closely. She wanted to learn more about this family that she hoped would soon become her own.

As Claudia relaxed in the warm water, a contented smile played on her lips. She'd passed Ariadne's inspection of the woman who interested her precious older brother. His beloved sister would raise no objection to her as a sister-in-law.

Chapter 33

Handsome in her Eyes

As Thessalonica shrank in the distance, Penelope stood at the rail with Philip.

"That was a wonderful visit. I'm glad I'll be living close enough to Ariadne to see her more often."

Philip draped his arm across her shoulders. "We run enough ships between the two towns that you should be able to visit as often as you want during the months when the sea is open."

Penelope looked up at Philip to see his response to her next statement.

"Ariadne liked Claudia a lot. She could see right away how much Claudia likes you. I can, too."

"I hear what you're not asking. Yes, I like her a lot, too. But I think you already knew that."

"Any thoughts about what you're going to do about it?"

"Yes." His eye was serious as he looked down at her. "I'm going to pray for God to make her a believer so I can ask her to marry me. Until she follows Jesus, that's all I can do."

"I'm joining you in those prayers, Philip. I'm sure Ariadne is, too."

Philip smiled at his baby sister and kissed her on the forehead. "Good."

Philip was sitting in the chair next to Claudia with his blind side toward her as he talked with Hector. When Hector left the canopy,

Claudia finally did what she'd been wanting to do for many days. She reached over and touched his scarred cheek. He couldn't see her hand coming, and he jumped at her touch.

Claudia's breath caught. "I'm sorry. Does it hurt when I touch it? I didn't mean to hurt you." Pity tinged her voice. It must be terrible for him if it still hurt after so many years.

"No. You just startled me. There's not much feeling at all."

She wanted to touch him again, but she was afraid to. He was looking at her like something did hurt. It would be terrible not to be able to touch your own cheek without pain. Had she hurt him, even though she didn't mean to?

"Don't look at me that way, Claudia."

"What way?"

"Like you're sorry for me. You don't need to be. I'm not sorry for myself."

He smiled at her, trying to look unconcerned, but no matter what his lips said, his eye told the truth. Her touch hadn't hurt his cheek, but her pity had hurt his heart.

"I'm not sorry for you. I admire you more than any man I've ever known."

"Then you haven't known many men."

❖

Philip was trying to joke away from this conversation that was so uncomfortable. For the second time in his life, he found himself wishing with all his heart that a woman could find him handsome. Claudia deserved a handsome man.

"I don't have to know many men to recognize how kind and smart you are. You're just like my father."

Her father. She meant that as the highest praise, but he didn't want her to think of him like her father. She liked him even with him being so ugly, but he still wanted her to see him as attractive, as the man she would actually want to look at every morning when she first woke up. A man who could fill her eyes with joy, not pity.

She touched his cheek again, and this time he didn't jump as she drew her fingers slowly over the ridges. He'd been wrong about the lack of feeling. Somehow her fingertips created tingling sensations unlike anything he'd felt before. She traced one of the swirls with her middle finger.

"You know, the scars don't make your face so terribly ugly, just rather...interesting. Hills and mountains are much more interesting than plains."

Her caressing fingertips heated his blood, and her words filled his heart with a lightness he'd never felt before. He had no idea how to answer, so he flipped it into a joke.

"That sounds like the inspiration for a poem. 'His cheek was like a mountain range, hers like the crystal sea...'"

He rubbed the stubble of the unshaven beard on his unscarred cheek. "Maybe you can add something about how the forest doesn't grow there."

Her eyes sparkled with delight as she burst out laughing. "You're a brilliant general, but I'm not sure you'll ever be a great poet."

"Then let's play some Conquest and give me a chance to achieve greatness in your eyes."

"You've already done that, even if I beat you this time."

Her eyes were still laughing as he rose to get the game. As he walked away from her, a beaming smile broke free. Maybe his face could bring a look of joy, not pity, to the right woman's eyes.

The lions still came every night, but it was bearable because of Philip. Every night Claudia went to him, and she could always go back to sleep quickly as long as she was holding his hand and listening to his deep voice as he read. She wasn't tired during the day anymore, but she still had Philip read her to sleep almost every afternoon.

It wasn't the sleep that she wanted so badly. It was the gentle touch of his fingers on her face and that wonderful smile as he looked down at her lying in his lap. They had long since finished the scroll about India, and now he was reading her one about travelling up the Nile.

She fluffed the pillow before laying it in his lap. As she lowered her head onto it, the happy gleam in his eye as he gazed down at her made her heart beat a little faster. Nothing could be better than his touch and his smile.

◆

Philip started to massage her temple and read. "'There are hidden dangers in the river. Crocodiles line the banks, waiting for unsuspecting prey. Equally dangerous is the mighty hippopotamus. His great gaping mouth...'"

As he paused to unroll the next panel of words, he glanced down at her face. Her eyes had been closed when he started, but they were open and watching him now.

"Is something wrong?"

"No." Her eyes warmed as her lips curved into a contented smile.

That pulled a smile from him. "Don't look at me. You're supposed to close your eyes and go to sleep."

"But I like looking at you."

His heart skipped a beat as his smile broadened. No one, not even his mother, had ever said that, although Mother had often told him he looked just fine. He never believed her. Mothers were known to tell their children things that weren't true out of love.

"Maybe so, but you still need to close your eyes if you're going to sleep."

"Whatever you say, Philip." She closed her eyes, and he resumed reading.

As he shifted to the next panel, he glanced down at her. She was looking at him again and smiling. She closed her eyes when she saw that he'd caught her watching him.

He kept reading and didn't say anything to her, but sheer joy pulsed through him. The impossible had happened. The blonde-haired beauty he loved to look at liked to look at him, too.

Chapter 34

No Man is Worth More

It was nearing the end of the good sailing season as they began the last leg of the voyage between Thessalonica and Perinthus, so it was not surprising when a storm blew up. Although the winds were not exceptionally high, they were blowing hard enough from the north that Hector decided to furl the sails on the main mast, trim the sail on the foremast, and lower the sea anchor to keep from being blown too far off his intended course.

It had been raining, so Claudia, Penelope, and Junia were sitting in Penelope's room out of the wind and wet.

Penelope opened the shutters a crack to peek out. "I really don't like it when the wind blows like this. My brothers still tease me about how I hid under the bunk the first time I was in a storm. I don't think they should. I was only ten at the time."

Claudia smiled at the image. "I'm sure Philip didn't laugh at you."

"He laughed the hardest. He'd been in a couple of really bad storms the summer before when he worked as a sailor. He actually likes it when the rain falls hard and the wind blows and there are flashes of lightening. He says he likes seeing the power of...well, he just likes it."

"The power of Jupiter? I'm sure he's joking about that." Claudia looked through the crack, too. "I hope he's being careful out there. I'd much rather he be in here with us."

"He'd never let his crew be out in the weather while he stayed inside. Besides, you never know when they might need an extra hand on deck, and he really does love being part of the crew."

When they heard the scream, Claudia was the first one to the small window in the galley that looked out over the deck. What she saw horrified her. A crewman had been walking along the yard on the main mast to get into position for lashing the square mainsail to the yard while others manned the lines on deck to furl the sail. Other times, she'd found it fascinating to watch a sailor scampering around up there as if he were on solid ground.

She usually enjoyed the sound of the wind flapping the sails, but a sudden strong gust must have slapped one of the triangular topsails into the crewman and caused him to lose his footing. Now he hung from the yard with his foot entangled in the lashing cordage. His leg was bent at a funny angle. With his broken leg, he couldn't raise himself back to the yard.

Claudia gasped and covered her eyes with her hands. "I can't watch. He'll die when he falls."

Penelope stood next to her, peering out through the rain. "He won't fall. Philip's going up to get him."

Claudia's fear as she watched the sailor twisting in the wind was nothing compared to the panic that gripped her as she watched Philip climb the mast with a coil of rope draped across his chest. When he reached the yard, he walked out to where the sailor was dangling. He tied the rope first to the yard, then wrapped it around his waist and chest, looping it down around his legs to make a harness. She almost screamed as he deliberately slipped off the yard to hang just below the injured man. Then he began pulling himself up hand over hand until the man could wrap his arms around Philip's neck.

She held her breath as Philip continued to pull both himself and the sailor back up the rope. When they reached the yard, the sailor managed to pull himself up to sit precariously on the wet wood. Philip hoisted himself up and straddled the yard while he untied the rope from it. He unwrapped his makeshift harness and reformed it around the sailor.

Then he wrapped the rope once around the yard and threw the end down to Hector on the deck below. Three crewmen grasped the rope. After the injured sailor slid off the yard, they lowered him to the deck. A cheer rose from the crew, and two men carried him forward to the crew cabin where his leg could be set.

Philip remained aloft, waiting for the sail to be drawn up so he could finish lashing it in place. When that task was completed, he descended to the deck. The two triangular topsails were lowered, and the work at the main mast was finished. Claudia thought he was coming to them in the cabin, but he walked past with three of the crew, heading to the stern where they lowered the sea anchor into the water. Finally, he entered the cabin, soaked to the skin with water trickling out of his hair.

As Claudia stepped toward him, he shook his head like a dog, splattering her with water. Then he grinned at her. "It's a little damp out there."

She threw her arms around him and clung to him. "I was so afraid for you up there. You might have been killed."

Philip laughed at her. "I know what I'm doing aloft, Claudia. There was nothing for you to worry about. This storm is nothing unusual. My ship has no trouble weathering much worse."

"But you shouldn't have risked yourself when your slaves can do the work. Why couldn't Hector or one of the other men have gone up to save him?"

Her arms were still wrapped around him, but he tilted her chin up to look into her eyes. His look was stern.

"No man's life is worth more than any other man's, Claudia. You should know that. I was the one with the strength and skill to be able to rescue Primus. Of course I would be the one to do it. I was in less danger getting Primus down than I was getting you away from Lucius. I would have ended up in the arena for kidnapping you if he'd caught us."

Her eyes saucered, and she fought the start of tears. It was the first time he'd ever spoken sharply to her.

He smiled to soften his rebuke. "Besides, my crewmen aren't slaves. They've all worked long enough for me to earn their freedom, and now they share in a portion of the profit as their wages."

She was stunned. The way he treated his slaves was even more generous than anything her father had ever done. Father had always treated his slaves well, but Malleolus was the only slave he'd actually freed.

Philip pushed a loose strand of hair behind her ear. "I'm soaking wet, and you got yourself all wet just hugging me. Let's both get into something dry, and then we can play some Conquest or read together while we wait for the rain to stop. I don't expect this rain to last until nightfall. If it clears in time, we should have a beautiful sunset."

"That's a wonderful idea."

Any idea that kept him inside with her, away from the danger, would be wonderful. She couldn't bear it if he were to die.

They'd played three games of Conquest and read the better part of the poetry codex they both liked best before the rain turned to a sprinkle and then stopped. The wind had died down enough to let Hector put the ship under sail again. She would have preferred that Philip not help with that, but with Primus unable to work with his broken leg, she wasn't surprised when he joined the crew until the sea anchor was stowed and the wind was in the sails again. She knew better than to say something to try to stop him.

Philip rejoined the women in the cabin. "Someone still needs to unlash the chairs and reset the canopy before dinner. Looks like you'll be inside for a while longer."

Claudia's lips curved into a teasing smile. She placed her hand on his arm. "Long enough for another game of Conquest? Unless you're afraid I'll beat you again."

He chuckled. "You certainly know how to make me an offer I can't resist."

She took his hand and led him back into her room, where they set up the board on her bed.

The first game went quicker than normal, and she smiled triumphantly as she took his last remaining fortress.

"If your brother is as good at strategy as you are, I would hate to face him in battle."

Philip bowed his head and extended his arms toward her, wrists together, as if to surrender.

"I yield to your superior skill, general."

When he tipped his head up and offered an impish grin, she couldn't help but laugh. "Oh, Philip. You're so different from other men."

"How so, great general?"

"You make me feel like I'm actually somebody."

He tipped his head sideways, his one bushy eyebrow raised. She almost laughed again at how funny he looked.

"But you are somebody—one of the few somebodies who can beat me at this game."

"Most men look at me like I'm something, not somebody. It's like I'm just a statue to be admired and possessed."

"Then most men are fools."

She was startled by the serious tone of his voice and an intense look in his eye that she'd never seen before. Then the twinkle reappeared, accompanied by a crooked grin.

"But they are right that you're very easy on the eyes."

He began placing the pieces back on the board.

"You have to give me a chance to regain my honor. Best two out of three. Loser goes first."

She watched him make the first move. It was good he lived in Perinthus. How could she ever bear having him disappear from her life when the ship reached port? In fact, the more time she spent with him, the more she wanted to be with him for the rest of their lives. Somehow, she had to get him to ask her to be his wife.

Chapter 35

LAST DAY AT SEA

Before this trip, Philip was always glad when the harbor at Perinthus came into view at the end of a voyage. This time was different. He would no longer spend every day with the first woman who looked at him and saw a dear friend who cared about her, not a rich man with ugly scars. He'd never expected to meet a woman who could write elegant poetry and beat him at Conquest, a woman who found his scars 'interesting' and not just ugly, a woman who told him that she liked looking at him and that he made her feel like somebody when no other man ever had.

The depth of her grief revealed a heart capable of true devotion to someone she loved. She was still haunted by her father's death, but Philip had helped her find pleasure in life again. She cared deeply for him as a friend; there were plenty of signs she might love him as a man. If she were a Christian, he would ask her brother for her hand in marriage within the week, and he would gladly pay any bride price Titus asked.

But she wasn't. She still blamed the followers of Jesus for leading her father to his death, and she wasn't ready to forgive. She wasn't ready to listen to why her father had chosen to follow Jesus and why she should follow Him, too. Philip couldn't share with her the most important part of his life.

He loved Claudia as a friend. He was in love with her as a woman, but until she followed Jesus, he could never ask her to be his wife.

Claudia stood at the rail, looking down the shoreline of Thracia, watching for the first sign of Perinthus. It had been a long voyage, but it hadn't been long enough. She was eager to see Titus, but...

She turned to look for Philip. She found him standing atop the cabin, talking with Hector. For the first time since she'd met him, he was dressed like the merchant prince he was. She'd grown so accustomed to seeing him in a short beige tunic like the rest of his crew that there was something surreal about him wearing long robes of rich, colorful fabric.

His blind side was toward her, and she could see all his scars. He was the ugliest man she'd ever seen, but he was also the most wonderful person she'd ever known. It was funny how she'd grown to like looking at the ridges and swirls of his scars. She liked touching them even more. There wasn't another face in the world she'd rather have smiling at her.

The thought of not spending most of her time in his company tore at her. How was she going to get through each day without him to read her to sleep after the horror of her nightmares or distract her from her grief with a few rounds of Conquest?

At least he lived in Perinthus, and she would be staying with Penelope and him for a few days until Titus got everything arranged. After that, she would have to learn to live without him near her all the time.

But she didn't want to...ever.

What if he didn't want her as much as she wanted him? What if he was content to have her move in with Titus and never see her again? As that thought wormed its way into her mind, the tears starting to pool in her eyes.

◆

Philip felt Claudia's gaze upon him. When he turned, her face had blanched with the stricken look that preceded a flood of tears.

"We'll discuss that later, Hector. I'm needed on deck."

Philip climbed down and walked over to stand beside her at the railing. The tears hadn't started yet. He had time to divert her thoughts before they did.

"We have a little more than half a day before we reach port." His smile teased. "Will you give a general one more chance to conquer? He might need two or three tries if you're really on your game today."

She flashed him a smile before she took his hand and led him toward the cabin. "Let's get the board, and we'll see if it's Greece or Rome that wins today. Best two out of three to decide the fate of the Empire."

They settled in under the canopy. She won the first game and was well on the way to winning the second.

"Philip?"

"Yes?"

"Promise me you'll come visit me."

"Of course. Penelope will insist on it."

"Often?"

"As often as you want."

Her face brightened at his answer.

He longed to ask her to never leave him so he wouldn't have to visit, but that was something he couldn't do as long as she still hated Christians...like him.

She won the second easily. His mind was not in the game. He was too distracted by the thought of her no longer being with him every day. He needed to focus, or she'd be asking him what was wrong. He didn't want to speak it aloud. The thought must be distressing to both of them.

"I'm not ready to concede your superiority today." He raised his eyebrow and tilted his head as his crooked grin teased her. "Best three out of five?"

Her eyes sparkled as she smiled back. "Very well. I'd like another chance to conquer you."

As he set up the board for the next game, he suppressed a sigh. She hadn't only conquered his armies in the game; she'd conquered his heart. How much he wanted to tell her and ask if she could love him, too. But until Jesus conquered her heart as well, that could never be.

Penelope and Junia were standing together at the railing, pointing out interesting sights to each other as the ship moved into the harbor at Perinthus. Claudia stood slightly apart, and the closer they got to the wharf, the paler she became.

Philip stood beside Hector, watching the crew as they prepared for the final docking procedures. He glanced down at Claudia and found her gripping the rail, white as a sheet. He climbed down the ladder and went to stand beside her. He laid his hand on one of hers and gently squeezed.

She looked up at him with enormous eyes.

"I'm afraid, Philip."

His brow furrowed. "But there's nothing to be afraid of. We're safely in the harbor, and docking isn't dangerous."

"What if you can't find Titus right away?"

"Then you'll stay with Penelope and me until I do find him."

"What if he can't have me live with him?"

"You'll stay on with us. If he can't take care of you, I will."

"But for how long? I can't ask you to do it forever."

"For as long as you need me to. You were entrusted to my care until Titus takes that responsibility from me. You don't have to be afraid that you'll be left alone."

"But what if—"

He placed his finger against her lips to silence her.

"No more what ifs. You're worrying about things you don't need to worry about. You don't have to be afraid. Trust me to make sure coming to Titus ends well for you."

He watched fear drain away and trembling lips curve into a smile. "I trust you, Philip. I'll try not to worry."

"Good." He squeezed her hand once more before rejoining Hector.

◆

As Claudia gazed up at the ugly face that had become what she loved most in the whole world to see, she breathed a sigh of relief. Philip had promised to make sure everything turned out well. No one, not even her father, was better at doing that than Philip.

Chapter 36

ARRIVING IN PERINTHUS

As Claudia walked down the gangplank onto the dock, once more she was entering a world unknown to her. In leaving Rome, she'd left all her friends and everything familiar. She'd felt so terribly alone. Arriving in Perinthus was different. Penelope and Junia were her friends. Titus was somewhere in the city, and the finest man in the world had promised to make sure all would be well.

Penelope turned to smile at her as they walked along the pier toward the road where Philip's carriage waited for them. "I'm glad you're going to be living here. I don't know anyone in Perinthus except you and Junia. I'm so glad I brought a friend with me."

Claudia couldn't agree more, so she nodded. Then she bit her lip. Did Titus live close enough to Philip's house that she could see them often?

Especially Philip. He'd promised they would visit, but it wasn't just visits she longed for. She wanted to spend every day with him and every evening, too. She wanted him to marry her.

For at least a few days, she'd be living at Philip's house. Would he realize how much she loved him and decide he didn't want her to go to her brother? All it would take was a word from him, and she would be the happiest woman in the world, in spite of losing her father, in spite of leaving everything she'd ever known behind.

She glanced back at his ship. They'd become close friends on the voyage, but what if he didn't want her as his wife? She still missed Father terribly, and the nightmares about how he died still tormented her every night. Only Philip was able to fill her days with smiles and laughter and to drive the lions from her mind at night. Only Philip.

Philip walked into the garrison at the provincial palace, looking for Titus. It was not a place he would normally choose to go. Being too close to Roman power was not comfortable for a leader of a Christian house church. The look the soldier guarding the entrance gave him did nothing to make this visit easier.

He approached the centurion in command of the guards that day.

"I have some important news for Titus Claudius Drusus. I understand he's a tribune serving the governor."

The centurion's gaze swept Philip from head to foot and back. Philip had dressed so it would be obvious he was wealthy. He carried himself so a guard would think he was someone important enough to justify summoning the officer he was requesting.

With a flick of his hand, the centurion summoned one of the soldiers. "Find Tribune Drusus. Tell him there's someone here with news for him."

The soldier saluted and disappeared into the building. In a few minutes, he reappeared with Titus.

Titus was not what Philip expected. Claudia had described him as a sweet, kind brother. The man who stood before him had the hard look of a seasoned Roman officer.

Titus crossed his arms and stood facing Philip with a slight frown. "You have news for me."

"Yes, and part of it is bad. I would speak to you in private."

Titus's frown deepened. "Follow me."

He led Philip into a room off the courtyard where they could converse undisturbed. He turned to face Philip and crossed his arms again. The frown had been joined by suspicious eyes.

Philip drew a deep breath. "First, I have brought your sister from Rome at her request. My ship docked this afternoon, and she's now on her way to my house with my sister Penelope. She hopes that you'll be able to take her under your protection and that she can live with you here in Perinthus."

Titus's jaw dropped as he stared at Philip. The hardness of the Roman officer had been replaced by the deep concern of a loving brother.

"Is she well? Why did she leave Father and come to me?"

"That's the bad news. Your father had become a Christian, and your brother Lucius reported him so he could take control. Your father has been killed in the arena. As the new head of your family, your brother planned to marry Claudia to Flavius Sabinus for a large bride price. She chose to come to you for protection rather than be sold into a bad marriage by your brother."

For a moment, Titus was stunned into silence. Then hot anger twisted his features. "Lucius. That cold-hearted, murdering son of a..." He checked himself. A steely look replaced the hot one. "He's a dead man when I return to Rome." He glared at Philip, even though he wasn't actually mad at him. "And how is it that you've come to bring my sister here?" His look and voice softened as he shook his head. "How is she, really? Father meant the world to her. His death must be crushing her."

From the pain in Titus's eyes, it was obvious Titus had loved their father almost as much as she had.

"One of your father's friends asked me to help her. She was about to kill herself when your father's steward suggested that she come to you instead." Philip locked his gaze on Titus's eyes as he asked the key question. "Will you be able to care for her as she hoped?"

Titus glared at him as if that was the stupidest question he'd ever heard. "Of course I'll care for my sister."

"I didn't mean to offend you. I'm not implying that you wouldn't want to. She's always been certain you would welcome her. I was concerned that your duties as an officer might mean you wouldn't be able to."

Titus's attitude softened. "This is my permanent station. I very seldom leave the capital, so it shouldn't be a problem. I'm living in rented lodgings outside the garrison now. I can get us a house instead. It shouldn't be too difficult."

Philip stifled a sigh. Her brother had no idea how much was involved in establishing a household suitable for his sister, or he would never have brushed aside the difficulty. Even though Philip was about to officially hand her over to her brother, the responsibility for making certain she was protected and properly cared for would remain his.

He would just have to find some tactful way to help her brother without him realizing how much help he was getting. Her brother seemed the typical Roman aristocrat, accustomed to having slaves do everything so he was ignorant of how much work simply living involved.

"I have connections throughout the city. It can be a challenge to find a suitable house to rent without them. If you will allow me to be of service to you, I can locate a house in a safe part of the city at the price you desire. I'd be very happy to do so. My sister and Claudia have become good friends during the voyage, and I expect they will want to continue the friendship. If Penelope is to visit your sister, I'd prefer it be somewhere I know is safe."

◆

Titus kept his eyebrows from rising. Such an offer was unexpected, but he welcomed it. He couldn't take much time off duty to search through the city for a home for them, and he really had no idea where to even start looking.

"My duties here prevent me from spending much time house hunting, so I accept your offer."

He paused as he did a quick mental tally of his normal monthly expenses, other than rent, and doubled them to support both Claudia and him. He'd have to buy some slaves: a steward, a cook, a maid for Claudia, someone to clean, someone for the stable. There were many more than five in his father's town house, but how many were really needed? And at what price? He'd never bought one, so...did a good slave cost about what a good horse did? And then he'd have to feed them, so he added in five times the cost of what he usually spent to feed himself.

There would be some expenses for furniture and all the other things needed to set up a household. He had no idea what that would cost. It was good he wasn't a heavy gambler. He had about eighteen hundred denarii saved and fifteen hundred each month in wages as a tribune, but one thing was certain. Money would be very tight.

"If you could find something with a monthly rent less than 150 denarii, that would be helpful. All Father's estates will have been seized. It sounds like Lucius got everything transferred to him somehow. All I'll have for the foreseeable future is my officer's pay."

◆

Philip blinked at the low figure. That would only rent something in a part of town that he considered too dangerous for the woman he loved. It was fortunate he'd made the offer. It gave him a chance to secretly subsidize the rent in a good part of town to keep her safe.

"I'm sure I can find something suitable for you and your sister in that price range. Your sister is welcome to stay with us as long as necessary for you to set up your household. Penelope is going to miss spending time with Claudia every day, so she would most certainly say the longer the better."

Titus simply nodded in response. It was clear he was distracted and deeply grieved by the news of his father's death. At least Philip hadn't been forced to report Claudia's death, too. This brother she loved so dearly loved her as well.

Titus squared his shoulders. "I'm on duty until the beginning of first watch this evening, so I'll need directions to your house for later. I want to see Claudia as soon as possible."

"Of course. I'll draw you a map. It's a short ride to the west from here. It would give me pleasure if you would join us for dinner, and we can discuss how I can best help you in getting your sister settled with you."

"Thank you, ..."

"Philip." Philip offered his arm, and Titus took it.

"I'm very grateful for what you've done for my sister, Philip."

"Penelope and I think she's a fine young woman. It's been our pleasure getting to know her during the voyage. We'll be happy to do anything we can to help her."

Her brother had no idea how happy Philip was that he would need to stay closely involved. The last thing he wanted was to lose frequent contact with Claudia.

He'd already decided where they should live. He owned a very nice house that he rented out. It was only a quarter mile from his own, an easy walking distance along a safe route. God had certainly provided since the previous tenant had recently moved back to Corinth and he hadn't rented it to someone else yet.

He would furnish and rent it to Titus for only slightly less than his maximum figure. He would have let her live there rent free, but if it cost too little, her brother might get suspicious. Titus could pay the rent to one of the brothers in his house church to conceal his generosity. Then, if Titus's wages were not enough, he'd find some way to give the rent back.

Chapter 37

Transfer to Titus

As Titus turned off the main road that evening and started up the street that led to Philip's house, he examined the houses lining each side. They were not as huge as the villas on the three family estates just outside Rome, but they were definitely upper class. All were behind tall mud-brick walls and appeared to have a good number of trees waving their fruit-laden branches.

His map showed Philip's house to be a little over three-quarters of a mile up the street from the main road. He could barely see the roof since it was surrounded by trees and set back from the roadside wall by some distance. As he rode through the gate, his brow furrowed. The gardens were fruit trees, grape vines, and food crops, and they surrounded a house that was smaller than most of the others he'd passed.

As he reached the house, he was met by a stable slave, who stood waiting for him to dismount and hand him the reins.

"Master Philip is waiting for you in the back garden. This way."

With a respectful bow, the man led Titus past the house to a more decorative garden at the back, where the stables also were.

As he rounded the corner of the house, he saw Claudia, Philip, and a dark-haired girl about Claudia's age sitting in some chairs under a large tree.

Philip said something to Claudia that he couldn't hear, and she sprang up and walked briskly toward him. Philip and his sister rose as well and followed her. As Claudia got closer to him, her walk turned into a run. When she reached him, she threw her arms around him and hugged him so tight it was hard to breathe. Then she tipped her head back, and he saw that beautiful smile he'd always enjoyed.

"Oh, Titus! It's so good to see you. I've missed you so much."

As Titus held his little sister, smiling down at her, something totally unexpected happened. She burst into tears and buried her face in his tunic.

"It's all right, Claudia. I'm here now. Don't cry."

He kept one arm wrapped around her as he stroked her hair with his free hand. Philip and his sister reached them, and Titus's eyebrows first lowered, then rose as his eyes asked Philip a wordless question.

Philip's lips tightened as he slowly nodded. The ugly Greek wasn't surprised by her tears. Like most men, Titus masked his emotions. He had no experience coping with weeping women. But the Greek had been four weeks in close company with Claudia. If anyone could tell him how to deal with her tears, it would be Philip. A private conversation before Titus left was in order.

Philip's sister rested her hand on Claudia's back, and Claudia released Titus.

She flicked some tears from her cheeks. "I'm sorry, Titus. I didn't mean to do that."

The dark-haired girl wrapped her arm around Claudia's shoulder. "Welcome to our home, Titus. I'm Philip's sister, Penelope." She waved her hand toward the chairs. "Let's go sit for a while. The dinner is almost ready, and someone will come get us when they're ready to serve."

Titus sat in the chair next to Claudia where Philip had been sitting. Philip stood behind Penelope with his hand resting on her shoulder. Philip's gaze shifted often between Titus and Claudia. For no reason obvious to Titus, the Greek seemed tense.

The Claudia Titus remembered had been relaxed and happy. Now she was like a lyre string stretched so tight that one more turn of the tuning key would snap it.

Titus took her hand. "I'm glad you came to me. What happened?"

"Oh, Titus. It was all so horrible. Father became a God-fearer about three years ago, and he was happy. Then someone convinced him to become a Christian. He was even happier, but I made the mistake of telling Lucius when he asked why Father was so happy. I never dreamed he would betray Father. He reported Father to one of his praetor friends. The soldiers came and took him away to the arena, and I never saw him again.

"When I told Lucius he was a murderer for betraying Father, he decided to make me marry Flavius Sabinus. That horrible old man beat his last wife to death. He was going to give Lucius 50,000 denarii if he'd make me marry him."

Her eyes swam in unshed tears. "Malleolus stopped me just before I killed myself. He went to one of Father's friends for help getting me away from Lucius. That friend arranged for Philip to help me escape and get to you."

The dam broke, and the tears trickled down her cheeks. "I want Lucius dead! I want those Christians dead! I want Father back!"

The trickle turned into a torrent. Titus rose and pulled her up into his arms. He'd expected her to be sad over Father's death, but to be crying in his arms while two relative strangers looked on?

◆

Philip could barely stand it as he watched Titus try unsuccessfully to console her. Those arms should be wrapped around his chest, not her brother's.

The tears slowed to a trickle and stopped. Penelope extracted Claudia from Titus's arms.

"We're going to go wash your face and freshen up. We'll be back in a few minutes for dinner."

Titus watched in silence until the two women disappeared into the house. Then he turned to Philip.

"Has she been this way since leaving Rome?"

"At the beginning of the voyage, yes. She was doing much better by the end of it. There were many days at the end when she didn't cry at all during the day. Nighttime is another matter. She has nightmares almost every night that wake her up, and she always cries for a while after those. Reading after the nightmares helps."

It would be unwise to tell Titus how she'd come to his bed each night to get him and how he'd helped her get some sleep lying in his lap as he caressed her temple almost every day. Her brother might be suspicious of his motives and misinterpret his actions.

"I'm concerned that she tried to kill herself. Was it just the one time?"

"No. After the first week, she tried to jump into the sea. I reached her in time to prevent it. She tried again with a knife the next morning. I told her what that would do to you, and she never tried again. I don't think she'll try here, either. She loves you very much and doesn't want to do anything that would hurt you."

◆

Titus took a deep breath and blew it out slowly. He would have bet anything that his happy little sister could never be so sad that she would seek to end her own life. Would she try again, or would being with him be enough to stop her?

"I owe you a debt of gratitude for stopping her and for getting her to me safely. I also owe you money for her passage. How much?"

"Nothing. I was sailing from Rome to Perinthus with an empty passenger berth. She merely filled it. She and Penelope have become close friends, and it gives me pleasure to help you both."

Their conversation ended when Penelope and Claudia emerged from the garden door. Claudia looked like the cloudburst was over. Penelope was holding Claudia's hand. If that was meant to encourage her, it was working.

Penelope's gaze shifted between him and Philip as she smiled "Shall we go in and eat? It's all ready."

◆

Titus took Claudia's hand and placed it on his arm. As they followed Penelope into the house, Philip wished it was his arm, not Titus's. It was too hard to give her to another, even to a brother who obviously loved her.

Claudia tried to be cheerful during dinner, and, for the most part, she succeeded. Each time she felt the tears starting, she looked at Philip. His encouraging smile helped her keep the tears in check. She really didn't want to worry Titus, and her earlier outburst had caused him great concern.

The final dishes were cleared from the table, and it was time for Titus to leave.

"It was an excellent dinner. I want to thank you for all you've done for my sister, Philip. As soon as your contacts can find me a house, I'll be able to take her home with me."

"No thanks are necessary. Penelope and I have thoroughly enjoyed her company as we brought her to you. We'll miss her when she leaves us."

Leave him. Claudia's throat tightened, and the tears his smiles had held in check broke free. The last thing she ever wanted to do was leave him, even if she was going to her beloved brother.

As silent tears began trickling down her cheeks, Penelope rose and moved over by Claudia. She placed her hand under Claudia's elbow to get her to rise as well.

"We'll leave you now. It's been wonderful meeting you, Titus. I'm sure we'll have many more opportunities to get to know you after you take Claudia to your house."

The rivulet of tears had become a steady stream as the thought of leaving Philip ripped into Claudia.

Titus stood. "Will you be all right, Claudia?"

She nodded, but the tears kept flowing.

Penelope put her arm around Claudia's shoulders. "Don't worry, Titus. Philip and I will take good care of her."

The two girls left the dining room and headed upstairs.

◆

Titus stood staring at the door for several seconds before turning to Philip.

"I'm sorry I have to leave her with you until I find a house and get it set up for her."

"Think nothing of it. We enjoy having her with us."

The men headed out to the stable.

As Titus waited for the stable slave to bring his horse, Philip crossed his arms. "My contacts have located a good furnished house for you. It's a quarter mile from here. In fact, you rode by it on your way up from the main road. If you want to see it tonight, my steward will get some torches and show it to you. If you'd rather see it in the daylight, he can show it to you tomorrow.

"If you decide you want it, he'll take care of all the necessary arrangements so you won't have to get time off duty. I hope you find it suitable. It's close enough that Penelope and Claudia can see each other daily. I think that might be very important for the happiness of your sister."

Titus's eyebrows rose. "That was fast. I can ride up around midday tomorrow. I appreciate your help with this, Philip."

"It's my pleasure to do it. You'll need a house steward as well. It can be very difficult to find someone with the proper skills that you can trust completely. I'd like to help you with that. I have a eunuch at one of my local estates who would be perfect for your needs. I'd be glad to lend him to you. He's familiar with the city, and he'll provide reliable oversight of the house slaves. He'll make sure Claudia is safe when you're on duty."

Titus's eyebrows shot up at this offer. He'd already been worrying about how he was going to find a good steward in a town where he knew only soldiers, government officials, and a few shopkeepers.

"That's a generous offer. Again, I'll gladly accept, but you must let me pay you for him."

"That's not necessary since I don't want to sell him. It's my pleasure to help you and your sister this way."

Titus was not a man who took unfair advantage of the generosity of friends. Normally, he would have insisted that Philip take something, but money would be very tight for the foreseeable future, even after he set up the household for Claudia. He would make an exception with Philip since the ugly Greek was rich enough that the expense meant nothing to him.

The stable slave brought Titus his horse. He mounted and looked down at Philip.

"I'll be coming midday to see the house and check on Claudia. Thank you again for everything you've done for her."

"No thanks are needed. Penelope and I are glad to have had the opportunity."

As Titus rode away, he twisted in the saddle to look back at Philip as he walked toward his house. It was a good thing Malleolus had found someone like him to bring Claudia from Rome. His little sister was precious, and he would have lost her without the ugly Greek.

It was a very good thing that Philip was the one who brought her.

As Junia turned back the covers on Claudia's bed, Claudia chewed her lip.

"What am I going to do when I wake up tonight? I can't go to Philip's room in his house like I did onboard, but I can't make it through the night without him."

"Don't worry about that, mistress. Just come to me, and I'll get Master Philip for you."

Claudia seized Junia's hand. "Oh, Junia! How am I ever going to make it without you all when I move in with Titus?"

Her eyes glistened as she fought to hold back the tears.

"Don't think about that now, mistress. I'm sure your brother will take care of everything you need. I think you'll be living just a short distance down the street from here, so you can visit often."

Claudia lay down on the bed, and Junia tucked the sheets around her.

"Go to sleep now, mistress. Everything will be all right."

Claudia closed her eyes. The night always started out all right, but then the lions came.

Claudia didn't get Junia when she awoke from the roars and screams. She would have to get through the night soon with no help. She buried her face in the pillow and tried to cry as quietly as she could.

She hadn't been crying for long when Philip entered her room with a lamp and a scroll.

Claudia sat up in bed and reached out for his hand. "I tried to make it without you, but I just can't. What am I going to do when I'm with Titus?"

Philip set the lamp on the bedstand and pulled a chair over by her bed. "Titus will care for you at least as well I have. He loves you very much."

She leaned over so she could stroke his scarred cheek. "No one, not even Titus, can take care of me like you do."

"I wouldn't be here all the time. I'm often away on business. Titus will be here every day. I do expect you to be living only a short distance from here. I've found a house for you and Titus just down the road. Penelope and I will see you often."

"It's not the same, Philip."

"I know. Now lie down, and I'll read you to sleep."

She took his hand and held it against her cheek as he began to read. How was she ever going to get through the nights when Philip was gone?

As Titus rode out the gate of the rental house the next day after meeting with Philip's steward, he was more optimistic about his financial situation.

The house Philip's contact had found was exactly what he needed. Philip's steward would arrange the details that afternoon, and he could begin preparing it for Claudia the next day. It already had the necessary furniture, so he wouldn't have to buy any before they could move in.

Best of all, the rent was only 145 denarii a month. Financially, he was in a tight situation, but it wasn't hopeless. With a low rent and no furniture to buy, it was better than he'd feared.

He hadn't been getting an allowance since his officer's pay was more than enough for a single man. That would have stopped with Father's death, anyway.

With Father's execution as a Christian, the family property would have been seized. The northern estate that was to have been his inheritance was his no longer. Lucius had arranged with his praetor friend to receive it all back as reward for his betrayal. All Titus now had was his tribune's pay, and he'd have to save as much as he could to live on after he finished serving.

Five more years—if he could save 1000 denarii a month, that would give him 60,000 denarii when he finished his tour of duty. Not enough to stay in the equestrian order, but enough to take care of him and Claudia, if she remained unmarried. He certainly couldn't ask Lucius for anything. He'd rent himself out as a mercenary before he'd take a bronze quadrans from that son of a snake, anyway. If he gave up his lodgings near the palace and lived with Claudia, he could manage the rent without any great difficulty. The rest of the household expenses… he'd have to figure out how to support it all on 350 denarii a month. That might not be easy, but it was doable.

Philip's eunuch would be at the house sometime later today. Tomorrow morning, he would go to the slave market and buy the other slaves he would need. Getting a household set up was proving to be easier than he'd expected, thanks to Philip. Now if it would just be cheap enough.

Before inspecting the house, he'd joined Penelope and Claudia for lunch. Claudia was in much better spirits. There wasn't a single tear during the whole meal. She did seem a little sad when he left, but at least she wasn't crying. He hated to watch her cry.

Chapter 38

Titus's stallion was saddled and waiting the next morning when he entered the garrison stable. Philip and Penelope were taking good care of Claudia for the moment, but nasty rumors could start if she stayed too long with an unmarried man with no blood relationship to her. He would move from his lodgings to the rented house that evening, but first he needed to staff it. He'd arranged to take the morning off and had withdrawn most of his savings from the paymaster.

Philip's loan of a trustworthy eunuch to be his steward had solved the most difficult dilemma of finding someone who would guarantee both her safety and her reputation when Titus was on duty. A decent steward would cost more than he even had, and he had no money to waste. Just buying enough ordinary slaves to properly care for Claudia would stretch his resources to their limit.

He'd never had to worry about the details of running a household before. As a soldier, taking care of himself was easy; figuring out how to care for her was another thing entirely. As a bare minimum, he needed to buy someone to cook, someone to clean and do other domestic chores, and someone to be her personal maid. With only one horse and so few house slaves to oversee, his steward could serve in the stable.

As he neared the slave market, Titus pulled a deep breath and blew it out slowly between pursed lips. He only had 1200 denarii—enough for three decent horses, but would it buy three good slaves?

200

He'd have to bargain very shrewdly to get everything they needed with so little. He couldn't stay for the afternoon auction, so he had to find what he needed that morning. Auction prices could run up higher than a direct purchase, anyway. A walk through the market to see what others were paying should give him an idea of the going rates for slaves in Perinthus. Horses he knew how to judge and set a value on, but he'd never had to buy a person before.

Miriam's arms hung at her side as she fingered her tunic. Of all the female slaves standing in line, waiting to be sold, she was the only one whose tunic swept the ground. With good reason. While the other owners were trying to lure buyers to pay higher prices by displaying their property's womanly curves, hers was trying to hide something.

She shifted her weight onto her bad leg for a moment, then back to her good one.

God, please let me be sold into a kind household.

She knew firsthand how hard it could be in a cruel one with a limp like hers. She'd been struck so many times for not moving fast enough to satisfy her first mistress, even though it was the mistress's own son who'd crippled her through his carelessness. Her shattered ankle had healed badly, and one leg was shorter because of it.

She'd been overjoyed when she was sold to Master Alexander when she was almost eleven. He was a Christian, and he treated his slaves like real people, not just property. Best of all, it was there she'd come to know Jesus was the Messiah so long awaited by her people, the Jews. But now Master Alexander was dead, and at the age of nineteen, she was being sold again.

She glanced at the wooden platform with the turntable, and her stomach knotted. Master Alexander had bought her directly from her first mistress, so she'd never been on the auction block before. Slaves would be displayed naked so potential buyers could see exactly what they were getting, and they could handle any part of a slave they wanted. Standing naked before a crowd...all the men who were buying and even those who weren't staring and touching her...She swallowed hard and fought the tears.

It had been horrible enough when the slave trader examined her so carefully to make sure she was a virgin before buying her. Her virginity was the main reason he bought her from the official who seized all Master Alexander's property before his execution. It might increase the value of a cripple enough to make her worth buying.

She had a very pretty face and a lovely figure, and those would draw the attention of all the men. Her deformed ankle would make buying her attractive only to those who couldn't afford to pay a higher price. The auction would be bad enough, but what came after...She fought the trembling that swept through her each time she thought about what would happen to her that night...unless God brought the kind master she'd been desperately praying for.

Her gaze was drawn to the proprietor of a local brothel as he made his way through the slave market, selecting young women to add to his stable of prostitutes. Last night, the woman in the holding cell with her had warned her about him. Not everyone wanted to go to the temple prostitutes, so he made a fortune satisfying the desires of a provincial capital that was also a seaport. Life was short in that brothel. He needed to buy new girls often.

What if her owner decided she might not bring a good price at auction? What if he decided to sell her to the brothel early for a guaranteed amount?

She closed her eyes. *Please, God! Deliver me from that fate. I'll gladly serve any household of decent people, but to be a plaything for lustful men? Please spare me from that...degradation.* She swallowed hard again. *I'd rather die.*

When she opened her eyes, she saw the handsome Roman officer wandering through the market, looking at female slaves. Intense relief flooded through her...relief straight from God. He'd brought the officer as the answer to her prayers.

But there was more than relief. There was a strange certainty. That officer needed to buy her for his sister at least as much as she needed him to buy her before the brothel owner came over.

He came closer...and closer. Finally, he was right in front of her.

And then he stepped past without even looking at her.

Stop him, God! Please make him buy me.

Mustering all the courage she had, she stepped out of the line and touched his arm.

◆

Titus spun to look at the slave who had presumed to touch him.

Before him stood a pretty young woman with thick brown hair and a pair of enormous brown eyes. Solemn eyes that seemed...wise.

"Your sister needs me. Please buy me for her."

His eyebrows dipped when she spoke to him. How did she know he was looking for slaves for his sister?

The slave trader turned at the sound of her voice. He stepped over and slapped her cheek.

"I am very sorry for the impudence of this one in speaking to you unbidden, noble sir. I bought her from a household that allowed such forwardness and coddled its slaves. She is actually very docile in spite of that. She will quickly learn that most masters do not treat their slaves like freeborn servants. Then she will be fine, excellent in fact."

Her response to the slap surprised Titus. He'd expected her to either cower before her owner or flash a look of defiance at him. Instead, she simply rubbed her cheek and continued to look at him with those earnest eyes.

His head tilted, and he rubbed his clean-shaven cheek. He'd planned to buy an older woman to care for Claudia's needs and to make sure she didn't hurt herself. This slave was not much older than his sister, but there was something about those eyes that made her seem like she was.

"So you think my sister needs you? Do you know how to help a Roman lady with her beauty preparations and other personal...activities?" He wasn't quite sure how to describe what a Roman lady's maid would do.

"I've never served a Roman, sir, but I did my Greek mistress's hair."

Greek hair, Roman hair. Was there a difference? He looked away from her and scanned the group of older women in the next stall. Maybe an older one would be better.

Her strangely calm voice drew his eyes back to the young one's pretty face. "I also know how to cook and keep house. Please buy me to do whatever your sister's household needs."

Titus rubbed his cheek again. She'd asked him to buy her, but her voice sounded unperturbed, almost as if she knew he would. She kept looking at him with those eyes that were calm but somehow compelling. Something about her intrigued him, but he couldn't quite put his finger on what it was.

He crossed his arms. "If you've never served a Roman lady, why do you think I should buy you?"

The dark eyes softened. "Because her heart is broken right now, and I can help it heal."

His head snapped back. How could she possibly have known that? What was it about her eyes that held his gaze? He rubbed the back of his neck.

The sincerity in them—he'd seen that in only a few slaves, and they'd all belonged to his father. Slaves were treated well in the Drusus household, and they responded with diligence and loyalty. It sounded like she may have come from such a household herself.

Money would be very tight for some time. If she could cook and clean and do Greek hair, perhaps she would be a good buy. She could do everything he needed as a house slave, and Claudia could train her to do what she needed as her personal attendant. After seeing the prices, he wasn't sure he had enough money even to buy two slaves that were any good. If she could do everything until after his next payday, that would solve a big problem.

The trader offered him an oily smile. "There are not many slaves who can do so many things. She is a Jew, but she speaks good Greek. She is strong for her size and healthy. If she does not do well serving your sister, you can always use her in the kitchen or for housecleaning or for entertainment. She can play the lyre and flute, and you can see she has a very pretty face." He bounced his eyebrows. "Your guests will find her very enjoyable."

He tapped her chin so she would open her mouth for Titus to inspect her teeth. Then he placed his hands on her shoulders and turned her around so Titus could view her at all angles.

"You can see that she was fed well by her last master. She is still a virgin, too." A chuckle accompanied his bouncing eyebrows. "I made sure of that myself. That is one good thing about buying slaves that are seized from Christian masters. They do not make full use of the females they own. Imagine the pleasure you can have being the first to enjoy this lovely body tonight."

The pretty Jew bowed her head and turned scarlet at that remark. Titus tightened his lips so the trader wouldn't suspect how appealing he found her.

"They're only virgin the first time. I'm not in the market for that right now, so it's not worth extra to me."

Titus was used to buying horses, not people. Still, horse trading had given him negotiating skills. He had some idea of the going prices from watching a few sales today, but he wasn't sure exactly how to gauge the price that he should offer for her.

"How much?"

"Five hundred denarii."

The trader's smile was too stiff. She was worth less, but how much less?

"That's too much by far. I can get a good horse for that, and, frankly, she's not that impressive. I would be taking a chance that she can do what I'm looking for since she hasn't done it before. The brothel would only pay you 350. That's my offer."

"The brothel is a regular customer, and I give them discounted prices for their faithful patronage. The price is higher for a single purchase."

Titus gazed again at those dark brown eyes in that pretty face. There was something about them. She might be just what he needed.

"I might be willing to pay 375 for her."

A twitch at corner of the trader's eye betrayed his disappointment that Titus was not as ignorant of the going rates as he'd hoped.

"I am sure you are a good judge of horseflesh, but this female is worth much more than 375. She is very pretty and a virgin, after all. Still, I always like to show how much I value the excellent service to our province by you Roman officers, and I like you. I would not be so generous to an ordinary buyer, but I would find 450 acceptable from an officer like yourself."

Titus appraised her one more time. He was drawn again into those eyes that had shone with compassion when she spoke of his sister's broken heart. If she could cook and keep house as well as tend to his sister's personal needs, she could be worth four hundred. Maybe he should make the counteroffer for her.

He began to nod his head. Buying her was the right thing to do. Four hundred wasn't too much for what he'd be getting. With her domestic skills, she should be all he'd have to buy for the moment. It was many days until his next payday, and he would be spending money much faster now there were two of them and a household to support. He could always sell her and shop again later if she wasn't able to do what she said.

"Four hundred would be acceptable. For four hundred, I'll buy her."

The slave trader's slight smile showed resignation to the price, and he offered Titus his arm to close the deal.

Titus took sixteen *aurei* from his purse and paid the man. In exchange, he received the bill of sale. Just like buying a horse. This had proven to be much easier than he'd expected when he first entered the slave market. He looked at his purchase. There was something about her that he was certain Claudia would like.

"What's your name?"

"Miriam, master."

He nodded. "Come." He turned and walked away.

◆

The trader's reserved smile morphed into a smug grin as he watched the tribune weave through the crowd with the limping girl behind him. He had received a much better price for her than he expected. The Roman officer had not been good at this. He should have been suspicious when a pretty young woman like her was fully clothed in a long tunic. He had not asked to see the placard that she would have worn around her neck during the auction that described her skills and defects, including her bad ankle. He had paid more than he had to, and he had not even checked her well enough to know that she limped.

Since her defect was so obvious if he had bothered to look, the Roman law that required a refund for unknown defects in the first six months would not apply, even if the officer demanded it. The quaestor overseeing slave sales in Perinthus would never believe that a buyer would not have looked at her closely enough before the purchase to see that bad ankle, and only defects not known at the time of sale must receive a refund.

There could be no charge of false claims since her limp would not keep her from doing everything he sold her to do. The officer was getting what he had asked for at the price he suggested himself, so perhaps he would be content with his purchase, anyway.

The trader rubbed his hands together. He liked dealing with fools, and this officer was the biggest one he had cheated in a long time.

Chapter 39

Not What He Paid For

Miriam's heart had danced at the officer's words when he said he wasn't in the market for a virgin and wouldn't pay extra for one. He must have been sent by God to buy her only for his sister. When the two men agreed on the four hundred denarii and the tribune took the bill of sale, songs of thanksgiving played in her mind.

Her rejoicing continued as Miriam limped after her new master. God must have made the officer choose her without checking everything. He hadn't examined her naked like most buyers would demand. Her deformed ankle might have made him think she was worth less than what the brothel would pay, and she would have been mortified to have him look at her body more closely than he had. If he'd wanted her for his own pleasure, he would have insisted on seeing and touching before he bought. He truly had bought her to serve his sister, and that she would do with her whole heart. She would prove to him that he got good value for his four hundred denarii.

He had a long stride, and he walked very fast. The thick crowd parted ahead of him and closed behind him. She'd fallen enough behind that she was having to dodge people. He wasn't wearing his helmet. As short as she was, it was hard to keep track of his head as so many people pressed around her, blocking her view.

What if she lost sight of him and then couldn't find him? What if he thought she was trying to run away?

"Wait, master."

◆

Titus turned to look back at his new slave. As she squeezed past the two men waving their arms as they argued, he saw the limp.

He frowned as she caught up with him. "That limp. How long have you had it?" He rubbed the back of his neck. "Is it getting better?"

"Since I was five, master. I will always limp." She bowed her head and stood very still.

A string of curses ended in plunging eyebrows. "I paid four hundred for a cripple?"

He rolled his eyes and shook his head. How could he have been so stupid as to buy her without checking for defects?

It was those eyes and what she said about his sister that made him do it. He would never have been so careless buying a horse. He'd been taken for a fool. With that limp, he could have argued the trader down to the 350 the brothel would have paid. She was worth buying at the lower price, but he didn't have an extra fifty denarii to waste.

◆

The master's cursing pulled Miriam's gaze from the paving stones to his face. Her stomach leaped, then knotted as disgust twisted his features. Disgust with his purchase...with her. Anger simmered in his eyes. She bowed her head and waited for another explosion.

A cripple—that's what she was, and the trader had cheated him. But if she'd revealed that and lost the sale, she would have paid dearly. She'd already seen how much the trader enjoyed caning one slave who showed disrespect by rolling his eyes. If the sale had fallen through, he would have made her pay with pain for the money she lost him. He'd left her alone because he thought a virgin would bring a higher price, but his desire to punish her would overcome that. The brothel wouldn't care at all if she was beaten and used before they bought her.

What if the officer took her back and demanded the return of his money? Surely the slave trader would be afraid to make a Roman officer angry by refusing. Then he'd beat her and take her for losing him the extra fifty denarii, and she'd end up in the brothel before nightfall.

Oh, God! Please! Make him want to keep me even with my limp.

She swallowed the lump rising in her throat. "Please don't take me back, master. I can't run well, but I was always able to do everything my old master wanted. Truly, I can cook fit for a banquet for a few sesterces and clean so even old things look new. I can do everything your sister might need as her maid. I promise I'll serve her with all my heart and work so hard you'll be glad you bought me."

Titus looked down at those dark brown eyes. They were no longer simply serious. Deep fear pulsed within them. The strange calmness in her voice was gone. Desperation put a quaver in it.

Her fear was justified. She'd never bring 350 at auction. She'd be sold directly to the brothel. That was a brutal place, and her bad ankle would provoke greater cruelty from any cruel man. She wouldn't last a month. Something about those eyes...he couldn't send her there now.

Father would never have taken her back when he learned she was a cripple. One time a slave lost half his leg in an accident at the northern estate. Father merely had the overseer find something the crippled man could still do.

It wasn't her fault he'd paid too much. Besides, a limp wouldn't keep her from doing what he'd bought her for. Gratitude for him keeping her should make her work hard for him and serve Claudia better. That might be worth an extra fifty denarii in the long run.

The corner of his mouth pulled up as he looked down at her pretty face. She was desperately eager to please him. He wanted a hard worker, and whatever she could do came in an appealing package, even with a bad leg. She was worth trying out before he made his final decision.

"I didn't buy you to compete in footraces, so your limp doesn't matter."

The look in her eyes as relief flooded through her was...joyful. Not what he expected from a new slave. Then one of the most beautiful smiles he'd ever seen lit her whole face.

"Thank you, master. I'll do everything I can to make you and your sister glad you bought me."

He nodded once. "It's a good thing I rode. It would be too slow a walk to the house otherwise. Come on."

He turned his back on her and walked to where his stallion was tied, but this time he shortened his stride enough for her to keep up. When they reached it, he turned to face her.

"Can you ride?"

The look of nervous uncertainty on her face as she stared at his stallion was quickly replaced by one of grim determination. "I can try to do anything you tell me."

His lips twitched as he suppressed the smile. It was likely she'd never been on a horse before, and his was a big one. She probably would try to do whatever he told her.

"Come here."

She limped over and stood right in front of him. He placed his hands on her waist and lifted her up to set her on the horse's back.

"Swing your leg over and slide forward to make room for me."

◆

Miriam did as the master told her. Her tunic was pushed up, revealing her bare legs and the odd shape of her ankle where shattered bones had healed wrong. He wrapped his hand around her calf and slid it down to feel her ankle, just as he would with a horse's leg. His touch was gentle, but she still had to fight against jerking away from him. His shrug as he removed his hand was somehow comforting. Her defect really must not matter to him, just as he said.

He laid the reins across his stallion's withers and reached across her leg to grab the mane before jumping up to toss his leg across the horse's rump. He wrapped one arm around her waist and pulled her snugly against him as he slid forward into position for riding.

She'd never been so close to a man before, and his muscular arm around her waist, his chest pressing against her back, and his legs touching hers made her stomach twist. She tried to slide forward a little to get away from him, but he pulled her back against his chest.

"Sit still."

She looked down as the heat overspread her cheeks and surged to the tips of her ears.

◆

Titus's mouth twisted into a crooked smile as he watched her ears turning bright pink. At least the slave trader hadn't lied about her being a virgin. She felt soft and womanly as he shifted his arm a little higher. A cook, a housemaid, a lady's maid…and his evening entertainment. A limp probably didn't matter when he was getting all that for four hundred denarii.

He nudged his horse into a walk and started the trip home.

Chapter 40

Asking the Impossible

Miriam breathed a sigh of relief when her new master finally rode through a gate into a walled outer courtyard and past a garden to the stable in the rear. To be held that close by a master...memories of what happened to her mother kept poking their way into her thoughts.

A man stepped out of the slave quarters attached to the stable. The master reined in as the man bowed.

"Master Titus, I'm Nestor. Master Philip sent me to serve you and your sister however you need."

That was the first time she'd heard the master's name. It fit him somehow.

Master Titus placed his hand on her shoulder and pushed. "Bend over."

She leaned over until her face was almost on the horse's neck. He swung his right leg over her head and slid off. Then he strode to his new steward, leaving Miriam mounted.

The stallion fidgeted as it watched the master and the strange man. The more it moved, the faster Miriam's heart beat. Finally, she could stand it no longer. As she had seen Master Titus do, she swung her leg over and slid off.

For a short woman sliding off a tall horse, it was a long way down. She stumbled as her feet hit the ground and fell back into its side. Her bottom hit the ground as the horse snorted and shied away from her.

She threw her arms up to cover her head, but its hooves were much too close. She squeezed her eyes shut.

Two strong hands were suddenly under her arms and lifting her back to her feet.

"You should have waited for me to take you down." He brushed the dust off her tunic as he spoke. She would rather have done that herself.

"Are you hurt?"

"No, master. I know now that I should have waited, but I thought he wanted me off. I won't do that again."

"No harm done as long as you haven't hurt yourself so you can't work."

"I'm ready to work, master. What did you want me to do first?"

"I want to move my sister Claudia into this house tomorrow. Do whatever it takes to get it ready for her."

"Yes, master." She bowed and headed for the kitchen door.

Did he really mean what she was sure she'd heard? Get a whole house ready by tomorrow? All by herself? There didn't appear to be anyone else there except the steward.

It was a large house. It would have several bedchambers on the second floor in addition to the women's room, plus at least a dining room, sitting room, bath area, and kitchen downstairs surrounding a central courtyard. That would be a huge task even if it was already quite clean.

Miriam drew a deep breath and blew it out slowly. She'd told him she could do whatever his sister needed, so she would try. Somehow, she must get it done. He could still change his mind about keeping her.

She squared her shoulders. If she had to work all night, so be it. Maybe he'd only beat her or use the lash if she didn't get it all done.

Anything would be better than being returned and sold to the brothel.

◆

Nestor watched the slave girl limp into the house. She would need help with the cleaning as soon as possible, or the house would never be ready in time.

He'd walked through all the rooms when he oversaw the delivery of everything Master Philip sent from his own house to ensure Claudia's comfort. The house had been empty for too long. It was in desperate need of a thorough cleaning. The previous renters hadn't bothered to keep it as clean as they should, so it needed scrubbing, not just dusting. But three or four slaves could get it ready by tomorrow morning.

Master Titus remounted and turned the stallion toward the gate.

"If you wish, master, I can get a cart from Master Philip's stable to bring back the cook and all the other house slaves in one trip. Then I'll take the cook to the market while the others start cleaning. The kitchen still needs stocking."

"I'm not going back to the slave market. Miriam is supposed to know how to cook. She'll do that as well as keeping the house and serving my sister's needs. If she works hard enough, I won't have to buy any more slaves right away. I hadn't planned on Claudia coming. It's half a month until my next payday, so this month money will be very tight. In the future, we need to keep expenses below 500 denarii a month, and 145 of that goes to the rent."

He untied the larger purse from his belt and tossed it to Nestor. "There's 800 in there. Take what you need for the market, and lock the rest up in the strongbox. Check with Philip's steward to find out where to pay the rent, then take care of it. It's two weeks until I get paid again. I'm not sure what else we still need to buy, but that will have to last until then."

The master's jaw clenched, and a scowl accompanied his next words. "When my brother arranged my father's death, he stole my inheritance as well. I need to save at least a thousand a month if I'm to build up reserves to support us after I finish my tour of duty in five years."

Nestor fought to blank his face so the master wouldn't see his utter astonishment. One small woman couldn't do the work of three. But if there was no money, it would do no good to point out that was impossible.

"Very well, master. It's some distance to the market. I'll take Miriam to get food and other supplies this morning, if you don't have anything more urgent you want me to do. The house will need many hours of cleaning, and she can get started on that this afternoon."

Without any help, Miriam could get the house ready. It would just take longer. A smile pulled at the corner of Nestor's mouth. Master Philip would welcome that delay of two or three days. Four would be even better.

From the back of his stallion, Master Titus looked down at Nestor.

"That sounds good. I'm going to check on Claudia before I head down to the palace garrison. I'll tell her she'll be moving in here with me tomorrow. I'll be back this evening."

As he headed toward the gate, the master turned in his saddle. "Tell Miriam to prepare a good dinner for me. I'd better taste her cooking before Claudia has to eat it tomorrow."

"Yes, master." Nestor was so shocked at this last command that he answered reflexively. Master Titus had trotted out the gate before Nestor could tell him it was impossible for one slave to clean everything by tomorrow and make dinner as well.

Nestor stared at the kitchen door. Poor Miriam. His new master had no idea how much time it took to prepare a dinner or a house. It was already mid-morning, and it would be mid-day before they could get back from the market.

He frowned as he shook his head. The master wanted her to do the full day's work of three in a single afternoon. It wasn't a steward's job to clean, but today he'd make an exception. Without his help, she'd never finish in time. With his help...his lips tightened. Even two couldn't do the work of three, but maybe they could do enough.

Would Master Titus beat or lash a slave for not doing exactly what he wanted, even if what he wanted was impossible? Nestor was only on loan, so he wasn't worried about being punished himself. But what would the master do to Miriam?

◆

As Titus rode down the street, a broad smile proclaimed his satisfaction. He had a house and two people to take care of it for him. One cost him nothing, and the other was damaged but would probably be worth what he'd paid. He hadn't expected to find a single slave who could take care of both the meals and his sister's needs.

All would be ready for Claudia's arrival tomorrow. As soon as she moved in, he could start helping her recover from the grief that was crushing her.

◆

Miriam walked from the kitchen through the storeroom into the dining room. With each step, her heart beat faster. The house had been empty for a while, and a coat of dust lay everywhere. The floors hadn't been scrubbed in a long time, and what should have been a bright mosaic floor in the dining room was dulled with grime. As she stood in the dining room door, her gaze swept the cobblestone courtyard and drew a sigh. The bumpy cobblestone surface was much more difficult to keep clean than brick or tile. She crossed the courtyard to check the bath and the sitting room. Filthy, just like everything else.

She climbed the stairs to the U-shaped balcony. There was one large bedchamber just to the right off the stairs. It was a corner room furnished with a bed, a chair, a woman's dressing table, an intricately carved chest, and a cupboard that matched. Two windows and a fresco of waterfalls and mountains made it a bright and cheery room for the mistress.

A large women's room with two looms and two padded wicker chairs was right past it. One small room opened at the head of the stairs and four small rooms off the left leg of the U. Four of the five small rooms were empty, but the largest of them on the corner opposite the mistress's room had two good-sized windows and was also furnished as a bedchamber. That must be the master's.

As she limped from room to room, her heart spiraled down. How was she ever going to get such a filthy house ready by tomorrow morning? There wasn't a single room that didn't need a thorough scrubbing to be what she considered clean enough.

A tear escaped as she stood in the master's room, and she brushed it aside. She dropped to her knees and raised her hands. "Please help me, Jesus. I can't fail him, or he might take me back. I'm sure you told me his sister needs me, so I have to make him want to keep me. But how am I ever going to do all this?" More tears trickled down her cheeks as she slumped back on her heels.

The footsteps behind her snapped her head around. The steward stood behind her, fists on his hips. How much had he heard? Her breath caught. What if he told the master she was a Christian?

Then his mouth curved into a smile. "Grace and peace to you in the name of our Lord, Jesus." He held out his hand to help her stand.

"And to you, my brother." She flicked the tears off her cheeks and put her hand in his. *Thank you, God, for giving me a brother here.* She'd missed the fellowship of believers so much since Master Alexander's house was seized and his slaves all sold to new masters.

"I know the master told you to do more than a single slave possibly could, but I'll help you with the cleaning after we get back from the market. I'll go with you today to show you where it is and to help you carry some of what we must buy. We'll carry what you'll need for tonight and tomorrow morning, and I'll arrange to get the rest tomorrow."

"Oh, thank you, Nestor! The whole house is filthy, and there's no way I could finish in time by myself."

With two of them working, there was at least a chance of getting the house presentable by tomorrow. She and Nestor could eat some bread and cheese that evening and keep working until he decided to quit. She'd work all night, if that was what it would take.

"I hate to add to your burden, but the master wants you to prepare him a good dinner tonight so he can test your cooking before his sister eats it. He'll need breakfast tomorrow, too."

Miriam's jaw dropped. She fought fresh tears. "Make a dinner, too? He's going to expect a three-course Roman meal. That takes hours to prepare. If I'm going to get any of the house cleaned, I can't do that."

She bowed her head and closed her eyes. *Oh God, please give me strength to do all that he asks. If I can't, please let him be satisfied with whatever I manage to do. Please don't let him take me back.*

She took a deep breath and stood up.

"I'll try to do everything he wants. God will give me strength for this. I think perhaps something simple but delicious will have to do for his dinner tonight. I make a pork stew that was my old master's favorite, and it doesn't take long to get started. Then it can simmer while we clean. There isn't enough time to both clean and cook a full dinner." She rubbed her cheek. "Do you think he'll want a clean house more than a Roman dinner?"

Nestor shrugged. "It's what I'd want if it was my sister. I know it's what Master Philip would choose for Mistress Claudia, and I still belong to him."

Miriam squared her shoulders. "I'll try to get it all cleaned, but first we'll clean the mistress's and the master's bedchambers and the kitchen. If you can sweep out the worst of the dust, then I can scrub the floors. Maybe we can both wipe down walls. I'm too short to reach all the way up to the ceilings. If you do the high part, I can finish the rest. I'll start on the kitchen while you sweep. After I start the stew, I can scrub the bedchamber floors while it simmers. Then we can work on the dining room and the bath."

She drew a deep breath and blew it out slowly. She had a plan, but was there enough time to complete it to the master's satisfaction? She ran her fingers through her hair. "Maybe I can get the women's room and the sitting room ready by tomorrow as well if I clean again after I serve him dinner."

Nestor shook his head. "It's too much to do it all today, but when we get back from the market, I'll help you clean as much as we can. Master Philip would consider whatever we get done enough and appreciate how hard we tried. Perhaps Master Titus is a reasonable man, too."

"I'll need bread for his dinner and breakfast, but there isn't enough time to both bake and clean. Is there a bakery where we can buy a loaf or two?"

"No, but there's usually someone selling fresh bread. We should start for the market now to make sure some will still be there."

"First I need to check what we have in the kitchen and the garden."

The corner of her mouth lifted. She couldn't walk well, but she was an expert in the kitchen. The master should feel she was worth more than he paid after he ate a few of her dinners.

Miriam followed Nestor back to the kitchen. He leaned against the door frame as she checked the cupboards and storeroom. She made a mental list of what she would need to buy for a delicious dinner and tasty breakfast for the master and a lunch suitable for the mistress, in case he brought her home early.

She found brooms, buckets, and rags that would do for the cleaning that awaited them. She found plenty of pots, pans, and utensils for cooking and all the dishes that she'd need for serving the food. Some of the dishes were surprisingly beautiful for a rented house.

What she didn't find was any food. She and Nestor would have to buy everything. The master had been angry about spending more on her than he had to, and he hadn't bought all the slaves the household needed. Was money a problem for him?

"I'm ready. Does the master have plenty of money, or do I need to be careful about how much I spend?"

Nestor's eyebrows rose, then lowered as a smile appeared. "Careful. The master needs us to run the household on 350 denarii or less a month. He wasn't planning to support his sister, and money will be tight until his next payday. There won't be much to spare even after that." He smiled down at her. "That's why he's hoping you can do the work of three people, at least for a while."

"I cost him 50 denarii more than he needed to pay for me. I'll try to be worth the extra money." She sighed. "He was sorry he bought me when he saw my limp. I'll try to do everything he wants so he won't be sorry he kept me. May God help me do it."

Chapter 41

Help for a Sister

Miriam surveyed the garden before she and Nestor headed toward the gate. Chickens for eggs. A large garden with all the usual vegetables. Fruit trees and grapevines just past the vegetables. Best of all, a well-planted herb garden. Her mother's skill as a cook depended on her creative use of herbs. She'd passed that knowledge on to Miriam. Add to that what Miriam had learned in Master Alexander's kitchen, and she was certain the master would love her cooking when she had time to prepare Roman meals.

"There's so much here. We shouldn't have to buy any vegetables now, and there's plenty for me to dry for winter."

"Tell me what kind of racks you need for that, and I'll see that we have them."

"Do you think the master can afford a cow? I can make our butter and some kinds of cheese, and that should save him money in the long run. Master Alexander didn't drink it, but some of his Roman guests liked cow's milk. And maybe the neighbors would buy some from us."

"I'll look into that." Nestor handed her a small basket and picked up two large ones. "I know where to get one for less than you might expect."

Miriam picked up another large one and placed the smaller one in it before hanging it on her arm. "I know what we need now. Let's go to market."

The house was on a street that ran uphill from the main road, so the first part of their walk was an easy half mile downhill. Then they followed the main road down the hill to the east for half a mile to where it turned and headed back to the west for another three quarters of a mile. The distance wouldn't have been a problem for most people, but her leg began bothering her a little by the time they reached the main road. By the time they reached the market, she was limping badly.

Miriam ran her hand through her hair as she scanned the stalls. "When will the master get paid?"

"He said two weeks."

"Then we'll need wheat, barley, olive oil, cheese, honey, and wine enough for two and a half weeks. I don't want to spend too much of what has to last until he's paid. I'll need pork for tonight's stew and a bottle of red wine for the master to drink, fruit and cheese for breakfast, and enough bread to last until I can bake tomorrow."

"We can carry enough for tonight and tomorrow ourselves. I'll borrow a cart from Master Philip to get the rest tomorrow. Just tell me what we need."

"I have all the herbs I need in the garden, but we'll have to buy some spices. I know they're expensive, but that's what makes my cooking taste so good. That and just enough wine to get the perfect flavor. I need red and white. I can pick some that taste good without being too expensive." She squared her shoulders. "Time to start bargaining." She grinned at him. "I like that part of shopping...getting a price that's low but still fair to everyone."

Nestor followed her from vendor to vendor as she tried to find the best value for each purchase. Finally, she had everything either ordered for the next day or placed in their baskets.

"You're good at this, Miriam. The master should be impressed when I tell him how much you saved him."

"But it's taken too long to get everything." A sigh escaped. "We have so much to do to get the house ready. I know we can't do it all before tomorrow, but I pray we can get enough done that he's satisfied. He was angry when he first saw how I limp. I promised him I could do everything he wanted in spite of it, but that was before I saw the house. God told me his sister needs me, and I really want the master to keep me."

"I want that, too. We'll get enough done to satisfy a reasonable master. Time will tell if he is one."

It was mid-day when they started back up the hill toward the house. Miriam's leg was hurting, and her limp was slowing them down. A short distance from the market, Nestor turned off the main road onto a narrow street.

"This is a good shortcut. It runs into the upper stretch of the main road just before our street. It probably cuts the distance in half from the market to the house. It's steeper but much quicker."

Relief drew her smile. "I'm glad we'll be going back a shorter way. I'm not a fast walker."

◆

As they started up the hill, Nestor shortened his stride to match hers. "This will be a good shortcut to remember. You'll probably be going to market at least once a week."

Not a fast walker was too generous. It had taken almost twice as long to get to the market as it did when he went by himself. He had long legs and a quick stride, but even considering that, she was slow.

Finally, they reached the house and entered the kitchen.

Miriam picked up a washrag and dusted the table. "We'll leave it all here until I get the storeroom cleaned."

Her shoulders drooped. "There isn't a single place in the whole house that doesn't need scrubbing."

Nestor could see her fighting tears again as she looked around the kitchen at the dust and grime. "I'll do the storeroom. You can start on the kitchen."

Her eyes brightened. "I can't thank you enough for being willing to help me like this. I know it's not a job for the house steward."

He rested his hand on her shoulder. "You don't have to thank me again, Miriam. Today I'm happy to help my sister bear this burden. Master Philip told me I was to do everything possible to make sure Mistress Claudia is well cared for, and helping you get this filthy house ready certainly fits that charge."

◆

Miriam headed toward the well in the inner courtyard to get some water as Nestor walked into the storeroom to begin dusting and sweeping. As soon as she got the kitchen counter clean, she could cut up the vegetables and pork for the stew. Once she had the stew simmering, she would scrub the kitchen floor. Then she could move on to the bedchambers. Her mother had always said the way to move a mountain was one boulder at a time. These were big boulders, but, with God's and Nestor's help, she would manage to move them all.

Chapter 42

WILLING TO BE PLEASED

For the first time, Septimus Corvinus walked through the gate into the stable yard of the Perinthus garrison. His brother Marcus had warned him about the rough seas that plagued voyages near the end of the sailing season, but a new tribune had little choice over where his first posting would be or when Rome would want him there. After too many days having trouble keeping food down, he was even looking forward to what a garrison cook called dinner as long as the ground didn't move.

As he glanced around the yard, his back straightened. Who should be there but the younger brother of Marcus's best friend, Lucius Drusus. Septimus had met Titus five years earlier when he'd stopped by the Drusus estate for lunch with his brother. He'd know Titus Drusus anywhere, and for him to be one of the more senior tribunes who could provide advice and maybe help in making the best of this posting was remarkably good fortune.

Titus strode toward him, and Septimus prepared to greet him. But Drusus only flicked a glance his way and walked past without even a nod of recognition.

Septimus's lips tightened. If Drusus thought himself too important to speak with him, that was Drusus's loss.

"I need a pack mule until tomorrow." Drusus's words to the centurion caught Septimus's attention.

"Yes, tribune. Soldier, get Tribune Drusus a pack mule."

Septimus turned to watch the man take a mule from the corral and put a pack saddle on it. Drusus also watched with his arms crossed. As the soldier finished cinching the saddle, Drusus walked to where his stallion was tied, mounted, and rode over to take the mule's lead. Then he kicked his horse into a trot and headed out the gate.

Septimus rubbed his cheek. Why would Drusus be needing a pack mule for only one night?

He strolled over to the centurion. "Wasn't that Claudius Drusus? He's the brother of my brother's friend. It's good to see him out here in Thracia. How long has he been here?"

"That's Drusus. Four years or so."

"Why the pack mule?"

"He's moving from a rented room into a house."

"A house? Is he getting married?"

"No. His sister just came from Rome, and she'll be living with him."

"That will be nice for both of them. His sister's a lovely girl."

The centurion nodded. It was clear that he considered the conversation ended as he turned his attention back to one of the horses that had just gone lame.

What a stroke of luck. Marcus gave a banquet just before Septimus's departure, and Lucius Drusus had been there. Many were talking about the unexpected disappearance of Lucius's sister, Claudia. Lucius was claiming she'd been kidnapped. He was offering a handsome reward for information leading to her return. A very different version of the story emerged when Lucius got drunk. Septimus overheard Lucius complaining privately to his brother that she'd run away to avoid marrying Flavius Sabinus. Sabinus was furious about that and told Lucius he'd better find her and drag her back to marry him if he knew what was good for him. He'd searched all over Rome and hadn't turned up any trace of her.

Septimus had inherited an estate when his father died, but it was a small one. His net worth exceeded the 100,000 denarii required to be a member of the equestrian order, but not by much. The 10,000-denarii reward would come in very handy.

He hurried to his room to write a letter to Lucius. If he could get it included in the mail dispatch being sent to Rome tomorrow, he could be a much wealthier man in less than a month's time. Lucius could pay his brother, who would get it to his own steward promptly.

He fought the grin that threatened to turn into a chuckle. This would be the easiest 10,000 he ever made.

When Titus rode through the gate and back to the stable area, he led the borrowed pack mule carrying everything he'd had in his lodgings. He wasn't a man who accumulated many things. It had been easy to pack everything onto a single mule. He only had a couple of boxes that contained his library, some civilian clothes, and assorted items of military clothing, armor, and weapons.

As he dismounted, Nestor came from the kitchen.

"Good evening, master." He looked at the mule. "Shall I take it all to your bedchamber?"

"Yes." Titus sniffed the air, and a smile appeared. "Is that what I think it is?"

"Yes, master. Miriam has prepared an excellent dinner for you."

"So I bought myself a cook after all. The trader hid her being a cripple, so I don't really know if she's anything he claimed."

Nestor untied the first box and lifted it onto his shoulder. "You would have been pleased to see her in the marketplace, master. She was very careful to get a good bargain for you on everything, and she spent only what was necessary to run your household until a little after your next payday."

"Good. What I really want to see is how good a job she's done cleaning. Our house in Rome was always spotless. I want Claudia to feel at home here."

As they passed through the kitchen, Titus tipped his head back as he inhaled the tantalizing aroma. The corner of his mouth lifted. It would be a good dinner tonight.

He glanced down as they entered the courtyard, and his mouth turned down. There was too much dirt on the cobblestones. Miriam needed to do a much better job if her cleaning was to be up to the standards that Claudia was accustomed to in Rome. Sloppy work was a sign of laziness, and that was not something he would tolerate, especially from a slave he'd paid too much for.

Nestor led the way up the stairs and along the balcony to the master's bedchamber. When the door swung open, Titus's frown vanished. The room was immaculate. It looked like the walls had even been washed. Clearly, she could do a good job if she tried.

Titus turned to Nestor. "I want to see Claudia's room."

"This way, master." Nestor lead Titus past four small rooms to the main bedchamber.

Nestor opened the door, and Titus entered. Again, he found an immaculate room with freshly washed walls. Titus's approving nod was accompanied by a slight smile. This was more like it. She'd done a thorough job on both his room and Claudia's. Maybe he just needed to tell her to keep the courtyard clean.

"Where is she?"

"Still cleaning, master. There are many hours of cleaning still needed to get the whole house clean. It was very dirty from sitting empty for some time. She's been working hard on it all afternoon, ever since we returned from the market."

They descended the stairs to look for her and found her in the room with the bath tub. The floor was already spotless, and she was washing the walls when Titus walked in.

Miriam spun to face him and bowed her head. "Master. Your dinner is ready. Did you want me to serve it now?"

"First I want to talk with you about the cleaning."

Her whole body tensed, and she kept her head bowed. Titus frowned. She was acting like she was afraid of him.

"Look at me when I'm talking to you."

She raised her head, and he found himself looking into those serious brown eyes again.

"Yes, master."

"I was not happy with the state of the courtyard when I saw it."

Fear filled her eyes. She sucked in a breath and bit her lip.

"But I'm pleased with how you've cleaned the two bedchambers. I'll expect you to clean everything that well in the future."

"Yes, master." She let the breath out. The fear faded from her eyes, and her mouth relaxed into a shy smile.

◆

In the future—those words were music to Miriam's ears. The master was satisfied enough with what she'd finished that he wasn't planning to return her.

Thank you, God, that he's patient enough to give me more time to finish. Thank you so much that he isn't like Mistress Xanthe.

Miriam always tried to do her best, but that had never been good enough for her first mistress. She'd enjoyed hitting Miriam for anything and even for nothing at all. Master Titus was a powerful man with a broad chest and muscular arms. If he liked to hit, he'd be a dangerous master.

"Now that's clear, you can go prepare to serve me dinner."

"Yes, master."

♦

The corner of Titus's mouth lifted. One word of praise and her pretty smile appeared. It seemed genuine, too, not just something to curry his favor.

She bowed and limped out the door ahead of him.

He turned his attention to Nestor again. "Take everything into my room, and tell her I'll be ready to dine as soon as I clean up."

Titus had been looking forward all day to the three-course dinner of the Roman upper classes. It had been too long since he'd eaten anything for dinner other than the porridges and stews prepared by the garrison cook or the cook at his lodging house. Those kept body and soul together, but that was about all that could be said for them.

Salad, some delicious meat dish as first table, a sweet dessert as second table. His mouth started watering at the mere thought. That scrumptious aroma that wrapped around him as he walked through the kitchen would have been from the second course, but it promised an evening of true dining pleasure. If the second smelled that good, what would the first and third be like?

♦

Nestor stopped beside Miriam as he headed out to get the rest of the master's belongings. "The master was very pleased with how you cleaned his room and that of the mistress. I think we'll find him to be a reasonable man."

"Oh, I hope so. I've served a mistress who was never satisfied. She used to hit me almost every time she saw me. I know God told me I was meant to be here to serve his sister, but I'm so glad He's given me a master who's willing to be pleased with something I do."

"Time will tell, but I think you have one." Nestor gave her an encouraging smile and headed out the door to fetch the remainder of the master's belongings.

Chapter 43

PROVING HER WORTH

A basin and a large pitcher of water were waiting for Titus on a table in the bath chamber. A full bath would have felt good just then, but he was eager enough for that three-course meal that he settled for washing his face and hands in the basin. He'd have Miriam fill the tub with hot water for a good soak after dinner.

Nestor was carrying the final box into the courtyard when Titus emerged from the bath chamber.

"Tell her to serve me now in the dining room."

"Yes, master." With the box still on his shoulder, Nestor stepped back into the kitchen.

◆

Nestor watched Miriam stir the stew before lifting the spoon to her mouth for a taste. The aroma was mouthwatering, possibly the most tempting Nestor had ever smelled. That was saying something since Philip had an excellent chef and under-chef.

"The master's ready for you to serve him." Nestor inhaled the heavenly aroma. "He should be delighted. I hope there will be some left over for me."

Her eyes warmed at his compliment. "I made plenty. Unless the master tells me otherwise, we'll always get to eat the leftovers." She dipped the spoon in the pot again and offered him a taste.

He blew on it and took a sip. His eyebrows shot up as he licked his lips. "Master Titus will love this. You could give Master Philip's chef lessons."

"Mother taught me most of what I know. She cooked for my first master until his wife sold her when I was ten."

Nestor's lips tightened. "I don't remember my mother, but serving in Master Philip's house gave me a new family."

"I'm sorry you had to leave them, but I'm so glad you're here. I can't thank you enough for everything you did today. I could never have gotten enough done without your help."

"Don't tell the master I helped clean. We want him to appreciate how valuable you are. You'd better serve him now. I still need to take the last of his things up."

Nestor returned to the courtyard and climbed the stairs to begin arranging the master's belongings in his chamber. A smile tugged at his lips as he remembered the taste of her stew. It was good that Master Philip had loaned him to Master Titus. It was an honor to be chosen to watch over the woman his master loved. Eating Miriam's cooking would be a fitting reward for his effort.

Upon entering the dining room, Titus was pleased to see it was as immaculate as the bed chambers had been. It contained the usual couches arranged around a low table for banquets, but it also contained a table and four chairs more suitable for use by Greek women and for less formal meals. He'd grown accustomed to dining at tables during his posting to Thracia, so he seated himself rather than reclining.

When she entered through the door to the storeroom that connected the dining room and kitchen, she carried a tray with a goblet, a bottle of wine, and a small pitcher of water for mixing to taste.

She placed the goblet before him and filled it to about half with water. Then she added about half as much wine and waited for him to taste it.

He took a sip and nodded approvingly. She'd selected good wine and diluted it exactly as he liked it. Not a bad beginning to a real dinner. She left the bottle and pitcher on the table, bowed deeply, and disappeared into the storeroom.

When she returned, the tray held a large, steaming bowl of stew and some bread. The rich aroma that had fueled his anticipation filled the room.

He took one look at the bowl, and a frown appeared as he raised his eyes from the bowl to her.

"Where's the first course?"

◆

Miriam's heart raced. She'd made a terrible mistake when she cleaned instead of making the three-course dinner the master expected. She bowed her head and stepped back from the table to get out of striking range.

"I beg pardon, master. There was time for cleaning or cooking but not both. I tried to guess which would be more important to you. I thought it would be preparing the house for your sister's arrival tomorrow. I know now it's the full Roman dinner, and I won't make that mistake again. I beg pardon for only making you a stew tonight."

She raised her head just enough to glance at him to see if he was still frowning, then she bowed even lower when she saw his frown had deepened. Her apology had done nothing to appease him. She stayed beyond his reach. Even one strike from that heavily muscled arm would hurt more than anything Mistress Xanthe had done. Bruises she'd lived with for her first ten years, but his blow might break a bone.

The spontaneous responses that had given some protection during those years with her cruel mistress kicked back in. She knew what it took to survive serving an angry master.

◆

Titus frowned and shook his head. She was too frightened whenever he was the least displeased. The trader may have lied about her coming from a household that treated its slaves well. Only frequent cruelty would make a slave that jumpy. No slave of his should cringe every time he spoke to her.

"Look at me, Miriam."

She raised her head. Fear pulsed in her eyes.

"Now come back to me at the table."

Her steps were halting, but she obeyed. She obviously knew she was getting close enough for him to hit her, and she was expecting it. Time to break her of that.

"Your guess was correct. It is more important to me that my sister is well served than for me to get the three-course meal I've been looking forward to all day. Your stew smells delicious, and it will do for tonight. I'll normally want the full meal when Claudia is here, but I'm not angry that you didn't get it made today."

She'd been as tight as a drawn bowstring when she came back to him, but her whole body relaxed as he spoke to her. Much better.

"However, you are doing something that I don't like."

There was fear in her eyes again before she bowed her head.

"What, master? I can stop it."

"You're doing it again. Look at me."

◆

Miriam raised her head to look into the master's eyes. No anger simmered there. They even seemed friendly, and the frown had been replaced by a slight smile.

"I don't like you acting like you think I'm going to hit you all the time. Cruelty had no place in my father's house; it won't have one in mine. I don't hit slaves for no good reason. As long as you try to do your best for me and work hard, you have no reason to fear me. That means no more cringing, no more bowing your head like you have been, no more stepping back quickly like you expect me to strike. And when I speak to you, I want you to look at me."

"Yes, master."

It sounded almost too good to be true. She'd asked God to place her in a kind household; the master's words promised that it would be.

God, please forgive me for being so afraid. You brought this tribune to keep me from the brothel. I should have known You'd give me a kind master who doesn't even mind me being a cripple.

His smile grew bigger. "Good. Now we have that settled, I can eat."

He closed his eyes and tilted his head back slightly as he inhaled the tantalizing aroma.

"If this tastes as good as it smells, I should enjoy what you've made me."

He filled his spoon, then blew on it to cool it a little before placing it in his mouth. His eyebrows rose, then dropped as a broad smile appeared.

"This is delicious. I'm glad you chose cleaning over cooking. I'll want this again."

"Yes, master." She bowed before returning to her post by the wall.

Master Titus finished his first bowl as she stood by the storeroom door, waiting to do whatever he asked.

"Very good. Bring me another serving."

"Yes, master." She stepped forward and picked up the bowl, bowing quickly before she carried it back to the kitchen.

Nestor was sitting at the table as she stepped out of the storeroom. His smile mirrored hers when she carried the empty bowl to the stew pot and refilled it.

"I see he liked your stew."

Miriam beamed. "Yes, and he said he'd like me to serve it again."

What a relief that he liked her stew and was satisfied with what she'd cleaned. She hadn't done everything the master told her to do, but he understood that she'd done the best she could in the time she had. She still hadn't cleaned the women's room or the sitting room, but she could complete those before his sister came if she worked all night.

He'd even talked about her cleaning better in the future and cooking the stew again. In the future and again—those words drew a smile. The master was planning to keep her.

Best of all, he'd said she had nothing to fear from him if she tried to do her best. She always did that, so he wouldn't be hitting her all the time like her first mistress, at least not if he meant what he said.

God had been so merciful in bringing Master Titus to buy her today.

She filled the bowl and carried it back to the dining room. When she set it down in front of him, his smile and nod triggered a silent song of thanksgiving in her heart.

As Titus finished the last of the stew and wiped his mouth, his gaze settled on Miriam as she stood awaiting his commands by the storeroom door. Whatever else she might be able to do, she certainly could cook. If the trader had known, she would have cost at least double what he'd paid.

She was a pretty thing, especially with that smile that broke out when he said she'd done something well. A delicious dinner, a relaxing bath, and a pretty slave to enjoy. This was turning into a much better evening than he'd expected.

"I'm ready for my bath now. I'll be in my bedchamber. Come get me when it's ready."

He rose and left the dining room.

◆

Miriam loaded the wine bottle and dirty dishes on the tray and carried them to the kitchen.

Nestor was finishing the second bowl of her stew. "Truly delicious, Miriam. Master Philip has a good cook, but this…it's amazing." His eyebrows dipped. "Is something wrong?"

"The master wants me to prepare his bath. I've never served a man in his bath before." Her cheeks turned scarlet as she anticipated pouring warm water over the master and bringing him a towel.

"You won't have to. If you prepare the water, I'll serve the master in the bath."

Grateful eyes mirrored the smile she gave Nestor. "Thank you so much, Nestor. I prayed so hard for a master who wouldn't..." She blushed again, and Nestor's nod meant she need say no more.

"That will also let me finish cleaning up the kitchen and start on cleaning the sitting room and the women's room. I want to get it all done before the master's breakfast in the morning. He might want to bring his sister home as soon as he eats."

She grabbed a bucket and limped to the well in the inner courtyard to draw the water to fill the tub the master would soak in. As soon as she'd filled it to the depth of her hand, she laid the kindling and wood in the firebox under the tub and lit it to start warming the water. She jumped when Nestor appeared beside her and poured a bucket of water into the tub.

"I've already placed the master's oils and scrapers on the shelf there. He may want to wash off first before soaking in this tub. In case he does, prepare a pitcher of hot water to put by that small washbasin. I'll finish filling the tub."

Miriam rested her hand on Nestor's arm. "I can't thank you enough for all you've done today."

His kind smile was accompanied by a pat on her shoulder. "It's my pleasure to help my sister in Christ."

◆

Titus was reading when Nestor appeared at his chamber door.

"Your bath is ready, master."

Titus's brow furrowed. "Where's Miriam?"

"Cleaning. I'll be attending your bath tonight and in the future."

"I see." A wry smile lifted one corner of his mouth. He didn't care who served him as long as he got his bath at the end of the day. He hadn't expected such modesty in a slave, even a virgin one, but she'd get over it after a few nights in his bed.

She was a funny little thing, but she tried hard to please him and certainly could cook. That alone was worth what he'd paid for her. Tomorrow he'd find out how well she would serve Claudia. After his bath, he'd find out how well she served him.

Titus felt refreshed and relaxed after a leisurely soak in the hot water. As he left the bath chamber and headed toward the stairs, he

heard quiet singing coming from the sitting room. He paused in the doorway. Miriam was on her knees by the far wall, scrubbing the floor. The contrast between the faded-looking dirty floor by the door and the bright mosaic pattern where she'd already washed was stark. For the first time, he had some appreciation for how much work she must have already put into the two bedchambers, the dining room, and the bath to have them looking as clean as they did.

The slave trader hadn't praised her domestic skills enough, but he had been truthful about one thing. She had a very pretty face, and any man would enjoy that lovely body. The cleaning could wait.

◆

A shiver rippled between Miriam's shoulders, and she stopped singing. Someone was watching her. When she looked back toward the door, her heart plunged. The master was standing in the doorway, bare-chested with only a towel wrapped around his waist.

No, God! Please, not this. I thought you'd delivered me from this. She dropped the rag into the pail and stood up. *Please don't let him.*

She bowed her head, closed her eyes, and waited for what she dreaded was coming.

"Come here, Miriam."

Those words sealed her fate.

◆

Titus leaned against the doorframe with his arms crossed, his smile growing as his anticipation grew. Miriam limped over and stopped four feet from him, her gaze fixed on the dirt-covered mosaic at his feet. His two steps closed the distance between them.

He placed his hands on her arms and slowly slid them up, then down. A jolt passed through her, and then the trembling began. If he hadn't tightened his grip, she would have crumpled at his feet.

What the...? He wasn't a man who took pleasure in a woman's pain. He was being gentle with her. Why was she so terrified of him?

He'd planned on her being his evening entertainment before Claudia came and later satisfying his needs after she finished helping his sister to bed. For some reason he couldn't explain, that no longer seemed so appealing. His little virgin slave would submit without a fight, but she would quench his pleasure with her shivers and silent tears.

"Look at me." When she raised those dark brown eyes to his, he saw desperate fear. She was losing her struggle to hold back tears. She swallowed hard as glistening eyes silently pleaded with him not to take her up the stairs.

"You can forget what your last owner said about me enjoying your lovely body tonight...or any other. I bought you to cook and clean and take care of Claudia. You won't have to be my nighttime entertainment as well. You don't have to be afraid of me as long as you try your best to do what I tell you and work hard."

"Yes, master."

The trembling stopped, and he released her arms. The relief flooding through her made her eyes sparkle and brought the beautiful smile he'd seen when he kept her despite being a cripple.

That smile made it almost too tempting to change his mind and take her. It really was part of why he bought her. Why had he made her that promise?

He prided himself on being a man of honor. A night of pleasure wasn't worth going back on his word, even to a slave. Now the promise had been made, he would keep it. Besides, how much pleasure could there be with a slave who was merely enduring his attentions because she had no choice?

"You've done a good job cleaning. If you continue to keep the house this well after Claudia comes, I'll be well pleased."

His approval of her work brought a happy glow to her eyes.

"You'll normally serve me breakfast just after dawn. Tomorrow morning, I'll explain what your special duties serving Claudia will be. You can go back to cleaning now."

"Yes, master." She bowed and returned to kneel by her pail. She wrung out the rag and started singing softly as she scrubbed more dirt from the mosaic floor.

As he turned to go upstairs, he glanced at her once more. Superb cook, hard worker, docile and eager to please. The slave trader hadn't taken advantage of him after all.

Miriam finished the sitting room a little before midnight and started on the women's room upstairs. It was the largest room in the house, so it took a long time to clean it as well as she wanted. She finished too late to bother going to bed. She wasn't sure where she was supposed to sleep, anyway. Nestor was sleeping in a room attached to the stables, but house slaves usually slept somewhere in the house. There were only two beds: one in the master's chamber and one for the mistress. She couldn't sleep in the bed that would be Mistress Claudia's. She'd ask Nestor where she should sleep tomorrow. As house steward, he would know.

Since the master said he wanted to eat right after dawn, she decided to start the bread and make his breakfast so it would be ready and waiting when he first came down. If he slept long enough, she might have hot bread straight from the oven for him. Surely that would be something to please even the pickiest master. She made scrumptious bread, even if she did say so herself.

Chapter 44

NOT YET

It was Claudia's last night under Philip's care. As she lay in her bed, the turmoil in her heart made it impossible to sleep. She still couldn't bear the thought that Father was gone, and now the man who'd become the light that pushed back the darkness wouldn't be with her either. How was she ever going to bear it when she didn't see him every day? How could she make it past the sadness without playing Conquest with him, reading poetry together, watching the sun set together?

The nightmares were as bad as ever, but holding Philip's hand while he read let her get back to sleep right away. First, she'd lost Father; now would she lose Philip? He'd become the most important person in her world, and she loved being with him, no matter what they were doing. He was the ugliest man she'd ever seen, but there was no one in the world she'd rather see.

There were so many things she loved about him: his kindness, his quick wit, the way he made her feel like she was somebody every time he talked with her or looked at her. She could be her real self with him. She didn't have to pretend she was happy when she was really sad or stupid when she really was as smart as he was. And he was so very smart. Talking with him was like talking with Father, except being close to him made her heart beat faster in a way she'd never felt before.

She was almost certain he loved her, too. So why hadn't he said anything about their future? If he loved her, shouldn't he have asked her to marry him? Had he not asked because he was afraid she'd reject him like Phoebe had? Should she tell him that she never wanted to leave him, that she wanted him to marry her? What would he say if she did?

But what if he only cared for her as a friend? What if he didn't love her as a woman, the way she loved him as a man?

The lions came, as usual, about midnight. Claudia would have to get past the nightmare herself tomorrow, so she tried. Tears flowed, but she buried her face in the pillow to muffle any sounds. She thought no one would hear, but suddenly Philip was at her bedside.

"Do you want me to read to you?"

She reached out to him.

"Maybe if you just hold my hand for a while."

"I can do that."

He pulled a chair up beside her bed and sat down. He took her hand in his, then caressed the back of it with his thumb.

The effect of the nightmare had passed, but he still held her hand.

After too short a time, he shifted on the chair. Before he could release her hand and rise, Claudia found the courage to ask the question burning in her heart and mind.

"Philip?"

"Yes?"

She drew a deep breath. The time was now. If she waited, she might never again have the chance to tell him how she felt.

"Titus is planning for me to move in with him tomorrow, but...I don't want to go. I want to stay with you."

There. She'd done it. She'd taken the risk of him saying what she didn't want to hear or saying what would make her heart sing.

◆

For a fleeting moment, the world froze for Philip. She'd just spoken the words that were uppermost in his own heart and mind, what he so longed to say to her as well.

His delight was beyond words, but then it was tempered by the obvious problem. She hated the followers of Jesus, and he loved Jesus with his whole heart.

"I want you to stay, too...but it isn't possible for me to marry you right now."

"If you want me to stay, why can't you marry me?" The pitch of her voice rose, and the slight tremor in it made the temptation to ask her harder to resist.

"I love you, Philip. It's not because you're rich, and I don't care if you're not handsome. I don't want to live without you...ever. I'm not sure I can."

She pulled his hand over against her cheek, and teardrops trickled across it, as they had so many times before.

He longed to say what she wanted to hear, but he couldn't. "I can't ask you to marry me...not yet."

"But why? Is it because you think I'm too poor now? I brought some jewelry so I do have something, but I thought you wouldn't care about that. I don't care at all what you have. I only want you. I want to be with you for the rest of our lives. Isn't it enough that I love you so much that the thought of living without you is unbearable? I can't stand the thought of losing you."

He was in agony as he heard the pain in her voice and felt her warm tears on his hand. He longed to take her into his arms and tell her they would be married within the month, that he would take care of her for the rest of their lives. But how could he do that while she still hated everything he believed in?

"Tell me, Philip. Why can't you marry me?"

"I can't tell you right now. If I did, you wouldn't like what you heard. It might make you hate me."

"I could never hate you."

She placed her hand on his scarred cheek and stroked it with her thumb. He placed his hand on hers and held it there for a long time as he closed his eye and leaned his cheek into her hand. When he finally lifted it from his cheek, he kissed her palm before placing it back on the bed.

"For now, you need to move in with Titus. You don't have to worry about losing me. You mean as much to me as I do to you, and I won't let you go out of my life. It's just not the right time for us to start our future together. Don't ask me why anymore. I can't tell you without risking everything. Please wait and try to trust me."

"I don't understand, but I trust you. I'll wait for as long as you want me to."

He stood and looked down at the beautiful young woman he loved more than any other person on earth. Somehow, he would change her mind about Jesus so he could have her as his wife. God would help him know when and how to tell her so she would hear God's call and come.

"Will you be all right now? I mean with the nightmares."

"Yes."

He leaned down and swept the last of her tears from her cheek with his fingertips.

"I'll be going out of town for a few days tomorrow morning. I need to visit the nearby estates to see what the final harvests are and to celebrate with my workers. I have to leave very early, but I'd like to see you before I go."

"I'll get up for breakfast with you. Please wake me."

"I will. Good night, Claudia."

He picked up her hand and kissed her palm again.

"Good night, Philip."

◆

Claudia watched him walk to the door, then turn to look at her in the moonlight before stepping out onto the balcony.

Her heart remained in turmoil. Philip wanted her, but there was something keeping him from her. What could it be? How long would it last? Would they have the future together that she longed for? He said to trust him. She couldn't imagine any man more deserving of trust than him. Somehow, Philip would make it all work out. She focused on that thought and finally drifted off to sleep.

Chapter 45

Caring for Claudia

Titus woke early, almost as tired as he'd been when he went to bed. He'd awakened repeatedly, each time to find himself worrying about Claudia. She'd been so glad to see him when he rode into the stable yard at Philip's house. She'd been smiling and hugging him when he first arrived, but within minutes he was holding her in his arms as she clung to him and sobbed.

While Penelope took her to freshen up after her tears, Philip had taken him aside and told him about her two attempts to kill herself during the voyage from Rome. He probably didn't have to worry about her trying to drown herself again, but her second attempt involved a knife. There were always plenty of knives and other sharp things around if she should decide to end her own life. Philip said he didn't expect her to try that again, either, but how could he be sure? The nightmares that made her want to die were still coming every night. He had no idea what he could do to make those go away.

During each interval of wakefulness, he heard soft music—a woman singing. It had to be Miriam still cleaning. He'd tried to listen to get his mind off Claudia's crushing grief. It would have helped if the words were some language he could understand. They weren't Greek or Latin, but it was pretty anyway. He found it soothing.

Claudia had always liked music. It usually made her cheerful when she listened to the lyre player in their garden in Rome. When he detailed Miriam's responsibilities at breakfast, he would try to remember to include singing.

The sky was still grey when he started down the stairs, but the aroma of fresh-baked bread wafted up to him. One eyebrow lifted, and then one corner of his mouth lifted, too. As late as he'd heard her singing while she cleaned, he didn't expect her to be up well before dawn to get fresh bread baked in time for his breakfast. She couldn't have gone to bed at all.

◆

Miriam had already washed the grapes and cut the cheese. Now she stood at the counter arranging them on the platter she would deliver to Master Titus in the dining room as soon as he came down for breakfast. The bread that she'd baked in the brick oven that was just outside the kitchen door filled the room with the tantalizing aroma that only bread freshly pulled from the oven and laced with rosemary could produce.

As she worked, she sang a psalm of thanksgiving. Early morning was her chance for some quiet time alone with God before everyone else showed up for breakfast. Today, with a new master who seemed both understanding and kind, she had so much to be thankful for.

◆

As Titus stood in the doorway, inhaling the smell of fresh-baked bread, a half-smile accompanied his nod. She was as hard a worker as he'd ever seen and an excellent cook. So far, she'd proven a worthwhile purchase. If she served Claudia as well as she'd performed her other duties, she would have been a bargain at three times what he paid for her.

"I'm ready for my breakfast in the dining room."

She startled and spun to face him. She bowed, but then she looked at his face, just as he'd told her to do.

"Yes, master."

He walked through the courtyard to the dining room door. As he entered and sat down at the table, she came through the storeroom carrying the platter. She bowed as she set it before him and retreated to stand by the door, awaiting his next command.

A satisfied smile curved his lips as he looked at the pretty arrangement of the food. He didn't care how the food looked himself, but it was something that would please Claudia. His smile broadened when he took the first bite of her rosemary-laced bread. The cleanliness of the rooms, the delicious food—Claudia would feel at home here.

"The bread is excellent, Miriam."

He smiled at her and received a happy smile in return.

"You've done a good job cleaning and cooking, but the most important part of your work will be serving my sister Claudia."

His brow furrowed. He wasn't quite sure how to describe the problem, but Miriam needed to understand as much as possible if she was to protect his sister from herself.

"In the market, you were right." He paused as he considered what to say. "My sister has a broken heart. Our father has just been killed. Our brother is responsible for his death, and Claudia has escaped him and come to me. She was very close to Father, and his death...well, nothing seems to console her. She tried to kill herself twice on the trip from Rome. The ship owner who brought her spent much of each day trying to keep her from grieving all the time.

"Your most important task is to keep her safe. At least for a while, you or Nestor must stay with her all the time when I'm not here. She can't have any opportunity to kill herself. Nighttime is the worst. She has terrible nightmares. You'll sleep in her room to make sure nothing happens."

◆

Miriam's eyes saucered as she stared at the master. He'd already given her the work of two slaves in cooking and cleaning. Now he was giving her one more task that could take all her time both day and night. The enormity of what he was asking—it was impossible for one slave to do it all. Could he not see that? He'd said he was a master who wouldn't beat her as long as she was trying to do her best, but even doing her best, she could never do the impossible. Would he understand that?

She took a deep breath, and let it out slowly so he wouldn't notice. God told her the master needed her to help his sister, so there must be some way she could do it all. God would guide her so she could do what his sister needed.

"I'll do everything I can to keep your sister safe, master."

She watched his eyes taking her measure. One quick nod told her he'd decided she would.

"I'll be getting her from Philip's house when I get off duty late this afternoon. You'll need to prepare a three-course meal for the two of us."

"Yes, master."

At least she'd have time to prepare the meal before her vigil over Claudia began that evening. No problem doing that. She had the morning to finish cleaning the four empty rooms and the courtyard. She'd do the courtyard and then see how many rooms she could complete by early afternoon. If she started the dinner then, the master and mistress would not be disappointed. But how on earth was she to complete her work tomorrow? Or any day after that, for that matter.

The master pushed back his chair and stood. Without another word, he left the dining room and headed for the stable.

Miriam leaned against the dining room wall and tipped back her head. Tears swam in her eyes, and one trickled down her cheek.

"Oh, Jesus, what am I going to do? He's asking more than is even possible. How am I ever going to do it? How am I going to do even half of it? His sister really does need me. Please, guide me so I can do everything he wants and still keep his sister safe."

Three times, she took a deep breath and let it out slowly. Then she squared her shoulders and flicked the tears from her cheeks. A sense of peace filled her. God would help her do what needed to be done each day. He'd told her the master's sister needed her. He would also tell her how to help the broken-hearted girl. Somehow it would all turn out the way the Lord intended.

Chapter 46

MISSING PHILIP

Claudia arose at dawn and put on a sky-blue tunic. Philip had said more than once it was his favorite color. She brushed her hair so it flowed down her back. She didn't bother with a headband. He liked hair natural. When he knocked on her door to invite her to breakfast, she opened it right away.

The warmth in Philip's eye wrapped around her like a blanket. "Good morning. You're a lovely sight to begin my day."

"I can't think of a better way to start my day than seeing your face, too."

He grinned at her. "It wouldn't take much of an imagination to think of something better to see than my face."

"Stop saying that. You're not as ugly as you claim to be." She rested her hand on his scarred cheek and drew her thumb across the ridges. "An eyepatch lends an air of distinction to a man."

A chuckle accompanied one shake of his head. "Maybe you do have a good imagination. I never heard anyone say that before."

◆

Philip loved it when Claudia touched his face like that. It was funny how his scars seemed to attract instead of repel her now.

He placed her hand on his arm and led her downstairs to the dining room. His servant immediately brought a platter of fruit and cheese and a loaf of fresh bread to the table.

He spoke very little while they ate. What could he say after her request last night? She said very little; maybe she was afraid to speak of it, too. But it was enough to just sit at the table together, looking at her often. It would be a week before he'd have the opportunity again, and he wanted to store up images to remember.

Finally, he pushed back his chair and stood.

"It's time. I have to leave now."

"So soon?"

Claudia's smile quivered ever-so-slightly, and her eyes looked too moist.

Philip leaned over the table and placed his hand on her cheek.

"Everything will be all right. You'll be with your brother, and he'll take good care of you while I'm gone. He's a good man, and he loves you very much."

"I know. I should try to be happy. Titus really wants me to be, and I don't want to be a burden to him by crying too much. But there's someplace I'd much rather be than with Titus."

Her wistful eyes tugged at his heart. "I know."

He knew where he wanted her, too, and it wasn't with her brother. It was sitting with him playing Conquest, or lying with her head in his lap as he massaged her temple, or even lying on her bed with her hand in his while he read so she could sleep after the nightmares.

But he hadn't figured out how he could tell her he was a Christian without driving her away. She still hated Christians because she blamed them for her father's death, and he really was partly responsible. She probably wouldn't say she hated him, but could she love him the same once she knew?

Somehow, he had to help her see that becoming a Christian was the best thing that ever happened to her father, even though it led to his death, and that it would be the best thing that could happen to her, too. Then he would tell her how much he loved her and ask her to make him the happiest man alive by becoming his wife.

He'd have a week to pray and think about that as he visited the estates. Maybe by the time he returned, he'd have some idea of what to do. If God intended her to be his wife, He would open her heart to Jesus so the only barrier to their marriage would be gone.

After Philip rose from the table, Claudia stood, too, and offered him her hand. He placed it on his arm, then rested his hand on top of it. She gazed up at his scarred face, and he felt the caress even though she didn't touch him.

He led her out into the stable yard. His stallion was already waiting for him. He was leaving later than he'd intended, but it was worth it to have spent time with her.

When he mounted his horse, he sat for a moment looking down at her. She placed her hand on his leg. Eyes moistened with unshed tears locked onto his own.

"When will I see you again?" The quaver in her voice was making the leave-taking so much harder.

"About a week."

"Will you let me know as soon as you come back? And then will you come visit me?"

"Of course." He grinned down at her, trying to deflect her attention from his departure. "I'll expect you to engage me in a few games of Conquest. Since discovering what a fine general you are, I'm not satisfied with anyone else as my opponent. It's not as much fun playing when I don't lose half the time."

She gave him a shaky smile. "Half the time? Wasn't it a bit more than that?"

He chuckled. "I stand corrected, mighty general. You do tend to win three out of five more times than I'd like."

The longer he talked with her, the harder it was becoming to leave. With one last grin, he kicked his horse and trotted away.

Claudia watched his broad shoulders as he guided the horse through the gate and turned south to catch the main road. She fought back tears as she began to count the days until she could see that wonderful scarred face smiling at her again.

Penelope was weaving while Claudia gazed out the window of the women's room, and Penelope was worried. She'd tried several times to get Claudia to join in her conversation with Junia, to no avail.

Claudia's silence was disturbing. Toward the end of the voyage, Claudia had happily sat and chatted with them. She'd seemed like a different person from the sad girl who boarded the ship in Portus. Now that sad girl had returned.

With great satisfaction, Penelope had watched Claudia and Philip fall in love. By the time they docked in Portus, she was certain Claudia would soon be her sister-in-law. There was still the problem of Claudia hating the Christians her father knew, but surely God would change that soon. She didn't know how, but as soon as He did, Philip would immediately make his official request to Titus. Philip always acted quickly once he decided what he wanted. She had no doubt that he wanted Claudia.

The collection of poems that Philip had been reading to Claudia yesterday lay on the small table beside the couch. Maybe that would cheer up her friend.

"Claudia, would you read to Junia and me for a while?"

◆

Claudia pulled herself out of her sad reflection. Father was dead, and Philip was gone. He was coming back soon, but it still hurt not to have him with her.

"What would you like me to read?"

Penelope waved her hand toward the codex by the couch. "I like that one. Especially those poems you two were reading yesterday."

Claudia smiled at the prospect. Reading had cheered her up every time she read with Philip. She picked up the codex and opened it to the first poem.

"'Ever the beauty of sunrise graces my eyes, filling my heart with joy. Oh, for the peace of...'"

She loved this poem. It was the first that she ever read for him that first afternoon when her mind was filled with thoughts of death and loss. She could see him now, leaning back in his chair with his legs stretched out and his clasped hands resting on the back of his head. She could see that contented smile as he watched her or sat with his eye closed, just listening to her voice.

As she continued to read, she longed to see him lounging there in his seaman's tunic, his brilliant scholar's mind in his muscled laborer's body. It was becoming harder to read as she missed him with increasing intensity.

"'The wind's caress stirred the grass and made the flowers dance. Such grace...'"

She'd reached the first poem that he read to her. It hurt to hear the words spoken in her voice instead of his.

The words on the page started to blur.

◆

Junia had been enjoying the poetry when Mistress Claudia's voice began to quaver. She glanced at her friend and saw that stricken look that was so common at the beginning of the voyage.

"Mistress, is something wrong?"

"Yes...I need Philip." A tear trickled down her cheek. "I'm sorry. I can't read anymore."

She clutched the codex to her breast and hurried from the room.

Junia left her loom and followed Claudia onto the balcony in time to see her enter her room and shut the door. Junia followed and knocked. There was no answer except the sound of Claudia once more crying her heart out as she missed someone she loved.

Chapter 47

Moving In

When Titus rode into Philip's stable yard, he saw a cart holding two trunks and a two-handled box. Nestor stood beside the cart, talking with a stable slave.

"Good evening, master. I've come to get the mistress's belongings. I'll take them down to the mistress's bedchamber now, unless you have other instructions."

Titus waved toward his house. "Go ahead. Tell Miriam I expect to bring Claudia down shortly. We'll want to eat soon after."

"Yes, master." Nestor bowed and flicked his hand to tell the stable slave to start the trek down the hill.

Titus tied his reins to a tree when no other slave appeared to take his stallion.

Philip had a peculiar household. He was one of the wealthiest men in the region, according to everything Titus heard when he asked around about him that day. Although the gardens surrounding the house on all sides were extensive and lush, the house itself was neither large nor ornate. It wasn't even twice as big as the one he was renting.

Maybe there were enough slaves to do what needed to be done, but there were fewer than Titus expected for the merchant prince Philip was reputed to be. Maybe it was because he was unmarried and didn't care much about his house. That would change when he took a wife. What woman would want him without the luxury his wealth could buy to make up for his ugliness?

When Titus entered the inner courtyard through the door that led to the gardens, he found Claudia and Penelope sitting together. Penelope was holding one of Claudia's hands, and Claudia's eyes looked puffy. Titus drew in a deep breath and let it out slowly. This was not an auspicious beginning to her first evening with him.

♦

When Claudia looked up and saw her brother, she forced a happy smile. He mustn't suspect she'd spent too much of the day crying because Philip was gone. She was determined not to let her grief be a burden on him. At least, she hoped she'd be able to keep it from being one. At least, she'd try...

Penelope took the lead. "We were just wondering when you would get here. Nestor has everything ready to move down to your house, and Claudia is ready to go." She reached over and took Claudia's other hand. "I'm so glad you two will be living just down the hill from me. We'll be able to get together often with it only being a short walk between our houses."

Titus nodded once. "I must thank Philip for finding something so convenient for the two of you. It would be lonely for Claudia if he hadn't."

Claudia forced another cheerful smile. "I hope Penelope and Philip will both come down often. We all became such good friends on the ship."

Penelope squeezed her hand. "I'm sure we will. You're my dear friend, and Philip will want to battle his favorite general."

Titus lifted one eyebrow at Claudia. She smiled at his perplexity.

"Philip taught me Conquest. It's a game where you try to take over the world. Almost no one can beat Philip at it. Well, except me. It turns out I'm very good at military strategy. We need to get the game, too, and I'll teach you. It's the most fun game I've ever played. Father would have loved it."

The remembrance of Father and the absence of Philip combined to start some tears pooling in her eyes. If she didn't change the subject, she'd be crying again.

She stood. "Shall we go? I'm ready."

Penelope stood as well, still holding Claudia's hand. "I'll walk you to the gate." She led them through the garden so Titus could get his horse.

The two girls strolled ahead of him to the gate in the tall wall that fronted the street. Penelope hugged Claudia before they started downhill toward Claudia's new home.

Claudia glanced back at Penelope, who still stood at the gate and waved. If only she was staying in Philip's house as his new wife, but he'd said "not yet." Still, he'd told her to trust him to make it all turn out right, and it couldn't ever be right for her until she was his wife. He knew that, and somehow he would make it happen when he thought it was the right time.

Miriam was in the storeroom when she heard the master and her new mistress enter the kitchen.

The master's voice sounded cheerful, something she hadn't heard before. "These Greek houses are laid out different from our townhouse or the villas, but it's not a bad design. Your bedchamber is upstairs. The two windows make it bright, and the wall paintings remind me of a garden."

Miriam stepped into the dining room to finish setting the table. She needed to hurry. Any moment, the master could be calling her to help his sister, and there were still a few things left to do before dinner was ready to serve.

"Miriam." The master's summons came too soon.

She took a deep breath, and stepped into the courtyard. "Yes, master?"

Master Titus was leaning over the balcony railing. "Come up. Claudia is here."

She caught a glimpse of the back of a slender woman with reddish blonde hair before he turned and followed his sister into her room.

Miriam climbed the stairs as quickly as her bad leg allowed. She was eager to meet the new mistress God had sent her to help. But since Master Titus told her about his sister's grief and her attempts on her own life, she wasn't sure what to expect.

When she entered the room, Mistress Claudia was looking out the window. "I can see Philip's trees from here."

Titus crossed his arms. "I'm glad Penelope lives close enough for you two to visit often. Every day if you want." His gaze shifted from his sister to Miriam. "This is Miriam. She'll be taking care of you."

Miriam bowed deeply before raising her eyes to her new mistress. The extraordinary beauty of the master's sister caught her breath.

Master Titus was a handsome man, but Mistress Claudia was the most beautiful woman she'd ever seen or even imagined.

"It's my pleasure to serve you in everything I can, mistress."

Mistress Claudia glanced over her shoulder at her. "You can begin by unpacking my trunks." Then she turned back to the window to gaze up the hill.

"Yes, mistress."

Miriam opened the two large trunks to see what was in each. She really ought to be downstairs cooking, but the mistress had said to unpack. The need to do two things at once—it had already begun.

Master Titus stepped in. "Miriam will have to unpack your things later. She's also our cook, and she probably needs to be in the kitchen right now."

Relief surged through her when the master said what she was afraid to.

"Pardon me, mistress. I do need to get back to the kitchen before anything burns." She bowed, and limped out of the room.

◆

With a sigh, Claudia turned from the window. Philip's house had lost most of its charm the moment Philip left. Perhaps it was better to be here with Titus than to wait in a house that felt too empty with its master gone.

Titus ran his hand across the lid of the larger trunk. "I'm sorry Miriam can't help you right now. She'll be cooking and taking care of the house as well as attending you. I only have her and our steward to take care of everything."

"That's not a problem. I won't be going anywhere except Penelope's, so I won't need much attending. She and I shared her maid on the ship, and I found it's just as easy to do many things for myself that Graecia used to do for me."

Claudia walked over to Titus and hugged his arm. "I understand how much my coming has changed everything for you. I know you weren't planning on having to pay for a household. Slaves are expensive, and we can make do with just two."

"Philip lent me Nestor. That was a huge help. I don't know how I would have found a good steward on my own. Miriam wasn't very expensive because of her limp. She's an excellent cook and a hard worker. So far, I'm satisfied with her eagerness to please me. I think she'll try hard to serve you well."

Titus took his sister's hand and led her toward the door. "Let's go have dinner as soon as I wash up. If yesterday's stew is any indication, you're in for a treat when you taste her cooking. I'm not sure we ever had as good a cook at home. I've been eating poor food for so long out here that I'd almost forgotten what it was like for something to be so delicious that you want to just let it sit in your mouth to make the taste last."

Claudia smiled at her brother because she knew that was what he wanted. No matter how delicious the food might be, she would much rather be sitting under the canopy eating bread and cheese with Philip beside her. He'd be back in about a week. Maybe whatever it was that was keeping them apart would change between now and then. Maybe…

Chapter 48

Two Broken Hearts

After the first bite of the main course, Claudia decided Titus had not been exaggerating when he praised Miriam's culinary skill. The sauce might well be the most delectable she'd ever tasted. She glanced at Miriam, who was watching for her reaction. Claudia smiled and nodded to convey her pleasure...and then forgot that Miriam was even standing there.

Miriam stood by the doorway, waiting to do whatever the master and mistress needed. It was gratifying to see the master nod his head and smile broadly as he took the first bite, and it was clear that the mistress appreciated the flavor almost as much. She'd expected them to like her cooking, but it still gave her pleasure to watch their enjoyment. She couldn't help but smile. God had been so good in bringing Master Titus to buy her, even if she must do the work of three.

It was to be expected that masters and mistresses would forget someone was listening while a slave waited patiently to serve. An attentive slave often knew more of what was going on in a household than any master. As Miriam stood by the doorway, forgotten by Master Titus and Mistress Claudia, she heard all their conversation, but what she heard was deeply disturbing.

The mistress's voice was strained. "It was all so horrible. Lucius turned Father in for becoming a Christian. The soldiers took him away to one of Lucius's friends who's a praetor, and I never saw him again.

What's even more horrible is I'm the one who told Lucius about Father becoming a Christian.

"Father was so happy, I mean really, really happy. I'd never seen him like that, smiling all the time for the two weeks after he decided to change from God-fearer to Christian. Then Lucius dropped by. He asked me why Father was so happy, and I told him. I never, ever dreamed that Lucius would use what I said to get Father killed. I didn't know he hated Father for making him be a faithful husband to Cornelia again. I didn't know he wanted Father dead so he could be in control of everything. I blame myself for giving Lucius what he needed to get Father killed."

Mistress Claudia kept flicking tears off her cheeks.

"And when I told him what I thought of him for doing that to Father, he decided to sell me to Flavius Sabinus for 50,000 denarii. Aemilia told me that horrible old man beat his last wife to death. I just couldn't stay in Rome and marry him. If Malleolus hadn't gone to Father's friend, who got Philip to bring me here, I would have killed myself."

The master leaned across the table and placed his hand on hers. "Don't blame yourself. You should have been able to tell our brother anything about our father. His treachery isn't your fault. I never especially liked Lucius, but I never expected he'd be a cold-blooded snake who'd betray Father like that. You had no reason to think he would."

The mistress wiped both cheeks with her free hand. "I hate Lucius so much. I want him dead more than anything in this world. I'd do almost anything to make him pay for killing Father."

"Father meant as much to me as he did to you. You were only a little girl, so you probably don't remember all the time Father spent with me and Decimus, teaching us about life—about love and loyalty and how to know what was important and what wasn't. Father should have been around to teach that to our children. Lucius took that from us."

Master Titus had been twirling a knife in his fingers. With the speed of a striking snake, he drove it into the table.

"I hate him as much as you do. I'll kill him when I get the chance. It's a good thing for him I'm stuck out here in Thracia for five more years. When I return to Rome, I'll avenge Father's death. I'll kill Lucius, and I won't do it quickly. He'll be lucky if he dies before I return."

Miriam almost jumped out of her skin when the knifepoint penetrated the table. Soldiers trained to kill, and this one was eager to kill his own brother. The venom in the master's voice terrified her. It could be fatal to get this master angry. Thank God he was ignoring her at that moment. He mustn't see her trembling. He'd told her several times to stop acting like she was afraid of him, but she wasn't acting. He truly frightened her as he spewed his hatred.

Master Titus threw himself back in his chair. "I'm sorry I wasn't there to protect Father. I would have found out who was telling him the Christian stories and turned them in before they convinced Father to believe all the lies about that dead Jewish carpenter. Thracia doesn't have the same policy as Bithynia about executing Christians who won't denounce their Jesus and sacrifice to Caesar, but it should. I didn't care before, but now I'd love to do my part in ridding the Empire of Christians before they spread any farther."

Miriam's stomach knotted. *Thank you, Jesus, that he doesn't know I follow You.* He'd sell her or kill her if he found out. As soon as she could, she'd warn Nestor to be careful so the master wouldn't learn he was a Christian as well.

Mistress Claudia's face twisted with hatred. "I wanted to kill Lucius myself. I thought about driving a dagger into his heart as he slept, but he doesn't deserve a quick death. I want him to know what it is to suffer like Father did. Slow poison would be better or feeding him to the lions."

Tears began pooling in her eyes again. "And that horrible man who convinced Father to become a Christian. If I knew who it was, I'd report him so he could die in the arena like Father did. If Father had only stayed a God-fearer, Lucius couldn't have had him killed. I hate them both. Why did I ever tell Lucius? Oh, Titus! No matter what you say, it's partly my fault for telling him."

The dam burst, and tears began pouring down her cheeks. She covered her face with her hands as her body shook. The master rose from the table and knelt beside her so he could wrap his arms around her.

"No, Claudia. It's not your fault at all. It's Lucius and that Christian, not you."

It was a long time before her tears stopped. The master knelt with his arms wrapped around her the whole time. He closed his eyes and looked almost as miserable as the mistress.

Miriam stood in silence by the door, watching her poor mistress's heart breaking. No wonder God had sent her into this household. The mistress was drowning in grief, guilt, and hatred. The master was suffering from his own grief and burning with hatred. They needed the peace and love of Jesus so desperately. But how was that possible if they wanted to kill anyone who might tell them about Him?

She was only a slave. They would never listen to her. If she tried, the master would kill her. *Jesus, how can I help without actually speaking about you?* She swallowed as the lump of fear grew in her throat. *I don't want to die if it won't even help save them.*

Finally, the tears were over. Master Titus released the mistress from his arms and returned to his chair. Worry twisted his face when it was turned away from his sister. He masked it before he turned so she wouldn't see.

"Miriam. Bring the second table."

Miriam bowed and removed the remains of the main course. She limped through the storeroom as she went to fetch the special pastries she'd prepared to welcome her mistress home.

When she returned to place the pastry tray on the table before the master, he didn't nod or smile. His gaze was locked on his sister. Her face twisted as she fought to hold back a fresh torrent of tears.

"I'm so sorry, Titus. Every time I think about what happened to Father, I can't stop crying...I miss him so much." The tears didn't start again, but she hung her head and buried her face in her hands.

The new lump in Miriam's throat was more from fighting tears than fear. The master's shoulders drooped as he watched his sister suffer. *Please, God. There's too much pain for both of them.*

◆

Claudia's heart ached for more reasons than Titus knew. Her thoughts had turned to Philip and how much she longed to have him with her at that moment. Only Philip knew how to turn her tears to smiles. She didn't tell Titus that she missed Philip even more than she missed their father.

She didn't tell him how much she missed the challenge of matching wits with Philip or lying with her head in his lap while he massaged her temple and read to her. She didn't tell him how she loved watching Philip watch her reading poetry with his legs stretched out, his hands clasped behind his head, and that contented smile lighting up the scarred face that had become so dear to her. She didn't tell Titus how Philip had helped her bear the horror of her dreams every night and how he'd managed to drive the darkness from her days.

She didn't tell Titus she was deeply in love with the man who'd saved her from Lucius, and it was mostly his absence that was breaking her heart.

Miriam had helped Mistress Claudia prepare for the night, but she returned to the unfinished work in the kitchen when the master came into his sister's room to tell her good night. As Miriam started down the stairs, the mistress started to cry. Since the master was with her, Miriam continued on to the kitchen.

One window of the mistress's room was directly above the window over the kitchen counter. As Miriam stood washing the dishes in a large basin, the muffled tones of their conversation reached her. First his deep voice, then her soft one, then the sound of a woman crying her heart out. Miriam couldn't make out the words, but he tried again and again to console his sister. Nothing stopped her tears. Weeping turned into hiccupping sobs, then died away.

When Miriam had put the last clean dish away, she blew out the lamp and headed for the stairs. She took off her sandals before beginning the climb. Any noise might awaken the sleeping girl.

At the door of Mistress Claudia's bedchamber, she startled. Master Titus sat on the chair by the bed with his elbows on his knees and his face buried in his hands. His head jerked up when she took a step. Fear clouded his eyes—fear for his sister.

She limped over and whispered, "I'll stand guard over her, master. You can rest now, if you want to."

He stared into her eyes for what seemed a long time, then nodded as if convinced. He rose from the chair and walked wearily to the door. He paused to look back at his sister as sadness filled his eyes. Then he sighed deeply and walked out with his head hanging.

Miriam's hand covered her mouth. The master may have thought the compassion in her eyes was for his sister, but it was mostly for him. His heart was breaking, too, not just from the loss of his father, but even more from watching his sister suffer.

She sat on the chair beside the bed. *God, please show me what to do to help my mistress. Please heal her heart...and his, too.*

When she was certain Claudia slept deeply. Miriam rose and crept over to the pallet in the corner that she'd prepared for herself. She lay down and drew the sheet over her. As she willed her breathing to slow, each breath became a prayer for the mistress and master until she drifted off to sleep.

<h1>Chapter 49</h1>

SOMETHING NEW BUT NOT ENOUGH

The first hint of pink brightened the clouds when Miriam awoke with a start. She rolled off her pallet and crept to Mistress Claudia's bedside. The mistress still slept soundly, so Miriam picked up her sandals and tiptoed out the door. She didn't put them on until she'd descended the stairs.

She had too much to do that day. The master would be down early for his breakfast before he went to the garrison, and she wanted to get the bread dough rising before her mistress woke up and needed help dressing. She wanted the mistress's breakfast ready before then, too.

The well in the courtyard between the dining room and the bath drew a smile. It was quick and easy to get water for rinsing the grapes she'd be serving him that morning. If she had to walk less, she could get more done. Her smile broadened. She wasn't a fast walker, but God had given her a master who didn't care.

Titus had spent another night in fitful sleep. He woke often, and each time he stayed awake too long worrying about Claudia before he dozed off again. Last night he didn't even have the soft sound of Miriam singing to distract him from his anxiety about his sister's safety.

As he descended the stairs, one of the melodies he'd liked the night before floated up to greet him. Through the kitchen door, he could see Miriam at the counter, kneading some dough and singing softly to herself. He stood in the doorway, leaning against the post as he watched her. She was a pretty little thing, and there was something about her that made the kitchen seem cheery and inviting. Maybe she'd have the same effect on Claudia.

She felt his gaze and turned. "Good morning, master. I'll take your breakfast to the dining room right away."

He watched her limp to the table and pick up the larger of two trays of bread, cheese, and grapes before he turned and walked to the dining room. As he seated himself, she placed the tray before him and bowed. Before she went to stand by the wall to await any commands, she paused.

"Do you want me to make a lunch for you to take with you, master?"

"No. You only have to make a good one for Claudia."

The corner of his mouth twitched up. A slave asking for extra work—that was a novel experience. Such eagerness to serve a master was rare. The more he saw of her, the more satisfied he was with spending the extra fifty denarii.

She retreated to the wall by the storeroom door and stood waiting for his command.

Titus glanced up from his food. She was a pleasure to look at, but it was a waste of her time to stand there while there was work to do.

"You can go back to your work. I don't need you to stand there at breakfast. If I need anything, I'll call you."

"Yes, master."

She disappeared through the storeroom door, and soon he heard her singing again. A little music with his breakfast was a pleasant way to start the morning. Sending her back to her work had been a good idea.

He ate quickly. He wanted to get to the garrison early to return the pack mule. As he walked through the kitchen on his way to the stable, he paused.

"I'm counting on you to protect Claudia. That's your most important duty. Don't let her be alone. After last night, I'm not sure it would be safe."

Miriam turned from the dough and focused dark brown eyes on him.

"Yes, master. I'll keep her safe."

Those eyes pulled him in, just like they had in the slave market. He wasn't sure what it was about them, but something made him certain he could trust her to protect Claudia from herself. He wouldn't have to worry about his sister today.

With a quick nod, he headed out to his waiting stallion.

◆

Miriam watched through the window as he mounted and headed for the gate. She pulled a deep breath and let it out slowly. It was good the master was more interested in her getting work done than in having her stand waiting for him to want something. Today would be the first day trying to do the work of three, and she needed every minute of it. Somehow, God would help her get everything done, even though she had to watch over the mistress. There must be some way.

As soon as she set the bread dough aside to rise, she climbed the stairs to check on Mistress Claudia. In the daylight, she could see how hard the mistress had cried. Even after a night of sleep, her eyes were still puffy. As Miriam stood gazing at the beautiful girl who was almost her own age, the mistress stirred and opened her eyes.

"It's Miriam, isn't it?"

"Yes, mistress. If you wish, I'll unpack your trunks now so you can choose what you want to wear this morning."

Mistress Claudia rolled onto her back and rested her arm across her forehead. "That's fine."

Miriam opened the ornately carved doors of the cupboard to reveal a set of drawers that would hold the mistress's jewelry and hair accessories. Even the inside of the doors and the front of each drawer were beautifully carved. This was a very expensive piece of furniture. Nestor had mentioned that the master rented the house already furnished. Who would put such lovely furniture in a rental house?

When she began to transfer the clothing from the rugged travel trunk to a trunk carved to match the cupboard, her breath caught at the sheer beauty of the fabric of almost every tunic and palla she lifted out. The textures were so soft. The fabrics draped so gracefully, and the colors were exquisite, like those of a rainbow. There was only one tunic in the whole chest that was an ordinary one.

"You have beautiful tunics, mistress. I've never seen so many lovely ones."

"Philip bought them all, except for that pale blue linen one. I had to leave everything behind except what I was wearing and that small box of poetry when I ran away."

"He must be a very generous man, mistress."

"The most generous man ever. He hadn't even met me when he gave Penelope money to go buy everything she thought I'd need."

Miriam's eyebrows rose. Was that the start of tears in Mistress Claudia's eyes?

"He's been so kind to me. It was wonderful making the trip with him...and Penelope, too, of course. I miss him...them so much."

"Nestor said their house is very close, so you can probably see them often, mistress. Perhaps invite them for dinner. I can prepare something special for you."

"He's out of town for a week."

Something in the mistress's voice told Miriam she'd better shift the subject before the mistress started crying again. It wasn't only the loss of her father that Mistress Claudia was grieving. She placed the last tunic in the ornate chest and lowered the lid.

"I have your breakfast ready for you downstairs. Did you want to dress before or after you eat?"

"After, I guess. No, before. It doesn't really matter."

"Which tunic would you like, mistress?"

"I don't care. You pick something. It doesn't matter. No one will see me."

Mistress Claudia had been sitting up, but she flopped back down on the bed and curled into a ball. She wasn't openly crying, but Miriam saw one small tear trickle down her cheek and disappear into her reddish-blonde hair.

Miriam selected a light green tunic that would be perfect with her hair. She took some gold tunic clips from the smaller travel trunk, and carried everything to the bed.

Suddenly the dam broke, and tears began cascading down the mistress's cheeks. Miriam laid the tunic at the foot of the bed and sat down beside her. She began rubbing her back. The mistress started shaking as she sobbed.

"Is there anything I can do to help, mistress?"

"No. Only Philip can."

Miriam's hand continued making slow circles on her back, and she began to hum a lullaby as she prayed for her mistress's tears to end. It wasn't long before the sobs turned back into tears and the tears stopped.

Claudia rolled onto her back, then sat up. She wrapped her arms around her knees.

"I didn't mean to do that, Miriam. Sometimes I just can't help it. I get thinking about Father being gone forever, and now Philip's gone." She flicked the tears off her cheek.

"But it's only a week until Master Philip will be back. That's not so long."

Claudia sniffed. "You're right. I can't keep crying like this. Don't tell Titus."

"I won't tell the master anything you don't want me to. He bought me to serve you more than to serve him."

Claudia stared into Miriam eyes, then a slow smile appeared. "I'm ready to get dressed now. The green one is a good choice."

As Miriam helped her mistress into the green tunic, she gave thanks that Mistress Claudia was already telling her some of the things in her heart. The more she knew, the sooner she could help her heal.

As Mistress Claudia went down the stairs in front of her, Miriam fought a frown. How was she ever going to get everything done if she had to keep an eye on the mistress all day? Even worse, she had to do it without the mistress suspecting. Any grown woman would resent being watched like a small child.

Mistress Claudia was heading toward the dining room when the answer popped into Miriam's head.

"Mistress, would you rather eat in the kitchen where you can watch me work or all alone in the dining room?"

The mistress paused, then turned. "That's an excellent idea. I'd much rather watch you than be alone right now."

With a welcoming smile, Miriam stepped back to let her mistress enter the kitchen ahead of her. Her breakfast tray was waiting on the table, so Mistress Claudia seated herself and began to eat.

Miriam returned to the counter where the dough had finished its first rise. She punched it to deflate it, then began shaping it into the loaves that she would bake in a half hour or so after the second rise.

When Miriam finished shaping the last loaf, she turned to check on Mistress Claudia. The mistress's elbow was on the table, and her cheek rested on her hand as she watched. The cloud of sadness that had hovered over the mistress earlier had been replaced by curiosity.

Miriam would start dinner preparations after lunch. Until then, she needed to start gathering and drying some of the heavy crop of apples that hung on the large tree at the back of the garden. If watching her make the bread had distracted the mistress...

"Would you like to come with me into the garden now, mistress? It's such a beautiful day to be outside. I need to start picking the apples to dry for winter."

◆

Everything Miriam was doing was new to Claudia. She'd never spent time in a kitchen before. Food always magically appeared fully prepared and prettily arranged on the serving platters or individual plates.

Miriam's question drew a shrug. "I suppose so."

She didn't have anything else she wanted to do. There wasn't a single poem in her library that she hadn't read to Philip or he hadn't read to her. After what happened when she read to Penelope yesterday, she was afraid to read when she was already missing him too much.

Miriam went into the storeroom and brought out two baskets.

"There's a nice chair under the big tree, mistress. You could watch from there."

◆

Miriam waited for Mistress Claudia to go outside ahead of her. After the mistress was settled in the chair, Miriam limped over to the apple tree, where Nestor had already placed a ladder for reaching the upper branches. With her basket slung from one arm, she began to climb. She had good enough balance on the ground, but climbing tall ladders with her bad leg...that made her heart beat faster. She was about one third of the way up when Nestor appeared below her.

"I'll pick the upper branches, and you can pick the lower ones. Come down now. You don't look very steady there."

She smiled down in gratitude. "I can do it if I have to, but I'd rather not climb too high. Thank you, Nestor."

He grinned. "Master Philip made me steward here. I'm going to protect every part of Master Titus's household, especially his chef. I like eating your cooking."

Miriam returned his grin as she stepped off the ladder. "And I like feeding you."

He picked up a basket and scampered up.

◆

As Claudia watched Nestor reach out for apples from the ladder top, visions of Philip on the mast in the rain and wind swirled in her mind. She'd been terrified that he'd get hurt. Was he somewhere now where he might get killed and never return to her? She closed her eyes and tried to push that thought out of her mind, but she couldn't quite do it.

"Hello!" Penelope's cheery voice pulled Claudia from her fear-filled thoughts. "We missed you and thought we'd visit."

Penelope and Junia, escorted by one of Philip's stable men, beamed as they walked toward her.

Miriam appeared at Claudia's side. "I'll fetch some fruit and something to drink out here, if you wish, mistress."

Nestor was already moving a bench under the tree to give extra seating.

"Yes. Do that." Claudia wiped her cheeks to be sure no tears remained and stepped forward to greet her friends.

A smile sprang to her lips. "I'm so glad you did. I've missed you, too." Palm up, she swept her hand toward the bench. "Miriam has gone to fetch refreshments. It will be almost like sitting under the canopy on the ship."

Almost, but not quite. The most important person was missing, and he would be for five more days. Her smile dimmed; then she forced it to brighten again. As Miriam had said, a week wasn't so long. Five days was even less...but even an hour wouldn't be too soon.

Philip had ridden to the farthest estate first and would work his way back. He had three to visit. It was a day and a half out to the first, then a day of accounting with the harvest celebration that evening. With half a day's ride between each and staying for an evening celebration with his workers, it would be five more days before he could be with Claudia again.

As he listened to the happy laughter shared by the women preparing the evening's feast, her trembling smile as he reined away from her kept slipping into his mind.

She was with her brother. Titus loved her and would try to take care of her. But it wasn't the same as doing it himself. She'd been his responsibility since Rome. She should be his responsibility as long as they both lived.

God, protect her. End her grief. Open her heart to hear and follow you.

He rubbed the back of his neck. *If Penelope's right that you brought her to be my wife, please let that be soon.*

Patience was one of the gifts of the Spirit, but this wasn't the way he wanted to practice his.

Chapter 50

THE NEW HELPER

Lunch was over, and it was time for Miriam to start dinner. Mistress Claudia sat at the table, watching her gather the pots and utensils she would use to prepare the master's Roman dinner.

"I need to go to the garden to gather some fruit, vegetables, and herbs for dinner. Then I need to get two sauces started. Would you like to come, mistress?"

Mistress Claudia hesitated, but the hopeful smile Miriam directed her way tipped the decision. "That sounds better than sitting here."

Miriam picked up the two small baskets she kept by the door and led Mistress Claudia into the vegetable garden.

The mistress bent down and fingered the lacy leaves of a carrot. "These were in the peristyle garden in Rome, but I just thought they were pretty. I didn't know they were food. The dinner last night was truly delicious. Titus loves good food, so I'm glad he bought you to cook for us. What are you going to make for tonight?"

"The master expects three-course Roman meals. For the salad course, I'll make carrots in one of my mother's special white wine sauces. For first table, pork in a red wine sauce that my last master loved. For second table, some pears in a white wine sauce I make with cinnamon and nutmeg."

She headed for the pear tree, and the mistress followed. Several perfectly ripened pears went into the basket. Then she gathered carrots, onions, celery, fennel, parsley, lovage, rosemary, and bay leaves.

The mistress lifted the sprig of rosemary from the basket and sniffed. "So many different things for a single sauce. I never would have guessed."

"I'm making both a vegetable stock and a pork stock, but there are many things in each. Time for me to cut everything up and start those simmering."

As Miriam stood at the counter washing the purple carrots before she peeled them, Mistress Claudia wandered over beside her.

Miriam lifted a small knife from the rack and began peeling.

Mistress Claudia rested her hand on the counter. "You do that so fast."

"I've done this since I was a child, mistress." The smile she gave the mistress failed to draw one in return. "Practice makes everything fast and easy."

As the mistress's hand started toward the knife rack, Miriam's eyes widened. The mistress took one of the largest ones out of the rack and felt the edge with her thumb.

While the mistress turned the knife in her hands, Miriam's heart raced. The master had said his sister tried to kill herself with a knife, and here she was in the kitchen with one of the sharpest knives in her hands. What would the master do if he knew she'd let his sister anywhere near a knife? What if she tried to use it?

"Mistress, it must be boring to have nothing in particular to do but watch me. It's much more fun to do something than to watch. Would you like to help me cut up the carrots? If not, I'm going to need that knife." She held out her hand and waited for Mistress Claudia to place it in her palm.

The mistress tilted her head, then a slight smile appeared. "You're right. It is boring. I'd like to help, but I've never done anything in the kitchen before. Teach me."

That was not the response Miriam expected, but as she watched Mistress Claudia perk up at the prospect of helping, a slow smile curved her lips. She could get her work done while keeping the mistress entertained and safe. God had given her a way to do two things at once.

Miriam carried the peeled carrots over to Mistress Claudia. Then she lifted down a cutting board that hung on the wall by the knife rack.

"For the salad and the pork stock, you cut them up into small pieces like this. Be careful. The knife is very sharp, and you don't want to cut your fingers. Hold the carrot like this so you won't." She cut two slices as the mistress watched.

"That looks easy enough."

While Miriam cut up the onions and celery for both the vegetable and pork stocks, Mistress Claudia carefully sliced the carrots.

By the time the mistress finished, Miriam had the stock pots filled with cut-up vegetables, herbs, and spices. She stirred the pork bones into the smaller one. They only needed the carrots to be ready to hang on the metal hooks that would hold them over the cooking fire to simmer.

"Is that all, Miriam?"

"No, mistress. After these cook about three hours, then they'll be ready for the next step in the recipes."

"You were right. It is more fun to do than to watch. Can I help some more?" The mistress's lips curved into the first real smile Miriam had seen.

"Yes, mistress, but I think the master wouldn't like it if you do too many things in the kitchen, even if they are fun. You can't be doing anything when it gets close to the time he comes home."

She'd only asked Mistress Claudia to help to distract her from using the knife on herself. How angry would the master be if he thought she was using the mistress as a kitchen helper?

"Titus doesn't have to know. I'll keep it a secret if you'll let me keep doing this."

Mistress Claudia's hopeful eyes made it impossible to refuse. "As you wish, mistress. You can help me when the master isn't here, and watch when he is."

The mistress's smile appeared again. "Philip loves working in the rigging of his ship, just like his crewmen. Penelope said he learned how when his father had him work a summer as a sailor. I was always busy in Rome, but I have almost nothing to do here. You can teach me to cook."

Miriam fought a grin. God had, indeed, provided. "I'll teach you whatever you want to learn, as long as the master doesn't forbid it."

"I don't think Titus would care, but we won't tell him, just in case. It will be fun to watch him eat what I've made, thinking it's one of your delightful creations. I'll try not to do anything that won't be up to your standards."

The mistress's smile was accompanied by a tilt of her head. "If you're going to teach me how to cook, let me teach you something. Can you speak Latin?"

"No, mistress. Only Aramaic and Greek, but I'd like to learn if you'd like to teach me. I can work on the apples while you do."

♦

Claudia's smile broadened. She didn't have Philip to fill her days with battles and poems and visions of distant countries, but she could keep her mind occupied with teaching and learning from Miriam. Miriam was right. It was much more fun to do than to watch.

When Titus took his first bite of the carrots sautéed in Miriam's peppered wine sauce, a delighted smile appeared. His little Jewish slave was some cook.

Claudia glanced at Miriam, and they exchanged smiles. Then she fixed her eyes on him. She rested her elbow on the table and leaned her chin on her hand. "Are the carrots good?"

"Delicious. Maybe the best I've ever had."

Titus glanced at Miriam, too. He'd been surprised to find Claudia sitting at the kitchen table when he walked in. He was even more surprised to find her smiling. She even said she had a good day when he asked. She didn't look like she'd been crying, so he believed her. His little cook had said she could help his sister. It looked like she was right.

Chapter 51

SHORTCUTS

The mistress was in good spirits when she went to bed, and she went to sleep quickly. Miriam went back downstairs to finish cleaning up the kitchen. She almost dropped the plate she was drying when she heard the blood-curdling scream.

Master Titus was in his room, so he reached the mistress before Miriam could make it up the stairs. She stood at the door watching as he sat on the edge of the bed and shook Claudia to wake her from the night terror. She jerked awake, then wrapped her arms around her brother. Burying her face in his tunic muffled the deep sobs.

"Don't cry, Claudia. It's only a dream." He stroked her hair. "It's only a dream."

It must have been a quarter hour before the sobs turned into simple tears. Then the tears continued for at least as long. He held her the whole time.

"Please, Claudia. Tell me what it is that scares you at night. I can't help if you don't."

She just shook her head. He kept holding her until tears led to exhaustion and finally brought her sleep.

Miriam stood with her back pressed against the wall, watching. She'd never seen a man so forlorn. When the master tried to lay the mistress down, she awoke. No more sobs, but the tears started again. He sat beside her, patting her back.

"It's only a dream, Claudia. If you'll tell me about it, maybe I can make it go away."

Miriam closed her eyes. *Please, God, take away the dreams that are tearing up Mistress Claudia.*

The small jerks that punctuated her silent tears finally ceased. Once more, Master Titus buried his face in his hands with his elbows resting on his knees. Miriam's heart ached for him as much as for the mistress.

The master rose and tiptoed to the door. He leaned down to whisper in Miriam's ear, "Your watch now."

Miriam nodded to acknowledge his command. Then she stood in the doorway, watching him walk away with his head bowed. He paused on the balcony just outside his door and looked back at his sister's room. One slow shake of his head, then he disappeared into his room.

Miriam pressed her palm against her cheek. The master loved his sister so much, and it was killing him to watch her suffer.

She tiptoed to the mistress's bedside to be sure she was deeply asleep. Then she crept to her pallet. Once more, she began her fervent prayers for the end of suffering for her mistress...and for her master as well.

The next morning, Claudia sat in the kitchen watching Miriam shape the loaves of bread. The happiness of yesterday had been erased by the agony of last night.

Miriam wiped some flour off her hands. "I don't want to leave you alone like this, mistress, but I have to go to market. Nestor's working in the garden today. Maybe you can watch him while I'm gone?"

Claudia sighed and nodded. "I guess so. Watching Nestor for a while might be interesting."

Miriam picked up two large baskets. "I need to go now, but I'll try to hurry. I want to make you a good lunch today."

Claudia managed a weak smile. She followed Miriam out the door. "Hurry back."

"I will, mistress."

Claudia watched Miriam limp through the gate and head downhill toward the market. Then she dragged herself over to the chair under the tree and settled in to watch Nestor and wait for Miriam.

It had been a long walk down the main road to the market, and Miriam's bad leg was already tired by the time she finished shopping. She would have taken the shortcut down to the market that Nestor had shown her, but she wasn't certain which street it was as she limped down the upper part of the road. She did know where it started going home. She would take the shortcut back since she wanted to get to their house as soon as possible. The mistress had been too sad that morning. Leaving her alone too long was a bad idea. Nestor was keeping an eye on her, but it wasn't the same as being there herself.

With her two baskets of groceries, she turned off the main road and started up the street that would put her on the road again a little to the east of the street that led to the house. Reducing the distance she had to walk by half would help her tired leg. More importantly, it would free Nestor from watching the mistress. From all she'd ever seen, men got distracted too easily and often missed what was going on even when they paid attention. If Nestor failed to catch the mistress before she hurt herself...

Just past the shortcut, two young men were loitering in the shade of a tree beside the road. When they saw the pretty young woman with the limp turn off the busy road and start up the deserted street, one poked the other with his elbow. He tipped his head toward the crippled girl as she disappeared from view. The second one nodded in response, and a lecherous smile spread across his face. They waited a moment to be certain no one else was heading up the street, then they strolled over and started to climb the hill behind her.

Miriam was glad she'd decided to take the shortcut. The street was narrow, and it zigzagged around houses and walled gardens, blocking any view of the main road in either direction. Still, it took her where she wanted to go much quicker than the road would, and it wasn't much steeper. She didn't notice the two men walking up the street behind her until she heard their footsteps. They were walking much faster than she was, so she stepped to the side to let them pass.

When one of them grabbed her arm, she dropped one of her baskets. He spun her around to face him. His eyes hardened as a sneer twisted his lips. Before she could scream, his hand sealed her mouth. He shoved her against a wall while his friend grabbed her other arm and flung her second basket to the side.

She tried to kick, but the first one pinned her against the wall so she couldn't move her legs.

God, help me!

The cruel face of the first man moved closer to her own, and she closed her eyes. *Now, God. Please!*

◆

Titus usually took the main road, but he was in a hurry to get home since he was only taking a break for lunch. Claudia had cried for so long last night; he was afraid she might still be grieving as deeply this morning. Joining her unexpectedly for lunch might cheer her up. He turned his horse into the narrow street that cut the distance in half.

Ahead of him was the sound of a struggle, but he was unprepared for what awaited him as he came around the corner of the house that had blocked his view. Two men had a woman pinned against the wall. When he drew his sword and rode toward them yelling, they hurled the woman into a pile of straw and ran, turning down a passageway that was too narrow for him to follow on horseback.

He turned back to the woman and dismounted to see if she was hurt. She was gathering up some fruit and placing it back into a basket.

"Miriam?"

◆

Master Titus seized Miriam's arm and jerked to make her face him squarely. His black scowl shot bolts of fear through her. She bowed her head and didn't look at his face. Looking into the eyes of an angry master was a good way to trigger a blow.

He'd told her the first night that he didn't like to hit his slaves, but a master might do anything if he was angry enough. Every time she cleaned the table, she saw the mark where he'd driven the knife in as he thought about his brother. Her first mistress used any excuse to strike her. Violence was second nature to a soldier, so why wouldn't a Roman officer hit when he was angry?

But what had she done that would make him so angry? She tensed, waiting for the blow that might be coming. Then he seized her chin and tilted her head until she was forced to look into his eyes.

"Are you hurt?" His tone was abrupt.

"No, master. Thank you for stopping them."

The scowl had relaxed into a frown, and her fear began to drain away. But the master was still unhappy about something.

"What are you doing on this street?"

"I went to market, but it takes me too long to walk the main road so I took the shortcut. I don't want to be late making my mistress her lunch, and I knew I could get home to her much faster this way."

"It is much faster, but it was a foolish choice for a woman alone. It's dangerous for you to get off the main road."

"Yes, master. I know that now. I won't do it again."

◆

Titus reached to remove a piece of straw that was caught in her hair. She cringed. She seemed more frightened of him than she'd been of her attackers.

His lips tightened. She shouldn't expect him to strike her when she'd only made a foolish choice with good intentions. Father had taught him that striking out in anger was the wrong way to treat anyone, even a slave. He'd already told her that the first night. The slave trader said she came from a kind household; her reactions continued to suggest otherwise. Maybe she'd been in a cruel one before that. Old habits must die hard.

He wasn't angry with her. He just didn't want her doing things that might get her killed. Claudia was much happier whenever she was around. What would his sister do if Miriam had died today?

"Stop doing that. I told you I'm not going to hit you."

He extended his hand more slowly, and she remained still as he extracted the straw. "You're not to use this shortcut again if you're not with Nestor. I paid a premium price for you, and I expect you to take better care of my property. Putting yourself at risk like this doesn't serve my sister well."

He picked up several of the fallen fruit and placed them in the basket she was holding.

"You'll ride home with me. I'm joining Claudia for lunch today."

When he whistled, his horse came to stand beside them. He took the basket from her hands and placed it next to the one she'd dropped.

"Up you go."

◆

The master wrapped his hands around Miriam's waist and lifted her onto the stallion's back. He picked up the baskets and waited to hand them to her as she swung her leg over and slid forward to make room for him. After he handed her the baskets, he mounted himself. He put his arm around her and pulled her against him as he slid forward into his normal riding position.

Today she was even less comfortable with his arm holding her against his chest than she'd been the day he bought her.

He'd said he wasn't planning to use her for his entertainment, and he had passed up the opportunity that first night, but she still didn't want him holding her. It didn't take much for a man to change his mind. Her mother had been bought just to cook, but that soon changed. Her mother's years of suffering might well have started with her master touching her for some innocent reason.

Contact was dangerous. She would much rather walk, even with her bad leg. But he was the master. She had no choice.

◆

As they rode up the narrow street, Titus glanced down at her profile. She was a pretty little thing, especially when she was singing. Those dark brown eyes sparkled then. Smart, too. Having Claudia watch her work in the kitchen had been a brilliant idea for distracting his sister from her sad thoughts, and Claudia was even laughing at something she'd said just before he walked into the kitchen after work yesterday. In fact, he hadn't seen Claudia cry at all yesterday until the night terror. Miriam had been right that his sister needed her. He'd made a good purchase, even if he did pay more than he had to.

But why had she put herself at risk just to get his sister's lunch ready on time? No one would expect a new slave to be so eager to serve. Such dedication was exactly what he wanted, but to see it so soon? Buying a cripple and making her grateful that he kept her was certainly paying off.

However, her bad ankle had its drawbacks. She did walk slowly, and that was a problem as long as she was the one going to market. He couldn't have her taking dangerous shortcuts.

"We need to do something different when you go to market."

She turned her head to look up at his face. "I could try to leave earlier so I can get back to make lunch, but I can't leave too early and still help my mistress when she gets up. And Nestor watches her while I'm gone, so he'd get less done, too." She looked down at the horse's neck. "I'm sorry I can't walk faster."

He shook his head to dismiss what she was saying.

"That can't be helped. I'm thinking we need a different way for you to get to market than walking. Maybe a donkey or a small horse."

She moved away from him and twisted to look up at his face with wide eyes. "You want me to learn to ride? I'm not sure how to do that and manage the baskets as well, but I'll try if that's what you want me to do."

She was right. That wouldn't work, but the mental image of her trying to balance two baskets and mount a horse drew a twisted smile.

That turned her cheeks a pretty shade of pink. She thought he was laughing at her, and he actually was. Not at what she'd said, but at how she blushed when she thought he was.

"No, I'm thinking more along the lines of a small cart. A donkey cart should work well for getting you down and back quickly with all your baskets. I'll have Nestor look into that for us."

He pulled her back against his chest and they rode on in silence.

◆

Miriam's stomach knotted when Master Titus took his arm away from her waist and lowered his hand to rest on her thigh. She'd seen him ride with one hand resting on his own thigh, so maybe he didn't mean anything by it. He was ignoring her otherwise. But she was still relieved when they crossed the main road and entered their street. Getting away from his touch couldn't come too soon.

When they reached the house, the master rode through the open gate and back to the stable. She bent over so he could swing his leg past her head and slide off. After he dismounted, he reached up to take her baskets before helping her down. This time she swung her right leg over and waited for him.

He placed his hands on her waist and lifted her down. She wasn't sure what was worse: his arm holding her close against him, his hand on her thigh, or his hands around her waist. He'd told her the first night she wouldn't have to serve him in bed, but Roman officers had a reputation for enjoying the intimate company of women. As soon as her feet were firmly planted on the ground, she moved away from him.

"I'll go prepare lunch for you and my mistress now." She bowed and hurried toward the kitchen door.

◆

Titus watched Claudia rise from the chair under the tree and walk toward him. Her smile looked a little shaky, but at least she wasn't crying. Maybe she'd be smiling more at dinner time after spending the afternoon with Miriam.

While he hugged his sister, he watched Miriam as she carried the two baskets into the kitchen. It had only been a few days since he bought her, and already he couldn't imagine living in this household without her. She'd cheered up Claudia considerably, and he was eating better than he had since he left Rome. That was the best four hundred denarii he ever spent.

Chapter 52

No More Lions

When Titus walked into the kitchen that evening, he found Claudia sitting at the table, leaning on her elbows and smiling as she watched Miriam arrange pastries on a tray. The aromas wafting through the kitchen were enough to make his mouth water. It was going to be another delectable meal.

Claudia stood to give him a hug. "Welcome home, Titus." The smile on her face when she released him made it hard to believe how long she'd cried inconsolably in his arms the night before.

"Just wait until you taste what Miriam has for you tonight." The smile she sent Miriam's way was accompanied by a wink.

His eyes narrowed. Some secret between them? Something funny about what Miriam would be serving him? Then he shrugged. Whatever it was, it would probably be tastier than anything he'd eaten before he bought her.

"I can tell from the smell that I'll have few regrets that I'm eating here instead of with my friends tonight." He kissed Claudia on the forehead before turning toward the door. "As soon as I've cleaned up, you can serve us, Miriam. I'm expecting another fine dinner from my excellent cook. I'm sure you won't disappoint me."

Claudia had seemed happy enough during dinner, and Titus was relieved. She'd been much too quiet at lunch, but the afternoon with

Miriam seemed to have brightened her mood. She'd actually grinned as she watched him enjoying the pastries.

He leaned back in his chair and wiped his mouth. "Definitely better than what Aulus and Gaius would have had at the inn."

"Did I keep you from an evening with your friends?" Regret tinged his sister's voice.

"Yes, but that's all right. I'd rather be here with you."

"But I don't want you to miss being with your friends all the time just to keep me company. I have Miriam, and I'll be fine tonight. Why don't you go join them for a while?"

Titus contemplated his sister. She was smiling at him, and it didn't seem to be one of the fake smiles she had been using to hide her sadness from him.

"Really, Titus. I want you to go. I'll be fine with Miriam here."

He glanced over at Miriam. She smiled and nodded. She thought his sister would be fine, just as Claudia was saying.

"All right. I will. You'll probably be asleep when I get back, so I'll say goodnight to you now."

He rose and kissed her forehead. Then he turned and fixed his eyes on Miriam. No doubt she understood his unspoken command to take good care of her mistress, and she nodded in reply.

"Go tell Nestor to get my horse ready." She headed toward the kitchen to carry out his command.

Titus tossed down one last mouthful of watered wine before he stepped into the courtyard. It would be good to have a night with friends without worrying about Claudia. Miriam would watch over her.

Mistress Claudia's scream jerked Miriam awake. She rolled off her pallet, rose to her feet, and ran as fast as her ankle would allow to her mistress's bedside. Claudia was sitting bolt upright on the bed. Stark terror filled her eyes as she clutched the sheet to her breast.

Miriam stood beside her and grasped her hands to stop them twisting the sheets.

"Mistress. What's wrong?"

The mistress's eyes were staring off into the distance, as if she didn't even realize Miriam was talking to her. Miriam climbed onto the bed and knelt next to the terrified girl. She wrapped her arms around her and drew her against her breast before resting her hand on Mistress

Claudia's head and gently pulling it down onto her own shoulder. *God, please help her. Please stop these dreams and bring peace to her heart.*

"It's all right, mistress. I'm here now, and nothing's going to hurt you."

Mistress Claudia startled and pulled away. Her eyes pulsed with pain, like a wounded animal. Then she let Miriam guide her head back onto her shoulder. Deep, racking sobs shook her whole body. Miriam began to rock her, just as she would a child. For too long, they remained like that.

"Please, mistress. Tell me your nightmare. Don't hold it inside. Telling me will help."

The mistress nodded, but the small jerks of half-suppressed sobs continued. Miriam kept the mistress wrapped in her arms, rocking her slowly. After releasing a shuddering breath, Mistress Claudia turned her eyes toward Miriam's.

"I never liked the games, but Lucius made me go with him once. He said it was something all Romans should do, and he wasn't going to let me be such a soft-hearted fool. I saw them turn the lions on some slaves who had run away. They were running and screaming as the lions jumped on them. They kept twisting and clawing at the ground trying to get free, and then the lions were ripping them apart. I can still hear their screams and see the blood. Lucius sent our father into the arena to die like that."

Anguish beyond measure filled her eyes. Miriam pushed a strand of hair behind Mistress Claudia's ear and laid her hand on her cheek.

"But that's not how it was, mistress. He would have stood or knelt with his arms raised in worship and faced the lions without fear. He died willingly, with praises and songs to his Lord Jesus, not screams. Now he's in heaven with Jesus, and he has no regrets about his choice. He wouldn't want you to grieve so deeply for him."

Mistress Claudia's head snapped back. "How can you be so sure that's how it was?"

Miriam began stroking her hair. "Because that's how Christians die, mistress. I've seen it myself." She blinked hard to push back her own tears as she saw once more the glowing smile on Master Alexander's face just before he was beheaded at the monument to Caesar.

"You've seen it? More than once?"

"Yes, mistress." Too many times more as Master Alexander, the mistress, their children, and each of the free servants were beheaded.

"So, he didn't die like those slaves?"

"No, mistress."

Mistress Claudia laid her head back on Miriam's shoulder. "I can see Father doing that. So that's how Christians die?"

Miriam rested her cheek on the mistress's hair and whispered, "Yes, mistress. That's how Christians die."

If she hadn't been a slave, she would have died that way along with the rest of Master Alexander's household. Her heart had shattered into a thousand pieces as she watched them all die while she still lived. She'd wanted to die with those she loved, but now she was glad she'd been sold and brought to Thracia where Christians were still allowed. God must have spared her for the mistress's sake.

Mistress Claudia nestled quietly in her arms. There were still a few tears, but the jerks were gone. Miriam closed her eyes and continued to pray for this broken heart to heal and to learn to love Jesus, just as her father had.

Titus had thoroughly enjoyed his late evening of talking and drinking with his fellow officers. It was his first since Claudia came, and he'd missed their company. He was just riding through the gate when he heard Claudia's sobs coming from her bedchamber window.

His jaw clenched. Getting drunk with friends wasn't worth the risk of her suicide. Miriam would try, but what if she couldn't stop her? Claudia was still struggling to live with what had happened to their father, and even Philip had barely prevented her from killing herself twice on the voyage from Rome. She'd seemed to be doing much better with Miriam here, and he'd thought it was safe to leave her. It was clear he'd been wrong.

As he rode by the house, the sobs stopped and he heard muffled voices. When he dismounted by the kitchen, he paused to listen. Claudia refused to tell him about the dreams, but maybe she was telling Miriam. He strained to hear what Claudia was saying, but he couldn't make out the words. Claudia's voice, Miriam's voice, some back and forth between them, and then silence.

He trotted through the kitchen and bounded up the stairs toward Claudia's bedchamber, but he stopped in the doorway and stared. What he saw stunned him. Claudia was cradled in Miriam's arms with her eyes closed and the trace of a smile on her lips. She looked more peaceful than he'd ever seen since she came from Rome. Miriam acknowledged his presence with a slight smile, but she continued to rock his sister. He nodded his approval and stepped back from the doorway. Claudia didn't need him with Miriam there.

He shook his head as he headed to his room. He had no idea what Miriam had just done, but it had calmed Claudia when everything he tried failed miserably. She'd told him in the market that she could help his sister's broken heart heal, and it looked like she was right. That day, he thought he'd paid more than she was worth, but he'd found a true bargain after all.

Chapter 53

More Music in the House

Titus had a beast of a headache from the night before as he descended the stairs and headed into the kitchen. He'd drunk more than he intended, and he was paying for it. Still, he was eager to know exactly what had happened last night with Claudia.

Miriam already had his breakfast of fruit and bread waiting on a tray. She was standing at the counter with her back to him, kneading the bread dough and singing to herself. He never understood the words of her songs. She was a Jew, so they must be Aramaic or something.

He sat at the table and began eating some of the grapes as he watched her kneading and singing, totally oblivious to his presence. He could see why Claudia liked having her around. There was a cheerful air about her that must lift Claudia's spirits. He had to admit she had the same effect on him.

When she finally turned, she startled.

"I'm sorry, master. I didn't hear you call." She limped to the table and picked up the tray. "Shall I carry it to the dining room for you now?"

"No, I'll eat it here. I have a question for you about last night."

"Yes, master?"

"What got Claudia so upset and what did you do that calmed her?"

Miriam set the tray back in front of him and took two steps back before she answered.

"She had a nightmare about your father's death."

"She has those every night, but she won't tell me what she dreams. She avoids answering all my questions, but if I don't know, I can't help her. Did she tell you?"

"Yes, master." She tensed, and that drew his frown.

"Well, what did she say?" Irritation sharpened his voice.

She seemed to be trying to avoid answering. Having such a bad headache did nothing to improve his patience.

"If my mistress doesn't want to tell you, I'm not sure I should, master."

She took two more steps back, which got her out of striking range. That irritated him more. What kind of man did she think he was?

"Come back here. I told you before that I'm not going to hit you, and you should stop acting like you think I'm going to. I don't treat slaves that way. My father always disapproved of that, and so do I."

"Yes, master."

She came back to the table and froze before him, not looking at his eyes.

"Now, tell me what makes Claudia so frightened at night. You don't have to tell me exactly what she said if you think she wouldn't want you to."

Her head tipped and she lowered her chin. Then she raised her eyes to look into his. "Your brother made her watch lions kill runaway slaves, and she thought that was how your father died."

"What did you say that calmed her so quickly?"

"I told her how her father really died."

His eyebrows dipped. "That is how he died."

"No, master. My mistress told me your father was killed for being a Christian. He would have died like one."

"And just telling her that calmed her?"

He was incredulous. As far as he could tell, all men died the same.

"Yes, master."

He frowned and shook his head. That made absolutely no sense, but if it worked to calm Claudia, that was good enough for him. His head hurt too much to think about it anymore.

He waved his hand toward the counter. "You can go back to your dough, now."

"Yes, master."

She returned to kneading the dough, but she didn't resume singing. As he sat watching her while he finished the last of his breakfast, he was sorry she didn't. She had a beautiful voice.

Claudia loved music, and Father always kept at least one slave who was a musician. Maybe it was partly the singing that was making her more cheerful. If he could get more music into the house, that would almost certainly be helpful.

"Miriam."

She turned from the dough to face him. "Yes, master?"

She pushed a loose strand of hair back from her forehead, leaving a dusting of flour in her dark brown hair.

"Is it true that you can play the lyre and flute?" Since the slave trader had passed off a cripple as an able-bodied slave, Titus didn't trust anything he'd said about her.

"Yes, master. My last master had me trained since it was something I could do for him that didn't need two good legs."

"Then I'll add that to your duties. Claudia loves music, and it should cheer her to have it every evening."

His eyebrow rose. A musician, too. She would still have been a bargain at four times what he paid for her.

"I'll find out where I can buy instruments and take you there to pick out what you'll play. I know nothing about lyres or flutes." He popped the last bite of bread into his mouth.

◆

Take her there. Miriam didn't like the sound of that. She hadn't seen any instrument sellers in the market where she bought their food, so it would have to be beyond walking distance.

"Will we take the donkey cart?"

The master rolled his eyes. "Of course not. We'll ride. You're light enough that my horse carries us both easily." He ate the last of his grapes and rose to leave. "Plan your work tomorrow around us going in the morning."

She watched him walk out the kitchen door and head to the stables. Then she blew out her breath between pursed lips. Riding with him again and who knew how far they would have to go. But getting the instruments would give her one more way to help Mistress Claudia, and that would be worth any price, even being held so close to the master as they rode.

As Miriam helped her get ready for bed, Claudia found herself looking forward to a good night's sleep. She still missed her father terribly, but when she thought of his death, she pictured him just as

Miriam had described, smiling and singing as he worshiped the God he loved and dying quickly without fear and unbearable pain. No roars and screams and blood would haunt her again.

The next morning, Miriam chewed her lip as she stood waiting for Master Titus to bring his horse from the stable. Mistress Claudia had been so excited about getting her instruments today that the master had decided to go immediately after breakfast. He'd arranged to be off duty all morning to have plenty of time for their excursion. The instrument maker's workshop was some distance west of the city, so it would be the longest ride she'd had to make with him yet.

Mistress Claudia stood facing Miriam. As the master was leading his horse over, she grasped Miriam's hand, and an excited smile brightened her whole face.

"Just think. Tonight I'll get to listen to lyre music again. There's almost nothing I love listening to more."

Miriam's smile mirrored the mistress's. "I hope I'll play well enough to please you, mistress."

"Everything you do for me is done well. I'm so glad Titus bought you."

◆

Titus laid his hand on Miriam's shoulder. She spun to face him as he stood close behind her. She barely came up to his chin, so she had to tip her head way back to look at his face.

"Up you go." He placed his hands on her waist and lifted her onto the horse's back. After she swung her leg over and slid forward, he mounted behind her and pulled her close as he settled in.

"We'll be back as soon as we can." He turned his horse and nudged him into a quick walk. Claudia waved at them until they disappeared through the gate.

As they started down the main road toward the edge of the city, Titus looked down at the small woman held close against him by his left arm. The night before last, she'd calmed Claudia's night terrors when he'd failed miserably. This morning, she had his sister smiling as if she were a child about to celebrate her birthday. So far, she truly had been what his sister needed.

Funny how she'd known that even before she met Claudia. To think he'd almost walked past her in the slave market. If she hadn't touched his arm and said his sister needed her, he would never have noticed her. He would have missed out on the best purchase he'd ever made.

◆

It was odd, but Miriam didn't feel as threatened by his arm around her as she had on their previous rides. It was probably because she knew him better. He really did love his sister, and he really had bought her to serve Mistress Claudia. That was why God had brought him to the slave market—so he could buy her before the brothel did and she could help the mistress's heart heal. God was answering her prayers for her mistress already.

They rode in silence for several minutes. Then the master moved his arm and placed his hand on his own thigh. Her back still rested against his chest, and she knew better than to try to move away from him after the last scold, but at least his arm wasn't around her. She didn't like that, even if it was only for her safety.

"I heard this craftsman makes beautiful lyres, but he always has flutes in stock as well. We should be able to get everything we need from him."

"We'll need to get spare strings as well, master, to avoid another trip. Strings break fairly often. We'll also need to pick a lyre that's easy to restring and tune."

"I'm glad the trader didn't lie about you being a musician. I'm planning to have you play and then pick something that's not too expensive but still sounds good. Maybe you can bargain for a lower price, too. Nestor said you do that well in the market. I don't know any more about buying lyres than I did about buying house slaves. I got a good deal on you, but I'm making you responsible for getting a good deal on the instruments today."

He looked down at her and smiled.

Miriam tried not to blush, but she couldn't quite stop it. She avoided looking into his eyes when he praised her, but it pleased her to know he'd gone from regretting how much he paid for her to thinking she was a good deal, even with her bad ankle.

"I've never done that before, but I'll try if that's what you want me to do."

He chuckled. "Did you know that's what you always say? Time for something else you've never done before." He wrapped his arm tightly around her ribcage and kicked his horse into a canter.

Her eyes widened, and she tensed as the horse gained speed. Then she relaxed as she got used to it.

As they approached the lyre-maker's shop, the master slowed his stallion to a walk. Miriam was almost sorry they were there. It was exhilarating to travel so fast with the wind blowing in her face and the scenery flying by. So much so that she'd forgotten about him holding her so closely and simply enjoyed the ride. After he dismounted, she waited until he lifted her down and set her carefully on her feet.

"Let's go see if you can get me that bargain."

She drew a deep breath. "I'll try, master."

He turned and walked into the workshop with her a few feet behind him.

◆

The lyre maker's eyebrows rose as two people entered his shop. A Roman officer with a crippled slave girl in tow? That was a first.

"Welcome. How may I help you today, noble sir?"

The tribune turned toward the girl and motioned her forward. "I have a musician here who needs to pick out a lyre and a flute. I leave the shopping to her."

Such a young woman being given the responsibility of choosing? The merchant tried to keep his smile from revealing too much. Here was a chance for an easy profit. The officer clearly knew nothing, and a slave girl wouldn't know a good deal from a bad one. Or care, for that matter.

He directed a patronizing smile at the girl and waved his arm toward an array of lyres. "Play any you wish and choose. Then we can discuss price."

"If you please, I would like to know the starting price for each before I play. Then if I find one that will suit my master's taste, we can discuss the real price."

◆

Titus fought a smile as shock registered on the merchant's face when his slave began the bargaining so astutely. Nestor was right. She'd picked up excellent trading skills somewhere. If she'd been buying herself, she would never have had to pay more than 350 denarii.

After playing every lyre in the shop and seeing how easily each tuned, she selected one that had a lovely sound but also had a gouge in the wood that marred its beauty.

Miriam cradled her chin as she rubbed her cheek. "This one sounds rather good, I suppose, but this gouge...I don't know...My master's guests might think it unfit to play at banquets. Many are more impressed by the beauty of the wood than the sound of the music. The gouge does make it ugly, and that's a problem.

"The wood of this cheaper one is much prettier, and the sound is almost as good, too. Maybe the cheaper one is a better choice...although my master might be willing to buy the ugly one if you reduce the price to just one tenth more than the much prettier cheaper one."

The lyre maker shifted his attention from the slave to her master. He stood with his arms crossed, nodding in agreement with what the girl had proposed. The lyre maker looked back at the more expensive lyre. She was right that the ugliness of the beautiful sounding instrument would make it hard to sell. The price she offered was reasonable for a lyre that might sit in his shop for many months or even years.

"I accept the offer. Now shall we look at the flutes?"

As they left the shop, Titus looked down at the smiling woman carrying the carefully wrapped lyre and flute.

"Very clever trading, Miriam. How did you know he would drop the price so low on the lyre you wanted? I would never have thought it possible if I hadn't watched you."

"Too many people judge only by appearance, so they can't see the true worth of something. I thought he might agree to the price if I just pointed that out to him."

As she limped beside him, a corner of his mouth lifted. If he'd taken her back as defective, he would never have owned an exceptional slave who could comfort and cheer his sister, prepare superb meals, play the lyre beautifully, and bargain with the best of them. She was right. Judging only by appearances could make a man miss out on something really worth having.

Chapter 54

PHILIP RETURNS

It was late afternoon when Philip turned off the main road and headed up the street toward his house. It had been a good trip. The harvest had been excellent. As was his custom, he'd given a share of the bounty to his workers, both slave and free, so everyone had cause to celebrate. The harvest celebrations were usually his favorite events of the year, and he often lingered awhile at each estate. This year, however, he was eager to get back to Perinthus. Celebrating with his workers could never match the charm of spending time with Claudia.

He'd left early and kept his horse at a steady trot for most of the distance. He wore a coat of road dust. He'd intended to clean up before going to the house he was renting to Titus, but as he approached the gate, he couldn't resist the urge to see her immediately.

Nestor was working in the garden when Philip rode through the gate. He reined in by Nestor and dismounted.

The corners of Nestor's mouth twitched as Philip brushed off some dust. "It's good to see you, master."

Philip handed his stallion's reins to Nestor. "It's good to be home. How is she?"

"These last two days, much better. Quite well, in fact. Master Titus bought a Christian slave girl to be her maid and cook. Mistress Claudia was crying often when she first came, but the more time she spends with Miriam, the better she seems to be doing. I don't think she cried at all yesterday or today."

Philip's eyebrow shot up. "Not even after the nightmares?"

"No, master. Those ended two nights ago."

A broad smile spread across Philip's face. He'd spent many hours praying about the problem preventing their marriage, and God had begun answering his prayers.

Titus had bought a Christian slave to serve her. Her brother couldn't have known the girl was a Christian. He probably hated Christians even more than Claudia did. He would never knowingly bring one into his household, not into a place where she might influence his sister.

Philip slapped Nestor's arm. "That is good news."

He needed to talk with this slave and enlist her aid. If she and Claudia became as close as Penelope and Junia were, it might not be long before Claudia would change her mind about the followers of Jesus and even want to become one herself.

◆

Claudia had just walked over to the counter to hand Miriam the carrots she'd been cutting up for the salad course. She almost dropped the bowl when she glanced out the window and saw Philip standing by his horse and talking with Nestor.

"He's back!" She placed the bowl on the counter before running out the kitchen door.

He heard her footsteps and barely had time to turn before she threw her arms around him and pressed her cheek into his chest.

"You're home! I missed you so much."

She stepped back and placed her hand on his scarred cheek. Her thumb stroked the ridges as she gazed at his adorably ugly face.

"I'm covered with dust, Claudia. You got yourself all dirty."

"I don't care. Come sit with me." She took his hand to lead him over to the chairs under the tree.

◆

Philip followed obediently. He couldn't have asked for a better homecoming. The happy smile on her face made her radiantly beautiful. She was as eager for his company as he was for hers. He'd made the right choice not waiting to clean up before he came.

◆

Miriam was surprised by Mistress Claudia's impetuous response to the arrival of the brawny man, but that was only until he turned around. With all those scars, there could be no mistake. It was the Philip that her mistress spoke of so often, and he was the same Philip she'd seen in the house of Master Alexander. He'd shared in their worship, so he was a Christian, too. Master Alexander had said more than once what a fine young man Philip of Perinthus was.

The two of them leaned toward each other while they talked. Mistress Claudia reached up and caressed his scarred cheek. It was obvious they were very much in love.

But the mistress spoke with such anger and hatred about the Christians in Rome who'd worshiped with her father. Master Titus was even more hostile, supporting the anti-Christian policy in Bithynia that led to the sacrifice of Master Alexander and his family. Was it possible for the mistress to be so in love with a Christian man if she knew he followed Jesus?

Miriam drew a deep breath and blew it out. She would take care to say nothing to the mistress of what she knew about Philip. If the mistress was to learn that Philip followed Jesus, it would be from his own lips, not hers.

It was close to the time when Titus was expected when Philip rose from the chair.

"Time for me to go. Your brother will be here soon."

Claudia rose with him. He placed her hand on his forearm before resting his own hand upon it. Her shoulder brushed his arm as they walked toward his horse.

"Can you come again tomorrow morning? We could play Conquest."

"No. I would much rather do battle with my favorite general, but I have business that needs my attention after my absence."

"Then come to dinner tomorrow, and bring Penelope. Our cook is wonderful, and I'll have a special surprise for you during dinner."

"Nothing would give me greater pleasure."

"And come early, before Titus gets home. We can all spend some time together, like on your ship."

They reached the stable, where Nestor had tied Philip's horse. As he prepared to mount, she placed her fingertips on his cheek and traced the swirls.

"I'm so glad you've returned. Now that I have the inspiration back with me, I can work on my poem about mountain ridges where the trees don't grow."

A huge grin split his face as he lifted her fingers from his cheek before kissing her palm.

"I look forward to reading the latest creation by my favorite poet."

Philip mounted the stallion and sat smiling down at her glowing face. It felt so good to be the man who could bring a look of joy to the right woman's eyes.

He nudged his horse into a walk and headed out the gate. He turned for one last look at her, and it filled his heart to see her waving and looking happy.

The anguish of losing her father seemed to be over. Now he could focus his prayers on her deciding to follow Jesus so their future together could begin.

Titus was hoping for a relaxing evening when he rode through the gate. Perhaps the good spirits Claudia had been in after he returned with Miriam and her new musical instruments would have survived the afternoon. It was too hard watching his sister cry.

When he entered the kitchen, Claudia sat at the table with a happy glow on her face as she watched Miriam complete the final preparations for their dinner.

She rose and gave him a hug. "I'm so glad you're home. Guess what!" She was beaming.

He hugged her back "I have no idea, but it must be something good."

"Oh, it is. Philip is back, and he and Penelope are coming to dinner tomorrow."

His sister's enthusiasm drew a smile. "That's good. I'm sure I'll enjoy getting to know Philip and his sister better."

"I know you will. Penelope is very sweet, and Philip, well, he's the nicest, smartest man in the whole world."

Titus would have to be deaf and blind not to notice that she liked the ugly Greek. Her affection surprised him at first since she'd always said she wanted a handsome man like him. All those scars made Philip ugly enough that his sister should have found him highly unattractive, even repulsive. But maybe four weeks on a ship with no one else for comparison had reduced her sensitivity, and Philip had been very kind to her. She'd always said kindness was important, too. Their father had been a kind man.

With all Philip had done to help when Claudia first came, the Greek was clearly a generous man as well. The loan of Nestor had solved a huge problem at no expense to himself, and Philip's connections had turned up a house that met their needs at a price he could afford. The Greek had even turned down his offer to pay for her passage from Rome.

Still, if this Philip was going to remain in their circle of friends, it would be good to get to know him better. Philip might well be one of the wealthiest men in Perinthus, but there was more than wealth to consider. Titus didn't want Claudia spending too much time with the wrong type of people, and there was something different about Philip. Something he couldn't quite put his finger on, but it was there.

It was the first time Miriam would play during dinner, and butterflies danced in her stomach. The mistress had told her to play some of her favorites, and then Mistress Claudia would pick what she wanted for Philip tomorrow.

She placed the salad on the table. Then she seated herself on one of the couches and picked up the lyre.

Of all the tasks she performed in Master Alexander's household, this was by far the one she loved most. As her fingers plucked the strings, she felt her spirit soar. She imagined herself as part of the heavenly host, offering the most sublime melodies in praise and thanksgiving to her Lord. Her eyes were almost closed as the music transported her heavenward.

When Miriam finished the first selection, she refocused on her master and mistress at the table. They had finished the salad course, so she set the lyre aside and rose to clear it and fetch the next.

Master Titus looked up at her as she reached to take his plate. "I don't know much about music, but that sounded good to me. It's hard to say whether you're a better cook or musician, Miriam."

Mistress Claudia beamed. "Well, I do know music, and it was superb. I don't think I've ever heard anything more beautiful. I can hardly wait to have you play for Philip and Penelope tomorrow. He's going to love it."

The corner of the master's mouth lifted. "You're full of surprises, Miriam. Whatever I ask you to do, you do it well for me. Your old owner would have insisted on a much higher price if he'd really known what you can do."

Miriam felt the heat spread from her cheeks to the tips of her ears. "I'm glad it pleased you, master."

She dipped her head before limping into the kitchen to fetch the second course. The echo of their words pulled the biggest smile as she passed through the storeroom. Nothing could be better than knowing she'd given such pleasure to the mistress who was becoming a friend and the kind master who'd saved her from the brothel. God had been so good when He brought Master Titus to buy her.

Chapter 55

MUCH MORE THAN GENEROSITY

As Titus descended the stairs the next morning, he heard Miriam singing in the kitchen, as usual. A satisfied smile appeared. His little Jewish slave was the best purchase he'd ever made.

He'd been so worried about Claudia when he held her, sobbing in his arms, that first evening at Philip's. The first night in his own house had been many times worse. Who would have thought she could have changed so much in a single week?

He gave all the credit to Miriam. Since he found her consoling Claudia that night he went drinking, the nightmares were gone. It made no sense that Miriam telling Claudia their father had died like a Christian would make any difference, but since that night, the dark cloud had cleared from his sister's mind.

He turned in at the kitchen and seated himself at the table, where his breakfast tray was already waiting. Miriam turned from her dough and smiled at him.

"Shall I carry the tray into the dining room now, master?"

"No. I'll eat here. You can keep working."

She turned back and resumed kneading the large mound of dough.

"And keep singing. I like the music."

As her voice floated around him, he settled back in the chair and popped the first grape into his mouth. Yes, indeed. The best purchase he'd ever made.

Mistress Claudia was dressed in Philip's favorite sky-blue tunic as she stood by the kitchen window, watching for him.

Miriam stirred the special sauce whose delectable aroma now filled the room. She'd been pleasantly surprised when the mistress told her they would leave her hair down so the reddish blonde tresses could simply cascade over her shoulders and down her back. Miriam had expected her to want a fancy Greek style since Philip was coming. That would have taken at least an hour to do.

She would never have said anything to Mistress Claudia, but she really wanted that extra time to work on the special dinner. The mistress was very eager for everything to be as close to perfect as possible for her first dinner for Philip.

Mistress Claudia stepped back from the window, ran her fingers into her hair, and shook them to make it look fuller before tucking it behind her ears. "They're here, Miriam. After we get settled under the tree, bring us something to drink." She hurried out the door to greet Philip and Penelope as Nestor led them back toward the chairs under the spreading tree in the garden.

◆

Penelope wrapped her arms around Claudia for a big hug before taking both her hands. "I've missed being together every day. I'm so glad you invited us down to dine with you."

"I'm glad Titus found us a house so close to yours that it's even a short walk."

Claudia released one of Penelope's hands and reached out to Philip. With a broad smile, he wrapped hers in his own. Then she led them to the bench and two chairs that were arranged in a semicircle under the tree.

Penelope took the end chair to encourage them to sit on the bench together. She needn't have worried. Claudia didn't release Philip's hand until she'd guided him down right next to her.

Philip handed Claudia a small bundle. "For my favorite general."

She laid it in her lap and removed the cloth wrapping. Inside was the folded board and the small box containing the pieces of the Conquest game they'd used on the ship.

"I can't take your game, Philip. What will you use?"

"Yes, you can. I can get another. I'll never find a better opponent, and using this set with someone who can't beat me just wouldn't feel right. If I give it to you, you'll have to invite me down often for a match."

"Perhaps we can play after dinner?"

"Whatever you say, mighty general. I seem to remember you beating me the last time we played, so I get to go first. I want a chance to regain my honor."

Penelope couldn't quite contain a sly smile. If Claudia didn't invite Philip, she would invite Claudia. She planned to do her part to make certain Philip ended up with the perfect woman for him.

Titus rode through the gate and around back to the stable. As he rounded the corner, his eyebrows popped up until he forced them down. Philip and Penelope were already there. He'd expected them to come late enough that he'd have time to clean up before their arrival.

His eyebrows lowered further. Penelope should have been sitting on the bench beside Claudia, not Philip. His sister should have had her hair in one of the elegant Greek styles that Miriam was supposed to know how to do. Instead, it was worn as simply as possible. She looked radiant as she talked with Philip, and the Greek didn't take his eye off her. Philip's sister looked very satisfied with the whole situation. The whole scene raised some serious questions.

Claudia heard the hoofbeats and turned her gaze from Philip to him.

"Titus. I'm glad you're home. Was it a good day?"

He rode over to them and slid off. He handed the reins to Nestor, who led the horse away for his rubdown.

"It was like any other day. Nothing exciting happened. It's good to see you again, Philip."

Philip smiled at him. "I can say the same, Titus."

Claudia took Titus's hand. "We've been having a lovely time getting caught up. Penelope and I have so missed our talks like we had on the ship."

She looked first at Penelope, but Titus saw how quickly her eyes focused back on Philip.

"I know you'll want to clean up before we eat. Take your time. We'll just sit here and talk until you're ready."

Titus got the feeling that the longer he took, the happier she might be. "I'll come get you when I'm ready."

Claudia flashed her smile at him, then turned her attention back to Philip. As Titus turned toward the kitchen door, he considered the implications of what he'd just seen. There might be more than generosity involved with Philip. Much more.

Miriam stared at the blue glass wine pitcher on the top shelf in the storeroom. The ordinary pitcher she used for the master wouldn't do for the mistress's special dinner for Philip. But even on tiptoes, she couldn't touch the bottom of the shelf. As she scanned the storeroom, her gaze fell on the small sacks of wheat and barley that Nestor had piled in the corner.

If she stacked three of them, she could reach it. She dragged the first over and patted it to level it out. Then she dragged each in turn to the pile and staggered them to make shallow steps. She gauged the height of the stack and the distance from her hand to the pitcher as she reached up for it. High enough.

The first sack was solid enough when she stepped on it. The second shifted a little when she put her weight on it. The third shifted more, but then it steadied. She stood on tiptoes and reached for the handle.

"Miriam."

She spun at the sudden sound of his voice. The top sack shifted, and she began to fall. The master jumped forward and caught her just before her head hit the opposite shelves.

"Don't do that again."

The master was holding her in his arms. His eyes were so close to hers, and his lips were smiling. She felt the heat rise to the tips of her ears. His smile broadened into a grin before she looked away.

"I'm sorry, master. I was just trying to get the pitcher down. I'm not quite tall enough."

He set her down so she was standing right in front of him. His chest bumped her as he reached over her head to lift the pitcher down from its place on the high shelf.

"Next time you need something from that shelf, get me or Nestor." His smile raised her heart rate as he handed her the pitcher. "I should have Nestor make you a stepstool so you won't have to be stacking sacks to reach something. I can't have the best cook in the city getting hurt. I don't want to eat ordinary food again."

"Yes, master."

She looked into his eyes like he'd said she was supposed to when he spoke. The blush that had been fading flared up again. That triggered his grin, and she blushed even more.

"Claudia's in no hurry to eat, but I am. If that smell is any indication, I'm expecting the best dinner yet as soon as I clean up." The master stepped back into the kitchen.

Miriam clutched the pitcher to her breast as a slow smile escaped. The master was so understanding when something was hard for her. God had surely blessed her with a master almost as good as Master Alexander.

Dinner would be served at the table instead of the couches, and Philip sat to Claudia's right. It made it easier for him to look at her, and only politeness made him look at anyone else. Then Titus's cook placed his plate in front of him.

His head bounced back. "Miriam? Why are you here?"

"Master Alexander was killed, and his slaves were all sold."

"And the rest of his family?"

"Dead."

Philip's lips tightened. "I'm sorry, Miriam."

Her eyes moistened as she nodded.

Philip turned to Titus. "You were certainly fortunate to get Miriam. I would have bought her myself if I'd known she was for sale in Perinthus. Alexander always considered her a treasure."

"I think she's a treasure, too." Claudia looked over at Miriam and smiled. "She's already helped me feel so much better. My nightmares are gone because of her. I couldn't bear to part with her."

Miriam blushed to hear herself described as a treasure. She didn't want to leave Mistress Claudia, either, even though she'd only known her for a little more than a week. They were already becoming more like friends than like mistress and slave.

"The way she cooks would make anyone glad to own her." Master Titus smiled at her as she set his plate in front of him, then turned his attention back to Philip. "She plays the lyre beautifully, too. You'll hear her as soon as she serves this course. I got a real bargain when I bought her."

Miriam's face warmed as she heard Master Titus's praising her to his guest. It felt so good to know he valued her service and no longer thought he'd paid too much for a crippled slave.

After delivering the last plate, Miriam sat on the couch, picked up her lyre, and began to play.

◆

Claudia watched Philip. As the elegant music filled the room, that special smile that signaled his delight appeared. As he watched Miriam play, Claudia reached over and touched his hand. He took his eye off Miriam and focused it on Claudia as he wrapped his fingers around hers. His eye spoke volumes before he turned it back on Miriam.

She couldn't have been happier with his response. To be able to offer him something that he could enjoy so much, even in her house with its few luxuries, made her heart sing.

◆

Titus blanked his face as he watched the silent conversation between his sister and the Greek. At first, he wasn't sure whether he liked what he was seeing. He hadn't realized before that night how it stood between them. Philip had told him that Penelope and Claudia had become good friends during the voyage. He'd said nothing at all about his attachment to her. Philip was looking at Claudia like a man in love. All the things the Greek had done to help him set up a household for Claudia now made sense.

From the sparkle in Claudia's eyes each time she looked at the ugly Greek, it was clear she was in love, too. He hadn't expected that, but maybe it wasn't so surprising. Philip had been very kind to her from the moment she boarded his ship, and Claudia was smart enough to value kindness over physical attractiveness once she got over the initial shock of him being so ugly.

As Titus watched the two of them together, he decided it might be a good thing. Philip was one of the wealthiest men in the area. He'd certainly be able to take care of her as his wife. He'd proven his genuine concern for her in all he'd done to help them since she arrived. If his interest should end in a request for her hand in marriage, Titus would not have to think long about what his answer would be.

Chapter 56

TIME WITH THE GENERAL

Claudia waited with eager anticipation for Penelope to come spend the next morning with her. What she hoped was that Philip might be free and would come, too.

She was in the kitchen with Miriam, watching out the window.

"I do so hope Philip can come to me this morning. It's been much too long since we played Conquest or read together. I wish we'd been able to stay together on the ship forever. I've never been happier than there."

Miriam's mouth was open to answer when Claudia interrupted.

"I see him." With a joyful smile, she left Miriam at the counter and hurried out the door to greet them.

Claudia gave Penelope a quick hug, then turned to take Philip's hands in her own.

"I'm so glad you could come. I've missed you so."

Penelope carried a codex. "I thought you two might want to play Conquest, so I brought my own entertainment." A mischievous smile played on her lips. "Don't pay any attention to me."

Claudia flashed her an appreciative grin. Penelope understood.

"Well, mighty general, I believe you won last time. I have until lunchtime to take the Empire from you."

Claudia had set a small table and the bundle containing the game by the chairs under the tree. She led Philip over and seated herself. As he began setting up the board, she leaned forward to slide his eyepatch up and off his face.

"I like the natural you better. You don't need this here."

The eyepatch dangled from her arm as her fingertips traced the ridges at the corner of his eye. The beaming smile that her gentle touch evoked warmed her heart.

"Are you trying to distract me so you'll win easier?"

She laughed. "How did you know?"

"You once said all's fair in love and war."

"So, is this love or war?"

His answer was a broad smile. "I think you know. On guard, Claudia. Prepare to lose your armies."

As she focused on the board, Philip gave thanks that God had given him the chance to save her from her brother. If only God would hurry up and save her from herself.

As Claudia escorted Philip and Penelope to the gate, she wrapped her arm around Philip's and leaned her head against his shoulder.

"I need the eyepatch now, Claudia."

When Philip held his hand out for it, she held it behind her back. She kept switching it back and forth between her hands as he unsuccessfully reached around her to get it. Finally, she let him catch her hand and take it.

As he positioned it on his face, she smiled up at him.

"So, is it time yet?"

"Time?"

"You know, time to start our future together?"

He'd hoped she wouldn't ask that question. He didn't want to dampen the joy of the morning. He pushed a strand of hair behind her ear.

"Not yet."

Her smile dimmed but remained. "I know you said not to ask why, so I won't. I just want you to know that I'm ready whenever you decide we can."

He rested his hand on her cheek and stroked it with his thumb. The love in his eye should tell her more than mere words ever could. Her dazzling smile said she would trust him and try to wait patiently.

Titus was in an exceptionally good mood as he approached the kitchen. He'd heard Claudia's laughter as he handed the reins to Nestor. His little Jewish slave had taken the dark clouds from his sister's mind and make her laugh again. He never thought she could do that so quickly, even though she'd told him she could help his sister's heart heal.

As he stepped through the door, the most tantalizing aroma wafted across his nostrils. Miriam was standing by the fire, leaning over to stir the pot that was the source of the scrumptious smell. He inhaled deeply, then let out his breath with a contented sigh. Time to show some appreciation to the best cook in the city.

She jerked when he wrapped his arm around her waist as he took the spoon from her hand.

"Hold still, Miriam. I don't want you getting burned."

He held her snuggly against his chest to keep her away from the fire as he leaned forward to scoop some of the sauce from the pot. After blowing on the steaming mouthful to cool it, he took a taste.

"You did it again. Another truly delicious one. Who would have thought I was buying the best cook in the city for only four hundred denarii?"

She was blushing when he finally released her and handed back the spoon. He took one look at the pink suffusing her cheeks and chuckled.

"Yes, indeed. Best cook in the city."

He kissed Claudia on the cheek before heading toward the bath to wash up for dinner.

Miriam returned to stirring the sauce, still blushing at the memory of him holding her that way. She was still uncomfortable with him touching her, even though she knew he didn't really mean anything by it. He'd promised she wouldn't be his nighttime entertainment. Still, it made her feel good to know the master appreciated her cooking that much. It was a joy to serve a master like him, and she thanked God yet again that Master Titus had bought her.

When Philip rode through the gate Monday morning, Claudia was holding a basket while Miriam pulled some carrots. She handed her basket to Miriam and hurried over to greet him as he slid from his horse.

"I'm so glad to see you. Ready to cross swords this morning?"

"Not today. I just stopped by to see you before I go out of town for a few days."

Worry lines creased her forehead. "I don't like it when you travel. Something might happen to you."

Philip chuckled before placing his hand on her cheek. "You don't have to worry about me, Claudia. I'm only going to my estates west of the city. The road there is perfectly safe."

"When will you return?"

"I need to be back in Perinthus to attend to some business next Monday."

"Then I want you and Penelope to come for dinner Monday night."

A smile tugged at the corner of his mouth. "I hoped you'd ask. Titus is right when he says Miriam's the best cook in town."

"Is that all you come here for?"

The smile morphed into a grin. "I think you know the answer to that."

He was actually going to be back Saturday night so he could teach at his house church Sunday. He was planning to drop in on her Sunday afternoon after everyone left. Waiting until Monday before he saw her again was out of the question.

He'd put some road dust on before he went to her house. When he returned from a trip, he always stopped to see her before he went home, so she'd expect to see him dusty.

She traced a curved scar on his cheek. "I'll be counting the days until you return."

He mounted and sat smiling down at her.

She rested her hand on his leg. "Be careful, and come back to me quickly."

"I'll be back before you know it." He turned his horse and headed toward the gate. When he twisted to look back at her before passing through, she was waving and smiling. He would be counting the days until his return, too.

Chapter 57

FROM HIS OWN MOUTH

Miriam had prepared Nestor some bread and cheese for his Sunday breakfast. Philip had lent him to Titus with the understanding that he would spend Sunday mornings at Philip's house. Master Titus thought he went there to perform some special tasks for his master. He was really going for Sunday worship.

"Thank you for the breakfast, Miriam. It should be a good day. Master Philip returned last night. It's always better when he's there."

Miriam smiled and waved as he headed out the door.

Mistress Claudia stepped into the kitchen just as he disappeared. Miriam's smile dimmed. The mistress had never come down before Miriam helped her dress.

"Philip is back early? Let's go to his house this morning and surprise him."

Miriam's breathing froze. That was a terrible idea. The house church was meeting at Philip's, and worship would be starting shortly after Nestor got there.

"I don't think that's a good idea, mistress. We should wait until Monday, when Master Philip told you he was expecting to drop by our house. He might have something else he needs to do today."

Claudia chuckled. "Philip is always as eager to see me as I am to see him. He'll be very pleased when I surprise him. I'm sure he can spare at least a few minutes for me to welcome him back home. Let's go get me ready."

With a sense of foreboding, Miriam watched the mistress hurry up the stairs. Going to Philip's on a Sunday while the mistress still hated Christians was a very bad idea, but how could she prevent it? Shaking her head, she followed her mistress.

When Miriam entered the bedchamber, Mistress Claudia had already picked a tunic in Philip's favorite shade of blue. She'd also placed a leather headband on the dressing table.

"I want my hair down, not even the gold net. Philip likes it best that way, and I want to be especially pretty for him when he first sees me."

Miriam helped her into the tunic and slowly brushed her hair. She was about to place the leather headband with the gold medallions over her hair when Claudia turned and beamed up at her.

"I've missed Philip so much. I can't wait to hear his voice. He thinks he's terribly ugly, but I don't think so. He's not handsome, but I like the way he smiles and that twinkle in his eye. I love the feel of his cheek and how he looks at me when I touch his scars."

She turned to look back at her mirror as Miriam finished arranging her reddish-blonde tresses and slid the headband into place. Her eyes sparkled as she inspected herself in the shiny silver surface.

"Pretty the way he likes, so I'm ready. Let's go."

Her mistress rose and hurried to the head of the stairs. She looked back at Miriam, who was moving slowly as she tried to think of some way to persuade Mistress Claudia not to go to Philip's that morning.

"Hurry, Miriam."

Reluctant but obedient, Miriam walked down the stairs as quickly as she safely could and followed her mistress through the kitchen and past the vegetable garden.

Mistress Claudia led them out the gate and started up the hill. They walked the quarter mile to Philip's house as quickly as Miriam's leg would allow. The pedestrian entrance through the roadside wall was locked, and there was no response to them knocking.

"Master Philip and Mistress Penelope may not be here, mistress. We should go home and try again tomorrow."

"Not yet. Let's try the carriage gate that leads to the stable. Maybe someone is there."

Miriam hoped the gatekeeper would tell them Philip was not available, but Nestor might have told him she was a Christian. Would he think she was bringing Claudia for the worship?

"Welcome, Miriam. Mistress Claudia. Come in."

He swung the gate open, and Mistress Claudia hurried through with Miriam close behind her.

"Mistress, are you sure this is a good idea? He isn't expecting us, and surprising him might not be what he wants."

"Don't be silly. He's never been anything but happy to see me since I met him. I'm not worried about him having another woman here or anything else that would make him not want to see me."

◆

They headed toward the garden at the rear of the house. Claudia's heart beat faster when she heard his deep voice. She couldn't quite make out the words until...

"Remember that Jesus warned us what following him might involve. The Apostle Matthew recorded the words of Jesus for us. 'Do not think that I have come to bring peace to the earth. I have not come to bring peace, but a sword.'

"'For I have come to set a man against his father, and a daughter against her mother, and a daughter-in-law against her mother-in-law. And a person's enemies will be those of his own household. Whoever loves father or mother more than me is not worthy of me, and whoever loves son or daughter more than me is not worthy of me. And whoever does not take his cross and follow me is not worthy of me. Whoever finds his life will lose it, and whoever loses his life for my sake will find it.'

"So, my brothers and sisters, let us always be in prayer for the ones we love who have not yet chosen to follow Jesus. So much depends on their choice, both for this world and the next."

Claudia froze. It couldn't be. The man she loved more than life itself was one of the people she hated most of all. It felt like a dagger had been driven into her heart by the one she trusted most in the world.

As tears sprang to her eyes, she covered her mouth with her hands and turned toward Miriam. Miriam reached out to take her hand, but before she could, Claudia whirled and ran.

The gatekeeper opened the gate before she reached him. She almost stumbled as she looked over her shoulder, back toward the garden where she'd dreamed of a future with the finest man she'd ever known, the garden where love and hate had collided and torn the heart out of her.

◆

Miriam ran after her mistress, but her limp made her fall far behind. Even when the mistress turned in at their own gate, her fear knew no relief. Miriam needed to catch up with her. There were too many knives there.

When she finally reached the house and passed through the kitchen to the inner courtyard, she could hear the mistress sobbing in her room. She rushed up the stairs as quickly as she could manage and found her mistress prostrate on the bed, her face buried in her arms and shaking as she cried.

Miriam limped over to the bed and sat beside her. She stroked Mistress Claudia's hair. *God, please give me the words that will help.*

"Don't cry, mistress. It's going to be all right."

The tears slowed, and Mistress Claudia rolled onto her back.

"It's never going to be all right. How could I have known him for so long without him telling me he was a Christian? How could he keep that secret from me and let me fall in love with him? Do you know how many times I've told him I hated Christians, that I wished they'd all die, especially the ones who got my father to follow Jesus?

"The very first day we met, I told him I could gladly watch Titus cutting them down and even kill them myself. I thought it was strange that he looked sad when I said that. It might have been Philip's father who made Father become a Christian. Malleolus said the man who would rescue me was one of Father's close friends, and no one I ever met at our house owned merchant ships. It had to be someone he worshiped with. Philip might even have had something to do with it. When we first met, he told me he'd talked with my father. Where could that have been except at a gathering of Christians?"

Mistress Claudia pressed her palms against her cheeks as she fought the silent jerks that threatened to release a new flood of tears. Miriam had only seen such pain in her eyes those first four days before the nightmares ended, when the mistress was consumed by grief over her father's death.

"How could Philip deceive me so?"

"I'm sure he didn't deliberately plan to deceive you, mistress. Maybe he didn't tell you because he knew it would hurt you to know before you were ready."

"Ready? Ready for what?"

"Ready to see that it wasn't the Christians or Jesus who killed your father. It was Rome."

"But he let me fall in love with him. He seemed so wonderful. So kind and patient, so wise, so happy in spite of all he'd suffered with his burns and scars."

"He is all of those things, mistress, and it's probably his faith in Jesus that made him into the man you love."

"The night before I came to Titus, I told Philip I wanted to marry him. He told me he couldn't marry me then even though he wanted to, that the reason might make me hate him. Was that because he's a Christian?"

"Probably, mistress."

"Oh, Miriam! I don't care if he's a Christian. I still love him, and I want him to marry me so much. But Titus hates Christians, too, and he'd never let me marry Philip if he knew. He'd probably kill Philip if he ever thought he had anything to do with Father's death."

"Then we just won't say anything to the master about Philip following Jesus."

Mistress Claudia had stopped crying, and Miriam wiped the remaining tears from her cheeks.

"The master might be coming home soon, and we don't want him to see that you've been crying. He might ask why, and I don't think you want to tell him. I'll get some cold water from the well, and you can wash your face and make yourself beautiful, like always."

Claudia sat up on the bed, drew in a deep breath, and let it out slowly.

"You're right. There's no reason why Titus needs to know. Philip and Penelope are coming to dinner tomorrow night. If I could spend so many weeks on the ship with them without discovering they were Christians, I'm sure Titus won't figure it out during a single dinner."

Worship had ended, and Philip was talking with one of the brothers about his new grandson. Then his gatekeeper approached and stood patiently waiting for him to finish the conversation.

"Is there something you want to tell me, Timothy?"

"Yes, master. In private."

Philip excused himself, and the two men walked away from the area where the fellowship meal was about to be served.

"What is it?"

"Something happened while you were teaching that you need to know."

Timothy paused and fixed his gaze on the ground.

Philip's eyebrow dipped. "Go ahead. Tell me."

"You told us not to let Mistress Claudia know we were Christians. Well…I'm afraid she knows now. She came to the gate with Miriam, and I let them in. I thought it would be all right since Miriam is a believer. I thought she was bringing Mistress Claudia to the worship service. When they got close enough to hear what you were saying, Mistress Claudia got very upset and ran back to her house. Miriam ran after her."

Philip's stomach knotted. Claudia had not just learned he was a Christian, but a leader in the church as well.

"Thank you for telling me, Timothy. I understand why you thought you should let Claudia in. I should have warned you before she came."

The gatekeeper bowed and returned to his post.

Philip closed his eye and ran his hand slowly through his hair as he stood shaking his head. During his last trip, he'd spent many hours praying for guidance on how and when to tell Claudia about his faith. He hadn't been shown a clear path, but this would certainly not have been the way he would have chosen. In fact, he couldn't imagine a worse way for her to find out.

She was expecting him and Penelope for dinner tomorrow. He'd planned to drop by after the worship to surprise her. He hadn't wanted to wait another day to see her, but now… Dropping in unexpectedly might be a terrible idea. What if she didn't want to see him now she knew he was a Christian? He couldn't bear her refusing him if he suddenly showed up. Maybe he should wait until tomorrow.

Normally, Philip enjoyed the time of fellowship after worship, but it was hard to pretend nothing was wrong. People were talking much too long and taking forever to leave. He needed to talk privately with Penelope about Claudia's disastrous visit that morning. Finally, the last person left, and he could go inside to find his sister.

◆

Penelope was sitting in the women's room, reading. She'd grown to love poetry while listening to Claudia and Philip read onboard. When her brother entered, she glanced up at him. The worried look on his face made her close her codex.

"Philip, what's wrong?"

He sat down on the chair next to her and stared at the floor. He ran his hand through his hair before taking off his eyepatch and hurling it as hard as he could against the wall.

"She knows."

"Knows what?"

He looked up at her with a pained expression. "She came this morning and heard me teaching." He rested his elbows on his knees and covered his face with his hands.

Penelope reached over and touched his shoulder. "It's all right, Philip. You were getting ready to tell her anyway."

He lifted his head to look at her. "But I hadn't figured out how. She still hates Christians. I was trying to find a way to tell her without her deciding she didn't want to have anything more to do with me because of my faith." He shook his head. "I can't imagine a worse way for her to find out than this."

Philip stood and walked over to the window. He stared down the hill toward Claudia's house. "It seemed too good to be true that someone like her would want to marry me." He turned to face Penelope. "She told me she wanted to stay with me forever the last night she was here. I wanted to ask her right then, but I can't marry an unbeliever. I was hoping to find the right way to tell her and then convince her to become a Christian, too." He looked back out the window. "Now that will never happen."

"You don't know that, Philip. If she really loves you, it won't matter to her that you follow Jesus. I think she loves you that way. You two just need to talk this out."

"I was going to visit her this afternoon, like I always do when I get back early. Now I don't think I can. What if she refuses to see me?"

"I don't think she'd ever do that. I see how she looks at you. She lights up every time she sees you."

A glimmer of hope appeared in his eye, then faded. "Maybe, but what if you're wrong?"

"I'm not wrong. I'm a woman, too. Trust me on this, Philip. She truly loves you, and you following Jesus isn't going to change that. You've been praying about how to tell her. Maybe this was God's way of letting her know without you having to tell her yourself. Be patient and see what comes next."

"Maybe, but I still don't think I can go to her today. Tomorrow we're having dinner with her and Titus. I'll see how things are then. I'll be praying that you're right."

His head and shoulders drooped as he walked out of the room.

Penelope walked to the door and watched her brother go into his room and close the door. Her heart ached for him. He'd finally taken the risk and fallen deeply in love. What if Claudia really did reject him over this? His heart would be broken a second time, and this time it would be so shattered that he'd never risk loving a woman again.

God, please don't let that happen. If any man ever deserved to love and be loved, it was Philip.

Claudia kept looking out the window of the women's room and up the street toward Philip's house. He must be through meeting with his Christian friends by late afternoon. Would he drop in unexpectedly, as he always did when he got back early from a trip?

But dinner time came and went, the sun set, and then it was time for everyone to retire. There was still no sign of Philip when it was time to go to bed.

She'd managed to put on a cheerful face during dinner so Titus wouldn't suspect there was a problem, but as Miriam helped her prepare for bed, the tears came.

"Oh, Miriam, why didn't he come? I know he's home, and he always has before. Do you think he knows we were there today, that I know his secret?"

"I don't know, mistress, but I'm sure he wants to see you."

"Then why didn't he come? I need to talk with him, to tell him it doesn't matter, that I still love him."

"I'm sure he'll be here tomorrow for dinner."

"But Titus will be here, too, and I can't talk freely with Philip when he might be listening."

"Maybe there will be some time for just the two of you to talk. If not, there will be time the next day when Master Titus is on duty. We'll just have to wait and see."

"Maybe he doesn't want to see me anymore; maybe he won't even come." The tears began to flow again.

Miriam stroked her hair. "I don't think anything can keep him away from you for long. I'm certain Master Philip loves you as much as you love him. Now it's time for you to get some sleep. Tomorrow will be fine. You'll see."

Mistress Claudia lay down on her bed, and Miriam headed downstairs to finish up some work in the kitchen.

She'd tried to keep the mistress from finding out that Philip was a Christian leader, but maybe it was God's plan for her to find out about Philip's faith exactly this way. God's ways were always the best ways, even when they weren't what she would have chosen.

She'd almost told the mistress she was a Christian, too, but something held her back. Was God telling her to wait, that the time wasn't yet right?

God, my mistress's heart is aching. Maybe Master Philip's is, too. If there's something I can do to help, please show me. If it's time for me to speak, please tell me. I want her to love you like Philip does, like I do.

A peaceful warmth flowed through her. She would know when it was time to tell the mistress she loved about the Master she loved even more, the Master she'd willingly die for.

Chapter 58

How Much It Matters

Claudia watched all morning, hoping that Philip would appear. He'd always enjoyed surprising her when he returned early. When he failed to come before lunchtime, she fought against tears as she helped Miriam gather the flowers that would decorate the dining room during dinner.

"What am I going to do, Miriam? He must know we were there yesterday, or he'd be here by now. What if he doesn't come tonight?"

"He'll come, mistress. He promised, and he always keeps his word."

"But what if he's only keeping his word, and he really doesn't want to be here?" A few tears escaped.

Miriam took her hand. "You need to stop crying, mistress. You don't want to make your eyes puffy before Master Philip comes. He wouldn't want you to be upset like this. Nothing that happened yesterday is going to change how he feels about you."

Claudia stepped back and swept the teardrops from her cheeks. "Do you really think so?"

"I'm sure of it, mistress. Master Philip loves you. He's probably more afraid of what you're thinking about him right now than you are of what he's thinking about you."

"I've said such horrible things about Christians, but surely he must know I could never mean those things about him."

"Maybe he doesn't yet, but I'm sure he will."

Claudia nodded and gave Miriam a shaky but hopeful smile. "You're probably right. As soon as I get to talk with him and tell him that it doesn't matter, everything will be like it was before. Even better. Now that I know he's a Christian, there's nothing that he needs to hide from me and no reason for him not to marry me."

◆

Miriam nodded, but she wasn't so sure about that. Mistress Claudia didn't understand. A leader of the church couldn't marry an unbeliever. As much as Philip loved the mistress, she was sure he loved Jesus more.

Claudia was counting on a talk with Philip before Titus got home. He and Penelope always came early, and that gave the three of them time to talk before Titus arrived. Penelope would know they needed to talk in private without being told.

She'd just come back into the kitchen after placing the flowers in the dining room when she heard the clip-clop of a horse's hooves. Her heart sank when she looked out the window. Titus was handing his reins to Nestor. Why had he picked today of all days to come home early? Now there would be no chance for that conversation with Philip she'd been longing for since yesterday.

Her eyes moistened despite several fast blinks.

Miriam took her hand. "Remember, mistress, we don't want Master Titus to think there's anything wrong. He might ask questions you don't want to answer today."

Claudia drew a deep breath. "You're right." She drew herself up to her full height. "Besides, if there isn't time today, I'll ask Philip to come tomorrow when Titus is gone. That might be better anyway. We'll have more time together."

She found her smile just as Titus walked through the door. "Titus. You're early."

He kissed his sister on the cheek. "I wanted to clean up before they came. Since Philip can't wait until a normal time to see you, I had to come home early."

He walked over and stood right behind Miriam. When she turned to look up at him, he reached around her and snatched a small pastry from the dessert tray she was arranging in a special pattern. He popped it into his mouth, and a delighted smile appeared.

"Best cook in the city. I'd like to see Philip top this even with his fully staffed kitchen."

◆

Miriam blushed at the praise, but she loved to hear the master speak the words.

He chuckled as her cheeks turned pink. "I messed up the pretty pattern, didn't I. Well, since I've already done that..." He reached around her with both hands, brushing his arms against hers and pulling her into him as he snatched more pastries. "I might as well take two more."

With another smile, he popped the first one into his mouth before he walked out of the kitchen.

Miriam began rearranging the remaining pastries into a different pattern. Her lips curved as she remembered that wonderful smile as he savored her special treats for tonight. She loved doing anything in the kitchen that gave the master special pleasure. Whenever he showed his appreciation by some kind words or a teasing smile, it made her feel warm and happy inside. Not even Master Alexander's highest praises could compete with one of Master Titus's playful smiles.

Philip and Penelope did arrive early, just as Claudia expected, but Titus greeted them immediately upon their arrival. Philip managed to mask his disappointment enough that Titus didn't see it, but Claudia saw how he looked at her with a mixture of uncertainty and eagerness. Miriam had been right about him wanting to come the day before but being afraid of how she'd receive him.

She was desperate to let Philip know she still wanted to marry him, but from the moment he arrived, Titus pulled him into a conversation about some problems on the eastern border with the Parthian Empire. Normally, she would have enjoyed seeing Philip impress her brother with his knowledge and depth of understanding, but today she wanted him to herself.

But if she couldn't talk with Philip, at least she could talk with Penelope without Titus listening.

"Come upstairs with me, Penelope. I want to show you something."

She took Penelope's hand and led her up the stairs to her room. She closed the door, then led her over to sit on the bed. She spoke in a near-whisper in case Titus came upstairs for something.

"Philip knows I know, doesn't he? He knows about me finding out he's a Christian?"

Penelope's smile vanished. "Yes, he does. He wanted to tell you himself. He was trying to decide how, but then you came yesterday and..."

"You're one, too, aren't you?"

Penelope nodded.

"I know I've said so many horrible things about hating Christians, but I never meant Philip and you. I need to talk to him, but not when Titus can hear. He mustn't know that you're Christians. I don't know what he'd do, but it might be something terrible."

Penelope took a deep breath. "I can see the danger of Titus knowing. I won't do anything to give us away."

"If I don't get a chance to tell Philip tonight, will you tell him I still love him more than anything and I still want to marry him?"

Penelope's straight lips were replaced by a broad smile. "I'd love to. I really want you as my sister, and the sooner the better."

Claudia paused. "He hasn't actually asked me yet. When I told him I wanted to stay with him instead of Titus, he said he wanted me to stay, but we couldn't get married just yet. But I know he wants to ask me, and I'm sure he will. There's no reason he can't now that I know about his faith."

◆

Penelope's smile dimmed. Philip was a church leader. He would only marry a believer, but for a long time now, she'd been counting on Claudia becoming one so he could marry her. Everything for the two of them depended on her making that decision.

Claudia's beaming smile betrayed her ignorance of how much it mattered. "If I don't get a chance to talk to him without Titus hearing, would you please tell him I don't care if he's a Christian and ask him to come see me tomorrow morning so we can talk?"

Penelope wrapped her arms around Claudia and hugged her. "Of course. Now let's go join the men. Even if Philip can't talk with you, he'll want to look at you."

She was eager to end the discussion. She didn't want to be the one to tell Claudia that Philip still wouldn't be able to marry her, at least not yet.

Chapter 59

No opportunity arose at dinner for the private conversation Claudia longed for. Titus drew Philip into seemingly endless discussions of the annexation of Armenia, the successes of Trajan's legions as they pushed into Mesopotamia, and what the eastward expansion of the Empire might mean for Thracia. Philip was too polite to break off conversing with his host, so Claudia had to settle for trying to speak with her eyes what she longed to say with her lips.

It was a good thing she'd asked Penelope to tell Philip what was in her heart. If Titus had deliberately planned to keep her from talking with the man she loved, he couldn't have done a better job. He even walked Philip and Penelope to the gate as they headed home.

As the mistress sat gazing at her reflection in the mirror, Miriam began brushing her hair.

"Tonight wasn't at all what I was hoping for. I wanted so much to tell Philip everything was all right between us, but Titus didn't give me a single chance to talk with him alone."

She sighed. "At least I got to tell Penelope. She's going to tell Philip to come tomorrow after Titus goes to the palace."

She turned to face Miriam. "As soon as I tell him it doesn't matter that he's a Christian, I'm sure he'll ask me to marry him. We didn't get to talk tonight, but I know from the way he kept looking at me that he wants me with him as much as I want to be with him."

"I'm sure he loves you, too, mistress." Miriam had seen everything Claudia had in Philip's face each time he looked at her, but she knew that nothing had really changed. Claudia was still not a believer, and Philip couldn't marry her while she wasn't.

As Claudia lay down on her bed, she smiled up at Miriam. "Tomorrow is going to be a wonderful day." With a contented sigh, she closed her eyes.

"I hope so, mistress."

Miriam pulled the blanket up and tucked it around her mistress. She still had some clean-up awaiting her in the dining room and kitchen before she would go to bed herself. As she stood in the doorway, she looked back at Claudia's happy, peaceful face. She hoped tomorrow would be a good day, but she was almost sure it wasn't going to be.

Claudia arose almost as early as Titus, but she watched out her window until she saw him ride through the gate. Had he known, he might have delayed his departure for the palace to eat with her, and she wanted him gone so she could talk with Philip as soon as he came. She didn't wait for Miriam to help her dress. She didn't want Philip to have to wait if he came early. He loved natural, and she could do that all by herself.

Miriam had a lovely breakfast tray ready when Claudia entered the kitchen, but one bite of cheese was all she could manage. Her foot kept tapping the floor as she sat at the kitchen table, watching Miriam knead the bread dough. She would have helped, but she didn't want any flour on his favorite sky-blue tunic.

Miriam glanced out the window. "He's here, mistress. He has three men with him, but they've gone into the garden to talk with Nestor."

Claudia leapt to her feet and met Philip at the door. She seized his hand as she beamed at him.

"I'm so glad you're here. It was horrible last night not getting to talk with you."

As she was talking, she led him into the inner courtyard.

Philip couldn't have looked happier. "I wanted to talk with you, too, but Titus...he's an interesting man, but last night a good conversation about the Empire was the last thing I wanted."

She wrapped her arms around him and gazed happily up at him. "At least Penelope was able to tell you what I wanted to say most, and now you're here with me."

His smile broadened, and love shone in his eye. Claudia reached up and slid his eyepatch up and off his face, letting it hang on her arm.

"You don't need this with me. I like you just the way you are. Nothing between my fingers and my favorite mountain ridges."

She laid her hand on his cheek and traced the swirls near his eye with her index finger. "I've missed doing this so much. I'll be glad when I can do it every single day."

"I've missed it, too. Almost as much as I've missed crossing swords with my favorite general."

She dropped her hand to rest on his chest. A strap was slung across it. Her gaze followed it down until she saw...a sword.

"Philip, what's this for?" Worry tinged her voice as she laid her hand on the scabbard slung at his side. Titus always wore a sword, but she'd never seen Philip with one before.

"I'm on my way to Odessus in Moesia. We grow wheat there, and I plan to enlarge our land holdings. I'm taking the road through the mountains to catch the main road along the Pontus Euxinus at Salmydessus. With an armed party, it's a safe shortcut. When we look prepared for trouble, it never happens." He pushed a strand of hair behind her ear. "It's nothing you need to worry about. I've made the trip several times without any problems."

"That's so far. How long will you be gone?"

"Four, maybe five weeks. It depends on how quickly I can buy the land I want."

"That's too long, but I guess it can't be helped. And you're certain it's safe?"

A corner of his mouth lifted. "I'm certain. We go with many prayers, and God protects us. You don't have to be worrying."

◆

Her finger traced a ridge on his cheek, raising Philip's heart rate and heating his blood. "I had hoped we could start our future sooner than that."

His stomach dropped like it did when the ship plunged into the trough of a giant wave. Dread of what she would say next coursed through him.

She stroked his cheek again. "Where's that smile I love? Penelope told you, didn't she? That I don't care that you're a Christian? That I want to marry you anyway?"

"Yes..." His mind raced as he sought the best way to tell her what she wasn't going to want to hear.

"What's wrong?"

He lifted her hand from his cheek and lowered it to hold it in both of his. He swallowed hard. What he was about to say was the hardest thing he'd ever had to say in his life.

"You know there's no one in this world I care for more than you. There's nothing on earth I want more than to have you with me, but..." *God, give me the right words.* He needed the ones that wouldn't hurt her too much, the ones that would make her want to consider following Jesus like he did.

Her mouth turned down when he paused "But what? How can there be any 'buts' when two people love each other like we do?" Her breaths came short and fast "You do love me, don't you, Philip?" Her voice started to quaver.

"As much as any man ever loved a woman." It tore at his heart to see her building toward tears.

"I know your secret about being a Christian, and it doesn't matter to me. We just can't tell Titus. That could be dangerous for you." Fear clouded her eyes. "That was all that kept you from asking me, wasn't it?"

"No. It was only part." He took a deep breath and let it out slowly. "I'm not just a Christian, Claudia. I'm a leader in the church."

He drew another deep breath. What he was about to say would hurt her, but he had to say it. With a desperate prayer that this wouldn't be the end of them, he forced out the painful words.

"I can only marry someone who loves Jesus like I do. You don't right now, but I've been praying since I met you that you'd come to love Him. Even more so now. I want to marry you more than anything in this world, but this world isn't all there is. I love you more than my own life, but I love Jesus even more."

She jerked her hand out of his. As she stared at him, tears of anger and pain pooled in her eyes.

"No, Philip. It isn't possible to love your god more than me. Not if you really love me. No one could ever choose a god over a person if they really love them."

He reached out to take her hand again, but she snatched it away.

"Your father did."

He couldn't have chosen anything to say that would have hurt her more. The look of anguish that he saw so often when she first came to his ship filled her eyes. At that moment, he would have endured boiling soup being poured over him again to unsay those three words.

"How can you say such a horrible thing to me? I never thought you could be so cruel." The agony in her shrill voice cut like a knife.

"Claudia, I—"

She placed her hands on his chest and shoved him away before he could even start to explain.

"No! If you love your god more than you love me, then you don't really love me at all. Maybe I should decide I don't love you either."

The dam broke, and the river of tears streamed down her cheeks. "If you don't really love me, I'm not sure I ever want to see you again."

She hurled his eyepatch at his head, and he barely caught it before it hit his face. She whirled and ran up the stairs. She didn't even pause to look at him before she ran into her bedchamber and slammed the door.

Once more, Philip heard the sounds of Claudia crying her heart out, but this was so much worse than ever before. This time he was the cause, and even if he went to her, it wouldn't change a thing.

No matter how much he loved her, he couldn't marry her until she loved Jesus, too.

Philip had thought his heart was broken when Phoebe rejected him as a monster seven years earlier. He'd thought he loved her, but he didn't know what love was then. Now he did. He knew what it was to love Claudia with the deep, unselfish, passionate love that should bind two people for a lifetime. But he'd just broken her heart, and she'd just shredded his.

In spite of all his prayers, all his hopes and dreams for a life with her had just shattered. Only God could fix this, but would He?

◆

Miriam kept kneading the dough as they talked in the courtyard outside the door. She heard every word, every gasp, every sob. She'd been afraid this meeting might not go as well as Claudia thought it would, but it had gone so much worse than anything she'd imagined.

Philip entered the kitchen with his head hanging. He gazed at the eyepatch in his hand before sliding it back on his head and adjusting it to get comfortable. So many times, Miriam had watched the mistress slide it off his face as her love-filled eyes caressed him. The happiness that brought to Philip's eye warmed Miriam's own heart. Would the mistress ever lift it from his face again?

"You heard?" Philip's jaw clenched.

"Yes." Did something glisten at the corner of his eye? She was struggling against tears herself.

"I have to leave this morning for maybe five weeks. I won't even have a chance to talk to her, to try to explain until I return. Please help us, Miriam. Do whatever you can to make her understand why I can't marry her even though I want to more than anything I've ever wanted in my whole life. Will you try to tell her about Jesus, convince her to follow Him like we do, like her father did? There's no hope for us if she won't."

Miriam had seen more than her share of suffering, but she'd never heard agony in a strong man's voice before.

"I'll try. I've been praying since I met her for the right time and the right words to tell her how much Jesus loves her. I love her, too, and I want her to know the joy we have. Five weeks is a long time. I'm sure God will give me a chance before you return."

With a smile filled with gratitude and at least some hope, Philip took both her hands in his. "Thank you, Miriam. Everything for us depends on her decision."

Miriam squeezed his hands and nodded.

◆

Philip took another deep breath and blew it out as he squared his shoulders. Miriam's promise gave him enough hope to sustain him for the next five weeks. Surely God wanted Claudia to come, and Miriam could find the way to lead her to Him. He spun and strode out the door and over to his horse.

He mounted before calling to his men, who were still talking with Nestor. "Let's go."

Philip swung his horse and started out the gate before they could even mount. He wanted to ride enough ahead of them that he had some time to regain his composure. The last thing he wanted was for his men to see how upset he was.

He willed his breathing to slow as he kicked his horse into a trot. He would try not to despair over what had just happened and pray instead that God could use it to reach Claudia. God could do anything. He needed to keep reminding himself of that. God could reach any heart and make it His own.

Chapter 60

NEVER ALONE AGAIN

Miriam climbed the stairs, praying for the right words as she paused on each step. She knocked on the door, but there was no answer except the mistress's sobs. Miriam opened the door and limped over to sit on the side of her bed.

Mistress Claudia lay with her face buried in her pillow. The bed moved with each jerk as she gasped for air. Miriam began to rub her back.

"Shhh. Don't cry, mistress. This will work out all right."

It seemed like the tears were never going to stop, but finally the mistress rolled onto her back so she could look at Miriam.

"Oh, Miriam! How can it possibly work out all right? How could Philip say he won't marry me because he loves Jesus and I don't? I thought he loved me as much as I love him. I'd do anything for him, give up anything for him, die for him. Why can't he do something as simple as marrying me?"

It was all Miriam could do not to cry as agony pulsed in Mistress Claudia's eyes. *God, what should I tell her?* No words came. She'd never loved a man like Philip loved Mistress Claudia, so how could she explain him loving Jesus more than her mistress, even more than his own life?

The mistress swung her legs off the bed and went to the window. Her lip quivered as she looked up the hill toward Philip's house. Then her jaw clenched before she turned to face Miriam with fists on her hips.

"No god is that important. I would never choose one over the man I love. A god isn't like a real person. What did that god ever do for him, anyway?"

Miriam could have answered that question, but a small voice inside her told her not to...not yet.

"Father taught me the Roman gods were just stories. Then he learned about the Jewish god, and he said that was different, that the Jewish god was real. But I never understood that. All I knew was believing that made him happy, and I wanted Father to be happy.

"And I didn't understand when he told me his god could only accept perfect people. No one is perfect. All his worrying about sin and the end of the sacrifices that let people approach his god...that didn't make sense either, because Father was so wonderful. He didn't need to change to be good enough for anyone, even the Jewish god, even if he was real. And then someone told him Jesus was the sacrifice for his sins. That never made sense, either, but it made him happier than I'd ever seen him."

Mistress Claudia covered her mouth with her hands as the tears welled up again. "And then he let Lucius's friend sentence him to death because he wouldn't offer a little incense to the emperor because his god said he couldn't worship any others. He chose his god over everything. And I lost him because of that."

Tears trickled down her cheeks. "I lost him, and I couldn't bear it. I wanted to kill the ones who took him from me. I wanted all the Christians to die before they talked anyone else into believing their lies. And then I met Philip, and somehow it didn't hurt so much. He was so wonderful, and I fell in love with him."

She swept the tears away. "And when I heard him teaching about Jesus...I know it must be partly his fault Father died, but I love him so much that it doesn't matter anymore. I thought he loved me that much, too. If I could forgive him for that, he should be able to do anything for me."

Her chest jerked, and she swallowed hard before her next words. "But today... When I told him no man would give up someone they really love for a god...he said my father did. How could he say that to me? How could he choose Jesus over me and then throw it in my face that Father chose him, too?"

The mistress wiped the tears from her cheeks, and a deeper sadness filled her eyes. "The really horrible thing is it's true. Father was everything to me. He knew how much I loved and needed him."

She sat down next to Miriam. "How could he choose to leave me all alone and die for Jesus when he didn't have to? All he had to do was offer a sacrifice to Caesar. He didn't have to mean it. That wasn't asking too much, was it? I shouldn't have had to lose him yet. It was too soon."

Miriam pushed some hair back from the mistress's face. "I lost someone I loved too soon, mistress. Mother was everything to me. She tried so hard to care for me and protect me, especially after I was crippled. It broke her heart to watch Mistress Xanthe hit me all the time when she couldn't do anything to stop it." Miriam bit her lip as the tears of the past threatened to flow again. "I lost her when I was ten."

"Sickness? That's different. She didn't choose to leave you."

"Sold because Mistress Xanthe hated her. No, she didn't choose to go, and she didn't want to leave me behind. She had to go where her new master took her, and he made her leave me."

Miriam blinked hard to stop the tears that started to build again. "She had to obey. Your father had to obey his master, too. He had to leave you behind, but he would want you to follow him there someday."

"Follow him where? He's dead and gone, and I'll never see him again." The tears pooled in Mistress Claudia's eyes once more. "I'd give anything to be with him one more time. All this talk about obeying his master...I know Christians call Jesus master and are supposed to die for him if they have to. Lucius counted on that to get Father killed. But Father was no slave. He didn't have to obey anyone. For him to believe dying for Jesus was the right thing to do...it makes no sense to me, but maybe he knew something I just can't see. Why would anyone as wise as Father give up everything and everyone they love and choose to die before they'd deny their god?"

Miriam took a deep breath and held it before letting it out slowly. *Is this it, God? The moment I've prayed for?* Peaceful excitement surged through her. Now was the time.

"I can tell you why, mistress. I would choose to give up everything and die before I'd deny my real master, too."

The mistress's brow furrowed. "You'd die for Titus?"

"Yes, but that's not what I meant." Miriam paused, took a deep breath, and plunged ahead. "I'd die for Jesus."

Mistress Claudia's eyes saucered. "You're a Christian, too? Oh, Miriam. You mustn't ever let Titus hear you say that. He hates Lucius for betraying our father to the authorities, but he hates the Christian who told him about Jesus at least as much. He'd kill both of them if he had the chance to avenge our father's death."

She pressed her palm against her cheek. "I'm afraid Philip and his father had something to do with it. Titus must never know that. He hates all Christians now. He's said he'd gladly kill them if he was serving in Bithynia. He'd even be happy to hunt them down. I don't know what he'll do to you if he finds out. I couldn't bear to have him hurt you."

"I heard him, mistress, but he's promised he'll never hurt me. I'm sure he wouldn't even if he knew I'm a Christian. I don't plan to say anything, but if he ever asks, I would never deny my Lord. My last master and his family died rather than deny Him. I would have gladly done the same if I'd been a free woman."

Tears began to trickle down Miriam's cheeks as the memories swirled within her, and she looked down at the floor. "I loved Master Alexander and his family. He treated me like a father would. To have to stand there and watch the executioner behead him…" She flicked the tears from her cheeks. "And then the mistress and their children and all the free servants." Again, she flicked away tears. "I watched all but one of the people I'd ever loved die that day. I asked God to let them kill me, too. I was ready to be with my Lord Jesus. I knew He'd paid for my sins, and I couldn't bear the thought of being left behind."

She raised her head to look at Mistress Claudia and smiled through her tears. "But God didn't want me to die that day. He left me here… for you."

◆

Claudia took Miriam's hand and held it between both of hers before she raised it to hold it against her cheek. "I'm so glad you didn't die. I needed you so much when I came to Titus. I still do."

She lowered their hands to her chest, but she still kept Miriam's hand wrapped in her own. "I remember that night when you told me how Father died. You said you'd watched Christians die—joyful, without fear. I was sure he died that way, too, and it ended my nightmares."

"That's how it was. I pray that I'll die that way if I ever have to."

Claudia pressed her palms against her cheeks. "Maybe I've been thinking about this all wrong. Father was so happy after he became a Christian. He was so eager to tell me about it, and I didn't let him. I saw how disappointed he was when I didn't, but I never dreamed it meant so much to him that he'd let them kill him for it. Then when they did, I felt so…alone, and I wanted to die, too.

"Philip changed that. He was always so cheerful, and he made me feel good just being with him. I didn't feel alone anymore. But now

I may have lost Philip, too, and everything is so…hopeless again." A teardrop tried to escape from the corner of her eye, but she flicked it away. "And I don't want to live like that. I want to stop hurting, to be happy again, like Father and Philip. And I think their happiness came from loving Jesus."

"Yes, mistress. But it's more joy than happiness. Joy no matter what, joy even when you're sad or suffering, even when you're about to die. Even more than that, you'll never be alone again."

"Father told me he met God, that God was right there with him."

"That's how it is, mistress, and that's why you'll never be alone."

"Oh, Miriam! I don't want to be sad and alone anymore. I want to know what Father knew, what Philip knows. Maybe then I'll understand why they chose Jesus over me. And if I do, maybe…well, maybe I should choose him, too."

Miriam's eyes lit up. "I've been wanting to tell you for so long how much Jesus loves you and why you should follow Him. He's done everything for me, and I want you to have the joy I have."

"Tell me now."

Miriam wrapped her second hand around Claudia's. "I didn't always follow Him, so let me tell you first how I came to.

"My father and mother were Jews, and they worshiped the God of Israel, the only true God, like your father did. They were separated just before I was born—sold to different masters when their owner died. Mother was a wonderful cook, and my first master bought her for that. She was very pretty, and after I was born, he decided he wanted her service at night, too.

"His wife hated Mother. The master wouldn't let her strike out at Mother, so she decided to take her anger out on me. She hit me whenever I got too close to her because she knew hurting me would hurt Mother, too. Mother couldn't do anything to stop the mistress, but she taught me to stay out of range and how to move as she struck so it would hurt less."

A shy smile brightened her face. "Master Titus hated it when I did that if he was unhappy when I first came here. I know now that he would never hit me, so I don't do that anymore. He's always kind to me."

The smile faded. "When I was five, Mistress Xanthe's son was driving the chariot, but he couldn't control the horses. He ran over me. That's when my ankle got crushed. The mistress said I should just be killed since it would never heal right and I'd be a cripple, but Mother begged the master to let her train me as a cook. I wouldn't need two good legs for that. He still liked her, so he kept me."

Claudia bit her lip. "That's terrible! To be so afraid of your mistress all the time. For her to want to kill you."

Miriam looked down at the floor. "The mistress hated me even more after that. Mother didn't tell me until I was a little older. Maybe she hoped the master would lose interest in her and the mistress would target his new favorite instead. When I was seven, I started serving in the house. Mistress Xanthe hit me whenever I was near her as long as the master wasn't watching. He protected me a little because of Mother."

"But he sold her when you were ten?"

Miriam nodded. "The master bought a younger slave who was prettier. Mother was well known as a great cook, so he sold her for a high price. But Mistress Xanthe had enough hate for both his new favorite and Mother. The last thing she told Mother as her new master was taking her away was that I would pay for what her husband had done."

Tears pooled in Claudia's eyes. "Oh, Miriam! How did you ever bear it?"

"Mother taught me about how my people, the Jews, were in bondage in Egypt for four hundred years, but God sent Moses as the deliverer. She taught me to ask God to help me bear my bondage until my deliverer came."

"Did God help you bear it?"

"He did even better. He brought a deliverer." Miriam closed her eyes for a moment. "I can still see Master Alexander like he was that day. When I was almost eleven, he came to see my master about something, but he had to wait with Mistress Xanthe until the master got home. I was serving the mistress, and she kept hitting me each time I brought her something. I think the way Master Alexander looked at her when she did that made her uncomfortable. She told him I was lazy and slow. She said she would sell me if she could get two hundred denarii, but a cripple like me wouldn't be worth even one hundred.

"I was standing by the door waiting for her next command, waiting for her to hit me again. Master Alexander came over and lifted my chin so I was looking into his eyes. I can still see them. There was such tenderness in them. It was like looking into Mother's eyes again. Then he turned to my mistress and told her he would give her 250 denarii for me. She couldn't say no to so much.

"After he finished with my master, he took me home with him. God had answered all my prayers, and my deliverer had come. But Master Alexander did more than deliver me from my cruel mistress. He led me to Messiah, who could deliver me from all my sins."

Miriam's face glowed as her smile broadened. "My life was so good with Master Alexander. Mother taught me special ways to use herbs and spices, and I learned even more in the master's kitchen. I learned to play the flute and lyre. But the most wonderful thing I learned was who Messiah was. My people were waiting for Messiah to free them from Rome, and Mother taught me all she knew about Him so I would know Him when He appeared.

"But Messiah wasn't coming to free us from Rome. He came to free us from our sins. I learned that God Himself had come as Jesus and freed me from paying for my own sins if I only believed in Him. Master Alexander and his whole household followed Jesus. That's why he looked at me with love like Mother had. It's why he rescued me. I loved serving the master's family. Everything I did let me show how much I loved them."

"That's exactly how you serve me. Like you love me."

"I do love you, mistress. That's why I want you to love Jesus, too. That's why Master Philip wants you to love Jesus like he does. Then you'll know the joy and peace of being right with God, not kept apart from Him by your sin. Master Philip wants you to share his life not just on earth, but forever in heaven."

Miriam leaned closer to the mistress. "Jesus promised that everyone who believes in Him would never die. We leave this life behind for an even better one with God in heaven. Jesus's blood covered our sins, so we don't have to be perfect on our own to go there."

"Is that why Father was so willing to die?"

"Yes. And when they killed him, he didn't really die. He just passed over into eternal life with Jesus."

Claudia massaged the back of her neck. "Father used to worry about how his sins could be paid for so he could approach God. Then he told me Jesus was the perfect sacrifice, that God himself made the payment. I couldn't see why payment was needed because I didn't realize no one is perfect enough for God. I was so naive; Father had protected me too well. Now I've seen evil in what Lucius did. I've seen it in myself the way I've hated and wanted to kill. I never used to think I needed anything to pay for my sins because I wasn't a sinner, but now I know I am."

"Then come follow Jesus, mistress. Just tell Him your sins and that you want to be forgiven and follow Him."

"But how do I do that?"

"Just talk to Him, like you're talking to me."

Claudia closed her eyes and took a deep breath. "Jesus, I want peace within myself and peace with God that my sins have been preventing. I didn't used to think I had any, but now I know better. I've hated people for what they've done and for things I thought they'd done when they hadn't. I've hated so much I wanted to kill them. I've wanted revenge on Lucius for what he did. I've wanted revenge on Your followers who told Father about You. I've thought I was a good person and that was all I needed to be. Now I know that's not enough. Please forgive me. I want to follow You like Father, Philip, and Miriam."

◆

Joy bubbled up inside Miriam as she watched Mistress Claudia begin to pray. Miriam's countless prayers asking God to claim her mistress's heart were answered before her eyes. A radiant smile told her the moment the Spirit of God filled her beloved mistress. When Mistress finally opened her eyes, sadness had been replaced by a sparkle even brighter than any Philip had caused.

"Oh, Miriam! It's wonderful! Father told me God was real, and I just met Him. I feel Him here with me."

"Yes, mistress, and you'll never be alone again."

Claudia threw her arms around Miriam and hugged her. Miriam's heart sang as she returned the embrace. They were no longer just mistress and slave or even friends. They were sisters in Christ, and they would be forever.

Chapter 61

SOMETHING DIFFERENT ABOUT HER

As Titus rode by the kitchen window, someone was singing. Miriam sang almost all the time when she was working by herself, but something sounded different. Then the voice he recognized joined in.

His spine straightened. The music was lovely, but that wasn't what surprised him. Claudia singing? He'd never heard her sing in Rome.

The corner of his mouth lifted. Miriam had turned his sister into a singer. Was there any limit to the ways she could find to lift his sister's spirits?

Nestor came to take the stallion as Titus dismounted.

Titus tipped his head toward the kitchen. "Pretty music. It's a good way to start my evening."

Nestor grinned. "Yes, master. I've been enjoying it all afternoon."

When Titus walked into the kitchen, the duet stopped.

"Titus! Welcome home." Claudia danced over and threw her arms around him and kissed his cheek before twirling away.

"Looks like you've had a good day."

"The best." Her glittering smile spoke the truth of it.

He had no idea what had made her so happy, but whatever it was, he was glad.

◆

Miriam looked up from the stew simmering on the fire. "Welcome home, master. I hope you'll like dinner tonight. I've made something different, and I hope it meets with your approval."

She leaned toward the pot and stirred the stew with a long-handled spoon.

Master Titus walked over and stood behind her. "I'm not willing to wait for a taste."

He rested his palm on her elbow, then slid it slowly down her arm to take the spoon. His touch made her tingle, and his closeness made her heart beat faster. He scooped some broth into the spoon and raised it to his lips. After blowing on it, he took a tiny sip. A huge smile spread across his face.

"Best cook in the city. Philip would love to have you in his kitchen, but he couldn't offer me enough to buy you. But he eats here almost as often as he eats at home when he's in town, so I guess he doesn't need to spend the money to enjoy your special sauces."

He threw a teasing look at Claudia. "Claudia thinks he comes to see her, but maybe he just wants more of your cooking."

Heat spread from Miriam's cheeks to her ears. The master grinned as he handed the spoon back to her. "Excellent, and I bet you have some pastry that's even better waiting for me."

As he headed into the courtyard, he looked back over his shoulder. "You're definitely not for sale."

When Titus entered the dining room, he expected a table set for four, but it was only set for two. As happy as Claudia had been when he came home, he would have bet Philip and Penelope were joining them for dinner.

Claudia entered the room in a beige tunic with her hair down and no jewelry. As she pulled out the chair and seated herself, Titus bounced his eyebrows at her.

"You'd better hurry and change into that blue tunic while Miriam sets for two more. You don't want to disappoint Philip. You usually treat him to a vision of loveliness when he comes."

"Philip and Penelope aren't coming tonight. He left for Moesia this morning. It's going to be four or five weeks before he returns, but I'll probably ask Penelope to dinner a few times before he gets back."

She leaned across the table and patted her brother's cheek. "It isn't that you're not good company, but I do like talking with Penelope, too."

Titus's eyebrows shot up at this news. Claudia usually moped for a few days after Philip left town, and her spirits didn't bounce back completely until he returned. Philip gone for maybe five weeks and his sister this happy? Odd, but he certainly wouldn't complain about it. It was good to see her so happy. He'd spent too much time watching her be sad.

Penelope was in her room the next morning when the servant came to announce Claudia's arrival. She'd been praying for Claudia and Philip ever since Philip went to talk with her before he left for Moesia. She was dying to find out what had come of their conversation. One look at Claudia's face was likely to tell her everything.

When she reached the inner courtyard where Claudia and Miriam stood waiting for her, she eagerly fixed her gaze on Claudia. There was a happy glow about her that was exactly what she'd hoped to see.

"I'm so glad you came." A smile tugged at the corner of her mouth. Claudia's sparkling eyes could only mean one thing.

"I have something wonderful to tell you, something I know you've wanted to hear for a long time." Claudia beamed. "I've decided to follow Jesus."

Penelope threw her arms around Claudia. "Philip must be so happy. I can hardly wait for him to return and make you my sister-in-law now you're my sister in Christ."

Claudia's smile dimmed as Penelope stepped back. "He doesn't know. It was after he left. He told me he couldn't marry me because I wasn't a Christian. When I told him no one would choose a god over the person they loved, he said my father did. He hurt me so much when he said that I wanted to hurt him, too."

Claudia pressed a hand to her cheek. "I told him I didn't want to see him again because he didn't really love me if he chose his god over me. But God used it all to open my heart, and Miriam told me everything I needed to hear to know I want to follow Jesus, too."

She took Penelope's hands in her own. "I didn't mean what I said at all, but I hurt him terribly when I said it. I'm afraid he won't feel he can come to me when he returns. If he doesn't, will you please tell him I want to see him more than anything and I have something to tell him that will change everything for us?"

"Of course, but I don't think you have to worry about him not coming to see you as soon as he returns. He'll never be able to ride by your house without seeing how you are."

Penelope pulled Claudia into another embrace. "I've wanted you for my sister-in-law ever since I saw Philip opening his heart to you on the ship. But even more, I've wanted you to be my sister in Christ. As soon as Philip returns, I expect you'll be both."

Chapter 62

DISCOVERY

Lucius had just returned from the Basilica Julia in central Rome. His regular Friday discussion with his friends had been enjoyable, but he wished he hadn't gone. Flavius Sabinus had been there. At first, Sabinus ignored him, and that was fine with him. In fact, he truly preferred that. Then someone talking with Sabinus called out his name, and the power broker couldn't pretend not to see him.

Sabinus inquired about his progress in locating his kidnapped sister, and he'd been forced to admit that he hadn't been able to find even the slightest trace of her since her disappearance more than seven weeks earlier. Lucius had hoped Sabinus's interest in acquiring Claudia might have faded after such a long time, but no such luck. Sabinus made several cryptic comments about any man who didn't deliver on his promises not being fit to live in Rome. Coupled with an uncomfortable silence as the crocodile stared at him, Lucius fully understood the threat.

As he sat at his father's desk rolling a stylus between his fingers, the door slave interrupted his troubled thoughts.

"Yes?"

"A letter for you, master."

The slave handed the letter to Lucius, then bowed before returning to his post.

Lucius slid the end of the stylus under the edge of the rolled sheet of papyrus and lifted to break the wax seal. He unrolled the sheet and laid it on the desk in front of him.

Septimus Valerius Corvinus to Lucius Claudius Drusus Fidelis, greetings. If you are well, then I am glad. I write to share good news. I know of your great concern for your missing sister, Claudia Drusilla, as shown by your most generous offer of 10,000 denarii to anyone who can find her. It is with great satisfaction that I tell you I have found her this day. She is now living in Perinthus with your brother Titus. Since it will be some time before I can return to Rome myself, I would be most grateful if you would give the 10,000 denarii to Marcus for him to transfer to the steward of my estate. I ask you also to tell my brother that all is well with me here in Perinthus, as I hope all is well with him. May the gods guard your safety.

Lucius took a deep breath and let it out in a sigh of relief. At last he'd found her. Since she was with Titus, she was almost certainly what Sabinus would consider "undamaged," so he should be able to fulfill his promise to the crocodile if he could bring her back.

He was about to summon Malleolus to discuss how best to retrieve her when he paused. Even though the old steward had spared no effort in trying to find her the first few days after her disappearance, Lucius got the impression he was secretly glad she'd escaped. As fond as the old man was of his sister, he wouldn't want to help drag her back from living safely with Titus to marry a man who would almost certainly hurt her.

Lucius would discuss how best to recover Claudia with his friend Marcus, and together they would find the right men to send to bring his sister back. If Malleolus somehow knew where she was, he might try to warn her before the agents arrived to drag her back to Rome.

He took a wax tablet from the drawer and was about to write to Sabinus to let him know that his sister had been found. As he began pressing the stylus into the wax, he hesitated. Then he returned the tablet to the drawer. It might be unwise to let Sabinus know he'd located Claudia until he actually had her back in Rome, ready to marry the old man. It could be fatal to disappoint a crocodile a second time.

Chapter 63

The Letter

Titus was about to head home for dinner when the postal slave entered the garrison and approached the centurion on duty. He glanced at the slave but took no real notice of him as he mounted his stallion.

"Claudius Drusus."

Titus turned to face the centurion. "Yes?"

"A letter for you, tribune." The centurion walked over and handed him the thick roll of papyrus sheets held shut by the wax seal. Titus's eyebrow rose. It was from Appius Manlius Torquatus. Torquatus had been one of his father's best friends, but why would he be writing?

When he broke the wax seal and unrolled the sheets, the greeting was like a slap in the face.

> Publius Claudius Drusus to Titus Claudius Drusus,
> my dear son, greetings.

Titus froze his face. Father's final message. He rolled it up and slipped it inside his tunic. He wouldn't risk reading it where anyone could watch him. Wouldn't risk revealing the lump in his throat, the pain in his heart, that the words "my dear son" caused.

Without a word, he kicked his horse into a trot and headed home. In the privacy of his own room, it wouldn't matter if he couldn't control his emotions as he heard one last time from the father he loved.

Miriam was alone in the kitchen when Master Titus entered.

"Welcome home, master."

Usually he smiled and greeted her. More often than not, he would sneak a taste of what she was preparing, tease her, and make her blush. Today was nothing like his usual homecoming. She'd never before seen him look grim when he came home.

"Smells good, Miriam. I'll be down to eat in a few minutes."

He walked through the kitchen and climbed the stairs. She stepped to the door to watch him as he strode along the balcony and entered his room, closing the door behind him. Something was wrong, very wrong, with the master.

Miriam began to pray.

Titus flipped the latch on the door before he drew the letter from his tunic. He took a deep breath before he unrolled it. He was eager to read it, but he was also afraid of what it might contain. There were many sheets, so it must contain something Father had considered very important. He sat down on his bed, and began to read.

> Publius Claudius Drusus to Titus Claudius Drusus, my dear son, greetings. Let me assure you that I truly am well, although what I am writing you might at first make you think otherwise. By the time you receive this letter, I will have been executed for refusing to deny my faith in Jesus of Nazareth and offer a sacrifice to Caesar. Everything I own will have been confiscated and given to Lucius. This letter is my only legacy for you, but what it contains is worth more than all my estates, more than all the wealth in the Empire. I pray you will come to treasure it for the truth it contains and as the final expression of my love for you.

Titus covered his mouth with his hand and took several deep but rapid breaths. He thumbed quickly through the several sheets of papyrus that had been rolled together and held by the wax seal. Father's final letter. His emotions churned as he clutched the sheets his father had held just before he died. Then he focused once more on his father's final words.

> I know this news comes as a shock and will cause you much grief, but I hope, after I tell you all that has happened to me since you posted to Thracia, that you will understand why I have chosen to die and why I tell you not to grieve too hard or too long. It is my deepest desire that you will choose to follow me in making the God of Israel your God and following Jesus as your Lord.

Titus's head snapped back. Follow Father by becoming what killed him? What rational man would do that? He rolled his eyes and read on.

> I begin with how I decided the God of Israel is the one true God. I had hoped to have this conversation in person during your next visit to Rome. Since that is not to be, I will try to write what I would have spoken to you then.
>
> The teaching of the great philosophers seemed true to me for a long time, but that was before I began to compare them to what my own eyes have seen of the world. After much thought, I came to the conclusion that a philosophy could only be of value if it described the way the world truly is. I discovered that the philosophers I had admired most contradicted what I had seen myself. Shortly after you sailed for Perinthus, I began my search for a new philosophy without those contradictions.
>
> I always considered Aristotle the wisest of philosophers, and I embraced his teaching wholeheartedly from my youth. At the core of his teaching was the existence of an effective cause for everything. I considered all I had seen of life, and if I looked deeply enough or back far enough in time, I could see the causes of almost everything. He also taught that nothing lasts forever, that everything changes over time. That was what I saw, too.

But I saw a terrible inconsistency in his teaching, and that disturbed me greatly. He taught that the universe was eternal, that it had no effective cause. But how could that be, that the universe as a whole was the opposite of all the parts within it?

Clearly, there was something wrong with this idea. The universe must also have an effective cause, so I began my search for a philosophy that taught the universe had a beginning and an effective cause that started it. I found it in the Jewish Scriptures. They tell how God created everything from nothing, how He is the effective cause of the whole universe.

Titus rubbed his cheek. Father was right. The parts and the whole should behave the same. He set the sheet aside and turned to the next.

I also considered Plato a great philosopher, but the more I saw of men and how they lived, the harder it became for me to agree with his teaching. He taught that cities and empires could be ruled by philosopher-kings: intelligent, self-controlled men who ruled based on wisdom and reason and placed the good of those they ruled above their own desires for power and wealth.

But as I examined history, I found men like this have never ruled. Emperor Trajan is as good a man as has ever ruled the Empire. By the standards of Rome, he's a shining example. He has even provided for the care of orphans with food and education in Italia, but what about the rest of the Empire? He leads his legions out to conquer, killing and enslaving, making new orphans who will starve.

From the histories of empires and kingdoms that we have both read, you know that great rulers have always done so. Trajan condemns the men he has conquered to die like animals in the arena for the entertainment of the crowds. Where is the wisdom and goodness in that? Plato was wrong about the nature of man, so how could his philosophy be true?

Man is not good and wise; he naturally chooses evil. There are a few who choose kindness and mercy, and I hope I have been one of them, but it is cruelty and lust for power that rule. Rome is rotten at her core, and she rules vast lands with an iron hand. Man's love of violence led to the games.

I expect to die in the arena tomorrow, killed by a lion or a gladiator's sword. Thousands of Romans, including many men whom I have known for years, will be watching and will consider it good entertainment. Again, I found this understanding in the Jewish Scriptures, that man is naturally evil, selfish, rebellious against God. Man is a sinful being.

Titus placed the second sheet on the one beside him. He stroked the stack to flatten the curl. So far, what Father had written made sense. He could almost hear Father's voice. Titus had spent so many hours with his best friend, Decimus, following Father's logic from point to point when they were still youths. His lips tightened. Never again, thanks to the treachery of his brother. His mouth turned down as he focused on the next sheet.

In the Jewish Scriptures, I found the philosophy that explained everything I knew to be true about the world, but it is much more than a philosophy. In those same Scriptures, I met the God who made the universe. I discovered that He cared about men enough to reveal Himself to them so they could know Him. I learned of Abraham, Isaac, and Jacob, and how each of them had met God.

I learned of Moses, who was told by God Himself to lead the people of Israel out of slavery in Egypt because God had promised the land of Judaea to Jacob's children. God cared so much for His people that He gave Moses the very laws by which they should live. I learned of the many men who were prophets to whom God Himself spoke so His people, who no longer knew and worshiped Him, would return to Him.

From the beginning, He always wanted men to know Him and love Him. So I became a God-fearer, worshiping the God of Abraham, Isaac, and Jacob, and I studied the Jewish Scriptures daily because I could learn about Him there.

Titus's brow furrowed. Father had always said the Roman gods weren't real, just characters in stories that were only believed by weak-minded men and women. So why would he think the Jewish god was any different? All gods had so-called prophets. Men could live well off what worshippers gave the so-called god they spoke for. For Father to think the Jewish god had real power to free the Jews from Egyptian slavery and give them their own land, that he actually cared about their welfare... That was nothing like what he'd taught Titus before. What was in the Jewish writings that led him to believe that?

He is a holy God, and He cannot tolerate sin in His presence. But sin is not just doing the things that He has forbidden or neglecting the things He has commanded; it is also choosing to treat God as if He didn't exist.

In the Law He gave to Moses, He told His people the way to approach Him by covering their sins through blood sacrifice in their temple in Jerusalem. For over a thousand years, His people made sacrifices so they could approach Him. That ended when the temple was destroyed 44 years ago by Titus when he was putting down the rebellion in Judaea.

That created a terrible problem, or so I thought. God said the payment for sin always required blood sacrifice, but He let His temple be destroyed by Rome, so how was sin to be paid for? I was at a loss to explain how the true God, the one so powerful that He could make the entire universe, could allow Rome to destroy His temple and take away what allowed His people to approach Him.

Then I met a man who could explain it all. He has become one of my closest friends, but I won't write his name here in case this letter is intercepted. I do not want to be the cause of his death in the arena, too. He told me of Jesus of Nazareth and how He came from heaven to make the final sacrifice for sins. He was the

Son of God. He was sinless, and He made Himself the perfect sacrifice for all sin when He was crucified. After three days, He rose from the dead, proving His claim to be God.

The grandfather of my friend actually knew men who had been with Jesus after He rose. There could be no doubt of the truth that Jesus was the Son of God and the final perfect sacrifice.

Titus ran his fingers through his hair. A god taking human form? That happened all the time in the stories of the Greek and Roman gods, but those were only stories. Even in those stories, the god-man did it for his own pleasure, usually with a woman, not to become a sacrifice to let people approach a god.

And to make that sacrifice on a cross? Titus wrinkled his nose. There was no worse way for a man to die. Many didn't even survive the flogging before, and those were the lucky ones.

And claiming a crucified man survived? Rome's execution squads knew their business. No one got off a cross alive. Rose after three days? By then the body would be a rotting, stinking corpse. How could that come back to life? He'd heard the Christians believed Jesus had risen, and the body did disappear. But the Jewish rulers claimed the body had been stolen. That was much more believable than him coming back to life.

The grandfather of Father's friend must have been fooled by lies those men told. And his friend had fooled Father. It had to be that.

He rubbed the back of his neck and picked up the next sheet.

At last I understood it all. The temple could be destroyed because God had made the perfect blood sacrifice Himself—Jesus on a cross more than 80 years ago. The temple and its sacrifices were no longer needed, so He had Rome destroy it so people would no longer cling to the old ways.

The coming of the Messiah, of Jesus, was foretold in the Jewish Scriptures hundreds of years before He came, and God kept the promise He made to His people. There was no need to continually sacrifice animals to cover my sin with their blood. To be saved from my sin, I only had to believe in Jesus as the sacrifice for all sins, including mine. It all made perfect sense, and I finally knew the truth.

When I went the first time to worship with my friend, I actually met God myself. I felt His love surround me, and now He lives in me. I am never alone. That day when I decided to believe, to repent of my sins and commit myself to Jesus as my Lord, all the worry and sadness in my life was replaced by peace and joy. For the first time, I knew what it was to be fully alive.

My son, more than anything I've ever wanted, I want you to experience this yourself. For you to know this perfect love deep in your soul—that will be my dying prayer.

Following Jesus is like a perfect marriage; denying Him would be like committing adultery against the most loving, beautiful, faithful wife a man could have. I could never betray my Lord that way. I have chosen death instead.

Titus gripped his head with both hands. No one could actually meet a god and then have him live inside him. Had Father gone crazy? But the writing was typical Father...just like a speech he would have made to his philosopher friends. It didn't read like the ravings of a mad man...except for his conclusion he'd met God and that dying for Jesus was a good thing.

He added the sheet to the stack and picked up the last one.

When he learned of my faith, Lucius reported me as a Christian. He betrayed me because he wanted to be free from my control over his life. He was unwilling to wait until I died a natural death. The praetor who heard my case is one of his friends and is well known to hate those who follow Jesus. His praetor friend did give everything to him as reward for turning me in, but Lucius's treachery was not simply to gain the Drusus fortune.

I have forgiven him, and I pray that somehow God will reach him and that he will choose to follow Jesus, too. I know you will want to avenge my death, but my last command as your father is to forbid that. You must even try to forgive your brother for turning me in. I know that will be hard, but I am praying that you will discover that forgiveness, not vengeance, is the only way to find peace with what your brother has done. Jesus has made it possible for me to forgive him. I pray that He will help you do the same.

Titus ground his teeth. Forgive that treacherous dog who'd used a Roman court to murder Father? Impossible.

I will die soon, but I have no regrets. I am content to die because it isn't death that matters. It is whether you have accepted Jesus as Savior. Death is terrible apart from Jesus. Without Jesus, I would be lost, in hell, forever separated from God. With Jesus as my Savior, death has no power over me, and I don't fear it. It will just usher me into life with Him in heaven.

Jesus told us that He is the way, the truth, and the life. He promised if a man would believe in Him and follow, he would know the truth, and the truth would set him free. If you let Him, Jesus will show you what is true. Open your mind to Him, Titus. Open your heart. Know the truth and be free like I am, even in this prison as I wait to die. I will be praying for all my children to choose to follow Jesus until I take my final breath and even after that, for life with Jesus is eternal.

I love you, my son, and I hope to be with you again someday in heaven. May grace, mercy, and peace from the one true God and from Jesus, my Savior and Lord, soon be yours.

Titus picked up the stack and placed the final sheet on the bottom. Then he stared at the letter as he held it in his hand. Conflicting emotions swirled through his mind. He would treasure this letter because it was the last message he would ever receive from his father, but its contents shook him to the core.

Father was trying to convince him to become what had led to his own death. He'd actually been glad to die. It was beyond understanding how a calm, rational man could be glad to die for a dead man who claimed to be the son of the Jewish god. It was even more ludicrous that Father would tell him that he should be willing to risk doing the same.

All that discussion of how seeking a true philosophy led him to be a God-fearer made sense, but the part about sin and sacrifice and following Jesus didn't make sense at all. How could a single man be the sacrifice for the sins of all men? And why would his father choose to die for such an idea?

And all that part about forgiving Lucius? Titus could never forgive that traitor for causing their father to be murdered. That was what it was. Murder. Lucius should be sewn in a leather sack with the viper, dog, rooster, and monkey and thrown in the Tiber, just like any other man who committed patricide. He would reluctantly obey his father's command not to kill his brother, but he could never forgive him. That was a ridiculous idea, and he wouldn't even try.

One thing was certain. He wouldn't let Claudia see the letter. Since Father had written it, she might think everything in it must be true. The last thing he wanted was for her to even think about becoming a Christian. He didn't want her killed, too.

He opened the chest where he kept important papers and buried the letter at the bottom. Then he put a smile on his face before he headed downstairs to join Claudia for dinner. He didn't want her to ask what was wrong, so he would act like the letter had never come. For both their sakes, he hoped his acting would be good enough.

Chapter 64

FEVER

Miriam stirred the sauce, then lifted the spoon to her lips for a taste. It was a little over a week since Mistress Claudia had decided to follow Jesus. They'd become friends before then, but spending their days together was even more enjoyable now they were sisters as well.

Mistress walked up beside her and leaned on the counter. "That smells so good. Titus is going to love it."

Miriam dipped and lifted the spoon again for Mistress to taste.

"Mmm. You'll have to show me how to make that one. Then I can tell Philip's chef how to do it."

Mistress twirled with her arms out. "Or maybe I'll have you teach him. I'm not sure how Titus and I are going to manage to share you. He's going to want to keep you as his cook, but you really should stay with me." Her smiled dimmed. "I wish I could tell him how wonderful life is and why. But he still hates the Christians who told Father about Jesus, and I'm afraid he'd be furious with you if he knew you'd told me."

She danced back to the table and picked up the bowl containing the sauce she'd made for the master's favorite pear dessert. "Oh. I just got some sauce on me. I'd better go change before Titus gets here." She giggled. "We have him so fooled about what I do all day. But he does expect me to be lounging in here, waiting to greet him. I don't want to disappoint him."

Mistress left the kitchen, and Miriam listened to her singing as she went up the stairs.

When Miriam looked out the window above the counter, she saw Master Titus dismount. He was home early. Never before had he rested his forehead against the saddle and just stood there. When Nestor came to take the stallion to the stable and rub him down, the master drooped as he walked toward the house.

She'd prepared one of his favorite dinners, and he always stopped to comment on the delicious smell or to steal a quick taste as he passed through the kitchen when he first got home. His eyes laughed as he teased her or Claudia. Today was different. When he entered the kitchen, his eyes looked dull, and his face was flushed.

"Are you well, master?" It was too obvious the answer was no.

"Not really. It smells good, but I won't be eating with Claudia tonight. I'm going to lie down for a while. Maybe I'll get some later."

His shoulders sagged as he headed into the courtyard and up the stairs on the way to his bedchamber. Tendrils of unease wrapped around Miriam. She'd seen fever before, and Master Titus looked like he had one. She'd get Nestor to check on him later if he didn't come ask for something to eat after he rested.

Claudia had finished dining and sat at the kitchen table watching Miriam clean up. If it were breakfast or lunch, she'd be helping, but they'd agreed that Titus shouldn't know how much time she spent doing household chores, so she never helped when he was home. He wouldn't think it was proper for a Roman lady to do such work, but doing something was so much more enjoyable than doing nothing.

"I wonder how Titus is feeling. I missed him at dinner."

She'd eaten with Miriam and Nestor instead of by herself. Titus wouldn't have thought that was proper, either.

Miriam dried her hands as she finished at the washbasin. "I was planning to ask Nestor to check on him before we go to bed."

Claudia stood. "I can do that now. I'll be right back."

Miriam was putting the plates and cups away on the shelves when she heard Mistress Claudia running along the balcony and down the courtyard stairs.

Mistress burst into the kitchen. "Titus was just lying there on his bed, and when I touched him, he felt like he was burning up."

Miriam took her hand and squeezed it. "I'll take a look at him. I've taken care of people with fevers before, and I know what to do."

Unfortunately, she did know what to do. There had been an outbreak of fever in Bithynia when she was in Master Alexander's household. Several of their neighbors fell ill, and Master Alexander and his servants tended them. Some lived, but some died. Miriam didn't tell Mistress that the woman she tended had been among those who died.

At the door to the master's bedchamber, Miriam placed her hand on Mistress's arm. "Fever is sometimes easy to catch, and I don't want you to come into the room with me. Stay here while I check him."

Mistress didn't object. She stood at the doorway, biting her lip.

When Miriam approached Master Titus's bedside, he rolled from his side to his back and moaned. His eyes opened at the soft sound of her footsteps.

"Miriam? What are you doing here?"

His surprise was understandable. She'd never entered his bedchamber when he was there before.

"Mistress said you weren't well, master. I came to see if I can help."

"Keep her away from me. There's fever in the garrison, and I have it now." He paused. "It's bad. Several of the men have died."

Worry clouded his eyes. Miriam laid her palm on his forehead. He was burning up.

"You don't have to worry about that, master. I've cared for fever before, and I know what to do." He didn't have to worry, but it worried her that it took some effort for him to speak.

"So I bought a nurse as well as a cook and musician." His mouth turned up a little. "I got a lot for four hundred."

"I always try to do whatever you need, master."

He gave her another weak smile.

She steeled herself to touch his bare shoulder. It felt even hotter. He'd removed his tunic before lying down. That was good; she needed his chest exposed if she was to bring down his temperature.

"You're a bit warm, master. I'm going to cool you to make you more comfortable."

Actually, he was alarmingly hot. This was not an ordinary fever. Mistress stood at the door on tiptoes, trying to get a better view of the master as Miriam walked back to her.

She spoke softly so Master Titus wouldn't hear. "He's very hot, but I know how to help that. He doesn't want you coming into the room because he's worried you might get sick, too. Keeping him from worrying is important. He'll rest better. Besides, I'll need someone to bring me things so I can stay here with him."

Mistress pressed her palms to her cheeks. "Is he going to be all right?"

Miriam forced a smile. "I've seen people who were much sicker get better."

She'd also seen people die who hadn't been this sick. That fact was best kept to herself.

"He should feel better after I start taking care of him."

She could make him more comfortable, but that didn't mean he might not die. It was best only she knew that as well. Besides, she didn't expect the master to die. Surely God would heal the man who protected and provided for both Mistress Claudia and her.

Mistress squared her shoulders. "Tell me what to do."

"First, I need some small towels, a sponge, a fan, and a bowl of water from the well. I'm going to try to cool him down. He'll feel much better when I do."

Mistress hurried off to fetch what Miriam had asked for.

Miriam returned to Master Titus and picked up his hand. He opened his eyes.

"I've sent for some cold water. I'm going to sponge you with the water to cool you and drape you with wet towels."

Her ears burned at the thought of touching his chest and face that way. All he had to do was brush her arm, and her heart beat faster. What she had to do to cool him down...she didn't want to think about it. But he was such a good master; she'd do anything it took to get him well.

◆

Miriam's flushed cheeks told Titus how uncomfortable she was with what she must do, but she'd do it anyway. Another time, he would have found her modesty entertaining and might have teased her about it. Not today. He simply squeezed her hand in appreciation.

He received a reassuring smile, but then he looked at her eyes. They were deadly serious. No need to worry? That clearly wasn't true.

His eyes widened. He tightened his grip on her hand and tried to sit up. "If I die, what will happen to Claudia? She can't go back to Lucius."

She placed her free hand on his shoulder and gently pushed. "Master Philip and Mistress Penelope will take her in and care for her, just like they did before, but you don't need to worry about that. I do know how to care for you, and you should get better."

He collapsed back on his pillow. His voice was quiet as he stared into her eyes. "Take care of Claudia, no matter what." He closed his eyes briefly, then opened them and smiled at her. "Don't know what we'd do without you."

"I'll take care of both of you, master. No need to worry."

Titus closed his eyes. A deep sigh escaped as he let his whole body relax. Miriam would make sure Claudia would be all right if he didn't recover. Philip would take care of her needs, and Miriam would take care of her heart.

◆

The master's last words warmed Miriam's cheeks and her heart. She loved Mistress Claudia like a sister, but she cared for Master Titus, too. He'd saved her from life in the brothel, and he always treated her like a person. Serving him gave her even more pleasure than serving Master Alexander had.

Miriam heard Mistress Claudia's footsteps on the balcony, so she limped over to meet her at the door.

Mistress handed her the bowl and other items. "Is this all I can do?"

"You or Nestor can bring me more cold water in a little while. I'll be cooling the master until his fever breaks, and that could be several hours."

"I'm going to stay here and watch with you, even if he won't let me come in. Just tell me when you need fresh water, and I'll get it right away."

"If you wish, mistress." Miriam wouldn't let her enter, but if the mistress wanted to stay by the doorway, it wasn't Miriam's place to tell her she shouldn't. "Why don't you get something to sit on? You can't help if you get too tired."

She limped back to the master's bedside and set the bowl on the floor. His eyes flickered open. They were dull and listless, and her concern ramped up. His temperature needed to come down as soon as possible. He seemed hotter than anyone she'd ever seen before.

She folded one of the small towels and soaked it in the cool water. After wringing out the excess, she wiped his face, then draped the towel on his forehead.

The master raised his arm and laid it across the top of his head. The corner of his mouth tipped up, but he didn't open his eyes.

Miriam dipped the sponge in the cold water and let the excess drip out before she wiped his chest and neck to thoroughly wet his skin. Then she picked up the fan. The evaporating water should cool him, but would it be enough?

When he spoke, it was barely above a whisper. "That does feel better...Got a real treasure when I bought you."

Miriam's heart swelled at the word "treasure." Mistress Claudia called her that all the time, but the master had never said it before. Being a treasure was so much better than being a bargain.

"I'm glad, master. I'll do this until you cool down enough. Rest now, and enjoy it."

Titus nodded once and relaxed. He didn't have to worry. Miriam knew what to do.

Miriam had made Mistress Claudia go to bed after bringing her a bucket of water so she wouldn't run out in the middle of the night. It was past midnight, and Master Titus was still much hotter than he should be. The master's breathing was all that broke the silence.

She turned over the cloth on his forehead to place the cool side against his skin. When she laid the back of her hand on his cheek, he still felt terribly hot, but at least he didn't seem to be getting hotter. Once more, she lifted the sponge from the bowl to let the excess drain. When she began to stroke his chest and neck with it, a sigh came from deep within him.

"Feels good, Miriam. Don't know what I'd do without you." His voice was barely above a whisper.

"Shhh. Don't talk, master. Just go to sleep. You should feel much better when you awake."

The corner of his mouth barely rose. His deep, slow breathing soon told her he was asleep.

She'd been praying for the master since she first felt his forehead. Tonight would be one of intense prayer. He was still much too hot, and he seemed weaker. She'd do all she could to help him feel better, but only God could heal. If only He would!

Titus awoke shortly before dawn. He expected to feel much better. He didn't. When he opened his eyes, Miriam was kneeling on the floor beside his bed with her arm that held the fan stretched out across his legs and her head lying on her arm.

When he stirred, she jerked awake.

"Forgive me, master. I didn't mean to stop." She stood and lifted the dry cloth from his forehead to dip it again in the cool water.

He closed his eyes. When she wiped his face with the cool, damp cloth before placing it back on his forehead, the corners of his mouth twitched up. He didn't have the energy for a full smile.

◆

When Miriam touched the master's cheek, he was still burning up. She lifted the sponge from the bowl and began again to wet his neck and chest.

God, please take this fever and heal him. She tried to push the thought away, but she knew a fever that raged this long and this hot usually ended in death.

They needed a miracle to save them all. Mistress Claudia didn't need to have her heart broken again, and Miriam didn't want any other master but him. But most important, the master didn't follow Jesus; he wasn't prepared to die.

Chapter 65

Not Prepared to Die

Miriam heard Mistress Claudia's footsteps scurrying down the balcony just after dawn.

"How is he, Miriam?" Hope brightened her face until she caught a glimpse of Master Titus. Then her eyes filled with fear.

Miriam limped over to the doorway so she could speak without the master hearing.

"He's still too hot, but he isn't getting any hotter, praise God! I'm going to keep cooling him with water, but I need Nestor to go the apothecary for some medicine. There are herbs that help cool a fever, and that would make him feel better."

Claudia rested a palm on her cheek. "I've been praying so hard for him. What if God doesn't listen to my prayers?"

"He always listens, mistress. Sometimes He just doesn't answer them quickly or in the way we want." She turned to look at the master. "I believe in my heart that God will heal him. I just don't know when. We must keep praying and listening for what God wants us to do to help him. Right now, that's cooling him and getting the medicine."

Claudia pushed a strand of hair behind her ear. "I'll find Nestor and tell him what we need. He can be at the apothecary waiting when they open."

Miriam limped back to the bed and resumed her efforts to bring the master's temperature down. As she stroked his neck with the wet sponge, she gazed at his closed eyes. What would happen if they lost him?

If she lost him.

Last night had been disturbing in more ways than one. After pouring her heart out to God for hours, begging for the master's healing, what she finally admitted to herself was a disturbing revelation.

She loved her mistress more than anyone she'd ever known. She loved her like the sister she'd never had. But just before dawn, she realized the way she cared for the master was different from how she'd ever felt about anyone.

He wasn't quite as kind as Master Alexander, but her former master had been a Christian. He'd treated her more like a father would than like a master. Still, Master Titus always had kind words for her, and any room seemed brighter whenever he was there.

Master Titus's smiles showed how glad he was to see her when he returned home. When he stole a bite of something, he'd deliberately brush against her hand or arm and then laugh when she got flustered. Sometimes he'd even stop and talk to her for a little while before going to find Mistress Claudia. Almost every day he told her he appreciated something she'd done for him or his sister.

Sometimes he even helped her when Nestor wasn't around and something was too hard to do by herself. His smile when she thanked him lit up her world.

He didn't mind that she was a cripple. When it took a little longer to do something because of her leg, he never complained. He usually said it didn't matter or joked about not buying her for footraces.

He was so strong, but he was always gentle with her. He'd promised he'd never hit her, and she couldn't imagine him ever doing anything to deliberately cause her pain.

Mistress Claudia loved Master Titus dearly as a brother, and who wouldn't? Miriam found herself loving him, too, but not just as a master who treated her well.

As the black of night lightened to a dark shade of gray, she finally admitted to herself that she loved him...as a man.

She'd never expected to love a man, but she'd fallen in love with this kind man who loved his sister so dearly that Miriam knew he had the best heart in the world.

Nothing would ever come of it. He was her master, and she was only his slave, but she'd grown to love him anyway. She'd do anything for him, even give up her own life to save his. She'd be as broken hearted as Mistress if he were to die.

She wet the cloth again. When she placed it back on his forehead, he didn't move at all. Her breath caught. He usually responded in some way, even if it was only the slightest smile.

"Master?"

She placed her hand on his shoulder and shook him. Still no response. Panic coursed through her. She laid her head on his chest and listened for a heartbeat.

What relief when she heard it, steady and strong, but his chest felt so hot against her cheek. Had anything she'd done lowered his temperature at all?

Her lips quivered. "Oh, God! Please! Spare him. We need him." *I love him...and he's not prepared to die.*

Tears trickled across her cheek, past her ear, and into the thick brown hair on his chest. She kept her cheek pressed against him, listening to his heartbeat as she cried out to God.

At long last, he stirred, and a soft sigh escaped.

"Miriam?" Mistress Claudia's voice quavered as she stood in the doorway. "Is he dead?"

Miriam sat up and turned toward Mistress. "No, but he is still hot. I need to keep cooling him."

"Nestor just left to get the medicine." The mistress's eyes swam in unshed tears. "Oh, Miriam. He's been hot much too long."

"Well, yes. It's longer than I would have hoped, but I've seen longer. Just keep praying."

She'd seen longer, and most of the ones who'd been this hot for this long had also died. But not all, and surely God could spare Master Titus like he had those.

She wet the sponge and once more began the cycle of sponging and fanning. He might not be getting cooler, but at least he wasn't getting hotter, and that was something to be thankful for.

It was mid-morning when Nestor returned with the herbs. Mistress Claudia was in the kitchen with him preparing the tea according to the directions from the apothecary.

Miriam pulled her shoulders back, stretching a back that was too tired from too many hours at his side, sponging and fanning until she thought her arm would fall off.

"Master? Can you look at me? I'll have some tea in just a little while that should make you feel better." Miriam shook his shoulder. "Try to look at me."

The master opened his eyes, and a slow smile appeared. "Pretty face...Shouldn't be...too hard...to look at."

Scarlet washed over her cheeks and up to her ears. He'd never said such a thing to her before. She didn't know what to say, so she just lifted the cloth from his forehead and dipped it in the cool water. After wringing it out, she wiped his face before replacing it. He sighed deeply.

She wasn't sure if he was getting better or worse. He still felt too hot, and he was so weak. But his eyes had seemed a little brighter before they closed. Watching the man she loved suffer hurt more than she'd ever imagined, but she'd never been in love before.

When Miriam heard Mistress Claudia's footsteps on the balcony, she met her at the door. Mistress had a cup of the herbal tea on a tray. When Miriam touched it, she snatched her hand back. It was still too hot for him to drink.

"Do you think this will break the fever?" Mistress bit her lip.

"I don't know, but I'm sure it will help. He seems a little more alert than he was, and I think that's a good sign. Maybe God has already started healing him."

Miriam didn't tell the mistress what the master said. His words were something precious that she wouldn't share with anyone.

Mistress blew on the tea to hasten its cooling. "I don't know what I'd do right now without Jesus. I'm so scared for Titus, but praying helps so much."

"I know. God has been giving me strength for taking care of him." She pushed a strand of hair back from her forehead. "I'm really not very strong myself."

Mistress's head snapped back. "Not strong? The only person I've ever known who's stronger than you is Philip. But I hadn't thought about how hard it is to keep tending him. Are you sure I can't take a turn so you can rest?"

Miriam shook her head. "Not until the fever breaks. He didn't want you to risk catching this. After it breaks, we'll see."

"But he's letting you risk it. Why can't I?"

Miriam's eyebrows rose. "Because I'm only his slave, and it won't matter that much to him if I catch it and die. He doesn't especially care about me."

It hurt to say that, but she knew it was true. Her love was not returned and never would be. Even though he treated her kindly, he only saw her as his slave.

"I can't believe that. It would break my heart to lose you. Titus must care, too."

Miriam's heart warmed at those words. To serve a mistress who loved her like a sister was pure joy.

"It would break my heart if I let you help and you got sick and died. I'd rather die myself." She would start crying if their conversation continued, so she stopped it.

"The tea is probably cool enough. Time for me to try to get him to drink it." She took the tray and returned to his bedside, where she placed it on a small table.

"Master? Time for your tea. I'm going to hold you up so you can drink it."

He opened his eyes again and slowly nodded.

She lifted his shoulders and slid herself behind him until she could lean his head back against her shoulder. She wrapped one arm around his chest to support him, then brought the cup of tea to his lips. He raised his hand to rest it on her arm, but he didn't try to take the cup.

"Drink this, master. It should help."

He opened his lips and let her give him the tea, sip by sip. When the cup was empty, his arm dropped back onto the bed. "Not...as good as...your dinners."

"I'll prepare your most favorite as soon as you're better." He was so weak. She fought tears. If she wasn't his slave, what it would be like to have him in her arms? Nothing like this.

"Best cook...in the city." He sighed again.

"Time for you to rest, master." She set the cup on the table and slid out from under him so he could lie back on the bed.

She replaced the cool cloth on his forehead. With the wet sponge in her hand, she resumed the fight against the fever. Only God could save the master. If only He would.

Miriam was pleased with the effect of the tea. Master Titus was still too hot, but he seemed cooler than he'd been since the first evening. She'd been trying to bring his temperature down for a full day, and she was desperately tired. Only her prayers had enabled her to stay awake to tend him. Except for that brief time when she dozed off, she hadn't slept at all. Mistress brought her bread, fruit, and cheese at meal times, so at least she hadn't gone hungry, too.

It was time to get the master to drink another cup of the tea. He'd been mostly sleeping even while she sponged him, which was probably a good thing. She lifted the cool cloth off his forehead and wiped his face. She laid her hand on his cheek and gazed at his closed eyelids. It would have been wonderful to touch his face as he looked at her with love in his eyes. But that was a dream that would never come true. It would have to be enough that she could show her love by caring for him.

"Master?" She shook his shoulder.

He opened his eyes and almost managed a smile. The tea had done nothing to help his weakness.

"Master, it's time for another cup of tea."

"Did it...help much?"

"I think you feel cooler, so yes, I think it did. I'm going to hold you up again."

"Nurse, too...for four hundred...real bargain." He tried to smile.

"I'm glad you think so, master."

Her voice cracked. The master was a little cooler, but he might die anyway. How could she watch the man she loved die, knowing he'd be lost forever because he didn't follow Jesus? Her eyes filled with tears, and one trickled down her cheek.

He reached up and caught the tear with his finger, sweeping it slowly off her cheek. His touch felt so wonderful. If only it were for another reason.

"Don't...scare Claudia."

"Yes, master." She flicked the rest of her tears away.

She rested his head against her shoulder as she had before and held the cup as he drank. He definitely felt a little cooler. Not cool enough yet, but definitely cooler.

When he finished, she lowered him back onto the bed.

"Rest now. I'll be here as long as you need me."

He barely nodded, then drifted off to sleep.

She replaced the cloth on his forehead and picked up the sponge again. She would never tell this man how much she loved him, but she could pour her heart into caring for him. The words would always remain unspoken, but she could show it by caring for him well. It was never words that revealed how deep love was.

It was another long night without sleep for Miriam. She thought she'd made it through without dozing, but she couldn't be sure. The master was still hot, but at least he'd slept peacefully through the night. Maybe he was starting to improve.

Mistress Claudia appeared shortly after dawn, so Miriam met her at the door.

"Is he better this morning?" Hope brightened Mistress's voice.

"I can't tell for sure, but maybe. I think he slept better."

"I've been praying and praying. I wish Titus believed in Jesus so he would be praying, too. Maybe then God would heal him."

◆

Titus was drifting in and out of a light sleep. He briefly opened his eyes to see Miriam at the door, talking with Claudia. His eyes were closed when he caught a fragment of their conversation.

"Jesus healed sick people all the time. They didn't all believe in him. Sometimes it was the people who loved them who believed."

"Well, I believe in Jesus, and you believe in Jesus, so maybe Titus will be healed because of our faith."

"God is merciful, and I still think He will heal him. I expect the fever to break soon."

He slipped back into deeper sleep and heard no more.

It was mid-morning when his fever broke. When Miriam was certain his temperature was falling, she dropped the sponge into the water and fell to her knees beside his bed. She raised her hands and sang a psalm of thanksgiving. God had been so merciful to the master and mistress...and her.

Master Titus would recover, Mistress Claudia wouldn't lose another person she loved, and she would still have the best master she'd ever had. Well, maybe the second best. Master Alexander really was a better master, but she hadn't loved him the same way she loved Master Titus.

From the doorway, Mistress saw her joyful face and heard her song.

"Miriam? Have all our prayers been answered?"

"Oh, yes! He's going to be fine in a few days. He just needs to eat well to get his strength back."

"Can I sit with him now while you go rest?"

Miriam was totally exhausted, or she would have stayed to see him awaken. To be with him when he opened his eyes and tell him he was going to be fine...nothing could delight her more. His smile of appreciation would brighten her world. Maybe he would even tell her again that she was a treasure. In her heart, she longed to be there, but in her head, she knew she desperately needed to get some rest or she might become sick herself. She couldn't keep Mistress Claudia from tending her, and she didn't want to risk Mistress getting sick because of her.

"Yes, but don't sit too close to the bed. He might still be afraid you'll get sick, and you don't want to make him worry. When he wakes up, get him to drink plenty of water with only a little wine mixed in. And see if he'll eat something. Some bread or cheese or grapes. I'll rest for a while, but don't forget to wake me to make dinner."

Claudia set a chair by the window and picked up a scroll that Titus had been reading.

"I'll do everything you say, Miriam."

Miriam paused in the doorway to look back at the peaceful face of her sleeping master. Her heart swelled with prayers of thanksgiving that God had chosen to spare the man she loved.

When Titus finally awoke late in the afternoon, Claudia was reading by the window.

"Where's Miriam? She was supposed to keep you out of here." His mouth turned down. "Tending me is her job, not yours. You go and send her back. This fever is too dangerous for you to be in here."

"She did keep me out until your fever broke several hours ago. She didn't leave your side until it did. Philip says no man is worth more than any other man, but Miriam is worth more than any other woman I've ever known. She's much better than me.

"Don't you remember all she did? She sat up with you two nights running and all day, too, trying to keep you from getting too hot. I don't know how she did it. I told her to get some rest after your fever broke so she wouldn't get sick herself. She wanted me to wake her so she can make dinner for us. I'm not going to. She really needs to rest. I can manage something simple."

She walked over to stand by his bed. "Really, Titus. I didn't expect you to wake up so grumpy and ungrateful that she risked her life to take such good care of you. She knew she could have caught the fever and died herself. She said that wouldn't matter to you, but I couldn't believe that. Now you're talking like she was right. Where's my cheerful, appreciative brother?"

Titus's eyebrow rose at her words. Miriam was only a slave. Their father had always treated his slaves well, but they were still only slaves. Philip had put some strange ideas into his sister's head.

She flashed a smile at him that drew one in return. Claudia was fond of Miriam. That's probably what colored her view of his slave.

"That's more like it. I like you much better when you're smiling."

He tried to sit up, but his head started spinning, so he lay back down. The fever had weakened him more than he expected.

Claudia poured a cup of water and handed it to him. "Miriam said you'd be weak until you get some good food into you. I'll bring some bread and cheese and maybe some grapes to get you started now. You can have one of her delicious meals tomorrow."

"That sounds good." He was hungrier than he expected, too.

Claudia patted his arm and walked toward the doorway. He watched her as she went. There was a confidence in her step, a sense of purpose that he didn't remember seeing before. That was good, but what could have caused it?

Chapter 66

A Very Different Claudia

The light supper Claudia brought to Titus's room satisfied his hunger. It wasn't one of Miriam's exquisitely delicious meals, but it was what he needed after being sick for so long. He already felt a little stronger, but it would take a few days before he fully recovered from the ravages of the fever. He'd send Nestor to the palace in the morning to report his survival and tell the governor and garrison commander that it would probably be a day or two before he was strong enough to report for duty.

Claudia had refused to awaken Miriam to wait on him that evening, so he had a chance to observe his sister in a way that simply eating dinner together never allowed. What he saw raised some questions.

Claudia was the most intelligent person he'd ever known, with the possible exception of their father. Despite her intelligence, she'd always been a sweet, helpless kind of person. In many ways, she'd been more of a child than a woman, even though she was sixteen. That was probably because Father had protected her like she was still a child. Many Roman women were already married and raising children of their own by her age.

Something had changed. Even in the few hours since his awakening, he'd seen a very different woman than he expected. She seemed calm, capable, strong—almost like a second Miriam. It was good to see her that way, but why hadn't he noticed it before? What could have caused the change?

She'd gone down to the well to fetch some fresh, cool water for him to drink before he went to sleep for the night. He could hear her humming as she came back along the balcony to his room. It sounded like one of the songs Miriam sang when she was kneading the dough while he ate breakfast.

Maybe the change was from being around Miriam. His little Jewish slave had ended Claudia's nightmares and helped her out of her crushing grief. Maybe she was helping the child become a woman as well.

Titus stayed home for the next two days as he regained his strength. It was an eye-opening experience. He'd thought he knew what was going on in his own household, but he discovered he was wrong.

Miriam had been able to calm and cheer his sister since their first day together. Claudia was very happy with her as her maid, and she found it entertaining to watch Miriam in the kitchen. No surprises there.

What he hadn't realized was how much influence Miriam had over his sister. If he hadn't known Miriam was only his slave, he would have said they were good friends or even sisters, and Miriam was definitely the older sister.

The first morning he stayed in bed. Miriam checked on him several times to see if he was hungry or thirsty, and she left his door open so she could hear him if he called. He spent part of his time reading and part sleeping. When he was awake, he could hear her and Claudia talking and laughing together. He heard Claudia teaching Latin to Miriam and Miriam teaching Claudia to sing one of the songs he enjoyed so much while he ate breakfast.

Miriam was a Jew, so he wasn't surprised when he heard her say something to Claudia about the song praising God. He assumed she was referring to the god of the Jews, who was legally worshipped. What he found surprising and a bit disturbing was then Claudia said something back where she was talking about praising God as well.

Like their father and him, Claudia had never believed in any of the Roman gods. It appeared she might have become a God-fearer, like Father. That would be all right, as long as it stopped there.

The problem was he wasn't sure it had. When he was drifting in and out as his fever burned, he'd thought he heard Claudia saying she believed in Jesus and Miriam did, too. After the fever broke, he figured he must have been delirious and imagined it. She couldn't possibly have become what killed their father and what she hated so passionately because of that. Or had she?

That afternoon, he moved from his bed to the chair under the tree in the garden.

Claudia kept him company, reading one of his histories while he read or dozed in the sun, so they hadn't talked much. Miriam only prepared one of her delicious stews for dinner. She said she didn't think he was ready for everything she would have prepared for a three-course meal. She was right. He'd been exhausted by the end of dinner and went straight to bed. Except for it being a lighter dinner than usual, the evening had seemed normal.

The second morning was another matter. He'd slept in, so Claudia had come to check on him. She'd roused him, but she didn't realize she had. That let him hear a conversation he was quite certain he wasn't supposed to.

"How is he, mistress?"

"He's still sound asleep, but he looks so much better today. God has been so merciful. I just want to keep singing thanks and praise for Him sparing Titus."

"Me, too, mistress. I'm so thankful God didn't let him die when he wasn't ready yet."

"I am, too."

The young women were walking away, and he didn't hear any more of their conversation. What Miriam said bothered him. What did she mean when she said he wasn't ready yet? Was anyone ever ready to die of a fever? What did she think made a man ready or not? Whatever it was, Claudia agreed with her.

He rose and went downstairs to find them in the kitchen. Claudia was leaning on the counter watching Miriam shape the loaves of bread. They didn't realize he was watching them from the doorway. Miriam would sing a few phrases in whatever language that was, then Claudia would sing a few, then they would sing something together. They went through the cycle several times before he stepped into the room and they became aware he was there. The singing stopped abruptly, and Claudia hurried over to give him a big hug.

"You look like you feel so much better today."

He kept his brows from lowering as he analyzed her face. Then his gaze shifted to Miriam.

She turned to face him. "Good morning, master. Where would you like your breakfast today?"

"In here." It would be wise to watch the two of them more closely. He'd be able to return to duty tomorrow, and he needed to figure out their relationship while he had a chance.

Unfortunately, they didn't let him. Claudia spent almost all her time under the tree with him, either reading quietly or telling him about something she found interesting in one of his scrolls that she was reading for the first time. Miriam started working on his three-course dinner right after lunch, so she was mostly out of sight in the kitchen. He was certain he wasn't seeing anything remotely like what usually went on when the two of them were alone.

By late afternoon, he felt frustrated. He'd have to get them to think he wasn't listening if he was to learn anything.

"I think I'll go up and rest awhile before dinner."

Claudia perked up at the prospect. That seemed suspicious. When he rose, she wrapped her arm around his and walked into the kitchen with him.

Miriam was shaping some pastries and looked up from the counter. "Can I get you anything, master?"

"No. Just come wake me when it's time for dinner."

"Yes, master." She returned to her work.

Claudia was still wrapped around his arm. "Would you like me to keep you company while you go to sleep?"

He smiled disarmingly at her. "No. I can manage just fine without you mothering me." She needed to stay downstairs so he could listen from the balcony.

"Sleep well." She flashed him that beautiful smile before unwrapping her arm and going over to the counter to watch Miriam.

As he stepped into the courtyard, he glanced back. Claudia had shifted her attention completely from him to Miriam. His time of observation could begin. He climbed the stairs and entered his room. Then he stood just inside the doorway, listening. Nothing unusual reached his ears, only some comments by Claudia about the sauce Miriam was stirring. A few minutes later he stepped back out onto the balcony. Whatever they were doing then, he didn't hear anything. After a few minutes, he returned to his room and took his nap.

Titus awoke to find Claudia shaking his shoulder.

"Ready for one of Miriam's delicious dinners?"

He sat up and smiled at her. "Always."

As he followed her downstairs, he ran his hand through his hair. Maybe he was worried over nothing. It was probably just delirium and his imagination playing tricks on him.

Dinner was perfectly normal. He was still a little tired, so he went right to bed. He'd be going to the garrison tomorrow, and a good night's sleep would probably be enough to get him ready for a normal day on duty.

Titus had dozed off, but he woke to hear them talking quietly as they climbed the stairs for Miriam to help Claudia get ready to retire.

First Claudia was speaking. "Titus is feeling so much better today. He's even planning to go to the garrison tomorrow. He was so close to dying, and now he's well. I'm so glad God heard all our prayers and spared him."

"I know, mistress. He always hears our prayers, and I praise Him for His answer."

"I know He saved Titus from the fever, and I'm praying He'll soon save him from his sins. I want him to be just like me and Father."

Her door closed, and he heard no more.

Titus's brow furrowed at what he'd just heard, and then the frown came. What did Claudia mean by her last comment? It could just mean she was a God-fearer; they worried about sin. But he had a bad feeling that wasn't the case. Father had written that he'd worried about how his god could forgive his sins without the temple sacrifices. His letter clearly said it was only by becoming a Christian that he'd actually been saved from them. But it didn't make sense that Claudia, who hated Christians for causing Father's death, would decide to take that step and become one herself.

Tomorrow morning, he would ask her. That was the only way to find out what was really going on. She would tell him the truth, whatever that happened to be.

Chapter 67

BLAMING MIRIAM

When Titus entered the kitchen, his breakfast tray awaited him on the table. Miriam was kneading the dough and singing, as usual.

"Good morning, master. I hope you're feeling all better this morning."

"Close enough. I'll be going to the garrison today."

He ate his breakfast quickly to leave time for a conversation before he left. Or, more accurately, an interrogation.

"Would Claudia be awake yet?" He'd wake her if she wasn't.

"Yes, master. I usually help her dress right after I finish with the bread dough."

He rose. "Good. I want to talk with her about something."

Miriam turned from the counter and watched the master head back into the courtyard and up the stairs. There had been a hard edge to his voice. What could the master want to say to Mistress Claudia that couldn't wait until dinnertime?

Claudia was already up and standing at her window, gazing out at the cloudless morning sky. It would be good to have a normal day helping and talking with Miriam. Doing nothing in particular for two days had been boring. She turned at the sudden sound of Titus entering her room.

"Titus. This is a nice surprise. I thought you'd left already."

"Not yet. I needed to ask you something."

"What's that?" He looked too serious. Was he feeling bad again?

"I've been watching and listening to you for the past two days, and you seem very different. I want to know why."

Her eyebrows shot up. "What do you mean, different?"

"Calm, confident...different."

Her head tilted. "And I wasn't that way before?"

"No. You weren't. I've heard you saying things, too. Things about giving thanks to God and about him saving me." He paused. "It sounds to me like you've become a God-fearer like Father was."

She beamed. "I have. I should have done it a long time ago. It always made Father so happy."

"Is that all you are, Claudia? Only a God-fearer?"

His face turned grim, and every muscle she had tensed. Then she relaxed. She hadn't intended to tell Titus she followed Jesus just yet. He still hated Christians. But was this God's way of getting him not to? God used a fight with Philip to open her eyes. Maybe He intended the same for Titus.

"No. I've become a Christian, just like Father. And it's so wonderful, Titus. I've met God, and He loves me, and life just couldn't be better."

Titus's face turned redder than she'd ever seen. The fury building in his eyes made her tremble. He gripped her arms so tightly it hurt. Then he erupted.

"How could you? They're still killing Christians in Rome. It's a death sentence in Bithynia. First Father, now you? Is everyone I love going to die because of this Jesus?"

He'd never, ever raised his voice at her. Now he was yelling.

"Please, Titus. Let me tell you why I just had to believe in Him, why you should, too."

"It's that slave of yours, isn't it! She talked you into believing in that Jewish carpenter." He shoved her away and stormed out of the room before Claudia could say another word.

◆

Miriam was laying out Claudia's breakfast tray when Master Titus stormed into the room. He grabbed her by the shoulders and spun her around to face him. He gripped both her arms and gave her a hard shake. His vice-like grip hurt, and the anger in his eyes made her heart pound.

"Did you make my sister a Christian?"

Her eyes saucered, and she trembled as she answered him. "No, master. God did that."

Black fury filled his eyes. He struck her hard with the back of his hand, knocking her to the floor. She rose and stared at him as her eyes filled with tears.

Miriam had been struck many times, but never by someone as strong as he was. Never hard enough to knock her down. She'd never even imagined a blow could hurt so much. She touched her cheek, then jerked her hand back as the screaming pain surged again.

But the pain in her face was nothing compared to the pain in her heart. So many times, the master had said he'd never hit her, and she'd come to believe him. If she'd thought he was about to, she'd have moved to lessen the impact. She'd figured out how during her many years with her first mistress. But she'd been so sure he would never strike that she'd done nothing to prepare for the blow.

"I bought you to help her, not get her killed."

"I only did what you bought me for, master. I helped her heart heal."

"By turning her into a Christian?" He clenched his teeth, and fury still burned in his eyes.

"Jesus is the only one who can heal a heart, master."

She stood motionless in front of him, looking him straight in the eye like he'd always told her to do. Black fury turned to red rage, and he drew back his arm. She saw it coming, and she tried to respond, but he was quicker. He struck her even harder, knocking her to the floor again and cutting her cheek with his signet ring.

This time Miriam remained crumpled on the floor as the master stood towering over her. She knew now it had been a mistake to stand up the first time. It was best to stay down and say nothing, or he would hit her again. If he did, he might not be able to stop. With her first mistress, the third strike always led to many more. It had been many years since she had a beating. He was so strong that one from him might kill her. His flaming eyes said he might want to kill her.

She knew how dangerous it was to look at an angry master. Still, she couldn't resist looking up at him. She saw only rage in his eyes.

◆

Titus saw deep pain and paralyzing fear in Miriam's, but in his wrath, he was unmoved.

Nestor had just brought the stallion from the stable. Now he stood in the doorway. Titus strode to the door, and Nestor jumped back to let him pass.

"I want her gone from this house when I return. Sell her."

"Yes, master."

Titus stormed out of the kitchen, mounted his horse, and kicked it into a trot.

◆

Claudia reached the kitchen just in time to see Titus strike Miriam the second time and order Nestor to sell her. She ran out the door after him.

"Titus! Wait! Please! You can't sell her."

He ignored her and disappeared through the gate before she could reach him. She stopped at the gate, staring at his back as he rode away. She would have run after him, but he'd already kicked his horse into a canter. She had no chance of catching him.

When she returned to the kitchen, she knelt beside Miriam and drew her into her arms. Tears streamed down both women's cheeks.

"Oh, Miriam, I can't lose you. What are we going to do?"

◆

Miriam clung to Mistress Claudia as deep, racking sobs shook her. How could she bear to leave the mistress she loved like a sister? And how could the master she'd come to trust and even love strike her so cruelly and sell her with no warning, like she meant less than nothing to him?

She thought nothing could ever hurt more than watching her beloved Master Alexander die. She was wrong.

Nestor stepped closer. "Don't worry, mistress. Master Philip will buy her and keep her safe until you can persuade the master to buy her back."

Mistress looked up, and hope lit her face. "You're right. Philip would want to protect Miriam until she can be with me again."

"He would do anything he possibly could for you, mistress. That's the only reason I'm here."

Mistress stood and helped Miriam to her feet. It was the first time she'd ever been helping Miriam instead of Miriam helping her.

"I'm sure I can convince Titus after he calms down. It should only be for a day or two."

Miriam's chin quivered. "I hope so, mistress." Tears still dribbled down her cheeks. "I don't want to serve anyone but you."

She'd loved serving the master as well, but that was over. His blows hadn't just bruised her face. They'd crushed her heart.

The mistress turned to Nestor with an air of authority Miriam had never seen before.

"All right then. Philip's not back yet, but go arrange it with his steward. Penelope will authorize it if he won't do it on your word alone. You can take Miriam there a little while before my brother is expected to return this evening. I want to keep my sister with me as long as I can today." She turned and stroked Miriam's hair. "Let's go take care of that cut."

"Yes, mistress." Nestor bowed and left for Philip's house.

Mistress Claudia kept her arm around Miriam as they climbed the stairs to her bedchamber to clean the blood from Miriam's face.

"My brother can be such a fool sometimes, but when he calms down, I'm sure he'll listen to reason and want you back."

Miriam had known the love she had for Master Titus would never be returned. She was only the slave, and he was the master. He joked enough about what he paid for her that she knew he always thought of her that way. She'd always shown him the deference due a master, even when he talked to her like she was a person instead of property. She'd never done anything to make him suspect her true feelings.

But she had thought he cared about her and appreciated how faithfully she served both him and the mistress. It pierced her heart to know someone she loved so much could value her so little that he'd sell her to anyone who wanted to buy her, no matter what they wanted her for. Only a few days ago, he'd called her a treasure, and now he'd cast her off like garbage.

She touched her cheek, and her finger came away with blood on it. She'd never been hit so hard, not even by her first cruel mistress. The master wouldn't even have treated his horse that way. Even if Mistress Claudia convinced him to buy her back, how could she bear to see him every day, knowing she meant nothing to him? There would be no more pleasure in serving him. Instead, she'd live in fear, never knowing when he'd strike again.

As Titus turned off their street onto the main road, his anger cooled. As it did, the enormity of what he'd just done struck him. He wasn't so much angry at Claudia for becoming a Christian as he was afraid of what that could mean for her safety, now and in the future.

He loved Claudia more than anything. He wanted her safe, but he also wanted her happy. What he'd just done was take away the person who mattered to her most.

What was selling her beloved slave going to do to Claudia? Miriam really had rescued his sister from her night terrors and the deep sadness that made her want to cry all the time. Would Claudia go back to the way she was before Miriam came? His sister really loved her, and whatever hurt Miriam would hurt his sister almost as much. Would she ever forgive him for selling her beloved companion who was so much more to her than a slave?

He was ashamed of himself for hitting Miriam, not once but twice and very hard both times. He'd prided himself on never hurting a slave in anger, and he'd done just that to the most loyal slave he'd ever known. She did anything he asked of her, even when her ankle made it hard. She deserved kind treatment if any slave ever did. The look in her eyes as she lay on the floor after his second blow haunted him. And then he'd ordered her sold.

What kind of person was going to buy a crippled slave, and what would they do with her? His stomach twisted at the thought of what might happen to her. By now, Nestor may have taken her to sell, and he didn't even know where. He might not have gone to the slave traders. He could get more money selling her himself, and Nestor always tried to get the best deal. But maybe Nestor hadn't taken her away yet, and he could still stop the sale if he got home soon enough.

He wheeled his horse and galloped back toward his house. He would just have to be late for duty today.

Titus rode through the gate and dismounted. There was no sign of Nestor in the stable area or gardens.

"Nestor!" Titus walked through the kitchen and into the inner courtyard. No answer. "Nestor!"

He climbed the stairs and trotted to the end of the balcony to see if he could spot him. If he could figure out which way Nestor had taken her, he might be able to catch up with them before the sale.

◆

Miriam was in Mistress Claudia's room when the two girls heard Titus searching. Mistress placed her finger on her lips to warn Miriam to make no sound as he hurried past her closed door. They heard him go to the end of the balcony, then trot back along the balcony past her door a second time.

"Nestor!" His voice came faintly through the window; he was back in the stable area.

Mistress took her hand. "I've been praying that Titus would change his mind, and here he is. He's come back to stop Nestor from selling you."

"Maybe, mistress, but he was so angry with me...I don't think he wants me anymore."

"Didn't you tell me God can change hearts? God knows we need you here. Titus needs you just as much as I do. It's just harder for men to see what they need."

Miriam offered a weak smile, but she wasn't convinced. She'd seen the fury in his eyes and felt the force of his blows. He didn't need or want her anymore, even if he once had.

◆

Titus took hold of his stallion's reins and rested his forehead against its back. He was too late. Nestor was gone, and he had no idea where to even start looking. If they'd gone to the main slave market, he should have passed them on the road. But Nestor knew shortcuts, so he might have missed them.

At that moment, Titus was sorry Nestor was a careful steward who always got the best deal he could. With her being a cripple, only the brothels were likely to pay a good price. Would Nestor be willing to sell a sweet girl like Miriam to one of those just to get the highest price? Had he taken her directly there to cut out the middle man? Would he have thought to sell her as a cook or musician instead? He'd told Nestor she had to be sold that day, so there wouldn't be time to shop her around to find a good place for her at a good price.

He closed his eyes as regret and shame coursed through him.

"Master. I didn't expect you back this morning."

Titus spun to see Nestor coming from the gate. He was alone. "Have you sold her already?"

"I've arranged for someone to buy her, but she's still here."

Titus breathed a deep sigh of relief. "Cancel the sale. Claudia can keep her. No one seems to be in the house, so they're probably together somewhere. Find them and tell them."

"Yes, master."

"And tell Miriam I'm looking forward to another of her delicious dinners tonight."

There. That should tell her he valued her service without him having to apologize for his stupid decision to sell her. It wouldn't be right to apologize to a slave.

He mounted his horse and cantered out the gate. If he hurried, he'd get to the palace only a little late. It was worth it to still have Miriam in his household.

◆

Nestor's smile morphed into a huge grin as Master Titus disappeared through the gate. God had solved that problem much quicker than he expected. Miriam was not leaving, and his real master, Philip, would be a very happy man when he returned to the news about Claudia. For having started so badly, it was turning into a very good day.

Chapter 68

STILL WANTED

Miriam stood at the counter, completing the finishing touches on dinner, when Master Titus walked into the kitchen. Her glance was fleeting before she turned away, focusing her attention on the garnish she was arranging on the platter. Looking directly at him might be dangerous. She'd made several of his favorite dishes, just as he'd told Nestor he wanted that morning. Maybe that would keep him from changing his mind about keeping her. Mistress Claudia wanted her there even if he didn't.

◆

Titus frowned at Miriam's response. He wasn't still angry with her. She should have known that when he kept her, but it would seem she didn't. A compliment on the pretty food should draw those brown eyes from the platter to his own; then she'd know. He walked up behind her and placed his hand on her shoulder. The moment he touched her, she startled, dropped her shoulder away from his hand, and stepped away from him. When she was beyond striking distance, she turned fear-filled eyes upon him, then bowed her head and locked her gaze on the floor.

His lips tightened. She was acting just like she had when he first bought her. He took a step toward her, and she backed away, staying out of striking range, still keeping her head bowed and her eyes downcast.

"Stop. I'm not going to hit you. Stand still and look at me."

She raised her head and looked into his eyes. He'd hurt her more than he'd realized. An ugly purple bruise and a cut the size of his signet ring marred her cheek under her right eye.

He took a step toward her and reached out to rest his hand on her shoulder. She didn't step back, but she flinched as his hand made contact. She lowered her eyes, and her whole body quivered. She expected him to strike her, and her trembling pierced his heart.

"Look at me." She turned her eyes back on his, as commanded.

He moved a strand of hair behind her ear and offered a sad smile. Then he rested his hand on the side of her face that he hadn't bruised and stroked her cheek with his thumb.

"I'm sorry I hit you. I told you I never would, and I meant it when I said it. I broke my word, and I don't blame you for not trusting me. I hope you'll believe me when I say I'll never hit you like that again." Fear still filled those dark brown eyes. "I didn't mean to hurt you like this. Will you forgive me?"

"Yes, master." She looked at the floor, then back at his eyes. "I have no choice."

Titus's brow furrowed. Why did she say that? Of course she had a choice. He could tell a slave what to do, but he couldn't control what she thought.

The fear started to fade from her eyes, and that drew his smile. He withdrew his hand from her cheek slowly, drawing his fingers along the bottom of her jaw.

"I already lost Father because he became a Christian. When Claudia told me she'd made the same choice, I was afraid I'd lose her, too, and I blamed you. I couldn't bear the thought of my sister being killed. She's all I have that matters now. But my fear was no excuse for hitting you like that." He paused. "Or for selling you."

She didn't say anything, but her eyes widened. Fear was replaced by uncertainty in those brown eyes he'd found so compelling in the slave market.

He didn't know what else to say, and he'd already said much more than he intended. He turned his gaze on the platter.

"Looks like it will be another great dinner tonight. It's a good thing I didn't sell the best cook in the city. I could never replace her."

He offered one more smile before striding into the inner courtyard.

◆

Miriam pressed her hand against her cheek where he'd touched her. He'd asked her forgiveness as if she were a real person. Wasn't she only the slave he wanted to sell? His eyes looked like he was truly sorry, like he actually cared if she forgave him.

She turned back to the platter, wondering at him telling her so much about the fears of his own heart, marveling that he cared enough to ask her forgiveness, remembering the gentle touch of his hand, and rejoicing that he said she was irreplaceable.

The dinner was as delicious as Titus had come to expect from her. Claudia beamed each time he smiled at Miriam and told her how delicious the food was when she served him the next dish. When the last course was served, Miriam disappeared into the kitchen, where she and Nestor would eat.

Claudia reached over and touched his hand. "Thank you, Titus."

"For what?"

"For letting me keep Miriam. I don't know what I'd do without her."

A deep sigh escaped as he shook his head. "I'm sorry I lost my temper with both of you. I wish you hadn't decided to follow Father in becoming a Christian, but I know I can't stop you. I just ask that you be very careful not to tell anyone. It's not illegal in this province now, but who knows what might happen with the next governor." Worry furrowed his brow. "I don't want anything to happen to you."

"I'll be careful. I know the danger, but it's worth it. I'm so happy now. Knowing Jesus is so wonderful, and—"

"Stop. I don't want to hear anything about your Jesus. If you want to talk about him, talk to Miriam."

Silence filled the room as he swirled the wine in his goblet.

"I'm sorry I hit her so hard. That bruise looks awful, and I'm sure it hurts. I never thought I'd do that to a slave."

"I'm sure she's forgiven you. Jesus said we must. She always forgave me for saying hurtful things to her."

"It's not the same. A few harsh words are nothing compared to what I did."

"Words can hurt more than any blow, Titus, especially if you love someone, and I'm sure Miriam loves me as much as I love her."

"That's another thing you shouldn't say to anyone but me. She's only a slave."

"How can you say that after the way she cared for you when you were so sick? She could have caught your fever and died, and she knew that. She wouldn't even let me or Nestor into the room because she was afraid we'd catch it. She'd do anything for you."

"Maybe." He stared into the goblet. "No, I know it's not maybe with her. You're right." He swirled his wine again. "I wish I could undo this morning."

He ran his fingers through his hair as he shook his head.

"At least I stopped Nestor before he sold her. A cripple like her... you have to get to know her to realize how much she's truly worth. If I hadn't bought her for you, she'd have ended up in the brothel. That's a brutal place. She might have died there by now, and even if she hadn't...it would crush a gentle person like her."

"I guess God took care of us both when He had you buy her for me."

"There you go, talking about the Christian god again."

"I'm only talking to you, Titus, and we've always been able to share anything we thought. I can't stop now."

He looked at her happy eyes and sighed. He'd been so worried she would kill herself when she was filled with despair. Now he had to worry about whether someone else might kill her because she was filled with joy.

Miriam was washing dishes when she felt someone watching her. When she turned, Master Titus was leaning against the doorframe, watching her with serious eyes and a frown.

"Do you need something, master?" She stepped back from the basin. He said he'd never hit her again, but she wouldn't get too close when he was frowning, just in case.

He walked over, placed his hands on both sides of her face, and turned it up until she was looking into his eyes. He was careful not to touch the bruise.

"That looks bad." He shook his head. "I can't do anything about the cut, but maybe I can help the bruise." His eyes warmed before he walked out the kitchen door toward the stable.

She'd been stunned by the way he touched her face before dinner, but that was nothing compared to him holding her face so gently now and seeming concerned about her pain. The painful blows and the gentle touches—she didn't know what to expect from him next. What was he planning to do that might help?

She kept one eye on the door when she turned back to the counter to continue washing.

When the master returned, he held a jar of ointment. He placed the stopper on the counter next to the wash basin.

"Face me, Miriam." His voice sounded gentler than she ever remembered hearing. She dried her hands and turned toward him.

"Close your eyes and don't move. I don't want to get this in your eyes. It would sting."

◆

Titus dipped his forefinger into the ointment, then began very gently rubbing it into the bruise. She flinched when he first touched her. Then the heat from the ointment began to relieve the pain, and she relaxed. When he finished, she still stood there with her face tipped upward and her eyes closed. A slight smile curved her lips.

He'd betrayed her trust that morning. How could she trust him this much so soon? He didn't deserve it. Was it her Christian heart that made it possible to forgive and trust him?

"Does that help?"

She opened her eyes. "Yes, master. Thank you."

"I'll do this again in the morning before I leave." He set the jar on the counter and capped it.

When he turned, he found Claudia watching him from the doorway, smiling broadly. He wrapped his arm around her and drew her into the courtyard as he left the kitchen. A few steps in, he glanced back at the kitchen. Miriam was singing softly.

It was good he'd stopped Nestor. The house wouldn't feel like home if she was gone.

As Titus descended the stairs the next morning, her bell-toned voice wrapped around him. Her songs were what made breakfast so enjoyable. To think he almost sold her...

He turned into the kitchen instead of going to the dining room, where she usually served his breakfast. It was already prepared and arranged on the tray she planned to present to him. She was kneading the day's bread as she sang.

He walked to the counter and picked up the ointment.

"Miriam."

She startled and spun around to face him. As she took a step back, she tripped on a sack of flour and began to fall backward.

He grabbed her hand with his empty one and pulled, stopping her fall and swinging her toward himself. He didn't want to drop the ointment, so instead of grabbing her with his second hand, he wrapped his free arm around her and pulled her close.

◆

Miriam's eyes saucered as the master held her so close, smiling at her. Her heart began to race as he held her for a moment. His smile grew warmer, and she felt her face warm as she blushed. She'd grown comfortable with his arm around her when they rode together, but she most definitely was not comfortable with him holding her so close in the kitchen.

When he released her, she took two steps back.

A smile tugged at the corner of the master's mouth. "Careful there. Don't let my cook get hurt. Who'd be fixing my dinner tonight? Claudia and I have come to expect the best, and I don't know who else would deliver that."

"I'll try to be more careful, master. You startled me."

She looked down, trying to hide the blush until it faded from her cheeks.

"Make sure you do. Now come closer so I can put some more ointment on that bruise."

Miriam would have preferred the master not touch her face just then. It felt too wonderful when he touched her so gently. She hadn't fully recovered from his arm holding her close, and she was afraid she couldn't keep from blushing again. But he was the master, so she obeyed.

He took her chin in his free hand and tilted her head back until she was looking into his eyes. The gentleness there surprised her.

"Now close your eyes, and don't move."

She was glad to close them. Looking into his eyes when he was standing so close made her heart beat too fast.

With the tip of his finger, he rubbed ointment into the bruise. When the gentle pressure from his finger stopped, she opened her eyes. A frown pulled his mouth down. Was he angry with her again?

"Don't be afraid of me, Miriam. I'm not going to hit you again."

"Yes, master." She wanted to believe him, but she couldn't...not yet.

He placed his hand on her unbruised cheek and stroked it with his thumb.

"I don't want to hurt you again...ever."

A sad smile accompanied the slow shake of his head as he looked at her cut, bruised cheek. Then he turned and sat at the table. He picked up a dried fig from his breakfast tray and popped it into his mouth.

"You can go back to your dough, and keep singing. I like to start my day with some music."

"Yes, master."

Her mouth curved as she turned back to the lump of dough. He was still treating her like a real person. He must truly care that he'd hurt her, and that thought warmed her heart.

It was easy to sing a psalm of thanksgiving as she resumed her kneading. The master she loved was being kind to her again. Her heart sang because, in spite of his order to sell her yesterday, he still wanted her there.

That evening, Miriam was still downstairs cleaning up after dinner when Claudia heard someone enter her room. She looked up to see Titus carrying a stack of papyrus sheets. He sighed as he handed them to her.

"Here. You might as well read this now. You've already become a Christian, so it can't do any harm for you to see Father's last letter to me. He wrote it the day before he died, when he was in the cell at the Amphitheater."

Claudia took the sheets of paper and eagerly read the entire contents before turning her face back toward Titus.

"Thank you so much for sharing this with me. Father tried to tell me this, but I was too busy to listen. I might not have understood him before, but I do now."

"Well, I don't understand him. I don't understand how he could forgive that treacherous son of a..." He paused. "That brother of ours. I still want to kill him, even though Father ordered me not to."

"I want to be like Father the way he forgave Lucius. Jesus commands us to love each other, even our enemies. God is making it easier for me every day. When my hatred made me think hurting Lucius could free my heart from pain, Philip told me that forgiveness was the way to freedom, not vengeance. I didn't understand then, but now I do. Jesus helps me forgive Lucius, and I really do feel free. Let it go, Titus. Hating Lucius won't bring Father back. Father forgave him. If he could forgive what Lucius did, we should, too."

"In my head, I know you're probably right, but in my heart...I can't do it."

"Yes, you can. Let Jesus in, follow him, and you'll be amazed at how liberating it is to forgive."

"Following your Jesus is what got Father killed. I'm not willing to do that, Claudia. I'll honor Father's wish that I don't avenge his death with my sword in Lucius's heart, but that's as far as I'm willing to go. You'll never convince me I shouldn't hate Lucius for what he did, even if I don't try to kill him."

"But you'll feel so much better yourself, and—"

"I don't intend to discuss this anymore, Claudia. You'll have to settle for me being willing not to kill him."

The coldness in his eyes and the firm set of his jaw told Claudia it was time to drop the subject, but that wouldn't keep her from praying for Titus to come to Jesus and learn to forgive.

It was three and a half weeks since Philip left Perinthus, and he was ready to be home. He leaned back in his chair as the harvest celebration at his Odessus estate swirled around him. Another good year for the livestock, another bountiful harvest of wheat...he should be happy.

But he wasn't. Too often, the words of his last conversation with Claudia played in his mind. The sound of her sobs echoed in his head.

He'd hoped to return in four weeks, but it had taken longer than he expected to find the land he wanted and make the deal. Finally, that part of his business was completed, but it was still a week's ride back to Perinthus. Four weeks had turned into four and a half, but was that long enough for Miriam to have found the right time to talk with Claudia?

He closed his eyes and pulled a deep breath. *God, tomorrow we head home. I thank you for the harvest and the success of the trip, and I ask you for a safe journey home.* His lips tightened. *But what will I find when I get there? Have you claimed her heart so I can ask for her hand?*

He opened his eyes to see the new wife of his Moesian steward offer her husband a platter of fruit. As two pairs of eyes locked in a silent caress, his own heart clenched. Would Claudia ever look at him like that again? And if she didn't, how was he to bear it? Even worse, what if she did, but she refused to follow his Lord and it must all come to nothing?

He forced a smile as the fruit platter was offered to him. One more week, and he would know.

It was two weeks since Master Titus learned the mistress was a Christian, and life in the household had returned to its usual rhythm. The bruise had faded, the cut had healed, and the master was still treating Miriam like a person. With each passing day, she found it a little easier to trust his promise to never hit her again.

Lunch was over. Miriam picked up a bucket and headed into the courtyard. She was lowering it into the well when Mistress Claudia stopped her.

"Come with me, Miriam. I thought of something much more fun to do than watch you scrub the floors today. When I was in Rome, my best friend Aemilia and I used to try on each other's clothes and jewelry. We'd play at styling hair, too."

She ran her fingers through Miriam's thick brown tresses, lifting them away from her face and letting them slowly fall back into place.

"You have beautiful hair. Let's go up to my room, and I'll style it for you."

"I should scrub the floors, mistress. The master expects me to keep the house clean for you." The mistress treating her like a Roman lady was not a good idea. Miriam knew her place in the master's eyes, and stepping out of her role as a slave was not something he'd like.

"They're already clean enough for me, and Titus won't know the difference." She ran her fingers through Miriam's hair again. "You're not just his slave, Miriam. You're my friend, too. I want to do this for you. When you brush and style my hair, it's very relaxing. It makes me feel good, and I want you to feel good, too."

"But the master wouldn't approve."

"Titus won't know we do it any more than he knows I help cook." Claudia smiled at her reluctance. "Do I have to order you to let me have fun doing this?"

"No, mistress."

"Good. Let's go have some fun, and don't worry about Titus. I'll make your hair look just like it does now before he sees you."

Claudia took Miriam's hand and led her upstairs.

Mistress pulled out the chair at the dressing table. "Sit here, and I'll get started."

As the mistress played with Miriam's hair, she hummed one of their favorite songs. Miriam watched Mistress Claudia's happy face in the silver mirror. It felt wonderful to have her hair brushed. It felt almost as good to have it braided and pinned up to make her look like a Roman lady. Miriam's discomfort with her mistress doing for her what she normally did for her mistress vanished when she saw how much fun Mistress had doing it.

Mistress put the final pins in place to complete the style. "There. I think you look lovely. Even prettier than Aemilia, and she's a pretty girl. If you were in one of my tunics, we could pass you off as a lady even in Rome."

As she spoke, Mistress reached for one of her perfume bottles. She tipped it upside down to get some on the stopper. Then she applied a little behind each of Miriam's ears. "That's better. Now you even smell like a Roman lady."

Miriam smiled at her kind mistress. She was right. It really had been a fun way to spend the afternoon, but now it was time to return to work.

"I need to start the master's dinner now."

Mistress began taking the pins out of Miriam's hair. "We're going to do this again. I like spending the afternoon this way."

After she pulled the last pin out, she ran her fingers through Miriam's hair and shook it back into its natural flowing style. "There. Titus will never know we did this."

"No, mistress."

"Let's go start dinner. I get to do the pastries." She chuckled. "That's another thing Titus never needs to know. We'll see if he likes my pastries better than your sauce."

She laughed again. "Titus loves your cooking. He thinks it's funny the way you blush when he praises you, but he isn't just teasing. You really are the best cook in the city."

Titus entered the kitchen ready for another delicious dinner after a long day. Miriam turned her head to smile at him as she continued to stir the sauce.

"Welcome home, master."

He walked over close behind her to steal his quick taste before going to wash up. As he began to reach past her to take the spoon, he sniffed.

"You smell as good as the sauce, Miriam." He nuzzled her neck as he inhaled the faint scent.

Miriam turned scarlet. She looked down and tried to step sideways to get away from him, but he blocked her way with his arm. He sniffed her neck one more time before he dropped his arm so she could escape.

Her skittishness drew a grin. Then he saw the fear as she glanced back up at him. His playful attention had really upset her. That hadn't been his intention.

"It's not what you're thinking, Miriam. I told you you're not my nighttime entertainment, and I'll keep my word. You don't have to be afraid of me."

"Yes, master. I mean, no, master."

"I know I broke my word once, but I won't do it again."

Titus stepped close to her again. Her eyes widened, then calmed when he only took the spoon from her hand. He stirred the sauce once, then lifted a small sample to his lips.

"Another exceptional one. All Philip's money can't buy better."

With an appreciative smile on his lips, he handed her the spoon before he headed across the courtyard to wash up before dinner.

◆

Miriam placed her hand on her chest, trying to slow her heartbeat. The master had no idea what exquisite agony such attention was for her. To love a man, to know he would never love her in return yet to have him tease her that way. His attention was so wonderful...and so painful.

She closed her eyes and took a deep breath. *Oh, God! Please help me with this. Please help me to love him only as a good master, not as a man.*

She sighed deeply and returned to stirring the sauce that she'd prepared to give him pleasure. God would give her strength to focus only on the pleasure of serving her master well, not on the pain of loving with no return.

After dinner and his bath, Titus climbed the stairs and entered his room. Once more, he closed his door and took his father's letter from the chest. Since the day he let Claudia read it, there was something about it that kept drawing him back to read it again and again. He couldn't stop thinking about his father's choices and why he'd made them.

It hadn't taken long for him to decide Father had been right in deciding to become a God-fearer. His logic was totally convincing. Although Titus had no intention of finding a synagogue and joining them in worship, he'd become a God-fearer himself. He'd seen enough of the world to know that men, including himself, were unfit to approach a holy God, so he understood his father's concern about how to pay for his sins so he could.

Several times Claudia had told him revenge could never undo their loss, that God had said vengeance belonged to Him alone. Father's letter said the same, but he still wanted to repay Lucius himself with a sword, not wait for God to do something.

Claudia said that was a big part of his problem, that he needed to forgive. Her eyes glowed every time she told him how good it felt to forgive Lucius and how she wished he would. She'd told him how Jesus had even asked God the Father to forgive the soldiers who crucified him. He couldn't imagine any ordinary man being able to do that as he hung on a cross. Maybe he really was the Son of God, like his father had written.

What he still questioned was why a god would ever sacrifice himself just to spare ordinary men from the punishment they deserved. How could anyone, god or otherwise, ever deliberately choose a horrible death so someone else wouldn't have to suffer? And why would any rational man choose to die when offering a meaningless pinch of incense would spare his life?

He returned the letter to the chest. He'd probably be looking at it again tomorrow, but he didn't intend to tell Claudia how much the whole thing kept bothering him. Maybe someday he'd figure it all out, and it wouldn't bother him anymore.

Chapter 70

SACRIFICIAL LOVE

Mistress Claudia had declared it another afternoon for dress-up. She sorted through her tunics to pick the one she wanted to try on Miriam.

"I think this green one would be nice. We haven't tried it yet."

"It's beautiful, mistress. The fabric is so soft."

"I used to wear green a lot in Rome. Aemilia thought it looked especially good with my hair, but Philip likes the sky-blue ones better."

Mistress stood holding the green tunic while Miriam took off her plain beige one. She lifted the green one over Miriam's head and let it cascade down around her.

"Oh, Miriam. This is the prettiest color on you yet. Now let's do your hair."

She brushed Miriam's thick brown hair, then wrapped it around her hand.

"I could braid it and wrap it at the back of your head, or twist it into little curls, or maybe today we should just use my gold hair net. The gold is so pretty against the dark brown. I don't think it looks nearly as good with my hair as it does on yours."

"Everything looks better on you, mistress. You're so beautiful; you make anything look good."

"Don't be silly. Everything doesn't look better on me. You're a very pretty woman, too."

Mistress wrapped Miriam's long, thick hair around itself to make it compact enough to pull the fine gold net up around it. Then she released it to fill the net before she pinned the rim of the net securely across Miriam's crown with small gold clips shaped like tiny butterflies. Finally, she hung a fine gold chain around her neck and slid her wide gold bracelet on Miriam's wrist.

"I like that. Look at yourself, Miriam. You're beautiful."

Miriam gazed at her image in the polished silver mirror. "I almost look like a Roman lady, mistress."

"Not almost. You really do. If we went to the Baths of Titus, like I used to, we could fool any of my friends."

The mistress picked up the perfume bottle.

"No, mistress. I don't want the master to smell your perfume on me again." Heat rushed from her cheeks to the tips of her ears as she remembered his face pressed against her neck.

"Then I'm done. Now stand up and let me see you. Go over by the window where the light is better and turn so I can see everything."

Miriam moved over to the window. As she looked out, two strange men walked through the gate. They were looking around in a way that seemed suspicious.

"Mistress. There are two strangers in the stable yard."

As she watched, Nestor came out of the stable and walked over to the two men. Suddenly, the tall man grabbed Nestor. While he pinned Nestor's arms, the shorter man drew his sword and struck Nestor hard with the handle. Nestor crumpled to the ground when the tall one released him.

Miriam stepped back from the window.

"Someone is going to try to take you, mistress. They've knocked out Nestor. Quick. I'm going to hide you under my blankets in the corner. You must lie as still and quiet as you can until they take me instead. Don't come out too soon, or they'll see you. Wait until we're gone. Then run up to Master Philip's house. You'll be safe there."

Claudia blanched. "Lucius. He's found me."

"But we won't let him take you. Hurry. Before they come into the house."

Miriam snatched one of the narrow fabric chestbands from the topmost cupboard drawer and began wrapping her bad ankle. "I'm going to be you, mistress. Hide now."

"I can't let you do that, Miriam."

"You have to. If they take both of us, then no one can help us. If they only take me, you can run to Master Philip's and be safe while you send someone to rescue me."

"But—"

"No time to argue, mistress. Quick. Under my blankets."

Miriam had finished wrapping her ankle. She began pushing Claudia over to her pallet in the corner of the room. She pulled it a little way out from the wall.

"Lie here next to the wall. Hurry, so I can get you covered before they get here."

Mistress Claudia did as Miriam ordered, and Miriam threw the blankets over her as if they'd been tossed back when someone got out of the bed.

As her mistress lay silently under the covers, trying to lie perfectly still, Miriam sat at the dressing table and waited for what was to come.

She heard them coming up the stairs. She could see the door in the mirror, and she watched the pair of them approaching. She picked up the perfume bottle and dabbed a small amount behind each ear.

"Miriam? I didn't expect you back so soon." She turned in her chair to face them. "Who are you?" She tried to sound commanding, like the mistress of a house might.

The shorter one stepped forward as the tall one blocked the door. He addressed her in Latin. "Are you Claudia Drusilla?"

Miriam drew herself up proudly while remaining seated. *Thank you, God, for Mistress teaching me Latin.* It was uncommon to hear it spoken in Thracia. Using it should convince them they had the real Claudia.

"Of course. Get out of my house." She stood and acted like it hurt to put weight on her wrapped ankle. She cried out as loudly as she could. "Nestor! There are men here."

The taller man uttered a cruel laugh. "It won't do you any good to call for Nestor. We already took care of him."

◆

Claudia was in agony as she listened, but Miriam had told her not to make a sound so they wouldn't find her. She struggled to obey. Tears pooled in her eyes, but she fought to keep them in check while she kept her breathing quiet and her body deathly still.

"Your brother Lucius has sent us to escort you back to Rome. You didn't have his permission to leave, and you're going back to him now."

"I don't need his permission. He's not the true head of my father's household. He murdered Father, and he should have been sewn in a leather bag and tossed in the river. Titus is my guardian, not Lucius."

"Not anymore. You're coming back to Rome with us."

◆

The agent stepped up to Miriam and took her arm.

"Take your filthy hand off me. Nestor! Help me!"

The agent clamped his free hand over her mouth. "One more shout from you, and we'll kill your man before we leave." Miriam's eyes saucered. "Is that what you want?"

She shook her head, so he uncovered her mouth.

He started to drag her forward, and she began hopping on one foot.

"Wait. I can't walk fast right now. I sprained my ankle. Please, go slower."

The short agent looked down, saw the fabric tightly wrapped around her ankle, and let out a string of curses. "Start walking."

Miriam took a short hop, then paused. "Wait."

He took her arm and tugged. She jerked it free. "I said keep your hands off me. You'll answer to my brother if you don't. I'm trying to go as I fast as I can."

The tall one took her other arm. "He said to bring you back no matter how hard you fight, so he won't do a thing. Get her other arm and lift when she hops. She'll go farther."

Miriam tried to hold them back, but they swung her three feet forward on each hop.

At the head of the stairs, the man with the deep voice paused. "I saw a big basket by the stable and a donkey cart."

The shorter one nodded. "When we get her outside, that should help." He scooped Miriam up, draped her across his shoulder, and carried her down the stairs.

"Put me down! Lucius will hear of the way you're treating me, and he won't be happy. He wants to sell me to Flavius Sabinus, and he won't get his money if you hurt me in any way."

◆

One of the men cursed again. Claudia strained to understand what they were saying, but their voices were getting fainter. She heard the one with the deep voice one more time. "Let's gag her, and use the basket."

What the other man muttered in response, she couldn't hear.

She stayed still as a statue as she tried to decide how long she should remain there before she ran for help. The house had become deathly quiet.

Miriam was gone.

Chapter 71

No Longer Impossible

It had been four and a half weeks since he'd broken her heart, and Philip felt his chest tighten as he turned off the main road and started up the street that ran past Claudia's house. He couldn't count how many times he'd begged God to claim her heart so she could become his wife. Most would consider him a brave man, but it took every ounce of courage he possessed to ride through her gate and risk her telling him to leave and never come back.

He didn't expect what he saw when he rode around the back of the house. He hoped to see Claudia in the garden or the kitchen with Miriam. Instead, Nestor was lying unconscious, bound, and gagged just outside the kitchen door.

A wave of his arm ordered his men to check Nestor as Philip slid from his horse. As he bolted through the kitchen and up the stairs to search for her, he kept praying that he would find her hiding somewhere, safe.

"Claudia! Are you here? Claudia!"

No answer.

He looped back through the dining room, store room, and kitchen. No sign of anyone.

As Philip emerged from the kitchen, his men were kneeling beside Nestor.

"He's alive, master. Just knocked out."

"Antyllus, stay with Nestor. Callias, Milo, come with me."

He hurled himself onto his horse and wheeled him to gallop out the gate. He headed up the hill to his own house, dreading what he might find there as well.

Philip cantered into his stable yard, and his pulse jumped as he caught sight of her reddish-blonde hair. He reined in and trotted to where Claudia stood by his steward. He swung his leg across his horse's neck and dismounted while it was still moving. He landed at a run and was by her side before she could fully turn to face him.

"I found Nestor. When you weren't at the house, I was so afraid..."

He pulled her into his arms. She wrapped her arms around his chest and pressed her cheek against his tunic before tipping her head back to gaze at him. Her eyes swam in tears.

"They took her, Philip. Lucius's men...they came for me, and they took Miriam. Just like Jesus...she took my place. We've got to find her and get her back."

Philip's heart leaped at the sound of her voice saying "just like Jesus." All his prayers for the last three months were answered in those three words.

He pushed her hair behind her ear and swept a teardrop from her cheek. He stepped back but left his hands on her arms.

"What happened?"

"Miriam saw them attack Nestor. She hid me under her blankets and told me to wait until they took her away before I came here for help. She was afraid they'd see me if I came out too soon. When I couldn't hear them anymore, I ran here as fast as I could."

"Which way did they go?"

"I don't know. First, I hid too long, and then I stopped to check Nestor, so I didn't see. I should have gone to the end of the balcony and watched to see which way they went. Why didn't I think of that? We've got to find her, Philip."

Philip turned to his steward. "Gather the men. Mount as many as you can. We're going to fan out and look for her."

His steward nodded and moved to obey.

Philip turned to his two armed men, who were still mounted. "They'll probably be heading west or toward the harbor. Check the western road for the first five miles out. They can't have gone farther than that."

His traveling companions wheeled their horses and cantered out the gate.

Philip's brow furrowed. By land or by sea? It was late in the season, so the large ships like his that sailed all the way to Rome were now moored until spring. Some smaller ships were making short coastal runs for another couple of weeks. They could take one as far west as Thessalonica and catch the Via Egnatia there. That would be his own choice if he'd kidnapped someone.

It was late afternoon, so they weren't likely to leave the harbor before morning. Most captains cast off early if they didn't have to time their departure with the tides, and Perinthus had almost no tidal variation in the harbor.

"If they're going by ship, I only need to find out who arranged for the row boats to pull them out of the harbor. Then we can search all the ships that are about to sail."

If the kidnappers went by land, there were too many possible routes. They must find her much quicker, or she would be gone. Claudia's worried eyes kept him from speaking that concern.

"We'll find her. I'll go to Titus, and he can have his troops look for her, too."

She managed a smile through her tears. "I'm so glad you're back. If anyone can find her, it's you." She laid her hand on his cheek and stroked his scars with her thumb. "I've missed you terribly. I'm so ashamed of what I said. I should never have hurt you like that. Please forgive me."

"Always, but there's nothing to forgive." He wiped more tears away. "Now, tell me what you know about the men. How could they have mistaken a slave for you?"

His eyebrow rose at that thought. How could anyone be so stupid?

Philip slid his hands up and down Claudia's arms. She took a deep breath, and when she released it, she seemed much calmer.

"The more you can tell me, the easier it will be to find her."

"I was having fun dressing Miriam up in some of my things. I had her in that lovely green tunic with my small gold necklace and my big gold bracelet. I'd just finished styling her hair with my gold hair net. She looked just like a Roman lady should. Her hair's brown, but a little dye could make mine match hers. She really is very pretty, so someone might think she was me."

"But her ankle and her limp..." Confusing the two of them was still beyond Philip's comprehension.

"She wrapped it to hide it and told them she'd sprained it."

The corner of Philip's mouth rose. "Clever. That should keep them from walking anywhere too fast. Did you hear a carriage?"

"No...and I would have recognized carriage sounds. I didn't hear horses, either. But maybe they'd left them down the street somewhere." Her face brightened. "One of them did say he saw a big basket and the donkey cart as they were taking her down the stairs. She was making them go very slowly because of her ankle. The last thing I heard was something about gagging her and using the basket."

"Does that basket have a cover?"

"Yes, and it would hold her. She's not very big."

Philip turned to one of his men. "Go see if the basket is still there and if the donkey cart is gone."

The man nodded, mounted one of the horses, and cantered out the gate.

"Can you remember anything else?"

"Yes. When they asked Miriam if she was me, they asked in good Latin. I've been teaching her Latin almost since Titus bought her, so she spoke it back to them. I'm sure that helped convince them they had me."

"So they might be Romans. That could help us find them. Anything else?"

"Well, there were two of them that came to my room. I don't know if there were any left in the courtyard, but it took long enough between when Miriam saw them knock out Nestor and when they came up the stairs that they probably tied him up themselves. If there were more men, I think they would have been upstairs faster."

Philip nodded. He rested his hand on her cheek and brushed away one of her last tears with his thumb. His brilliant little general had observed plenty to help them find her.

"One had a deep voice. Not as deep as yours, but close. The other sounded more like Titus. He's the one who asked Miriam if she was me. One had heavy footsteps, too, so maybe he's tall or fat. I didn't see anything, though."

The man he'd sent to check on the donkey cart trotted through the gate and rode directly to Philip.

"The basket is gone, and so is the donkey cart."

"Good. See if you can follow the cart tracks down to the main road and tell if the cart turned left back into town or right to go west." The man nodded and headed back through the gate.

Philip stroked Claudia's hair. "It looks like they took her away in a basket using the donkey cart. We should soon know which way they went. Then I'll go to Titus, and we can all start looking for them."

She'd stopped crying, but fear still clouded her eyes.

"But what if we don't find her? If they take her to Lucius..." The tears started to pool in her eyes again.

"I don't think it will come to that. God will help us find her. You just need to be praying that we'll find her soon."

"Oh, I am. When Titus was so sick with fever and now...I don't know what I'd do without Jesus."

Philip took her hands in his as he gazed at the beautiful woman who was now his sister in Christ. "You'll never have to find out."

He took a deep breath before his next question. He was almost sure he knew what the answer would be, but he was still nervous asking.

"This might not be the best time to ask, but I don't want to wait any longer. You've told me before that you want to stay with me forever. If you still do..." He paused before plunging ahead. "Will you be my wife?"

◆

Claudia pulled one hand free to reach up and caress his scars. "I want that more now than ever."

She'd loved looking at this ugly man for many weeks, but his look of sheer joy at her answer made him the handsomest man her eyes had ever beheld.

She slid her hand behind his head and guided his lips down to meet her own. In that first lingering kiss was the promise of years of joy together as husband and wife.

She stepped back and gazed up at him. "I've dreamed of that for so long." She caressed his scars again. "I'm so thankful God gave you scars so no other woman would win your heart before I could."

He grinned at her as he moved a strand of hair behind her ear. "My heart is all yours, mighty general."

◆

Philip pulled Claudia back into his arms and held her tight as his unscarred cheek felt the softness of her hair. He'd held her many times when she was broken-hearted, and it had made him glad when he could comfort her. To hold her like this when she was joyful was precious beyond words. He might never have let her go if his man hadn't returned to report.

"Master. The tracks headed back toward town. And Nestor is awake now. He can give us a good description of the two men and the donkey cart."

"Excellent. Gather the men. We'll hear from Nestor, and then we hunt."

Philip turned back to Claudia. "They've probably taken her to the harbor. The time is wrong for setting sail, so we should have plenty of time to find her before they can leave. I'll have your precious Miriam back to you in time for her to help you prepare for our wedding. Stay here with Penelope so you'll be safe."

Claudia caressed his scars again. "I've always trusted you to make things turn out right. I know you will again, with God's help."

Philip mounted and turned his horse toward the gate. He looked back at her as he passed through. Even in the midst of her fear for Miriam, she was smiling at him. Penelope had been right. God had brought someone special into his life when he least expected it, and the impossible had happened. The most beautiful woman in the Empire was thrilled to be marrying the ugliest man.

Chapter 72

Hunting for Miriam

Philip left his men at the wharfs with instructions to find out from the harbor master which ships had requested the rowboats for the next day. They were each to pick one of the ships and watch for signs of Miriam. He then rode on to the garrison to find Titus.

Philip still wore his sword, and the centurion in command of the guards drew his own at the sight of an armed man riding fast toward him. He slid it back into its scabbard when he saw Philip's scars. The corner of Philip's mouth lifted. The guard probably recognized him as the ugly man who'd come with news for Tribune Drusus a few weeks before.

Philip dismounted before speaking. "I have urgent news for Claudius Drusus about his sister."

The centurion turned to a guard. "Find Tribune Drusus and bring him here."

Philip felt like pacing as he awaited Titus's appearance, but he didn't. The centurion was watching him too closely. Even though Titus had become his friend, he was still uneasy this close to Roman power.

Concern pulled Titus's face into a scowl as he approached.

"Philip? Why are you here? What's going on with Claudia?"

"I've just come from your house. Lucius sent men to get her."

Titus's back stiffened. "Did they take her?"

"No. She's safe at my house. Miriam hid her and let your brother's agents think she was Claudia, so they took her instead. I've come for your help in getting her back."

"They've taken Miriam?"

Titus's stomach knotted. Miriam in Lucius's hands. If they took her to Rome, Lucius would be furious with her for fooling his men. What would his scum of a brother do to make her pay for the deception? Tendrils of dread wrapped around his heart.

The intensity of his response was eye-opening. She'd become truly important to him, not because she was his talented cook and Claudia's beloved companion. Having her in his house made it a home instead of a building. He had to get her back.

"Any idea who they are and where they've taken her?"

"Two men, one very tall. They spoke good Latin, so maybe Romans. They appear to have put her in a basket and carried her toward the harbor using your donkey cart. I think they're planning to smuggle her out of the city on a ship, but I might be wrong. If they try to take her by land, I'm hoping your troops can stop them."

Titus turned to the centurion. "Assemble the troops. I want men stationed on each road at the edge of town to search everyone leaving until we find them."

When the troops were assembled, Philip provided the detailed description of the men, Miriam, and the cart.

Then he turned to Titus. "My men will have found out which ships are planning to leave tomorrow by the time I get back to the harbor. I think that's where we'll find her. Come with me and bring a few men, but not too many. We don't want to make them nervous when they still have time to get rid of her and escape. My men and I can check the ships without giving them cause for alarm. When we find the right ship, you can take over."

Titus ran his hand through his hair. The wisdom of Philip's plan was obvious. He gave the command to dispatch the troops who would prevent their escape by land. Then he called for his own horse and told six of the men to come with him. He and Philip mounted and headed for the harbor.

Titus's jaw clenched as they held their horses at a walk so the men on foot could keep up. If Lucius's men had hurt her...Roman citizens or not, he would deal with the kidnappers himself when they were caught.

Miriam lay on some canvas, the musty smell of damp wood wrapping around her in the dark. Lucius's agents had trussed her up like an animal after they blindfolded and gagged her. They'd tied her wrists so any attempt to raise her hands to remove the gag jerked on her bound ankles, and that shot screaming pain through her. Had she broken her good ankle when she jumped from the ship to the dock or only sprained it?

Even if someone was hunting for her, they'd never think to look in the belly of a boat too small to sail the open sea to Rome. For herself, escape was impossible, but at least she'd convinced them she was Mistress Claudia. The short one had apologized over and over for having to keep her in the hold after her escape attempt. Lucius must have told them to be careful with his sister, and they would take good care of her until they reached Rome. But when they presented her to Lucius...

A shudder coursed through her. Lucius would be furious that she'd thwarted his plans to kidnap Mistress Claudia. Any man who would murder his father and sell his sister to a brutal old man would likely vent his anger by making her suffer as much as he could before he killed her.

She dragged her thoughts away from the agonies of the future and focused on the joys of the present. When Master Philip returned, he would marry Mistress. A slow smile lifted the corners of Miriam's mouth as much as the gag allowed. It would be a day of celebration beginning a lifetime of joy. *Thank you, God, for letting me give her that.*

One month, maybe two, and her end would come in Rome. She fought the tears and lost, but the blindfold kept them from dribbling down her cheeks.

What would Master Titus do after their marriage? Would he stay in the house or go back to lodgings? If he stayed, would he find a cook who'd make his favorites, like she had? Or would he only get them when he dined with his sister? His face drifted into focus in her mind, his eyes laughing and a crooked smile tugging at his lips after he took a bite of his favorite stew, the one she made the first night he owned her.

Thank you for bringing Master Titus to buy me. Please claim his heart, like you did Mistress's.

Death awaited her in Rome. Soon she'd be reunited with Master Alexander and all his household. Someday she'd be with Mistress Claudia and Nestor again. If only the man she loved with all her heart would join them all.

Titus leaned on one of the posts that stood beside the road above the wharfs and scanned the ships tied to the piers. His men stood at ease beneath one of the trees nearby. He'd never found it so hard to wait patiently and do nothing. Philip and his men were searching the wharf area so casually that no one would ever think they were looking for something. Casual was the way not to alarm Lucius's agents, but it also took longer. It grated to stand there doing nothing when Miriam was in danger.

When he heard the clip-clop of a mule team, he glanced over his shoulder, then jerked upright. It was Nestor handling the reins.

"What are you doing here?"

"Mistress Claudia couldn't stand waiting at the house without knowing what was being done to get Miriam back, and Mistress Penelope told me to bring her to Master Philip so she could find out."

"Penelope? Both of them should have known better than for Claudia to come down here. It's too dangerous for her. Why did you do what she told you? How many people do you take orders from?"

"Almost everyone, it seems, master. Mistress Claudia was talking about riding a horse here by herself until Mistress Penelope convinced her to come in the covered carriage so no one would see her." He paused. "Does she even know how to ride?"

"I don't know what my sister's learned when I'm not home. It seems I'm the last to know what's going on in my own house."

The curtain on the door window was drawn back, and Titus saw his sister's face peeking out.

"Titus? Come in here and tell me what's going on. Any signs of where they took her?"

Titus opened the carriage door and climbed inside. He sat across from Claudia and took her hands.

"Not yet. I have troops stationed on all the roads out of town, and Philip and his men are checking the ships to find any that might take her out of Perinthus. I'm waiting here to see what he finds."

Claudia bit her lip. "We've got to find her, Titus. It's all my fault they took her. She saw them knock Nestor out, and she made me hide by the wall under her blankets while she pretended to be me. She knew exactly what they were going to do, and she sacrificed herself to save me from Lucius. If they take her to him in Rome…I keep imagining all the horrible things he might do to her for fooling his men."

Titus's lips tightened. "I never expected a slave to sacrifice herself like this. If they take her back to Lucius, he'll kill her for sure, and he won't do it quick or easy. Philip thinks she's here. It's taking longer than I'd like, but it is safer for her if only his men look around the harbor. If my troops start searching ships, Lucius's men might kill her to get rid of the witness before they try to escape."

He wished he hadn't said they might kill Miriam when he saw the stricken look it brought to Claudia's eyes. He rested his hand on her cheek.

"I expect to get her back unharmed. I know she's a treasure to you. I know you two love each other like sisters. I don't want to lose her, either. I'd never find another slave as good as her. She couldn't be harder working or more willing to do whatever I need."

He valued her much more than he was willing to say aloud, even to Claudia. He wanted her back at least as much as his sister did.

Claudia's lips tightened. "Another slave as good as her? Is that all she is to you? She doesn't just love me. Can't you see she loves you, too? Not like her old master, but as a man. I know what it's like to love a man with every fiber of my being, and that's what I see in Miriam's eyes when she thinks you're ignoring her. She looks at you with such longing. She puts on a mask so you won't know because she thinks you'll only ever see her as your slave."

Titus's head snapped back. With how she blushed and withdrew from him whenever he touched her, he never suspected she felt anything toward him except loyalty.

"She looks at me with longing? So, you think she wants me to take her to my bed? I'd be glad to. She's a pretty little thing. I've thought about it many times, but I told her the first day I didn't buy her for that, and I've kept my word to her. If she wants me, that could change."

"If you do, I'll never forgive you. That's not the kind of longing I mean. How can you even think of using her that way? You'd be no better than Lucius or her first master who did that to her mother. That's why his wife was so cruel to her for years. She doesn't just want you; she wants you to love her, too."

Titus's eyebrows shot up. "Love her? She's my slave, Claudia. What would you have me do, free her and marry her?"

"Why not? You'll never find a woman more worthy of you, who loves you with more devotion."

He opened his mouth to tell her what a ludicrous idea it was to suggest that a Claudius Drusus should marry a crippled Jewish slave girl, but as he was about to speak, he paused.

Why not, indeed? Maybe Claudia was right. His father had married a woman chosen for him based on bloodline, status, and wealth, and he'd regretted it for the rest of his life. Father had wanted his sons to choose for themselves so they wouldn't suffer the same miserable fate.

The last thing he would ever want was a wife like his own mother—selfish, cold-hearted, even cruel in the way she abandoned Claudia. He wanted a woman whose love was real. One he could count on for the rest of his life. He was still single because he hadn't found one... until now. Miriam truly was that kind of woman.

◆

Claudia watched her brother start to open his mouth, then stop. He tipped his head slightly as a frown appeared. Then he raised his eyebrows as the frown was replaced by a wry smile.

"You always were the smartest one. You might be right. I'm never going to find a more faithful woman than Miriam. Maybe I should marry her. I'll have to give that some serious thought."

His smile broadened. "And I wouldn't even have to pay a bride price, so she fits into the household budget. Actually, I guess I already did pay it. She cost me four hundred denarii."

Claudia smiled, but she still slapped her brother's arm. "Very funny, but don't you ever tell her that."

His face grew serious. "But first I have to find her."

He placed his hand on her cheek. "Go back to Philip's house. There's nothing you can do here, and I want you safe. I'll bring her to you as soon as we find her."

He climbed out of the carriage. "Take her back to Philip's and keep her there, Nestor. Keep her safe."

As the carriage drove away, he turned toward the harbor and focused once more on finding the woman who made his house a home.

Chapter 73

FINDING A TREASURE

Titus was tired of standing, so he started strolling along the road. It was taking too long. How many ships could there be that Philip's men had to check out? As he walked, he scanned the ships tied to the piers. Then a donkey's bray drew his attention across the road to an alley.

There, parked between a shipping office and a maritime supply shop, was his donkey cart.

His eyes scanned the immediate vicinity. A short distance down the road was a beggar with only one leg. He was sitting on the ground, leaning against the wall of the shipping office. That pulled a smile. So often people would talk and act as if they saw a beggar as a rock or a bush, if they even saw him at all. More than once he'd learned exactly what he needed from a beggar who heard with ears that no one realized were listening.

He strode over and squatted down by the man before throwing a coin into his cup.

"Thank you, tribune." The man glanced at the coin and offered a sad smile.

"I have some questions for you." The beggar focused his gaze on Titus. "That donkey cart over there between the buildings. Were you here when it was left there today?"

"Yes, tribune."

"Tell me about the people with it and what they did."

"There were two men, one tall, the other about your height. They led the donkey into the alley and left it there."

"Was there anything in the cart?"

"A big basket."

"What did they do with it?"

"Carried it down that ramp to the pier." He pointed a short distance farther down the road. "It looked heavy. They set it down once before they got to the ramp."

"Which ship did they go to?"

"There's only one ship down there right now."

Titus took three denarii from his purse and dropped them in the cup.

The beggar's eyebrows shot up as a broad smile appeared. "Thank you, tribune."

Titus was already striding back to where his men waited. He had the clue he needed. It was time to do some searching himself.

Titus stood with two of his men at the top of the ramp the beggar had pointed out to him. A small, dirty-looking merchant ship was tied to the pier below. He watched it for a few minutes to gauge what awaited them there. A single deckhand was visible, a scrawny youth of about fifteen who appeared to be standing guard. There was no sign of a captain or the two agents. Titus signaled to his men. They walked down the ramp and along the pier to where the ship was tied.

When Titus put his foot on the gangplank, the scrawny deckhand's spine straightened. When the two soldiers followed Titus up the plank and onto the deck, the sailor's eyes widened as he swallowed hard.

Titus marched up to him and crossed his arms. "I want to speak with your captain."

The youth fidgeted under Titus's fixed gaze. "He's not here, tribune."

"When will he return?"

"I don't know." Fast blinks and another hard swallow betrayed his growing fear.

"We're going to search this ship for a stolen female slave."

"There's no female slave on board, tribune. Only a Roman lady."

"Take me to her." Titus's gaze locked on the cabin.

The young deckhand hesitated. "She's not in there."

The deckhand's eyes darted between Titus, his men, and the gangplank.

"I'll see for myself."

As Titus took his first step toward the cabin, the deckhand broke for the gangplank. The younger soldier tackled him. After jerking the sailor to his feet, he pinned his arms behind him while the older soldier held a sword to his chest. Titus stepped close to his face and glared at him.

"Where is she now?"

The youth blanched. "I didn't do anything. It was the two Romans. I didn't have anything to do with her getting hurt."

Titus's stomach knotted at the word 'hurt'. He put his hand around the youth's throat and squeezed.

"Where is she?"

The youth was struggling to breathe until Titus released his grip. He gasped and coughed before he could speak enough to answer.

"In the hold. But it's the Roman lady, not a slave."

Titus frowned at his men. "Hold him. If he tries to escape, break his leg, but don't kill him...yet."

He strode to the cover over the hold and dragged it back to reveal a set of stairs. He took a deep breath as he placed his foot on the first of the narrow, steep steps. A chill ran up his spine. What would he find in the darkness below?

Miriam heard the commotion on the deck above her, but she couldn't tell what was happening. She raised her bound feet, and thumped them once on the floor. Pain shot up her leg and exploded in her brain. She wouldn't try that again. No one on deck was likely to hear her, anyway.

Silence was followed by a scraping sound. She tried to call out, but the gag muffled her voice enough that no one would hear her outside the hold.

Even with the blindfold over her eyes, she could see more light. Again, she tried to call out, praying that whoever was coming down the stairs was not one of her captors.

Rapid footsteps came down the stairs and raced toward her. Someone knelt beside her.

When the blindfold was pulled off, she stared into the eyes of the one man she longed to see. The master's fingers worked the knot behind her head and pulled the cloth from her mouth.

"Master. You came for me."

Joy bubbled up inside her. It hadn't mattered how well the kidnappers hid her. Master Titus had searched for her until he found her.

He pulled out his knife and cut the leather thong that bound her wrists. Then he held both her hands as he helped her sit up.

A broad grin lit his eyes. "Of course I came for you. I paid four hundred denarii for you, and you're the best cook in the city."

His words quenched her joy as if he had thrown a full bucket of water on a sputtering candle. She was still nothing more than property to him and always would be, no matter how much she loved him, no matter what she did to show her love.

But what more could a slave expect from her master? How foolish to even dream otherwise.

She lowered her head and gazed at the floor. The master placed his fingers under her chin and lifted it until her eyes were looking into his again.

"What's wrong, Miriam?"

She would have looked down at the floor again, but he was still holding her chin.

"Something's wrong. What is it? Did they hurt you?"

His words came quickly, and deep concern roughened his voice. He was looking at her like he'd looked at Claudia when she first came.

Her eyes widened. Could it be that he saw her as a woman he cared about instead of a slave he owned?

"No, master. They thought I was Claudia, and your brother told them to be careful with her. I hurt my ankle myself. They had me tied up in the cabin, but I got loose. I tried to get back to you and my mistress. I hurt it jumping off the boat."

The corner of his mouth pulled up as he shook his head. "That's my Miriam. Always trying to do what I want."

He pushed a strand of hair behind her ear before he rested his hand on her cheek and stroked it with his thumb. "I can't think of anything I want more than to have you back with us."

Miriam's heart raced at his touch. The master's smile—it was almost like Philip's when he watched Mistress Claudia after he returned from a trip. But it couldn't mean the same thing. He'd just said she was only his cook who cost him four hundred denarii.

The master turned to cut the leather thong that bound her ankles together. He sucked air between his teeth when he saw the greenish purple color and the swelling of her normally good ankle.

"This doesn't look good." He frowned as he glanced at her face. But that looked like worry, not anger in his eyes.

"I landed wrong. Then I could hardly walk at all, and they caught me before I could even get off the pier. That's when they tied me up better and put me down here until we were out to sea."

He took her ankle in his hands and raised his eyes to hers. Again, it was as if he was looking at Mistress.

"I'm afraid this will hurt, but I need to see if it's broken."

"Do what you must, master."

She winced even though he felt her ankle as gently as he could. He breathed a sigh of relief when he finished.

"Nothing feels broken. It's only a sprain. Let's get you home where I can take care of it properly. It shouldn't be long before you'll be able to walk as well as ever."

"That's not saying much, master. I've never been a good walker for you."

"How many times have I told you I didn't buy you to run footraces, so that really doesn't matter?"

The lightness of his voice drew her eyes to his. They were laughing, and a teasing smile played on his lips. He took her hands and helped her to her feet; then he scooped her up in his arms.

As he cradled her there, his smile broadened. Her cheeks heated, and she looked away.

"I can see why Lucius's men were fooled. In Claudia's tunic and jewelry, I could pass you off as a lady, even in Rome. You're always a pretty woman, but you're even prettier when your cheeks turn pink."

The heat spread to the tips of her ears.

◆

"That's even better." Titus almost laughed aloud at her response. There was a lightness in his heart over finding her that made everything about her amuse him.

He carried her up the stairs, then set her feet on the deck.

"Sit." He held her hands to support her as she lowered herself onto the hold cover. He stroked her hair once and lifted her chin so he could smile into her eyes before turning back to the deckhand.

"You." Terror filled the youth's eyes as he stood with his arms pinned behind his back by one soldier while the second one pressed a sword tip into his side.

Titus scowled at him. "If you help me catch the men who did this, I will overlook you not reporting this kidnapping and let you live."

"What can I do?" The youth trembled as he faced Titus's frown.

"You will stay here at your post as if nothing has happened. You will pretend the woman is still down there. When the men who brought her come back to the ship, you will signal my men, who will be hiding over there." He pointed at a large stack of crates where several soldiers could easily be concealed from view until someone was on the ship. "If the men are caught, I won't arrest you for your part in this crime."

"I'll do everything you say."

"See to it." Titus nodded at the soldier, who released the young deckhand's arms. "If you try to escape or do anything to warn them, you're a dead man."

The youth's head bobbed up and down in his eagerness to do whatever it took to save his own life.

Titus turned to the older soldier. "I'll send the rest of the men to join you. I want these kidnappers alive. As soon as you have them, let Philip know we found her. Take them to the garrison, have the rest of the troops recalled, and send a messenger to my house. If I'm not at home, I'll be at the house belonging to Philip about a quarter mile up the hill from mine."

The soldier's fist struck his chest. "Yes, tribune."

Titus turned back to Miriam and held out his hands. When she placed hers in his, he pulled her to her feet and scooped her into his arms again.

"It's a good thing I rode. It would be a long, slow walk home otherwise."

Miriam snuggled against his chest and rested her head on his shoulder as he carried her down the gangplank. As he walked along the pier, her contented sigh was music in his ears.

His brow furrowed. She felt small and vulnerable, but she was so strong when she cared for the people she loved. She risked death when she nursed him through his fever. She'd just sacrificed herself to save Claudia. She knew what kind of man Lucius was. She'd lived with cruelty before. She knew she was sailing to her death or worse when the agents delivered their imposter Claudia to him.

Claudia was right. Miriam was a woman whose love could be counted on.

He carried her up the ramp to the road where he'd left his stallion. He glanced over where the donkey waited with the cart. He could have her drive herself home, but that was not what he wanted. He'd send Nestor or one of Philip's slaves back to get it. She was not getting out of his reach again.

When he set her on the horse's back, she swung her leg over and slid forward to make room for him. He mounted and pulled her against him as he settled in. It had been some time since he kept his arm around her when they rode together, but he wanted to hold her close today. He'd almost lost her.

Miriam was irreplaceable. No house could be a home without her. But what should that mean for the future? Whatever he decided, he would make certain nothing bad ever happened to her again.

"Let's go home and make Claudia happy."

◆

Miriam twisted her neck around and leaned her head back to look at Master Titus's face. Every moment of being held so closely was sheer bliss. She felt like a woman he cared for, not just some stolen property he'd recovered.

The master looked happy himself. Was finding her as important to him as it seemed? Maybe he only hunted for her because he loved her cooking, but there seemed to be something new in his eyes when he looked at her, something that made her heart beat faster when she returned his gaze.

Chapter 74

Dreams That Can Never Be

It was a good distance from the harbor to Master Titus's house, but it wasn't far enough for Miriam. The security of his muscled arm around her waist, the warmth of his chest against her back—she'd once felt very different about those things. Instead of wishing for the ride to end, she wanted it to take as long as possible to reach home.

Too soon they were in sight of the house. She expected to turn into their gate, but Master Titus rode past and continued up the street.

She turned her head to look at his face.

"Where are we going, master?"

"Philip's house. I sent Claudia there to be sure she'd be safe. Lucius knows nothing about him, and his agents would never think to look for her there. If I hadn't left her at Philip's, he would have filled my house with guards to protect her." He smiled down at her. "I wanted all his men out looking for you."

A knowing smile tugged at Miriam's lips. So Philip was finally back, and she knew what that meant. Now that Claudia followed Jesus, nothing stood in the way of their deep love for each other. He would ask the master for her hand in marriage before the end of the week, if not before the end of the day.

Master Titus rode through Philip's gate and around the house to the stable yard in the rear. A stable slave scurried over to take his horse. He dismounted and stood close, waiting for Miriam to swing her leg over so he could lift her down. Then he scooped her up in his arms again.

She looked into gentle eyes as he smiled at her.

"Not a day for you to be trying to walk anywhere."

She certainly wasn't going to argue with him. Anything that kept her in his arms for a few moments longer was fine with her. She rested her head on his shoulder again.

He carried her through the door from the garden that opened into the inner courtyard.

"Claudia!"

Mistress Claudia ran out of the women's room on the second floor, calling as she ran. "Did you find her? Is she all right?"

"I'm here, mistress, and I'm fine."

Mistress ran along the balcony and down the stairs to throw her arms around Miriam even though the master still held her.

"I'm so glad Titus found you. I've been praying and praying." Mistress beamed as she lay her cheek against Miriam's. "I don't know what I'd do without my sister."

Titus shifted her a little in his arms. "She's not fine. We'll need to take care of her instead of her taking care of us for a few days."

The mistress's hands shot up to cover her mouth. "Oh, Miriam. What did they do to you?"

"Nothing. I hurt my ankle myself."

The master's eyes warmed as he smiled down at her. "Trying to get home to us. She knew we needed her."

He still held her in his arms. He probably meant nothing by it, but his eyes seemed to say he did. "Where shall I take her? I want to tend to that ankle now." The master shifted her in his arms, but he still held her close.

"Bring her upstairs to my old room." Mistress held onto Miriam's hand as she led them to the stairs. She scampered up the stairs ahead of them and took Miriam's hand again at the top to lead them along the balcony. After they entered her room, Master Titus set Miriam on the bed.

"There should be liniment and something for wrapping your ankle in the stable. Don't try to do anything until I get back."

"I won't, master."

He placed his hand on her cheek and stroked it with his thumb. She closed her eyes, savoring the touch of his hand.

"I'll be back as quickly as I can." He drew his fingers along the bottom of her jaw before leaving the room.

Mistress Claudia knelt in front of Miriam, her eyes sparkling. She took Miriam's hands and held them to her chest.

"I have the most wonderful thing to tell you now that Titus can't hear. Philip wants to marry me as soon as possible. Now that we both follow Jesus, there's nothing to keep us apart."

"I knew he would ask the moment he saw you again. If anyone could deserve you, it's him. When will you marry?"

Claudia blew her breath out between pursed lips. "Well, there's still one problem. Titus doesn't want anyone to find out I'm a Christian. I'm not sure he'll give his permission if he thinks that will expose me, but I don't know how to tell him Philip is a Christian so he doesn't have to worry about that."

"Surely the master can see what a good man Master Philip is and how much he loves you. I think the master will trust him and say yes."

Claudia bit her lip as she looked at Miriam.

"Maybe, but there's another problem. We'll marry in a Christian ceremony. There's no way Titus won't know then, and he still hates Christians except for you and me. He still blames them for Father's death, like I used to. When he learns Philip is a Christian, I'm not sure what he'll do."

Claudia cradled her face in her palms. "But that's not the worst. He still wants to kill the Christian who first told Father about Jesus. Penelope told me it was her own father, but Philip was the teacher at the first Christian worship Father went to, and he declared his faith and received the Holy Spirit there. It was Philip's father that our steward asked to get me to Titus. I can't have him wanting to kill Philip and his father. He might try to do it. I've prayed and prayed for him to begin to forgive, but he doesn't even want to try to forgive Lucius or Philip's father. Maybe he can't. Not without Jesus's help, and he can't have that if he won't believe in Jesus himself."

"Can you tell him Master Philip follows Jesus without telling him he knew your father?"

"He already knows Philip's father was our father's friend. Once he knows Philip is a Christian, he'll put it all together, and he'll know."

"Maybe he'll be so grateful for them saving you from Lucius that he'll forgive them. Maybe he'll say yes, and none of it will matter after you finally tell him everything."

◆

Titus returned from the stable in time to hear Miriam's words. He stopped in the doorway with crossed arms.

"Maybe I'll say yes and none of what will matter after you finally tell me everything? What are you trying to hide from me?" He looked first at Miriam, who looked down at the floor, then at Claudia. His frown deepened.

Claudia took a deep breath, obviously steeling herself for a confession. "Philip asked me to marry him, and I said yes. He'll be asking your permission later today."

"I'll give my permission. He's a good man, and I have no doubt how much he loves you. He'll take good care of you. But that still doesn't answer my question. What are you hiding from me?"

"Promise me you won't do anything to hurt him, and I'll tell you."

Titus's frown turned into a scowl. "What has he done that would make me want to hurt him?"

"It isn't what he's done. It's what he is."

"Go on."

"You haven't promised yet. Please, Titus. Promise me, and then I'll tell you."

He entered the room and planted himself in front of Claudia with his legs spread and his arms crossed. His eyebrows scrunched as he looked at his little sister. She used to be a sweet, fragile girl. Now she was a strong young woman. Without the promise, she would never tell him.

"All right. I promise."

"He's just like Miriam and me...He's a Christian."

Titus rolled his eyes as a deep sigh escaped. He really liked Philip, and now this. "Another one? How can he keep you safe if the next governor decides to kill Christians?"

"Maybe the point of life isn't just to be safe. Maybe it's to live it fully right now and then forever with Jesus."

Titus's lips tightened as he shook his head. She looked so happy and hopeful. She was like Father had described himself in his final letter. He'd been furious when she became a Christian, but had it made her into the exceptional woman standing before him? Philip was possibly the best man he'd ever met. They deserved each other.

"You have my permission, even if he is a Christian. At least I won't have to worry about you having someone to talk to about your Jesus. If you two could keep that from me for so long, you can probably keep it secret from anyone else."

He lifted Claudia's chin so she was looking up into his eyes. "You don't have to worry about me trying to kill any of the Christians I know. You're probably hiding even more of them, but I like the three I know best. Father was wiser than I once thought when he became one, too."

The beaming smile his words brought to Claudia's lips was exactly what he expected. He'd see a similar response from Philip when he spoke with him that evening. He had every expectation that they'd be blissfully happy together for however long Rome left them alone. Maybe that was enough to ask for.

"After you marry, Philip will have to get you a new maid. I'm planning to keep Miriam at our house until I move back near the palace. I need to find the right lodgings so I can keep her with me after I move, and that might take a while. I'm not going to eat ordinary food again."

It wasn't just her cooking he'd miss if he didn't have her with him. No house could ever feel like home if she wasn't there, but he still hadn't decided what he ought to do about that.

He knelt by Miriam. "Now let's take care of my favorite cook. Give me your ankle so I can wrap it."

◆

Take care of his cook. Those words drove a dagger into Miriam's heart, but they forced her to face what must be.

When Master Titus cradled her in his arms while his gaze felt like a caress, she'd dreamed that maybe, just maybe, he might see her as more than his slave. He'd looked at her like a man looks at a woman he truly cares for...or so it seemed. How foolish she'd been. He would never see her as more than the maid for his sister and the cook he kept calling the best in the city.

She blinked to push back the tears that wanted to escape. Then she watched the master's hands as he applied the liniment and rubbed it into her sprained ankle. As he began to wrap it, she watched his face. She'd never expected to see him again as she lay in the black belly of the ship. But he'd tried hard to find her, so he did value her. Even if he would never love her, he was still glad to get her back. He wasn't going to let Claudia take her because he wanted her himself.

It was good to be back with him, even if he would always see her as his slave.

Still, she wished it were otherwise. Everything was turning out just as it should for Master Philip and Mistress Claudia. Their love was so deep and pure, and now they would marry and spend their lives together. It was too hard when you loved someone with all your heart, but your dreams for a life together as husband and wife would never be more than dreams.

She closed her eyes. *God, please help me be content with what must be.* There could be pleasure in serving the one you love, even if he would never know how much you love him. When you truly love someone, happiness can come from doing everything you can for him...even when he doesn't love you in return.

Chapter 75

Difficult Decisions

Claudia's gaze snapped onto Titus. She'd expected him to tell Miriam he intended to marry her. She wasn't sure why he didn't, and she was more than a little concerned that he hadn't.

She'd told him how much Miriam loved him. He seemed convinced Miriam was the right woman for him, so why didn't he tell Miriam? Claudia would gladly give up Miriam to be her brother's wife, but not if he only wanted to keep her as his slave.

As Titus finished wrapping Miriam's ankle, Claudia placed her hand on his shoulder. "Come with me to the kitchen. I may need help with something."

He stood and lifted Miriam's chin so she was looking into his eyes. "Don't try to get up and do anything."

"Yes, master."

Titus followed Claudia along the balcony until she turned into one of the bedchambers. She motioned him to follow her in, then closed the door behind him.

"Why do you want to keep Miriam? If you're not planning to marry her, you shouldn't keep her." She rested her fists on her hips. "Are you going to marry her, Titus?"

"I haven't decided yet. I'd always expected to marry someone like us, not a freed slave. I'm not sure it's the right thing to do."

"The right thing for whom? For you? What about what's right for Miriam? How can you be so cruel and just keep her as your slave?"

"Why do you think it's cruel? She seems happy just the way we've been."

"Do you know how much it hurts to love someone who doesn't appreciate that love? Can't you see the kind of love she has for you? She risked death to care for you when you were so terribly sick. You would have died without her. You saw the way she took my place so I wouldn't have to suffer. She's willing to suffer whatever it takes to spare someone she loves. Sacrificial love—that's the kind of love that's worth more than anything."

Titus ran his fingers through his hair. "I can't argue against what you're saying. If it were just for me, I'd marry her, but how can a Claudius Drusus take a crippled Jewish slave girl as his wife? There are obligations to family honor and Roman pride that I have to consider. I should marry someone from at least the equestrian order. What would Father have said if I don't?"

Claudia flicked her hand to sweep away the stupid words he'd just spoken. "I know exactly what Father would say. He'd say marry her because she'll make you truly happy. Father never wanted to be in the Senate, and Grandfather died before he could be, so there's no reason you can't marry her. Are you going to sacrifice your happiness and hers to stupid pride? How could you ever think she's not as good as us just because she's not from a noble Roman family? She's better than either you or me."

She took his hand as she stared intently into his eyes.

"Please don't make that mistake. It's only the heart of the person that matters, not the outside or where they came from. I used to be so stupid, thinking that only a handsome Roman would be good enough to marry me. I wouldn't have given Philip a second glance if God hadn't put me on his ship so I got to see what a truly worthy man looks like. Miriam's just like Philip; once you see the treasure within, why would you settle for someone who only looks good on the outside or has the right ancestors?"

Titus rubbed the back of his neck. "I hear what you're saying, but how can I take her back to Rome as my wife? Do you know how our friends and relatives would treat her? What they would say about her? About both of us?"

"Then don't go back to Rome. Stay here when you finish your service. What do you want in Rome that you can't have here?" Her lips tightened. "What's so wonderful about Rome, anyway? It's so full of pride and violence and greed and...I never want to go there again."

She frowned and shook her head. "Pride is the greatest sin of all, Titus. It's keeping you from the finest woman you'll ever know."

As Claudia stared into her brother's eyes, a still, small voice whispered within her. *Is it time, Lord?* She'd prayed for countless hours, asking God to reach Titus's heart since the morning He'd reached her own. The whisper grew louder...and somehow, she knew. Titus was ready to listen and decide.

"Even worse, pride keeps us from turning to Jesus because we think we're good enough on our own, because we don't want to admit we need Him to save us. But we do need Him, and He loved us enough to die to save us, even though we don't deserve anything from Him."

Titus tightened his lips and shook his head. "You don't have to tell me I'm not perfect, Claudia. I already know it. Father would have told me I'm a sinner because I had no desire to follow the Jewish god like he did. His last letter laid it all out. I know he thought his god wants me to love him, that his god loves me already, and that Jesus died as a sacrifice for sin because of that love. I've spent many hours thinking about what he wrote, but I don't understand how that could be."

Claudia took his hand. "What don't you understand?"

"For a god to become a man, not like in the Greek stories but for real, he'd have to give up so much power and freedom and...everything that made him a god. But why would he do that? Why didn't he just leave the temple in place and use the animal sacrifices to let his people approach him? Why be the final sacrifice himself? And why on a cross? You've never seen that type of death, but I have. It makes what Father suffered in the arena seem kind."

"Penelope told me the animal sacrifices were only to teach people how serious sin was, that it needed blood to cover it before God. But animal blood only covered it; it didn't erase the sin. The plan from the beginning was for Jesus to come and make the final, perfect sacrifice when people could understand it. He took on all the sins of everyone who ever lived or will live and paid for them all. He did it out of love."

Titus rubbed the back of his neck. "But to choose to die on a cross... how could anyone, god or otherwise, love people he didn't even know enough to do that? It can take days, and it's pure torture the whole time a man's up there." He rested his hand on her cheek. "I could choose to die to spare you, but you're my sister. I love you. For some stranger? No. That kind of love is earned."

Claudia lifted his hand from her cheek and held it as she gazed up into her brother's eyes.

"The deepest, truest love isn't. Just look at Miriam. She tries to love us like Jesus loves us, even when we haven't done anything to deserve it, even when you hurt her terribly. You've seen how she's forgiven you after you hit her so hard and told Nestor to sell her when all she'd ever done was love and care for us."

Titus frowned and slowly nodded. Claudia fought the smile. He'd always done that when he was really listening to Father.

"She was willing to suffer anything to save you when you were so sick with fever. She didn't care if she caught it and died if that was what it took to get you better."

She watched his frown begin to turn into a slight smile as he listened. His nods became faster and deeper.

"You were so ungrateful that afternoon when you finally woke up. I'm glad she never heard what you said, but she already knew that was what you felt. She told me you didn't really care what happened to her, but she kept loving you anyway. Jesus loves us even when we don't love Him back, and He never stops loving us even when we say or do things we shouldn't. He even gives His followers the power to love like He did.

"Miriam loves me like that, too. She wanted to go to Lucius in my place, and you know he would have made her suffer unbearably before he killed her in some horrible way. She knew that, too, but she was willing to pay any price so I wouldn't have to suffer. She was willing to die to buy my freedom.

"God loves us even more. Jesus suffered to pay for everyone's sins so we wouldn't have to. On that cross, He paid for Father's sins, for my sins, for your sins to end our separation from God. He freed us out of love."

She raised his hand and held it against her cheek. "I wish you'd follow me and Father and become a Christian, too."

He pulled his hands from hers, crossed his arms, and stared at the floor. "Ever since I received Father's letter, I've been thinking about why he made his choice. I can't tell you how many times I've read and reread that letter. His reasons for becoming a God-fearer make perfect sense. They convinced me the Jewish god really is God, so I guess you'd have to call me a God-fearer, too. His worry about how to replace the Jerusalem temple sacrifices made sense. After a while, so did his conclusion that a man who was also God could make the perfect sacrifice and end the need for any more. What I couldn't understand was why

Father chose to die when offering a little incense to Caesar could save him."

He rubbed his mouth with the back of his hand before he shrugged. "But maybe that makes sense, too. Loyalty and love for the one who saved you by his own death is the most reasonable thing in the world. Refusing to deny the one who loves you that much…that makes sense, too, even if you have to die for it."

Titus crossed his arms again. "The surest proof of love really is going to certain death to spare the ones you love, even if they don't love you in return." He raised his eyes to gaze into hers. "If a woman like Miriam can love that much, surely God can love even more. I can believe Jesus did just that."

He tipped his head to the side, and a thoughtful smile appeared. "The three smartest people I've ever known are you, Father, and Philip, and you all decided to believe Jesus died to save you. Perhaps it's time I join you."

Claudia bounced on her toes. "Really? Oh, Titus! I'm so happy for you. For me, too, because now you and I and Father will all be together in heaven someday with Jesus. Nothing can part us forever."

"I still have some questions, but I expect Philip can answer them all as well as Father would have." He stroked her cheek with the back of his fingers. "We'll have that conversation after I give him my permission to marry you when he gets back from the harbor. Or maybe before I give permission, just to prolong the suspense for him."

Claudia caught her brother's hand and held it against her cheek. "I want to be there. Promise me you won't start without me."

Titus chuckled. "He won't want you out of his sight, so I'm certain he'll have no objection to that."

Claudia's sly smile crept out. Titus was in for a big surprise. Her brother had decided to follow Jesus with his head, but soon he'd open his heart to receive the Holy Spirit. Life was so much sweeter when you moved past knowing about God to meeting Him yourself.

She'd only been this happy twice before in her life: the morning she decided to follow Jesus and the moment Philip asked her to be his wife. Titus had made the first decision she'd prayed for. Now to get him to make the second.

"Now what about Miriam?"

He gazed into her eager eyes, and a crooked grin appeared.

"You're going to have to find yourself a new maid. If you want to eat as well as me, you'll have to come visit. Even after she's my wife,

I'm going to have her direct the kitchen. I've become too spoiled to switch cooks now."

Claudia bounced on her toes again when he said 'after she's my wife.' That was exactly what she wanted to hear. Her brother wasn't so stupid after all.

Chapter 76

BETTER THAN VENGEANCE

Titus had scarcely finished sharing the two most important decisions of his life with his beloved sister when the messenger came from the garrison to report that Lucius's men had been caught. He told the soldier he would be along shortly, and the soldier saluted and left.

Claudia placed her hand on Titus's arm. "What are you going to do to them, Titus?"

The corner of his mouth turned up. "This afternoon, when I first learned they'd taken Miriam, I wanted to coat my *gladius* with their blood for daring to hurt someone I care about. Now, well, I guess I'm a different man. Father was right about me needing to forgive Lucius, not just for him but for me. I don't want revenge anymore, on Lucius or on these men who are just doing what he ordered. I have a better way to deal with them. A way that will please God while solving your problem with Lucius once and for all."

She smiled up at him. "I'm glad."

"I have to finish my business with them, then I'll be back to set some things straight with Miriam."

Claudia bounced on her toes and clapped her hands when he said that.

Titus tightened his lips to stop the grin. "Don't you let her know what I have planned. I want the fun of watching her face when I tell her."

"I won't. I can keep a secret with the best of them, and this is the best secret I've ever had to keep."

Titus stood in the garrison stable yard with his arms crossed, scowling at Lucius's agents. He could have them killed, but that wouldn't keep Lucius from simply sending someone else. He had a better plan.

"By the authority of the governor, your fate is in my hands. While stealing my slave is simple theft, that was not your intention. You thought she was my sister Claudia. Taking Claudia against her will would be kidnapping. If you had taken her, you would be better off dead right now. You have admitted you are peregrines, not citizens of Rome, so what I choose to do is not limited by Roman law. This is Thracia, not Rome. Kidnapping is not tolerated in this province, and the governor will allow me to crucify you for merely trying to kidnap a Roman citizen, even though you bungled the attempt."

Titus raked them with his angriest stare until the panic in their eyes reached the desired level.

"I could order my centurion to kill you right here, right now...but I'm not going to. Instead, I'm sending you back to Lucius with a message from me. First, he is never to try to kidnap Claudia again. He can forget about getting money from Flavius Sabinus or anyone else in Rome who wants her. The governor has made me her guardian instead of Lucius. Before you reach Rome, she'll be married to the man we have chosen. Lucius deserves nothing since the role he played in finding her husband was not what he intended. Still, her betrothed is willing to pay him the same amount that I gave for the woman I'm planning to marry. You will deliver it to him."

He tossed them a sack that had been sewn shut and then sewn inside a second sack. Inside was four hundred denarii in *dupondii*, so the 3200 brass coins made it very heavy. Titus fought a smile. Too bad he wouldn't see the emotions on Lucius's face when he opened it. Surprise, then fury. It was likely to be quite amusing.

"Second, I expect him to admit that the estate north of Rome is now mine, as Father always intended. He is to send me proof that ownership has been legally transferred to me. You will tell him that I'm certain he wouldn't want all Rome to know that he cheated his brother and tried to sell his sister after arranging to murder his father. I will make certain all the people he cares about in Rome know if he refuses to give me what is rightfully mine. Malleolus is to continue overseeing the estate for me. I'll expect an accounting from him twice a year."

He spoke to the soldier standing right behind them. "Untie them."

"Third, you are to tell him that neither Claudia nor I plan to seek revenge on him for killing Father or trying to hurt her. Father forgave Lucius for his betrayal; we are choosing to forgive him, too."

The two agents stood before him, rubbing their wrists where the ropes had cut into them.

"Now go. Deliver my message to Lucius, and be thankful that I'm a merciful man."

Titus left the incredulous men staring at him as he spun and walked to his horse. He mounted and kicked the stallion into a trot. He'd already been away from Philip's house too long. Two women he loved were waiting for him.

Miriam and Mistress Claudia were sitting together in the mistress's room when they heard Master Titus's footsteps on the balcony. Both looked up to see him standing at the door with an odd smile on his face.

Then the smile flipped into a frown. "Claudia, I need to speak with Miriam alone. I'll come get you when I'm through with her."

The mistress covered her mouth with her hand. "I'll be next door. Call me when you want me."

Miriam looked first at Master Titus, then at Mistress Claudia, then back at the master. The set of his mouth was grim, his eyes deadly serious. Something was wrong, dreadfully wrong.

Mistress headed for the door, but she patted the master's arm as she passed.

He offered his hands. "Stand up, Miriam. I have something to tell you."

She took both his hands and stood, keeping her weight off her sprained ankle. What could be so serious that he wanted her to stand? She swallowed hard.

"Claudia and I have a problem. I own you, but we both want you. She wants you as her companion. I want you as my cook. There is one thing we agree on, however. We both want you to be her sister. I see only one solution that will satisfy us both so..."

Sadness wrapped around her heart as she waited for the master to decree her fate. No matter what he decided to do with her, she would no longer be spending every day with one of the two people she loved.

The master paused as he reached out to push a strand of hair behind her ear. Then he rested his palm on her cheek and stroked it with his thumb. She fought against the tears that were trying to escape.

As much as she loved his gentle touch, she wished he wasn't touching her that way. Her heart longed to stay with the man she loved, but nothing would ever come of that love. Someday the master would marry, and she wasn't sure she could bear watching him love another woman. It would be much better in the long run if she could stay with the mistress who loved her like a sister.

"You've always been willing to try something new when I ask you to."

"I'll try to do whatever you tell me, master. What do you want me to do?"

"Look at me, Miriam."

She obeyed because, no matter how hard it was, he was still the master.

His gaze felt like a caress. Her eyebrows rose. Why had his tightened lips been replaced by a teasing smile?

"I want you to become my wife. I'm going to set you free, and then you're going to marry me. You've shown me what faithful love is, and I want us to love each other that way for the rest of our lives."

Her eyes saucered as she heard the words she'd only dreamed of. Had he really spoken them? She'd never even prayed for this because she thought it was impossible. Wasn't she only the great cook who cost him four hundred denarii?

She froze, speechless, gazing up at him.

"Of course, under Roman law, you have no choice since I'm freeing you for that purpose, but Claudia tells me she thinks you might want to do it anyway."

◆

Titus let his grin escape. His little Jewish slave stood with her head tipped back, blinking faster as her lips parted. It took all his self-control not to kiss them before she answered.

"Do you want to marry me, Miriam?"

Her blinks slowed, but no words came.

"Well? Aren't you going to answer me?" His grin broadened. She was a funny little thing sometimes. He would enjoy the years with her beside him.

Finally, she found her voice. "Oh, yes, master. Yes!"

He placed both hands on her face and tilted it to just the right angle.

"Titus, not master."

As captivating brown eyes stared up at him, he slid his hands down her neck and across her shoulders before pulling her against him. For the first time, she didn't blush or try to move away when he touched her. Her dark eyes were luminous, and there was that beautiful smile he found so enchanting. He lowered his lips to hers, and she wrapped her arms around him as she melted against him in their first embrace.

When he finally withdrew from their first kiss, he placed his fingertips under her chin to keep her face tilted upward. The love in her eyes deepened in response to his own.

"That's more like it. I consider myself released from my promise not to make you my nighttime entertainment. I expect you to entertain me day and night for the rest of our lives."

He rested his hand on her cheek and stroked it with his thumb. She leaned her face into his hand and closed her eyes until he spoke again.

"There is one thing you do now that you'll still have to do after we marry."

Her head tilted. "What's that, mast...Titus?"

"You're still going to direct the kitchen. I'm not willing to give up having the best cook in the city just to have the best wife."

Her eyes sparkled. "I wouldn't want you to. I'll always try to do anything you want."

The corner of his mouth lifted. "I know. I got the greatest treasure for only four hundred denarii."

Her smile mirrored his own. "I'm glad you think so, m...Titus."

As he drew her back into his embrace and once more lowered his lips to hers, Titus found himself thanking God...for Lucius.

It was ironic. What his brother had intended for evil, God had used for good. Good for Claudia and Philip, good for Miriam and him. Maybe, in the long run, there would even be good for Lucius. He would pray for that. Vengeance belonged to the Lord, and only God knew how best to repay.

Coming Soon

If you're not ready to say goodbye to the people in *The Legacy*, you'll have a chance to spend more time with them eight years later in the sequel. Go to the next page for a sneak peek at the start of *Second Chances*.

Second Chances

Sometimes it takes more than love to conquer all.

In AD 122, Cornelia Scipia, proud daughter of one of the noblest Roman families, learns her adulterous husband plans to betroth their daughter to the vicious son of his best friend. Only over her dead body! Cornelia divorces him, reclaims her enormous dowry, and kidnaps her own daughter. She plans to start over with Drusilla a thousand miles away. No more husbands for her! But she hadn't counted on meeting Hector, the widowed Greek captain of the ship carrying them to their new life.

Devastated by the loss of his wife and daughter, Hector's heart begins to heal as he befriends Drusilla. Cornelia's sacrificial love for Drusilla and her courage and humor in the face of the unknown earn his admiration...as a friend. Is he ready for more?

Marriage to the kind, honest sea captain would finally give Drusilla the father she deserves...and Cornelia the faithful husband she's always longed for. But there are secrets in his past and unspoken misunderstandings born of the chasms between their social classes and different faiths. Will they keep two lonely hearts from the second chance at happiness that God so unexpectedly offers?

Join the people you met in *The Legacy* eight years later in this tale of hope and a future never imagined until God opens the door.

Legacies have impact even before someone dies. If you wonder about the consequences of Lucius's treachery in the lives of his sons when they're grown, you'll find that story in *Forgiven*.

If you're curious about Decimus's story, you can find it in *Blind Ambition*.

Chapter 1

Husbands and Fathers

Mare Nostrum, AD 122

Hector awoke, once more drenched in sweat. He lay on his bunk, staring at the wall as the ship rose and fell on the waves. He willed his breathing to match the rhythm of the ship.

The nightmares of his childhood were long past, the pain that caused them mostly forgotten. But now his dreams were red and raw, a stark reminder of reality, and they tore his heart each time he had one.

The dreams started well enough. It was the end of the final voyage of autumn. As his ship glided up against the pier and his crew prepared to secure it with ropes, his beloved Damara and their ten-year-old Charissa waved from the road above the wharfs. Even after seventeen years of marriage, his heart beat faster as he thought about spending the cold winter nights in the warm embrace of the incredible woman God had given him to make him whole.

As the gangplank was lowered, they started down the ramp. He trotted down the plank and loped up the pier. As he dodged the crates and barrels waiting to be loaded, he lost sight of them. When he finally stepped clear of the stacks of cargo, Philip stood before him. He placed his hand on Hector's shoulder, tightened his lips, and shook his head.

Philip dissolved in a swirl of smoke, and Hector remained on the dock...alone.

He'd known loneliness before God brought Damara into his life, or so he'd thought. But when two have become one, and suddenly one is gone... Those first four months when the sea was closed and he'd been home at his farm, where they'd planned on growing old together—that was when the sweet memories of what he'd lost engulfed him, tormenting his days and haunting his nights.

It hadn't been as bad when he was back at sea, at least not during the daytime. He'd often been gone for weeks at a time, and he didn't expect to see Damara smiling at him when he turned around on deck or Charissa running to wrap her arms around him when he walked through the cabin doorway.

Hector rubbed his forehead with the back of his hand. If only Damara hadn't heard his ship might reach home port early and come to the wharfs to see. If only he'd thought to tell her to stay well away from where the wagons unloaded, no matter how much Charissa begged to get closer to watch.

It had been almost a year since the accident, and the pain still cut deep. The shipping season was almost over. One more stop in Rome, then home to Perinthus...and another winter in a cold bed with empty arms.

Experience told him that sleep would not come again that night, so he rose and headed out to the ship's rail. There, alone in the moonlight, he watched his ship cutting through the waves and once more asked God why.

Rome

Tertius didn't want to believe what his best friend, Gaius, had just told him. It shouldn't be true, but given what his father was like, he was afraid not to ask. He wasn't going to let his sister be killed if he could prevent it.

His father, Lucius Drusus Fidelis, was reading at his desk when Tertius walked into the library. Tertius's entrance drew a smile.

"I hadn't expected to see you today. I thought you were staying with Gaius at the Corvinus estate this week." His father set the scroll down and turned his attention to the youngest of his three sons.

"I hadn't expected to come, Father, but Gaius just told me you were talking with his father about betrothing Drusilla to Gnaeus."

"That's true. Marcus told me he's looking for the right girl to betroth to Gnaeus now that he's fourteen. Drusilla's ten now, so she'll be exactly the right age to marry him in five or six years."

"You can't do that, Father. Gaius told me his brother is dangerous. Just last year, he and Gaius were riding out at their estate. His horse stumbled and threw him. He took a hoe from one of the slaves, and when he was through, Gaius had to slit its throat to put it out of its misery. He's already beaten one of the house slaves to death and almost killed one of the slave girls after taking her. Don't betroth Drusilla to him. He's vicious, and she's going to get hurt or killed."

His father picked up a stylus and rolled it between his fingers while he listened, then shrugged. "Marcus is my closest friend, and he hasn't found anyone else who wants his daughter to be married to the boy. I have a daughter the right age, so I can solve Marcus's problem."

Tertius was stunned. "You can't be serious about marrying Drusilla to a monster."

His father's brows dipped as a frown appeared. "What I choose to do with Drusilla is none of your business, Tertius. Marcus wants a wife for Gnaeus, and I can give him one. Gnaeus is no worse than many boys his age. Even if he did want to hurt her, Marcus wouldn't let him. She'll be safe enough."

Tertius was appalled, but he knew better than to let it show. "I hope you're right, Father. Drusilla's a sweet little thing. You'd really like her if you spent more time at the eastern estate. Mother and I would hate to see anything bad happen to her."

A sneer flitted across Lucius's lips. "What your mother thinks means less than nothing to me. Marcus will make sure nothing happens to Drusilla. Her safety is not your concern." He fixed irritated eyes on his son. "We won't discuss this again."

"As you wish, Father. I need to leave now, anyway. I'm meeting Gaius at the Circus Maximus for the afternoon races."

"I hope your team wins. Enjoy yourself." His father turned his attention back to his scroll as Tertius walked out of the room.

When his father could no longer see him, Tertius's brow furrowed as his lips tightened. He should have known it would be pointless trying to convince Father not to put Drusilla in mortal danger. Time for a different approach to protect the little sister he loved.

Chapter 2

TIME FOR A CHANGE

Tertius told his father he was going to the chariot races, but he headed to the eastern estate instead. Although he mostly stayed in Rome now he was eighteen, his mother and sister never came to the town house that had been Grandfather's before Father arranged for him to be killed in the arena for his Christian faith. Aunt Claudia had accused Father of murder. To punish her, Father had tried to marry her to a rich, sadistic old man from one of the noblest Roman families. Mother had tried to stop him, and they'd hardly spoken to each other in the eight years since.

Drusilla meant the world to Mother. It took no imagination to believe Father would let something terrible happen to her just to hurt Mother. But Father wouldn't hurt Drusilla if he could stop it.

Tertius trotted into the stable yard, and a slave scurried over to take his horse. He threw his leg over the horse's neck and slid to the ground. "Where's my mother?"

"In the garden, Master Tertius."

He tossed the reins to the slave and strode through the archway that separated the garden from the stable area. "Mother? Are you here?"

◆

Cornelia Scipia's eyes snapped up from her codex when she heard Tertius calling. She rose from the seat under the grape arbor and waved at him. When he reached her, she embraced her youngest son.

"What a pleasant surprise. I hadn't expected to see you until next week."

"I had to come today because there's something you need to know."

The grim set of his mouth ramped up Cornelia's heart rate. "What's wrong? Are you well?"

"I'm fine, but Drusilla won't be if we don't do something to protect her."

A cold hand of foreboding gripped her heart. "What's going to happen to Drusilla?"

"Father is planning to betroth her to Gnaeus Corvinus."

"To Marcus's youngest son? Are you sure?" She'd heard too many rumors about the boy.

"After Gaius told me, I went to Father and asked him. I told him how dangerous Gnaeus is, and he didn't care. He's planning to do it anyway just to help out his friend. We can't let him do that, Mother. She'll end up hurt or dead if she marries him."

Cornelia drew herself up to her full height, and her mouth set into a determined line. "Your father is a traitor to this family. He murdered your grandfather, he would have hurt Claudia if she hadn't escaped, and now he's planning to get Drusilla killed. Well, I won't let him. I'll do whatever it takes to protect her."

"How can I help?" Eager intensity lit his eyes as he squared his shoulders.

Cornelia's brow furrowed as she pursed her lips. "First, don't tell your father you came here. He mustn't know I've been warned, or he'll take her away from me before I can do anything."

"I can't tell him. Father already told me we wouldn't discuss this again." His lips twisted up in a wry smile. "If I'm to be a good son, I must never say anything to him about it."

If Drusilla hadn't been in mortal danger, Cornelia would have laughed at her son's twisted interpretation of the duty to a *paterfamilias* that grown sons continue to obey their fathers in everything. Her mouth turned up a little anyway.

Cornelia clenched her left hand and tapped the side of her forefinger against her pursed lips. "I've stayed married to your father only so he wouldn't take you all away from me, but you boys are all grown. It's been eight years since he completely abandoned me for other women. It's time I divorce him and reclaim my dowry. Then I can take Drusilla where he can't get to her."

"But children always belong to the father in a divorce. Where could you go that he couldn't get her?"

"Away from Rome. Maybe even away from Italia. Far enough away that he might decide it's not worth the effort to find her and bring her back."

"I want to help. Just tell me what to do."

Cornelia covered her mouth and stroked her cheek with her forefinger. "I think, for now, it's best that you not know what I'm going to do. If he thinks you're not part of this, we might get advance warning of what he's doing to get her back. Later, I'll let you know where we are so you can warn me of anything he might be planning."

She wrapped her arms around Tertius's chest and stretched up to kiss his cheek. "I'm so proud of you and your brother Lucius. Two of my sons grew into fine men like your grandfather Publius. Marcus... well, he's too much like his father."

Tertius hugged her back. "If I can't help right now, I should go back to the Circus Maximus. I told Father I was going there to meet Gaius, and I'd better know who won."

"Go. I already have an idea what to do, but I need to think about it more."

Tertius kissed his mother's cheek and left.

Cornelia began pacing. She would need her whole dowry. As steward and overseer of all the Drusus estates and Lucius's under-the-table business ventures, Malleolus was the only person who could help her do that quickly and without Lucius knowing what she was planning. The moment he knew she was divorcing him, he'd come to get Drusilla.

Secrecy was vital, but she could trust Malleolus to keep everything secret. Even though Lucius Fidelis was now the head of the Claudius Drusus family, the old steward's loyalty still belonged to Publius, even eight years after his death. Saving Publius's granddaughter was something he'd be eager to do.

Breakfast was over, and Aristarchus and Helena walked Hector to the stable. It was a four-hour ride from Aristarchus's house near the eastern edge of Rome back to the ship in Portus. In a few days, Hector would sail back to Thracia, where he would spend the four months that the sea was closed due to winter storms at his farm near Perinthus.

Aristarchus expected his captain of the *Claudia* to dine with them and spend the night whenever he brought the ship to Rome. Hector was, without doubt, the most deserving young man he had ever bought and freed. He had served in the family's merchant fleet for twenty five years, first as a slave, then as a freedman whose maritime skills had elevated him to the rank of captain. He was loyal and honest to a fault, and he had been the best friend of Aristarchus's youngest son, Philip, since they worked together one summer fifteen years ago.

Each time Hector had visited that shipping season, Aristarchus saw the dark shadow enveloping him. He was worried about his captain, who was more son than employee. It had been hard for Hector since his wife and daughter died just before he reached home last fall. The deep grief had a grip on him that he could not shake. His smiles were sad, and his eyes seemed weary. He was barely forty, but his sorrow made him seem much older this visit.

Helena, Aristarchus's wife of over forty years, wrapped her arm around Hector's as they walked him to the horse he had rented for the ride from the coast.

"I'm so glad you came up to see us. We love having you here." She stood on tiptoes and kissed his bearded cheek. "You're my sixth son. I'll be praying for you until I see you again."

Hector smiled in response, but there was no joy in his eyes. "God truly blessed me with both of you."

Aristarchus wrapped his arms around Hector in a crushing hug and slapped his arm when he let go. "May God be with you on your voyage and bring you happiness again."

"And may He continue to bless you both with a long life together."

The tightness at the corner of his smile and the two quick blinks that stopped any tears betrayed Hector's longing for the years with Damara that would never be.

Hector mounted and waved before kicking the horse into a trot and heading down the street. Helena wrapped her arm around Aristarchus's and leaned her head against his shoulder as she watched Hector ride away.

"It breaks my heart to see him suffering so. I don't know if it's Damara or Charissa he's missing more. To lose them both at once..." She sighed. "He has so much love to give, and he needs someone to give it to. He needs another woman who'll love him with her whole heart and a child he can give the love he would have given Charissa. A dead child can never be replaced, but another child can begin to fill the void. He needs to remarry and have more children."

Aristarchus shook his head as his mouth turned down. "That is not so easy for a man who has known the joy of having the perfect wife. I am not sure I could remarry if you died."

She slapped his arm before she hugged it. "Don't say that. I would want you to remarry and find happiness again, God willing. I'm going to be praying for that for Hector. I'm going to ask God to bring a woman to heal his heart before we see him again next spring."

Aristarchus smiled down at the sweet, godly woman who had graced his life for so long. She might think a man can just remarry to replace a lost love, but some women were irreplaceable. He would know. He was married to one.

Chapter 3

THE PERFECT ALLY

Early the next morning, Malleolus rode up to the stable at the eastern estate. It wasn't so easy to ride anymore. These days, his knees told him how far the ride from the town house was. It might not be long before he would need to take a litter in the daytime or drive the two-wheeled *cisium* when the ban on wagons on the streets of Rome ended at dusk. That would be a sad day. He was still a man of thirty from the inside looking out, but riding reminded him that the wrinkled old man in the mirror with the fringe of silver hair was him and not his father.

Although he came every week, he never found much needing his attention. Cornelia ran the estate herself better than the overseers at the other Drusus estates. The main reason he came was to visit with Cornelia and Drusilla. Cornelia had become a dear friend in the eight years since Publius's murder, and Drusilla loved him like a grandfather. It felt good to spend a few hours with people who were just like family. He had none of his own.

After he dismounted, he placed his hands on his knees and bent forward to limber up for walking. He flexed his rein fingers a few times. Too bad there wasn't axle grease for the joints of a man nearing seventy.

The stable slave bowed as he took the reins. "Mistress Cornelia said you were to come to her in the garden the moment you arrived."

Malleolus's face remained impassive when he heard the command, but he was concerned. He'd never been met with such a message before. He arched his back to loosen a few more muscles and walked as fast as was almost comfortable to find his mistress and friend.

When she saw him walk through the archway, Cornelia rose and held both hands out to him. "I'm glad you came early today. I have

440

something important to ask of you, and it's vital that you start on it as soon as possible."

Malleolus's gaze swept the garden near them to see if any ears were listening.

Cornelia followed his gaze. "I've already given orders that no one is to come into this part of the garden until I say. I've been watching, and no one is here. Our conversation needs to be totally private. Drusilla's life depends on it."

Malleolus was a difficult man to upset, and he was a master at concealing his thoughts even when he was. Her words broke through his unflappable demeanor, and his eyebrows rose.

"Drusilla's life? What's going on?"

"That loathsome husband of mine is planning to betroth her to Gnaeus Corvinus. I'm sure you've heard all the rumors about the boy. I know at least some of the worst of them are true. We can't let that betrothal happen."

His brows dipped downward as he tightened his lips. "No, we can't."

She sat back down and patted the bench so he would sit down next to her.

"I've decided to divorce him and take her away from Rome before he commits her to that marriage. I need my dowry money as soon as possible, and I need your help in getting it without him knowing I'm getting ready to leave."

Malleolus cupped his chin in his hand and stroked his cheek with his thumb. "Normally it would take some time to get you that much money, but as luck would have it, I can do it as soon as this afternoon. I was about to buy two estates ten miles up the Via Aurelia to make one large one. I've already arranged to have more than enough gold at my disposal to make the purchases. I only need to have most of it delivered here instead." One corner of his mouth rose in a wry smile. "Lucius is required by law to return your entire dowry immediately when you divorce him. I guess he'll have to wait to get his new estate northwest of Rome."

She leaned over and embraced him. "I knew you'd be able to help." The smile that had appeared at the news of the gold dimmed. "The next part might be harder, and I'm not sure how to go about doing it." She scanned the garden to make doubly certain no one was listening. "I'm planning to go to Thracia where Titus and Claudia are living. I'm sure they'll be glad to let me stay with them for a short time while I find an estate of my own to buy where no one will recognize us."

Her brow furrowed. "I want to go by sea, but I'm not sure how to arrange everything. You've shipped things all over the empire. Can you find a good ship for us without Lucius suspecting anything before we sail?"

He cupped his chin and stroked his cheek again. "If he's still living in Rome, I know exactly the man to ask to help with this." The corner of his mouth lifted. "The same man helped me sneak Claudia out from under Lucius's nose eight years ago. Actually, help isn't the right word. He did everything. Publius called him a good friend, and he couldn't have been a better one. I think he'll be just as willing to help save Publius's granddaughter."

He rose. "I'll go now to see if he can help. When I return, we can make final plans."

Historical Note

PATERFAMILIAS: THE ABSOLUTE POWER
OF THE ROMAN PATRIARCH

Honor your father and mother. When God delivered His Ten Commandments to the people of Israel through Moses, this was the only one that included a promise: "Honor your father and your mother, that your days may be long in the land that the LORD your God is giving you." Exodus 20:12 (ESV)

Respect and affection within an extended family certainly contribute to an enjoyable life. But "honor" does not mean "obey absolutely." While a Jewish father might expect a lifetime of respect from his children, he did not exercise total control once his sons and daughters were grown.

For Roman citizens, the expectations of a father were quite different. The oldest surviving male was the *paterfamilias*, the legal head of the family that might include several generations. The power of a Roman patriarch was absolute within the family for as long as he lived. Under Roman law, the oldest male owned all the property and could dictate everything his sons could do, no matter how old they might be. Only a father's death gave true independence to a son.

A man in his sixties might have sons in their forties and grown grandsons in their twenties, but those grown children were still under his control as if they were young children. All property belonged to the *paterfamilias*. Grown sons lived on an allowance, and any material goods they gained belonged to the *paterfamilias*, not them. The "family" over which he ruled included his sons and daughters (married or not), his sons' offspring, and any slaves he owned. A wife remained under the authority of her own *paterfamilias* as long as he lived. Since any offspring belonged to a husband's *paterfamilias*, a mother had no rights to her own children. If her husband died, she might be kept from ever seeing her children again if the *paterfamilias* chose to exclude her.

While a son gained independence upon his father's death, a daughter did not. She came under the guardianship of another male relative, who was himself a *paterfamilias*. She could petition a judge (*praetor*) to have an alternative guardian appointed if the current one was unsuitable, but she was required to have one. The Emperor Augustus wanted to encourage the upper classes to have more children, so he introduced a law where a married woman would no longer need a guardian if she had borne three or more children.

The *paterfamilias* could tell his children what they could and could not do, and they had to abide by his rules. When a baby was born to anyone in the family, he made the decision about whether the child would live or die. If he refused to take the child when it was offered to him, the baby was abandoned to die, usually in a public place. Anyone could pick up such abandoned children and raise them, either to be their own child or, more commonly, to be a slave. During the Republic, the paterfamilias also had the right to kill his adult child without any legal penalty. Even in the early Empire, that right remained, although it was not practiced and would have been generally condemned if it were.

One can well imagine the friction that could arise when grown men, married with children of their own, had to subordinate their own desires to the will of the patriarch. The temptation to do whatever it took to break free of that control must have been great at times. Perhaps that contributed to the Roman attitude toward killing a parent and the severity of the punishment for murdering one's father.

Patricide was considered one of the most heinous crimes, and a unique punishment for the crime was practiced. Following a flogging, the murderer was sewn into a leather sack with a snake, a dog, a monkey, and a rooster. If in Rome, he was then thrown into the Tiber River to drown or suffocate, if the bag was sufficiently water-tight. If not in Rome, another river, a lake, or the ocean could be used.

In *The Legacy*, Publius is the *paterfamilias* of the Claudius Drusus family. When he becomes a God-fearer, he adopts many of the Jewish laws for living. He commands his oldest son Lucius to give up his womanizing ways and be a faithful husband, as required by Mosaic law. Lucius wants Publius dead so he can become the *paterfamilias* himself and resume his licentious lifestyle. Although he is unwilling to risk the consequences of murdering his father, Lucius leaps at the chance to get his father executed for treason when Publius becomes a Christian.

For more about life in the Roman Empire at its peak, please go to carolashby.com.

Discussion Guide

1) Publius was offered the chance to save his own life by rejecting his Christian faith and offering a sacrifice to the emperor. He chose to remain loyal to Jesus, even though it meant leaving his precious daughter in the hands of the son who betrayed him. Have you or someone you know ever been faced with the choice between loyalty to a beloved family member or loyalty to Jesus?

2) Lucius betrayed his own father to the authorities, knowing it would lead to his father's death. Why did he do that? When Publius learned his own son wanted him dead, how did he respond? Do you think you could have responded as Publius did?

3) Claudia was devastated by the loss of her father, and that was made worse by feelings of guilt because she unwittingly gave her brother what he needed to destroy their father. She was consumed with hatred for her brother, who was guilty, and for her father's Christian friends, who weren't. Have you ever seen someone direct their hatred toward someone who wasn't to blame? Was there anything you could have done to help?

4) Philip's disfiguring scars had led him to believe no woman could love him, but he finds that isn't true when Claudia loves him for the man he is behind the ugly exterior. In Claudia, Philip finds the desire of his heart, but he's willing to sacrifice satisfying that desire if it means not living up to God's standards for a leader in the church. Have you or anyone you know ever been faced with a similar choice?

5) Titus loved his father and sister, and Lucius's betrayal of them both spawned hatred and a burning desire for vengeance. He has no desire to forgive anything. What does that do to him?

6) Miriam experienced both brutality and kindness during her life as a slave in Roman times, when slaves were legally classified as "mor-

tal things" or "voiced implements." How did her faith help her live her difficult life as a slave? Are there parallels today?

7) Publius wrote a letter to Titus to share what he considered the most important thing in his life, the faith he was willing to die for. Have you ever faced the problem of sharing your faith with someone you love but no longer have regular contact with? What did you do?

8) Miriam's sacrificial love played a large role in Titus opening his heart to God. Her faithful love with no expectation of it being returned also played a role in Titus opening his heart toward her. Have you ever seen the same in your own experience?

9) At the end of the novel, Claudia and Titus decide to forgive Lucius, just as their father had. How do you think Lucius will respond to Titus's message that they have forgiven him? Have you ever offered forgiveness to someone who refuses to believe or accept it? What did you do then?

10) *The Legacy* is a story of the power of love to open two hearts hardened by hatred of someone who destroyed a person they loved. What touched you most? What made you think about what your own choices would be?

What does the future hold for Lucius Fidelis and his family?

Lucius Fidelis got his father executed so he could take control of his own life and the family fortune. At the time of *The Legacy*, his sons, Lucius, Marcus, and Tertius, are sixteen, fourteen, and ten, and his daughter Drusilla is two. Lucius and Marcus are old enough to understand what their father has done, and the consequences play out eight years in the future in *Forgiven*. Lucius Fidelis will also return in 2018 in *Second Chances*. But I haven't yet decided what Fidelis's ultimate end will be. Will he continue on his present path, or choose a different way? I'd love to hear your thoughts about that. Please go to Contact Carol at carol-ashby.com (my blog) or carolashby.com (my Roman history site) and share your thoughts in the comment box. I hope I hear from you!

Glossary

aureus	gold coin worth 25 denarii
cisium	two-wheeled cart with forward-facing seat located above the axis
corbita	merchant ship, typical size 90 feet long, 25 feet wide with one large sail midship and a second small angled sail in the bow
denarius	coin equal to about one day's wage for a worker.
dupondius	coin worth 1/8 denarius
first table	the main (second) course of a three-course Roman dinner
gladius	short thrusting sword used by Roman military
palla	woman's large rectangular shawl (60 x 120 inches) worn wrapped around the body and sometimes over the head
paterfamilias	legal head of a Roman family with absolute control over all his children, even when grown or married
peregrine	a person who is not a Roman citizen
praetor	a judge in the Roman court system; the second level magistrate in the senatorial course of honors
quadrans	smallest denomination Roman coin worth 1/64 denarius
raeda	a four-wheeled closed-in carriage
second table	the dessert (third) course of a three-course Roman dinner
sestertius	coin worth 1/4 denarius
stola	a long robe worn by married women fastened by clasps at the shoulder and worn over a tunic
strigil	a metal scraper used to remove oil, sweat, and dirt
vestibulum	short hall between the entrance and atrium of a Roman town house

Scripture References

Scripture quotations marked ESV are from the Holy Bible, English Standard Version, copyright © 2001, 2007, 2011, 2016 by Crossway Bibles, a division of Good News Publishers. Used by permission. All rights reserved.

Scripture quotations marked CSB are taken from the Christian Standard Bible®, Copyright © 2017 by Holman Bible Publishers. Used by permission. Christian Standard Bible® and CSB® are federally registered trademarks of Holman Bible Publishers.

Chapter 5: John 11:25-26 (ESV) and John 14:26-27 (CSB)
Chapter 57: Matthew 10:34-39 (ESV)

Acknowledgements

First, I want to thank God for blessing me with the opportunity to write stories about difficult friendships and life-changing decisions in dangerous times, where forgiveness and love open hearts to discover their own faith in Christ. Nothing could be better than spending so much time with characters whose love for Jesus powers their lives, even in the hardest times.

It would never be possible to write the best book I can without the help of many others. Special thanks go to my critique partner, Katie Powner, who's an award-winning author herself. I'm especially thankful for the deep wisdom and spiritual insight of my trio of beta readers: alpha beta Regina Fujitani, who gets so many things tried out on her more than once, and my kindred spirits, Lisa Garcia, and Patti Stouter. I'm also thankful for my New Mexico compatriot and fellow author, Andrew Budek-Schmeisser, who lets me test the life-changing conversations on him to make sure they feel like the real deal between people, not just characters in a book.

Many thanks also to my wonderful friends who love to read and gave me many helpful comments. Some willingly read the earliest versions of The Legacy when I was first starting to write novels and it had a different name. My deepest thanks go out to each, and here they are alphabetically: Seaborn Ashby, Martha Kreklow. Christopher Miller, and Antoinette Smith. Your insights and suggestions made the characters more real and the situations more authentic. Many thanks!

Many thanks to my marvelous editor, Wendy Chorot, whose spiritual insights and editorial skills helped me refine the turning-point conversations so they have the ring of truth. On top of that, she's a blast to work with!

Yet again, I want to thank Roseanna White for making another gorgeous cover that captures the theme of the series, the Light in the Empire. She made a truly beautiful cover even when I told her it had to include the "ugliest man in the Empire." Her elegant use of light and shadow makes it sheer pleasure to look at. I can hardly wait to see what she creates for the next novel in the series.

I also want to acknowledge the invaluable advice for refining the cover design from Hy Tran and Andrew Budek-Schmeisser, without whose insights I might never have figured out what keeps the cover of a historical novel about spiritual transformations with a romantic sub-plot from looking too much like a simple romance that turns off male readers. Thanks, guys!

I especially want to thank my wonderful family. My son Paul been writing himself since 8th grade, so he's my kindred spirit who understands how addictive it is. My daughter Lydia does her part to keep me from writing all the time by being so much fun to do things with.

The best characters are inspired by real people, and my husband Jim is the inspiration for the best characteristics of my heroes. What could be a greater blessing than being married for decades to a man who is smart, kind, funny, and able to put up with me? God truly blessed me when He brought Jim from Texas to Idaho to get his wife!

About the Author

Carol Ashby has been a professional writer for most of her life, but her articles and books were about lasers and compound semiconductors (the electronics that make cell phones, laser pointers, and LED displays work). She still writes about light, but her Light in the Empire series tells stories of difficult friendships and life-changing decisions in dangerous times, where forgiveness and love open hearts to discover their own faith in Christ. Her fascination with the Roman Empire was born during her first middle-school Latin class. A research career in New Mexico inspires her to get every historical detail right so she can spin stories that make her readers feel like they're living under the Caesars themselves.

Read her articles about many facets of life in the Roman Empire at carolashby.com, or join her at her blog, The Beauty of Truth, at carol-ashby.com.

Light in the Empire Series

The Light in the Empire Series follows the interconnected lives of four Roman families during the reigns of Trajan and Hadrian. Join them as they travel the Empire, from Germania and Britannia to Thracia, Dacia, and Judaea and, of course, to Rome itself.

Now Available

Forgiven

Are some wounds too deep to forgive?

With a ruthless father who murdered for the family inheritance, Marcus Drusus plans to do the same. In AD 122, Marcus follows his brother Lucius to Judaea and plots to frame a zealot for his older brother's death. But the plan goes awry, and Lucius is rescued by a Messianic Jewish woman. Her oldest brother is a zealot and a Roman soldier killed her twin, but Rachel still persuades her father Joseph to put his love for Jesus above his anger with Rome and hide Lucius until he heals.

Rachel cares for the enemy, and more than broken bones heal as duty turns to love. Lucius embraces Joseph's faith in Jesus, but sharing a faith doesn't heal all wounds. Even before revealed secrets slice open old scars, Joseph wants no Roman son-in-law. With Rachel's zealot brother suspecting he's a Roman officer and his own brother planning to kill him when he returns, can Lucius survive long enough to change Joseph's mind?

Blind Ambition

Sometimes you have to almost die to discover how you want to live.

It's AD 114 in the Roman province of Germania Superior, and being a Christian carries a death sentence. Tribune Decimus Lentulus is on the fast track for a stellar political career back in Rome. When he's robbed, blinded, and left for dead, a young German woman who follows the Way finds him. Valeria knows it's his duty to have her and her family killed, but she chooses to obey Jesus's command to love her enemy and takes him home to care for him.

It's not his miraculous recovery that shakes Decimus to his core. It's the way they love him like family and their unconcealed love for Jesus. In spite of himself, he falls in love with the Christian woman Rome wants him to kill. Can Valeria hide her faith to follow him into the circles of Roman power? Or should he abandon his ambition to help rule the Empire and choose to follow a different way?

Faithful

Is the price of true friendship ever too high?

In AD 122, Adela, the fiery daughter of a Germanic chieftain, is kidnapped and taken across the Roman frontier to be sold as a slave. When horse-trader Otto wins her while gambling with her kidnappers, he entrusts her to his friend and trading partner, Galen. Then Otto is kidnapped by the same men, and Galen must track them half way across the Empire before his best friend loses a fight to the death in a Roman arena.

Adela joins Galen in the chase, hungry for vengeance. As the perilous journey deepens their friendship, will the kind, faithful man open her eyes to a life she never dreamed she'd want?

A trip to the heart of the Empire poses mortal danger to a man who follows Jesus, especially when he must seek the help of an enemy of the faith for Otto to survive. Tiberius hunted Christians when he governed Germania Superior and banished his own son when he became one.

When Tiberius learns sparing Galen offers a chance at reconciliation, he joins the trio on their journey home. Can his animosity toward the followers of Jesus survive a trip with the Christian man whose courage and faithfulness demand his respect?

Follow the continuing saga of the people you met in *Blind Ambition* from the frontier of Germany to the heart of the Empire.

Second Chances

*Must the shadows of the past destroy
the hope of the future?*

In AD 122, Cornelia Scipia, proud daughter of one of Rome's noblest families, learns her adulterous husband plans to betroth their daughter to the vicious son of his best friend. Over her dead body! Cornelia divorces him, reclaims her enormous dowry, and kidnaps her own daughter. She plans to start over with Drusilla a thousand miles away. No more husbands for her. But she didn't count on meeting Hector, the widowed Greek captain of the ship carrying her to her new life.

Devastated by the loss of his wife and daughter, Hector's heart begins to heal as he befriends Drusilla. Cornelia's sacrificial love for Drusilla and her courage and humor in the face of the unknown earn his admiration...as a friend. Is he ready for more?

Marriage to the kind, honest sea captain would give Drusilla the father she deserves...and Cornelia the faithful husband she's always longed for. But while her ex-husband hunts them to drag Drusilla back to Rome, secrets in Hector's past and the chasms between their social classes and different faiths erect complicated barriers to any future together. Will God give two lonely hearts a second chance at happiness?

Join the people you met in *The Legacy* eight years later in this tale of hope and a future never imagined until God opens the door.

True Freedom

*The chains we cannot see
can be the hardest ones to break.*

When Aulus runs up a gambling debt to his father's political enemy, he's desperate to pay it off before his father returns to Rome. His best friend Marcus suggests they fake the kidnapping of Aulus's sister Julia and use the ransom money. But when the man they hired kidnaps her for real, Aulus is catapulted into a desperate search to find her.

Torn from his childhood home by Rome's conquering armies and sold as a farm slave to labor until he dies, Dacius's faith gives him strength to bear what he must and serve without complaining. After a deadly accident makes him one of Julia's litter bearers, he overhears Marcus advising her brother to kidnap her. When Dacius almost dies thwarting the kidnapping, a Christian couple pretend Julia and Dacius are their children to keep her brother from finding them before her father returns.

But pretending to be free again makes returning to slavery more than Dacius can bear, while acting like a common woman opens Julia's eyes to dreams and destinies she never knew existed. With her brother closing in and her father almost home, can she find a way around Roman law and custom to free them both for the future they long for?

Find out what happens to Ariana's brother Diegis twelve years later in this tale of hope and a future never imagined until God opens the door.

Hope Unchained

Can the deepest loss bring the greatest gain?

Rome's conquering army took Ariana's family and freedom, but nothing can take her faith in Jesus. When she rescues a tribune's wife from certain death, her reward is freedom and a chance to free her brother and sister. But first she must catch up with the slave caravan before they vanish forever, and tracking them from Dacia to the coast seems impossible for one woman alone.

Discharged from the legion with a hand crippled by a Dacian knife, Donatus faces a future without hope. When the tribune asks him to escort Ariana on her quest, it's the only work he can find. It means four weeks with a Dacian woman and a gladiator bodyguard, but it takes money to eat. A man without options must take what he can get.

But a lot can happen in four weeks. Even battle-hardened men can be touched by love and forgiveness, and it's easier to face an enemy with a sword than to face the truth. When his moment of truth comes, what will Donatus choose, and what will that mean for both of them?

Honor Bound

When the honorable path isn't clear, how do you find your way?

Marcus Brutus owns estates, ships, and gladiator schools that increase his fortune daily, but his greatest treasures are his honor and his wife. When she reveals her faith in Jesus before dying after the birth of their son, he's consumed by hatred for the unnamed Christian woman who led his beloved to abandon the Roman gods, making him lose her in this life and the next.

For fifteen years, Licinia's father hid her Christian faith. But now her father is dead, and a ruthless political enemy is hunting for anything to destroy her brother's career. When she becomes the target, her brother sends her to their estate in Germania. But is that far enough to protect her from an evil man who will stop at nothing?

When a carriage accident leaves Brutus injured and his best friend near death after rescuing Brutus's son, Licinia welcomes and cares for them. But her strange habits and his friend's unexpected recovery make Brutus suspect she's the Christian who corrupted his wife. When her brother's enemies come for her, does honor require him to protect her or turn her over as an enemy of Rome? And when Licinia's heart is drawn toward the pagan man who makes money off death, can she reconcile her growing affection with her love for Christ?

Join some of the people you met in *True Freedom* four years later in this tale of loss and discovery, anger and forgiveness, and the truth that sets people free.

I'd Love to Hear from You!

If you enjoyed this book, it would be a real gift to me if you would post a review at the retailer you purchased it from. A good review is like a jewel set in gold for an author. Other great places to share reviews are Goodreads and BookBub. If you've read others in the series, it would be great if you post a review of those, too.

I'd also love to hear from you at carol-ashby.com or directly at carolashbyauthor@gmail.com.

Want to hear about upcoming releases in the Light in the Empire series and free gifts only for newsletter subscribers?

For free gifts and other special offers, advance notices of upcoming releases, and info about my latest writing adventures, I hope you'll sign up for my newsletter at carol-ashby.com.

Carol Ashby